#1 *New York Times* best

KRESLEY C

wows with the Immortals After Dark series

KISS OF A DEMON KING

"Perennial favorite Cole continues to round out her Immortals After Dark world with kick-butt action and scorching passion!"

—*Romantic Times*

"Kresley Cole knows what paranormal romance readers crave and superbly delivers on every page."

—Single Titles

"Full of magic, mayhem, sorcery, and sensuality. Readers will not want to miss one word of this memorable and enchanting tale. The closer to the end I got the slower I read because I knew once the story ended I would be left craving more of this brilliant and emotionally gripping saga. . . . It is truly one of the most amazing tales Kresley Cole has ever released."

—Wild On Books

"Cole deftly blends danger and desire into a brilliantly original contemporary paranormal romance. She neatly tempers the scorchingly sexy romance between Sabine and Rydstrom with a generous measure of sharp humor, and the combination of a cleverly constructed plot and an inventive cast of characters in *Kiss of a Demon King* is simply irresistible."

—ReaderToReader.com

***Demon from the Dark* is also available as an eBook**

DARK DESIRES AFTER DUSK

"The snappy dialogue and sensual tormenting make this the best in the Immortals After Dark series so far!"

—*Romantic Times*

"Kresley Cole is a gifted author with a knack for witty dialogue, smart heroines, fantastic alpha males, and yes, it has to be said, some of the hottest love scenes you'll read in mainstream romance. . . . You're in for a treat if you've never read a Kresley Cole book."

—RomanceNovel.tv

"A wonderfully romantic tale of two people from the opposite sides of their immortal world. . . . I'm sure I will reread *Dark Desires After Dusk,* the love story of Cadeon the rage demon and Holly the halfling Valkyrie, many, many times as it was everything I had hoped it to be and so much more!"

—Queue My Review

DARK NEEDS AT NIGHT'S EDGE

"Poignant and daring. You can trust Cole to always deliver sizzling sexy interludes within a darkly passionate romance."

—*Romantic Times*

"The evolution of this romance is among the most believable and engrossing I've ever read. Cole's Immortals After Dark series continues stronger than ever with this latest installment."

—Fresh Fiction

KRESLEY COLE

DEMON FROM THE DARK

POCKET
BOOKS

LONDON • SYDNEY • NEW YORK • TORONTO

First published in Great Britain by Pocket Books, 2010
An imprint of Simon & Schuster UK Ltd
A CBS COMPANY

3 5 7 9 10 8 6 4 2

Simon & Schuster UK Ltd
1st Floor
222 Gray's Inn Road
London WC1X 8HB

Simon & Schuster Australia
Sydney

A CIP catalogue record for this book is available
from the British Library

ISBN: 978-1-84983-037-9
Export ISBN: 978-1-84739-752-2

Printed in the UK by CPI Cox & Wyman, Reading, Berkshire RG1 8EX

Dedicated with all my heartfelt thanks to Louise Burke, publisher extraordinaire.

I'm on a man-fast. Why bother with them? The good ones are always taken. Or they're weirdly uninterested in a capricious wild child with continuous legal problems.

—Carrow Graie, a.k.a. Carrow the Incarcerated, mercenary of the Wiccae, practitioner of love spells

My enemies have deemed me fearless. 'Tis no compliment. The only males who know no fear are the ones who have nothing to lose.

—Malkom Slaine, leader of the Trothan rebellion

Glossary of Terms
from

THE LIVING BOOK OF LORE

THE LORE

". . . and those sentient creatures that are not human shall be united in one stratum, coexisting with, yet secret from, man's."

- Most are immortal and can regenerate from injuries. The stronger breeds can only be killed by mystical fire or beheading.
- Their eyes change with intense emotion, often to a breed-specific color.

THE HOUSE OF WITCHES

". . . immortal possessors of magical talents, practitioners of good and evil."

- Mystical mercenaries who sell their spells.
- Separated into five castes: warrior, healer, enchantress, conjurer, and seeress.
- Led by Mariketa the Awaited.

THE ORDER

"The immortal takers. Once captured by the Order, immortals do not return. . . ."

- A multinational mortal operation created to study—and exterminate—immortals.
- Thought to be an urban legend.

THE SCÂRBĂ

"Abominations, created rather than born, with unnatural powers—and hungers. . . ."

- Demons poisoned with vampire blood who retain the traits of both species.
- Previously thought to be truly mythical; considered abominations by most in the Lore.
- Strongest of any sentient immortal being.
- Colloquially known as *vemons*.

THE VAMPIRES

- Two warring factions, the Horde and the Forbearer Army.
- Each vampire seeks his *Bride*, his eternal wife, and walks as the living dead until he finds her.
- A Bride will render his body fully alive, giving him breath and making his heart beat, a process known as *blooding*.
- *The Fallen* are vampires who have killed by drinking a victim to death. Distinguished by their red eyes.

THE ACCESSION

"And a time shall come to pass when all immortal beings in the Lore, from the Valkyrie, vampire, Lykae, and demon factions to the witches, shifters, fey, and sirens . . . must fight and destroy each other."

- A kind of mystical checks-and-balances system for an ever-growing population of immortals.
- Occurs every five hundred years. Or right now . . .

DEMON FROM THE DARK

1

Demon plane of Oblivion, City of Ash
Year 192 in the Rule of the Dead

"*D*o we go to our death—or worse?"

Malkom Slaine gazed over at his best friend, Prince Kallen the Just, wishing he had a better answer for him, anything to ease the apprehension in Kallen's eyes.

As the vampire guards shoved them along, deeper into their stronghold, Malkom suspected death might be welcome before the night was out.

"The rumors are likely untrue," he lied, putting up a renewed resistance as the dozen guards forced them down a flight of stone steps. But his bonds were mystical; Malkom was unable to teleport or break free.

At the base of the stairs lay a subterranean chamber with an ornate throne on a dais. Though the floor was of packed earth, the walls were hung with rich silks and tapestries. Rare crystal and glass adorned the room.

At once, Malkom began analyzing every inch of the area for an escape. Ahead, a pair of winded demon slaves stood beside a freshly dug grave. More guards lined the walls, with swords at the ready. In the back, a black-robed sorcerer worked at a vial-cluttered table.

Gods, let the rumors be untrue . . . those whispers of the Scârbă—the abominations.

Kallen muttered, "Can you see a way out of this?"

Normally, Malkom could. Without fail, he figured his way out of seemingly impossible predicaments. "Not as of yet."

The guards shoved Kallen and Malkom to their knees before the grave.

"Ronath will pay for this once I get free," Kallen grated. Ronath the Armorer was a seasoned warrior, the strongest demon after Malkom. He'd once been Kallen's favored commander. "The traitor will not see another night."

'Twas Ronath who'd turned Malkom over to the vampires. Disastrous enough. But without Malkom's unwavering defense, Kallen's fortress had fallen just a week later. The Trothans' beloved prince had been captured.

Blinded by his hatred for Malkom—a slave turned commander—Ronath had unwittingly doomed Kallen and all the Trothans.

Malkom had already planned his own revenge. As he was neither noble nor good like Kallen, his retribution would be far more vicious than the prince could ever envision.

Without warning, a vampire traced into the room, teleporting directly onto the throne. Clad in costly silk robes, the male was pallid, his skin untouched by Oblivion's blistering sun. His eyes were wholly red, his visage twisted by madness.

The Viceroy.

When the vampires had conquered Oblivion and turned it into a colony, they'd dispatched the Viceroy, their most malicious leader, to act as ruler of the plane.

"Ah, my two new prisoners," he said in *Anglish*.

Though Malkom and Kallen both were fluent in the language, they refused to speak anything other than their native Demonish—even as the use of that tongue was now punishable by death.

The vampire rubbed his narrow, clean-shaven chin. "At last, you have both been captured."

Malkom and the prince were the leaders of the rebellion, and to break them would be to break the resistance. The vampire overlords had searched for them relentlessly.

When the Viceroy snapped his fingers, the two slaves exited the room, returning moments later with an unconscious demon boy. One of their own, handed over for a vampire's refreshment. *A leisurely repast.*

Malkom started sweating. He strained even harder against his bonds but couldn't get free before the vampire collected the boy in his arms, then bent over his neck.

At the sight, rage spiked within Malkom. Those sucking sounds . . .

He bared his fangs, overwhelmed with memories of his childhood as a blood slave. His only consolation was that this boy was unconscious, a luxury he himself had never been afforded. Nor had Malkom's neck been taken, for that skin would have been readily seen—and he hadn't been kept only for his blood.

"Steady, Malkom," Kallen murmured in Demonish. "Keep your wits about you."

How many times had Kallen said those exact words? *The prince has long kept me sane.*

The Viceroy dropped the boy from the dais to the ground like refuse, then dabbed at his lips with a crisp handkerchief. "I confess, you two fascinate me." His red eyes burned with curiosity. "A friendship between a beloved royal and his brutal guard dog. The highest of the high, and . . ." He flicked his hand at Malkom.

No one had been more perplexed by their friendship than Malkom. Kallen was the crown prince of the Trothan Demonarchy, hundreds of years old, and filled with wisdom.

Malkom was the illiterate thirty-year-old son of a whore, raised as a vampire's slave—and filled with rage.

Yet somehow he and Kallen had become comrades in arms, brothers by choice if not by blood. Kallen had said he'd recognized something in Malkom, an innate nobility. As if he'd known how badly Malkom wanted to be noble.

"Penniless, ignorant, and fatherless," the Viceroy intoned. "The son of a demon whore who sold her body." With a sneer, he added, "Until she could sell one of her offspring."

Malkom could deny nothing.

"How easily you sprang to life, when you should have been no more than seeping waste in a back alley."

"If Malkom is not noble in blood," Kallen said, "then he is noble in deed."

Kallen, still defending me.

The Viceroy seemed amused. "I can imagine none so lowly, yet you had the gall to resist us, knowing death awaited. Amazingly, you very nearly routed us from your world, demon."

Malkom could scarcely comprehend this. Though he'd won numerous battles, he hadn't imagined his foes were on the brink of surrender. Malkom had never known an Oblivion without the walking-dead vampires here.

Decades before his birth, they had arrived from an alien plane filled with myriad breeds of immortals and mortals, settling here for one reason.

Blood.

When the vampires consumed Trothan blood, it made them more powerful than they'd ever been, made them heal from injuries more swiftly. Blood had eventually become the currency in Oblivion.

"So very nearly," the Viceroy continued. "But in the end, breeding will tell." The vampire traced to stand just beside them. "You can dress in your fine warrior clothing." He reached down to rip Malkom's rich cloak from him. "But you can only mask what you truly are. Under those manacles at your wrists, I bet I would find bite scars."

Again Malkom voiced no denial. He normally wore silver cuffs to conceal those shaming marks.

The details of his past weren't necessarily held secret. All the demons in Ash knew how Malkom had earned his bread as a boy, how he'd eaten from their trash once he'd grown too old for a vampire lord's tastes.

But for this vampire to know as well ...

"Does not matter how you appear, demon—you are still nothing."

"Do not listen to him, Malkom," Kallen said. "You are a good man. A stalwart leader."

"Who was betrayed at the earliest opportunity?" the vampire said.

A gang led by the powerful and devious Ronath had tricked Malkom. Before he could trace or attack, he'd been caught in a metal net and stabbed through repeatedly.

"You rose up high for the briefest time. But I will break you down once more."

Malkom craned his head up to face the Viceroy. "Break me down?"

"You submitted to a vampire master once. You will do so again."

"Is that why we live still? For me, save yourself time and kill me now." Nothing this vampire could do would be worse than what the slave master of Malkom's childhood had done. Malkom gazed at the demon boy, unconscious in the dirt. *Nothing.*

"'Tis not so simple," the Viceroy said. "It never is with our kind." Had he signaled something to the sorcerer at the back of the chamber? "You've destroyed so many of my soldiers that I have decided to create more, starting with you two, the strongest of your kind. You shall be transformed, remade in my image."

The rumors ... 'Twas said that the overlords had developed a rite to transform Trothans into Scârbă—demonic vampires who thirsted for the blood of their own. *A demon and a vampire united, an abomination stronger than both.*

The Viceroy drew his sword from a scabbard at his hip. "You will drink my blood, and it will open your veins to the ritual. Your deaths will be the catalyst." He ran a finger over the edge of his sword, while in the shadows his sorcerer began to chant, fueling a sinister curse.

Power emanated from the sorcerer with every utterance, filling the room with forbidden black magics. Some unseen force seemed to wrap around Malkom's body, digging in.

Even more guards closed in, heaving tight on Malkom's and Kallen's chains. One of the largest vampires jammed his knee into Kallen's spine, forcing his head backward, while another wedged a bit between Kallen's teeth.

"No, no!" Malkom roared, twisting violently.

The Viceroy sliced his own wrist. "'Tis a gift I'm giving you. The *Thirst*. I am going to make blood sing for you, make you dine on demon flesh every day for eternity." He shoved the streaming gash to Kallen's pried-open mouth. "You will become like us, and be loyal only to me. It begins now."

"Do not drink it, Kallen!" Malkom bellowed, but they forced him to swallow it.

They set upon Malkom next, stabbing him until he was too weakened to resist. The Viceroy's thick, vile blood was forced down his throat as well.

Then the vampire raised his sword. Malkom thrashed against the chains with every ounce of power left in his body, but neither he nor Kallen could get loose.

Kallen met Malkom's gaze for a harrowing moment—just before the Viceroy's sword sliced clean through Kallen's neck. His body collapsed backward, his head tumbling into the grave. Dazed, sightless eyes stared up at Malkom. The prince's brows were still drawn, his teeth gritted.

Malkom gaped in disbelief while years of their shared memories flashed in his mind.

The two demons' countless battles, more victories than defeats. The dozens of times Malkom had saved Kallen's life; the thousands of times Kallen had praised him, encouraging him to better himself.

"You are a fearless warrior who's more than his past." "Of course you've the intelligence to learn how to read! Who the devil convinced you otherwise?" "You are stronger and faster than the others, your will to live greater than any I've known. You see details others are blind to. Uniqueness is a kind of nobility, is it not, brother?"

Throughout, Malkom had begun to shed the taint of his past. He'd dared to entertain dreams of a better life.

Now Kallen was dead. Malkom roared with impotent fury, his eyes going wet with loss. Kallen. Dead.

Or worse.

The sorcerer cast a layer of black dust over Kallen's body.

"No!" Malkom bit out. "Leave him in peace!"

More chanting, more *power*.

Malkom's lips parted. Kallen's body was lifeless no more. With each of the sorcerer's words, it began to twitch, to . . . move in the dirt.

Not from death spasms. But writhing with *life*. The headless neck pumped blood anew.

The Viceroy again snapped his fingers for the demon slaves. Once the pair had kicked Kallen's body into the grave, the sorcerer scattered more of that dust over all. To make Kallen whole once more?

When smoke snaked up from the depths, the Viceroy raised his bloody sword. "Now 'tis your turn, Slaine. And I promise you, rising from the dead—if it takes—will be the easy part. If you live, I will break you."

Malkom silently prayed for a true end, beseeching the gods who had never once answered his most desperate entreaties. *Please, do not let me rise—*

The sword whistled through the air. He perceived the scantest bite of blade.

Then nothing.

Despite Malkom's prayers, he and Kallen had both risen two nights later, waking into a nightmare of darkness, deep in the earth. After clawing through the dirt, inching their way to the surface, they'd been thrown in a murky cell in the Viceroy's dungeon.

They hadn't suffocated as they'd risen because they now drew no breaths. Nor did their hearts beat.

The walking dead. *Vampire. I am a vampire.*

No! Malkom still hadn't accepted his fate, was ready to rage and fight it. Even as he recognized how much he'd been altered.

Though he wore no cuffs to prevent him from tracing, he no longer had that ability. His clammy skin felt as if a thousand spiders crawled all over him. His upper fangs had elongated and narrowed, throbbing painfully. Even in the low light, merely opening his sensitive eyes was an agony.

His very hearing was different, more acute. He could detect insects boring in the ground beneath him.

From the moment he'd awakened in the grave, the burgeoning need for blood had lashed him. Confusion and anguish roiled within him.

In Kallen, too. He stared at the filthy cell walls, hollow-eyed and unblinking.

"We will fight our way free," Malkom assured him now, "then return home."

"We are Scârbă. Brother, no demons will ever take us among them."

He was likely right. The two were worse even than the vampires. They were defiled demons, cursed to feed off their own kind. They were the monsters of legend feared by all.

Kallen rasped, "There is no reason to go on."

"There is *always* a reason." How many times had Malkom had to convince himself of this? "If for nothing else, you can seek vengeance." He himself would not rest until retribution was meted.

He would slaughter the sorcerer who'd muttered his curses in the background, the guards who'd held them down, and the bloodthirsty Viceroy whose sick will had set them all into motion.

Then he would return to destroy Ronath.

Those who betrayed Malkom did it only once.

When all was done, he would find a way to erase every vampire trait from himself, to rid his veins of the Viceroy's blood and return to what he'd been.

Or he'd greet the sun. Malkom frowned. Would that kill a Scârbă?

"Live for vengeance?" Kallen said. "Tell me, will that be enough?"

How to answer that question when Malkom's own dreams appeared so ridiculous now?

He'd wanted a home that no one could ever force him to leave. He'd wanted as much food and water as he could ever enjoy. But more than anything, he'd secretly longed to be respected like Kallen—a noble like him—gifted with a blood far better than his own.

Malkom's only fortune was that no one else had ever discovered how much he yearned to be highborn. "Then live for your fated female," he urged Kallen. "She will accept you. She must."

"Is that what you seek, Malkom? Your fated one?"

"I've no such expectations." What use had he for a woman of his own? He'd needed no offspring for a noble line or sons to work the water mines with him.

"No? Then why have you never taken a demoness from the camps?"

Malkom's gaze flicked away. Never had he known a female. Those who followed the army could be had for a price, but Malkom had never used one. No matter how urgent his need, no matter how badly his curiosity burned, he physically *couldn't*.

They smelled of other males, reminding him of his

childhood. Nothing extinguished his lusts like the scent of seed.

So he'd put females from his mind. As a boy, he disciplined himself not to dream about food. He'd applied that same discipline to keep from fantasizing about intercourse.

At length, Malkom answered, "Because war has become everything for me—"

The Viceroy traced into their cell, his eyes lit with pleasure. "Remade in my image," he said. The vampire wasn't shocked the ritual had worked—he was brimming with pride. So how many had they created here? "And this is just the beginning. Do you feel the Thirst? It's sacred to us, as death is." His gaze fell first on Kallen, then on Malkom. "Only the one who kills—or answers the Thirst—will ever leave this cell alive."

Just as Malkom tensed to attack, the Viceroy disappeared.

Once their situation sank in and he'd found his voice, Malkom said, "We will not fight each other." They both knew that when he said *fight,* he meant *drink* or *kill.* "I will not fight my brother." But if anyone was freed, it should be Kallen. *He's all that is good.*

"Nor I," Kallen vowed.

"We will not," Malkom repeated, wondering if he sought to convince Kallen—or himself.

Three weeks later . . .

Malkom weakly stood before the bars, expending precious energy just to remain on his feet, yet unable to lie down as though defeated.

Day after day had passed with no food, water, or—
dark gods help them—blood. His thirst intensified
hourly, his fangs throbbing until he'd silently wept.
He'd caught himself staring at Kallen's neck, the skin
there taunting him.

At times, Malkom had flushed to find Kallen's gaze
on his own neck.

Never had he hungered like this. Last night, Malkom
had waited until Kallen fitfully dozed. Then he'd sunk
his aching fangs into his own arm, sucking, disgusted
by how rich he'd found the taste. How delicious, how
blistering the *pleasure*...

Endless days passed as their bodies withered but
would not die. With no industry to be had, no battles
to be fought, Malkom was beset by memories cloying
in his mind. For someone who held survival para-
mount, he'd begun to have doubts. How important
was living?

Living means more betrayal.

His first betrayal had been dealt by his own mother. At
six years of age, he'd complained of hunger so acute he'd
nearly blacked out. She'd railed that he was never satisfied, then sold him to a vampire who would feed him all
he wanted if he was an "obedient and *affectionate*" boy.

His second betrayal? That same vampire had cast
him out at fourteen, deeming Malkom too old to stir
his lusts.

Back to the gutter, back to hunger. But against all
odds, Malkom had grown increasingly strong, until
he'd finally been ready to exact revenge on the master.
Malkom had always been observant, and he'd noted

every protection guarding that vampire's home. He'd found it easy to steal back inside, take out the guards, and murder the master who'd tormented his youth and twisted him as a man.

And it'd felt so good, so *glorious,* to kill one of their kind, he'd hunted another, and another.

Soon, word of his deeds had reached Kallen's ears. The prince had invited him to his stronghold, then spent months convincing Malkom to join their rebellion, even to lead it.

Eventually Malkom had been acknowledged in the street, asked to dinner by Kallen, paid in riches and fine clothing—merely for risking a life Malkom had cared naught about. For so long, shame had been his companion, but at last he'd dragged himself from the gutter.

He'd known his people didn't love him, but he'd thought he was earning their respect each time he saved their miserable lives.

Weeks ago when he'd noticed a tension among them, he'd chastised himself for reading too much into others' reactions, telling himself he needed to listen to Kallen and stop expecting betrayal at every turn. *No matter how many times I have been dealt it.*

"And now what is going on in that head of yours, Malkom?" Kallen asked from across the cell, his voice faint. "You've that dangerous look on your face."

"My thoughts are dark."

"As are mine. I fear we near the end."

"There is no end." Malkom faced him. "Not until *I* decide it."

A sad smile creased Kallen's gaunt face. "Fierce as ever." He rose unsteadily, then limped to stand before Malkom. "For me, I've decided this cannot go on." His eyes flickered black with emotion. "So embrace me, my friend." He wrapped his arms around Malkom.

His own arms hanging by his sides, Malkom peered up at the ceiling in confusion. *I've never been embraced like this before.* Touching meant using.

Was this giving instead? *Am I too scarred to recognize it?* Hesitantly, Malkom wrapped his arms around Kallen as well. *Not so bad.*

When he felt Kallen's lips against his neck, Malkom frowned. Kallen loved females, enjoyed a new demoness nightly. So what was this? *You are merely ignorant in the ways of affection—*

Kallen's lips parted.

He was going to drink. With the realization, Malkom started to sweat, his eyes darting, the will to survive rising up. But if he was truly steadfast, he'd sacrifice himself for the prince, for the good of the crown. How much had Kallen done for him? He'd taught him how to control his rage, to channel it.

He'd given Malkom purpose. *If not noble in blood, then in deed . . .*

But memories arose within him, sordid scenes with a vampire who'd used him for years. The feedings in the dark . . . the way the master's skin would grow warm against his own. . . .

No, no! "Do not do this thing, Kallen." Malkom's voice was hoarse. "Do not betray our friendship." *Don't betray me.*

"I am sorry," he said, his tone defeated. "I do not have a choice."

Kallen is all that is good. Though Malkom had vowed he would never be bitten again, he somehow held himself still as the prince's splayed fingers dug into his back, clutching him even closer.

A final sacrifice for my friend? Can I control my will to live?

Or would the prince's brutal guard dog finally turn on him?

When Malkom's jaw clenched, his every muscle tensing, Kallen rasped, *"Steady, Malkom."* Then he plunged his fangs into Malkom's neck, giving a wretched groan of pleasure as he sucked. And the sound was so familiar, the shuddering of his body just like the master's.

Kallen's chilled skin began to warm against Malkom's.

Betrayal. Rage erupted, and he roared with it. *Cannot control this.*

Seizing Kallen by the shoulders, Malkom shoved him back. He looked down at the prince and knew that, for him, this was the end. "Forgive me, brother...."

But those who betray me do it only once.

2

Immortal Internment Compound
Present day

When Carrow Graie had awakened from her abduction a week ago, she'd had a raging headache, cotton mouth, and a metal collar affixed around her neck.

Things had only gone downhill from there.

Tonight I might be hitting rock bottom, she thought as warden Fegley—a billy club-carrying, no-balled loser—forced her down the corridor of cells to her doom.

"Dead Wicca walking," the centaurs' leader sneered from their cell as Carrow passed. He, like every other Lore creature imprisoned here in the immortal menagerie, suspected she was about to be offed.

"Shut the fuck up, Mr. Ed," she said, earning a harsh yank on her collar from Fegley. Glaring at the mortal, she struggled against her cuffs. "Once I get my powers back, *Fug*ley, I'll curse you to fall in love. With your own bodily functions. If it comes out of your body, your heart will long for it."

"Then I guess I'm lucky you've got this on." He again

jerked on the band at her neck—the mortals called it a *torque*. It mystically nullified her abilities and weakened her physically. Every species here had been hobbled in some way, making them controllable, even by mortals like Fegley. "Besides, witch, what makes you so sure you're going to make it past the next hour?"

If these people execute me, I'm going to be sooo pissed. Unfortunately, that appeared to be in the cards. At the very least, she was about to be tortured or experimented on.

Hell, maybe then she could find out why anyone would have gone to the trouble of abducting her.

Carrow was a rare three-caste witch, but she was by no means the most powerful, not like her best friend Mariketa the Awaited. Though overjoyed that Mari hadn't been taken, Carrow didn't understand why *she'd* been targeted....

What would Ripley do? When in a jam, Carrow often thought of how Ellen Ripley, the legendary badasstress of the *Alien* quadrilogy, would figure her way out.

Ripley would analyze the enemy, take stock of her surroundings and resources, use her wits to defeat her foes and escape, then nuke everything in her wake.

Analyze the enemy. From what Carrow had heard from other inmates, this place was run by the Order, a mysterious league of mortal soldiers and scientists led by a magister named Declan Chase, a.k.a. the Blademan, along with his trusty bitch, Dr. Dixon.

Carrow's sorceress cellmate had told her the Order was bent on eradicating all the immortal miscreations, or *miscreats.*

My surroundings? A diabolically designed prison, with cells made of foot-thick steel on three sides and unbreakable, two-foot-thick glass on the front. Each cell had four bunks, with a toilet and a sink behind a screen—and no real privacy. The Order recorded their every action from ceiling cams.

This incarceration was like nothing she'd ever known—and she'd known more than her share of *two hots and a cot.* Carrow hadn't enjoyed a single shower or change of clothes. She still wore her club duds: halter top, black leather miniskirt, and thigh-high boots.

Each day inside brought more shitty food and *bad lighting.*

Along with experiments on immortals, some of whom were her friends.

Resources? Carrow had precisely zero-point-zero resources. Despite the fact that she could usually charm prison guards, these mortal soldiers seemed immune to her. Except for Fegley, who for some reason appeared to resent her deeply, as if they had a history.

Though each of her steps carried her potentially closer to her demise, she observed as much as she could, determined to escape. Yet one reinforced corridor bulkhead after another doused her hopes of breaking out.

The layout was labyrinthine, the halls riddled with cameras and the cells all booked up. Lykae, Valkyrie, and the noble fey—all allies of a sort—were mixed amid the evil Invidia, fallen vampires, and fire demons.

In one cell, contagious ghouls snapped at each other,

tearing at their own yellow skin. In another, succubae wasted away from sexual hunger.

The Order had snared more beings than could be named, many of which were notorious and deadly.

Like the brutal werewolf Uilleam MacRieve. The Lykae were among the physically strongest creatures in the Lore, but with that torque on his neck, Uilleam couldn't access the beast within him.

For fun, the warden rapped the glass with his club. Maddened by the captivity, Uilleam charged, hitting the glass headfirst, splitting his scalp to the skull right before her eyes. The surface was unharmed while blood poured down his tense face.

In the next cell stood a huge berserker, a savage warrior male that Carrow had seen around New Orleans. He looked on the verge of going berserk.

Carrow swallowed to see his neighboring inmate—a Fury, with uncanny violet eyes and bared fangs. The Furies were female avengers, embodiments of wrath. And this one was a rare Archfury, raven-winged and lethal.

The Order certainly didn't pull their punches. Some of the beings here were even infamous. Like the vampire Lothaire, the Enemy of Old, with his white-blond hair and eerily sinister hotness. Whenever the guards sedated him and dragged him down the ward, his pale red eyes promised pain to those who'd dared to touch him.

"Step on it, witch," Fegley said. "Or I'll introduce you to Billy."

"I might like him, heard he's wittier than you are." She gritted her teeth when he shoved her again.

Once they'd reached the prison ward's main entrance, another long corridor branched off, this one filled with offices and labs. Without a word, Fegley hauled her into the last room, what looked like a modernist den. *No lab? No electrodes or bone saws?*

A plain-Jane brunette sat behind an executive desk. She sported an *I'm a bitch, so deal* look behind unstylish glasses. Must be Dr. Dixon.

Behind her, a towering dark-haired male stood at the window. He gazed out into the turbulent night, revealing only a shadowy profile.

Carrow peered outside to get an idea of their location, but rain pelted the window. According to inmate whispers, this facility was on a giant island, thousands of miles from land in any direction. *Natch.*

"Free her hands," the tall man said without turning. Though he'd spoken only three words, Carrow recognized Declan Chase's voice—that low, hateful tone with the faintest hint of an Irish accent.

Fegley unlocked her cuffs the same way he'd locked them—with his thumbprint—then he exited through a concealed panel door in a side wall.

Everything in this place, including her torque, was locked with a person's right hand thumb. Which meant Carrow needed to cut off Fegley's. *Beauty.* Something to look forward to. "I remember you, Blademan," she told Chase. "Yeah, from when you and your men *electrocuted* me."

Those bastards had posted bail for Carrow's latest disorderly conduct charge—*proudly earned!*—and then lain in wait outside the Orleans Parish Correctional. As she headed home, they'd blown her down a city block with charge throwers, gagged her, and forced a black bag over her head. "Was the hood supposed to instill dread in me or something?"

'Cause it'd worked.

Without deigning to reply, Chase faced her briefly, yet he didn't look *at* her, more like *through* her. His pitch-black hair was straight, longish. Several hanks hung over one side of his face, and she thought she saw scars jagging beneath them. His eyes, at least the one she could see, were gray.

He was dressed in somber hues from head to toe, concealing any exposed skin on his body with the help of his leather gloves and high-collared jacket. By all outward appearances, he seemed cold as ice, even as his aura screamed *I'm unbalanced!*

This was the man who took Carrow's friend Regin the Radiant out of her cell, time and again, to be tortured. Whenever he hurt Regin, her Valkyrie lightning struck outside and the compound's lights surged from her radiant energy.

He hurt her *a lot.*

"So, Chase, you get off torturing women?" It made a kind of sick sense that a man so cold would fixate on the normally joyful Regin, with her glowing beauty and lust for life.

Carrow thought she saw his lips curl, as if this statement held particular significance to him. "*Women?* I only torture one woman at a time."

"And you've decided to go steady with Regin the Radiant for now?" Out of the corner of her eye, Carrow saw Dixon frowning at Chase, as if she suspected some untoward interest as well. Ah, so that was the way of it—Dixon carried a torch for the Blademan.

Carrow supposed some might consider his features attractive, for a sadistic human, but his half-hidden countenance resembled a pale, deadened mask.

All the best with that, you crazy kids. Tommy-used-to-work-on-the-docks and mazel tov.

Chase merely shrugged, turning back to the window. But the tension in his shoulders was so marked, she wondered how he remained upright.

"You've got stones to nab a Valkyrie, I'll give you that," Carrow said. "But her sisters will come for her. For that matter, you really shouldn't have pissed off the House of Witches. The covens will find your little jail. They'll descend on this place." Though she sounded confident, she'd begun to suspect that the island was cloaked somehow. By now, Mariketa would know she'd been abducted, and if her powerful friend hadn't yet scried her location—or gotten a soothsayer to uncover it—then it couldn't be found.

"Will they, indeed?" His tone was smug, *too* smug. "Then I'll add to my collection."

"Collection?"

Dixon hastily said, "Magister Chase is only doing what must be done. We all are. Whenever immortals begin to plot, we sentinels rise up, as we have for centuries."

"Plot?"

Dixon nodded. "You're planning to annihilate mankind and take over the earth."

Carrow's lips parted in disbelief. "That's what this is all about? My gods, it's too ridiculous! You wanna know a secret? There's no plan to kill you all, because you're beneath our notice!"

Ugh—fanatical humans! Sometimes she hated them so much.

"We know that a war between us is coming," Dixon insisted. "If your kind isn't contained, you'll destroy us all."

Carrow squinted at her. "I'm warming to the idea. Especially with mortals like you. Don't you get it? Human fanatics are more monster than any of the Lore."

"More than the Libitinae?"

The Libitinae often forced men to self-castrate or die—for fun.

"Or maybe the Neoptera?" Dixon continued.

Insectlike humanoids, the stuff of nightmares. At the mention of the latter, Chase tensed even more, the muscle in his jaw bulging. Interesting.

Watching for any reaction, Carrow slowly said, "No, I'll grant you that the Neoptera are depraved. They don't kill their quarry; they keep it, tormenting it hour after hour."

Had sweat beaded on Chase's upper lip? If those creatures had gotten hold of this man . . . Well, Carrow knew what they did for shits and giggles, what they did to their victim's *skin,* and it made her stomach turn.

Was that why Chase had covered as much of his body as possible? How was he still sane? *Was* he?

The inmates gossiped about this man constantly; apparently, he hated to be touched, had once clocked an orderly who'd made the mistake of tapping his shoulder.

That would explain the gloves.

She almost felt a shred of pity for him, until he grated, "And the witch believes she's better than they are."

And the witch is talking to a madman. "Okay, clearly you two are beyond rational debate, so let's just get to it. Why did you take me?"

Dixon answered, "Our aim is not only to study you, but to conceal your existence. Most immortals fly under the radar. You flaunt your powers in front of humans."

Carrow had been repeatedly chastised by her coven for this. But, as she'd often argued, she never used her powers around *sober* humans. "So why'd you bring me here tonight?"

"You're going to help us capture a vampiric demon, a male named Malkom Slaine."

Heh. Twenty large says I'm not. "A vemon? You really think they exist?" she asked innocently. Vemons had been thought an impossibility, a "true myth"—*oxymoron, hello?*—until one had been unleashed on New Orleans last year.

Unimaginably strong, he'd defeated several fierce Valkyrie, who'd survived only by chance. He'd barely been destroyed by the powerful Lykae king, and only because he'd been threatening the werewolf's mate.

"They're rare, but we have knowledge of one's existence," Dixon said. "You'll seek out this male, then lead him to us."

"You want me to go out and coax some poor sap to his death?"

"We don't intend to kill him," she said. "We want to discover his weaknesses—"

"And how he was made, huh?"

Dixon held up her palms. "We *are* interested in the anomalous beings among the Lore."

Anomalous. What a mild way of putting it.

"He lives in Oblivion, a demon hell plane."

The demon planes weren't parallel universes, but self-contained, hidden territories with their own climates, cultures, and demonarchies. Most of their societies were feudal and old-fashioned. Not exactly hotbeds of technology—or, say, women's liberties.

"I've heard of it," Carrow said. A wasteland once used as a gulag for Lore criminals, Oblivion was the former home of the Trothan Demonarchy. Before the vampires overthrew their royal line.

"We've been able to compile information about your target, taken from detained Trothan demons."

Carrow raised her brows. "You torture them to spill the beans?"

"They volunteered the details gladly. He's reviled among his kind, a bogeyman of sorts. You'll like him no better. He is illiterate, filthy, and brutish. Mentally, he is severely disturbed."

"You're calling someone 'severely disturbed' with this dude in the room?" Carrow hiked a thumb at Chase. The tension in his shoulders and neck ratcheted up, if that was possible. "You know, Dix, you're not exactly selling me on this."

Dixon pursed her lips. "To succeed, you will need to know exactly what you're up against."

"Why me?"

"You're from the enchantress caste of witches, and

you're attractive. The males on that plane have probably never seen a female like you."

"That plane? Honey, try this universe. Oh, and easily *this room*."

"We have your history as well," Dixon snapped, losing patience with her. "In your forty-nine years of life, you've routinely done things that are very brave—and very stupid. This should suit you perfectly."

No argument there. And she'd only grown bolder since she'd become fully immortal twenty-three years before. "Why can't you go and get him yourselves?"

"He's sequestered in deep mines within a mountain and has choked the few passes with traps. He guards his domain ruthlessly. If we can't take him out, we can *lead* him out."

With her playing the part of Delilah? *Don't think so.* "As much as I appreciate the invitation to help out with your vemon-retrieval problem, I'm afraid I'm going to have to R.S.V.F.U."

Over his shoulder, Chase said, "Is that your final decision?"

"Yep. Even if I wanted to help you, I'm not special-ops—I'm front line." She was a general among her kind, leading armies of spellcasters. "So if you've got some urban warfare, we can talk. But not so much with the tromping around on a mountain in a hell plane." Carrow *loathed* the outdoors, Gulf Coast beaches excepted.

Chase said, "We thought you might be misguided in this." Were his pupils dilated? "I have something that will give you perspective." He crossed to an intercom panel on the wall, pressing a button beside it.

That concealed panel door slid open once more, and Fegley walked in. He had his arms full—with a young girl, unconscious and limp in his hold. Her mane of long black hair covered her face. She had on a dark T-shirt and leggings, a tiny black puff tutu, and miniature combat boots.

Carrow felt a stab of foreboding. *Don't let it be Ruby.* She glared at Chase. "You're taking kids prisoner?" *How many little girls dress like that?*

Fegley sneered, "When one of them tortures and murders twenty soldiers?" Then he tossed the girl to Carrow.

She dove forward to catch her, shooting the man a killing look before gazing down. *Don't be her.*

Carrow hissed in a breath. Ruby. A seven-year-old from her own coven, related to her by blood.

"Where's her mother?" Amanda, a warrior-caste witch, would never have been separated from her little girl. "Answer me, you prick!"

Fegley snidely said, "She lost her head."

Amanda dead? "I'd already planned to end you, Fegley," Carrow choked out. "Now I'm going to make it *slow.*"

Fegley merely shrugged and sauntered out, making Carrow grit her teeth with frustration. In the past, she could have electrocuted him with a touch of her hand, could've rendered him to dust as an afterthought.

Struggling to get her emotions under control, she turned her attention back to the child, petting her face. "Ruby, wake up!"

Nothing.

Dixon said, "She's only sedated."

Carrow gathered the girl closer. Her breaths and heartbeat did sound regular. "Ruby, sweet, open your eyes." Of all the young witches for them to have . . .

Within the coven, there were *tanda,* social groups of similar ages. Ruby was in a group of baby witches, or a "gang" as they called themselves—a gang more in the sense of Little Rascals than of Crips and Bloods, but it was cute.

Carrow and Mariketa often took them to sweets shops, getting them jacked up on sucrose before setting them loose on the coven. Ring the doorbell, drop them off, then run like hell, cackling all the way.

Carrow and Mariketa—Crow and Kettle, as they'd been dubbed—were the gang's favorite "aunts." Ruby was secretly Carrow's favorite as well. How could she not be? Ruby was fearless and bright, an adorable little girl dressed in ballerina punk.

Dixon frowned. "She could pass as your own."

Like many in a coven, Carrow and Ruby were related, though more closely than usual. The girl was her second cousin, and she belonged to the exact three castes that Carrow did, with her strength in the warrior caste. *Just like me.*

Ruby's green eyes blinked open. "Crow?"

"I'm right here, sweetheart." When Ruby's tears welled, Carrow felt a pang like a blade in her heart. "I've got you."

Ruby's body tensed against hers. Eyes wild, she cried, "Mommy t-told me not to kill them! B-but when they hurt her, it . . . it just happened." She was beginning to pant, her breaths shallowing.

"Shh, you're all right now. Just breathe easy." When Ruby got overly excited, she would hyperventilate, even passing out on occasion. "It's okay, everything's going to be all right," Carrow lied, rocking her. "Just breathe."

"They swung a sword at her neck!" Her chest heaved for air. "I saw her . . . d-die. She's *dead*—" Ruby went limp once more and her head fell back. Unconscious.

"Ruby! Ah, gods." Amanda was truly gone? And Ruby's father had been murdered by rogue warlocks before she'd even been born.

Orphan.

The coven didn't usually spell out things like godparents or custody. Immortals not actively at war didn't have to worry much about leaving behind orphans. But if Amanda had gone to battle, she would have expected the closest blood relation in the coven to care for her daughter.

That'd be Carrow, the House hellion. *Poor Ruby.*

Though Carrow had been treated so callously by her own parents, she would do right by her responsibilities. She stared down at the girl's ashen face with a new recognition, a momentous feeling of a *shared* future.

Carrow had long had a unique and curious talent— the ability to sense when another had just become a part of her life forever, when their destinies would eventually be intertwined and shared.

In that instant, Carrow became *witch plus one.*

But she couldn't even get herself out of this shithole, much less a child!

"Action and reaction," Chase said. "You get us our target, and the two of you will go free." Though tension thrummed off him, his voice was monotone, his accent barely perceptible. "Otherwise, she dies."

Carrow stiffened. Against Ruby's hair, she murmured, "I'm going to take you home soon, baby." She turned to Chase. "I'll have the use of my powers?"

"Your torque will be deactivated for the mission," he said.

Not that Carrow would be able to spellcast even without her torque. She *needed* crowds and laughter for power to fuel her spells. Here she'd been tapped out, as useless as an empty keg.

"You'll depart tomorrow, remaining in Oblivion for six days." Dixon continued over Carrow's sputtering, "Tonight I'll assist you in collecting your gear. You'll be allowed a shower, and we'll provide you with a dossier on your target."

"Nearly a week in hell? How am I even supposed to get to Oblivion?"

Dixon answered, "Your sorceress cellmate, Melanthe, the Queen of Persuasion, can create a portal."

That's right. Lanthe could open thresholds to anywhere.

"We'll briefly deactivate her torque—under SWAT supervision. And of course, we'll keep Ruby here to make sure all goes according to our plans."

There went that idea. "I want Lanthe and Regin released as well."

The doctor shook her head. "Impossible."

If they truly set Carrow free, then she'd come back

for the two of them soon enough. "I want the Order's word about releasing me and Ruby."

The woman said, "You have it."

"Don't want yours," Carrow said in a scoffing tone. "I want *his*."

Chase turned to her once more. After a hesitation, he gave a nod.

"Then we have a deal," Carrow said.

He narrowed his eyes, as if she'd just proven a point. "Not even a *qualm* about betraying one of your own species?"

"A demon is *not* one of my own species," Carrow snapped. "You make us sound like animals."

Without another look at her or the girl in her arms, he strode out of the room, saying in a chilling tone, "Because that's all you are."

3

"*She's not coming back, is she?*" Ruby whispered as Carrow held her, rocking her in the bottom bunk. She'd awakened just a couple of hours ago, immediately bursting into tears.

"Amanda's gone to Hekate, sweetheart."

"Can we bring her back?"

"*No.* You know that's forbidden." At times, Carrow forgot the magics stored in Ruby's trembling little form. The girl had exceeded even Mariketa's abilities until Mari had recently come into her powers.

Apparently, the last time Ruby had cast a spell, she'd tortured and killed twenty men.

"Don't go tomorrow, Crow."

Carrow had explained that she was setting out to hunt a demon. In exchange, these mortals would free Carrow and Ruby. "I don't want to leave, but I don't really have a choice. Hey, in a way, this is just a mercenary mission. I go out and do some magic, and I get something in return." The girl would understand an arrangement like this. The witches were mercenaries, taught at an early age to sell their magic. "And the sorceress will take good care of you."

From the top bunk, Lanthe gave a feigned pissy exhalation.

Earlier, with a clipped "Oh, very well," she'd agreed to look out for Ruby. Carrow suspected Lanthe might actually like kids but kept that fact secret, protecting her street cred as a wicked sorceress.

After all, she was the notorious Queen of Persuasion, a sorceress who could compel others to do whatever she bade them. To be deemed a "queen" meant that she was the best at her talent in all the Lore.

Though Sorceri and witches shared a common ancestry, many of the Sorceri class belonged to the Pravus, an alliance of evil factions that warred with the Vertas, the relatively good alliance that Carrow affiliated with.

Before allying, loosely, with the Vertas, Lanthe and her sister had fought on the Pravus front line.

Still, Carrow felt a level of trust toward Lanthe. She usually had a good sense about people, and the week she and Lanthe had spent confined together in this cell felt like a lifetime.

They'd played tic-tac-toe in the condensation on the steel walls, gabbed about the hotness known as King Rydstrom, Lanthe's new demon brother-in-law, and commiserated about the man drought they were both presently gasping through.

Carrow had had lovers—more than a couple, less than a handful—and a single night on Bourbon Street could score her another one. But she had her reasons for her current coitus hiatus. . . .

"What will happen when you get us free?" Ruby asked.

How much confidence the girl had in her. "I'm going to take care of you myself. You'll live with me." *Mental checklist, item eighty: find us some new digs.*

Witches with kids didn't get to live at Andoain. Carrow had felt a pang at the thought of giving up her sorority-style life there—and her coveted suite with a private bath—but when she'd looked at Ruby's tearstained little face, she'd easily decided that it didn't matter.

"We'll get a pad near Andoain so you can still go to spell school there. I'll pack lunch"—bag leftover pizza—"for you every morning."

Lanthe made a sound of disbelief from overhead.

"I *will*. And when you get old enough, I'm going to teach you all about the Street that is Bourbon."

Ruby yawned, her puffy lids drooping. "I heard some witches talking about you a couple of weeks ago. They said you were rutterless."

Now a chuckle from the top bunk.

"Ru*dd*erless?" *So true.* "Maybe so. But I'm not going to be anymore." *How's it feel to be a rudder, kiddo?*

"Will you hold my hand until I fall asleep? And stay here till I wake up?"

"You got it." Maybe the reason she'd never done well with responsibilities in her personal life was that she'd never had any practice? Carrow had led armies—but she'd never had another depend solely on her.

In minutes, Ruby was out, her countenance relaxing, her brow smoothing. Carrow waited a little while, then eased from the bed to recheck her pack and begin studying the dossier.

When Lanthe slunk down from her bunk, Carrow noted yet again that the sorceress looked flawless, displaying no signs of a week's worth of stress, discomposure, or even wrinkles. But then Lanthe wore typical Sorceri garb: a metal bustier and a mesh skirt, held together with bits of leather.

Her dark hair was a mass of braids in the wild Sorceri style. The only things missing were her metal gloves—with built-in claws—and the half mask that would normally adorn her face.

Carrow found it interesting that the mortals left their prisoners in their own street wear for the most part. She herself still wore her jewelry and club duds.

"They're going to double-cross you," Lanthe said.

Did Carrow suspect Chase would go back on his word? Of course. But she also knew she had to operate under the assumption that he would release her and Ruby. What were two witches to them? And more importantly, what other choice did Carrow have? "I don't know that for certain," she said as she began rooting through the pack Dixon had offered her earlier.

At once, Carrow had demanded to go to the facility's PX store for her own supplies. While the Order might have a dandy assault pack for soldiers to make an incursion, they didn't have an all-purpose Carrow pack for witches bent on seduction.

So after a few hygienic tweaks to her gear—and her first shower in a week while her clothes were dry-cleaned—she was ready.

"In any event, witch, I think you waste your time."

"Look, I might not trust that they'll keep their

word about releasing us," Carrow said. "But I trust one hundred percent that they'll keep it about killing her."

Lanthe sighed, gazing over at Ruby. "Well, then, let's see this dossier."

They sat on the floor with their backs against the wall. *Fitting.* Carrow opened the folder to the first page, a summary of her destination and its peoples.

"I still can't believe they're sending you to *Oblivion*." Lanthe shivered.

"Come on, it's the only place you can get fresh vemons this time of year."

Oblivion was one of the hell planes, a place of such limited resources that only the harshest demons could survive. In this case, water was scarce. No rain fell, and the few collections of water were underground.

According to the dossier, the Trothan culture was a chaotic mix of slavery, violence, and cruelty—its members brutal. Yet they had a deeply entrenched class system in their society.

Carrow's lips thinned. She wasn't a big fan of classes in *any* form—educational *or* social. She herself hailed from a "noble" family, but had buried that little tidbit about herself. *And it's not like my folks will out me.*

When Carrow turned the page to the summary of Malkom Slaine, her "target," Lanthe said, "A *vemon,* the most dangerous of all Lore creatures, was created out of a *Trothan,* one of the most barbaric species of immortal?"

Though Carrow knew demons who were civil, engaging, and *hot,* she'd never met a Trothan.

"And you're going into hell to get him? This is like *Escape from New York,* except you're bringing out the baddie."

"Snake Plissken, at your service," Carrow said as she began perusing Slaine's information, organized in handy bullet points.

Description: Light blue eyes. Defined musculature. Over six and a half feet tall. Black horns, curving back from just above his ears. Identifying marks: A large, winding tattoo on his right flank, typical demon piercings.

Background: Born more than four hundred years ago to a prostitute demon mother. Father unknown.

Carrow felt a flare of pity for him. Living in Oblivion was bad enough, and he hadn't exactly gotten a great start.

Led rebellion against vampire invaders until his capture. Transformed into a Scârbă—a vampiric demon. Before escaping the vampire stronghold, he beheaded Kallen the Just, the Trothans' demon prince, as well as the Viceroy, the vampires' emissary.

Carrow frowned. "Why would Slaine have assassinated the two potential leaders, then *not* taken control of the demonarchy?"

Lanthe said, "Sounds to me like a failure to capitalize."

Fugitive from Trothans for over three centuries. No known associates. Unwed. Most current activities: Defending his territories, the water mines of Oblivion. Special skills: Battle-trained, survival, military command experience.

"Unwed?" Carrow said. "Their kind marries?" Many demon breeds didn't, especially if their species had one fated mate.

"At least you won't have to worry about competition."

"Unless he's got a demon harem in those mines. A little honey or two holed up underground?" Carrow said, raising a brow at the next bullet point.

Language: Demonish, some Latin. There had been an isolated report of his speaking English, but it couldn't be confirmed.

"How am I supposed to communicate with him?" Carrow's Demonish was sparse. She knew mostly curses and how to order liquor.

"The language of love?" Lanthe suggested.

"Check out his psych profile." *Easily enraged, reacts with a marked ferocity. Violent and territorial . . .*

"Psych profile? Isn't that what they do with serial killers?"

Carrow nodded. "Dixon said he was the Trothan version of the bogeyman."

"Well, then. Tell me they'll deactivate your torque for this mission."

"They will." *A lot of good it'll do me if the folks in hell aren't happy.* Whereas Mariketa's magic was based on adrenaline, Carrow's own was fueled by emotions, specifically happiness. The raucous revelry of a crowd was like an exquisite feast for her powers.

"Then you can just do a love spell on him," Lanthe said.

"It doesn't work for me." Many people knew Carrow sold love spells for a living—they just didn't know she sold them for folks to use *on themselves*. Like when a guy knew he had a good woman but was tempted to stray, he'd order a Carrow Graie special. "I probably won't have much power to do magic anyway."

"Cruising Oblivion with no magic, witch? I suppose you'll just use your brute strength to defend yourself?"

Wiccae and Sorceri were among the physically weakest in the Lore.

"And what about the vemon?" Lanthe continued. "If you can't lure him to the portal, he could just keep you in hell as his little witch pet."

"I've had worse relationships," Carrow deadpanned.

They snickered. Gallows humor.

After they'd flipped through all the pages, Lanthe summed up Malkom Slaine: "A dangerous, devious, demon non grata." Gazing at Carrow with curiosity, she asked, "You're really going through with this?"

"I've got this down cold," she answered confidently. Carrow had always followed her instincts and landed on her feet. Sometimes she landed on her feet in County, but it always worked out in the end. "But if for some reason, I don't"—she glanced over at Ruby—"will you make sure she gets back to the House of Witches?"

Lanthe said, "I will. Just try not to let it come to that—"

A sudden bellow echoed down the ward.

"I guess he don't like the corn bread, either," Carrow quipped.

When a fight ensued and they heard loud *whooshing* sounds, Lanthe shot to her feet. "A Vrekener."

Vrekeners were fierce, demonic "angels," with wings, horns, and fangs.

Shortly after, the guards dragged a limping, winged male past their cell. He stared at Lanthe, his eyes haunted, his lips drawn back from his fangs. His scarred wings had been bound. He said only one word as they passed: *"Soon . . ."*

Lanthe shuddered.

"I take it you two know each other?" Carrow asked.

"Would you believe that Thronos and I were child-hood friends?"

Carrow raised her brows. "I'd hate to see your child-hood enemies."

"The bastard probably let himself get caught, just to get closer to me."

"You want to tell me what for?"

"Maybe one day. For now, let's focus on your own menacing male."

Carrow sighed, growing serious. "I might not make it back from this."

Instead of assuring her that she would, Lanthe said, "It isn't likely. . . ."

Wastelands, Oblivion
Year 601, Trothan Restoration

They'll come to kill me soon, Malkom thought as he ad-justed the tension on one of his spring traps.

After concealing the contraption, he climbed to a blustery vantage on his mountain, gazing out over the Forest of Bone and the vast desert beyond—the sun-scorched desert he could never cross again. His vam-pire nature made it impossible.

Far in the distance, in the city of Ash, sacrificial

pyres burned bright. The dwellers there were making yet more offerings to their dark gods for an end to Malkom. He'd been judged a twisted murderer, a fugitive from justice, an abomination.

All true.

They would like nothing more than to sacrifice Malkom himself on a pyre. More so now than ever since they were desperate for water. And he controlled every drop.

Soon they'd come for him; their stores were nearly gone. They'd have no choice but to cross the desert that had protected them from Malkom.

Though he could travel over his dust-shrouded mountain in the hazy light of day, the desert and city were void of wind and shade. He couldn't cross that expanse and return within a single night. The sole time he'd successfully traversed it—fleeing a mob of Trothans more than three hundred years ago—he'd nearly died.

All his attempts over the centuries had failed. Each time, he'd been so weakened by the midpoint that he couldn't continue, much less contend with his powerful foes.

So he'd cut off the dwellers' water supply to draw them near, knowing they would be led by Ronath the Armorer—the demon who'd taken over after the leaderless vampires fled from this plane.

The traitor who now lived in the Viceroy's opulent fortress.

I removed all of his obstacles. Kallen and eventually the Viceroy both fell because of me.

Malkom had despised the vampires, but at least they had acted according to their nature. The armorer and his men? Malkom remembered their feigned greetings to him just before they'd attacked, just before they'd doomed their prince.

Kallen, my sole friend.

At the memory of his death, bitter-tinged grief swept over Malkom. *As fresh as the day I killed him.*

When the winds increased, heralding dusk, Malkom gave a low curse. They would never come in the dark.

Now a long, solitary night stretched before him. He'd endured lifetimes of them.

He turned away, heading toward his lair down in the mines—where he would wait, alone, in silence, staring at the damp walls. Time passed slowly deep in the mountain, and the isolation weighed on him.

Malkom consoled himself with the knowledge that one way or another, his miserable existence was about to end.

4

"You can't come, sweetheart," Carrow told the irate seven-year-old seated on the bunk before her. "Oblivion's not a place for kids."

Sometime between last night and this morning, Ruby had decided she would *not* be separated from Carrow.

Throughout the night, Carrow had lain awake, wanting to be there if she woke missing her mother. Carrow had been exhausted and knew she needed to be strong for her mission, but putting Ruby's needs above her own affected her in ways she wasn't ready to analyze.

Once, the girl had sleepily mumbled, "Mommy?"

Tears threatening, Carrow had said, "It's okay, baby. Go back to sleep."

But since Ruby had awakened this morning, there'd been nonstop hissy. At least she hadn't passed out so far.

"Why do you have to leave *this* morning?" Ruby demanded.

"The sooner I leave, the sooner I can return. Now, Dr. Dixon is going to sit you until Lanthe gets back, okay?"

Ruby crossed her little arms over her chest, jutting her chin. "You're not leaving me behind. Or I'll do a spell to make you smell like ass. Forever."

Carrow raised her brows. "Harsh, Ruby, *harsh*." *I think I'm the one who taught her to say "smell like ass."* "And you can't do spells, anyway. Remember what I said about the collar?"

From behind Carrow, Lanthe quietly said, "You need to be firmer with the child."

Over her shoulder, Carrow muttered, "Come on, think about what she's been through." And Carrow had no way to comfort her, none of her old tricks to pull.

Before when Ruby had cried, Carrow had been able to solve all with strategic bouts of consumerism. An all-expenses paid trip to Disney World for her and her posse of friends, a monkey, a robot, a half-pipe skating ramp. Easy, peasy, lemon squeezy.

Lanthe scoffed. "I lost my parents when I was not much older than she is."

Funny, so did I, Carrow thought. But she shook away those memories. She didn't have the luxury of wallowing in the past. As she looked down at Ruby, it struck Carrow yet again that she now had *a responsibility.* Someone depending solely on her. "You're going to be good for Miss Lanthe, right?"

"Miss Lanthe?" the sorceress repeated, her blue eyes gleaming dangerously. "Why don't you just buy me a minivan, zip me into mom jeans, and shoot me in the face?"

Carrow shrugged. "I'll make this up to you when we all get out, yeah?"

The sorceress played with one of her dark plaits. "Melanthe's sitting service has rates of one hundred K an hour."

"Put it on my tab."

Footsteps sounded down the corridor. *Coming for me.* Ruby heard them as well; she launched herself from the bunk at Carrow's legs.

Carrow caught her up, swinging the girl into a hug. Ruby clung with her little arms, her face streaked with tears as she pressed it against Carrow's neck. Carrow stared at the ceiling, struggling to keep from bawling with her.

"Promise you'll come back," Ruby whispered.

Her words sounded slurred, babyish even. Promise came out as *pwomise.* Carrow knew precisely jack-point-jack about raising kids, but she didn't think this reversion could be a good thing, in light of the circumstances.

Carrow eased Ruby back to meet her eyes. "I vow to the Lore that I will come back for you. You believe me, don't you?"

A slight nod.

Fegley, Dr. Dixon, and a contingent of guards arrived, opening the cell's glass door. The woman reached for Ruby, but Carrow hugged her even closer.

"Anything happens to her, it's on your head, Dixon." She cast the doctor a warning look, knowing her irises would flicker. Carrow's eyes didn't change color with emotion. They changed brightness, glittering like stars. Right now, she was literally starry-eyed, and it was freaking the mortal out.

Dixon stared, absently replying, "L-like we agreed . . ."

Ten minutes later, Carrow sat in a military Humvee, one of five that made up Fegley's convoy. As the truck bounced down a rutted road outside the facility, Carrow gazed out of the rain-slicked window, still in turmoil, replaying the sound of Ruby screaming for her. *How can I miss her like this already, as if I've left my heart behind?*

Giving herself an inward shake, Carrow forced herself to study her surroundings.

The road wound through a moist forest overflowing with fir trees. Lichen and moss coated fallen trunks and anything stationary, making everything appear fuzzy, any sharp edges smothered by green. The area looked like it could be in the Pacific Northwest.

Or Tasmania.

Way to narrow it down, Carrow.

The landscape was definitely coastal, which lent credence to the latest rumor going around—that the Order chummed the surrounding seas to attract great white sharks, ensuring no immortal could escape by water. . . .

As her eyes darted over geographic details, she tried to mentally prepare for her mission, reflecting on all she'd learned from the dossier.

She was filled with curiosity about Malkom Slaine. What had happened when he'd been turned into a Scârbă? Had he become the walking dead or had his demon nature remained dominant? Had he been alone for all those years?

Did the Order just assume she'd have sex with him to lure him back?

Carrow couldn't remember the last time she'd taken a lover. She would've enjoyed more, but she'd learned that sex didn't necessarily make all men happy. It made them feel good, relaxed, but not necessarily joyful. There was angry sex, insecure sex, preening sex. Some men needed validation, others vindication, but most thought of wild-child Carrow as a conquest.

If she knew she wouldn't get *all* her needs met, she didn't go all the way.

Now she might not have the luxury of being choosy. . . .

Eventually, the convoy parked around a large clearing encircled by five equal-sized boulders. As she climbed from the truck, Carrow sensed power there, sacredness.

Then she glared up at the steady deluge of rain that wetted her leather boots and skirt, reminding Carrow how much she loathed the wilderness. For her, the "great outdoors" was as much an oxymoron as "true myth."

Last night, Dixon had suggested combat boots in place of Carrow's own—her two-thousand-dollar, gathered-leather, over-the-knee boots. "Do you want me to go in as an enchantress or a warrior?" Carrow had asked testily. "Pick a caste, any caste, mortal. I myself think I have the best chance as an enchantress. And fuck-me boots are standard-issue."

Carrow gazed down at the mud creeping around her soles. *Oh, well.* She would rather die than admit a mortal was right.

Furthering his own doom, Fegley yanked Lanthe out of another Humvee by her collar, shoving her into the clearing. His continued cruelty gave Carrow insight into the skin-bag of waste that was Fegley. She'd decided he was a deeply insecure man who hated women.

This gig gave him power over females he would never otherwise possess.

Enjoy it while you can. Only a matter of time before he went down. Once Carrow got Ruby settled at Andoain, she would return here and go wicked on their asses.

"Get to it," Fegley ordered Lanthe. "You have two minutes. Try anything and the snipers will plug your skull."

With a killing look, the sorceress raised her hands. Soon an iridescent blue light glowed from her palms. Her face pinched with strain as she created a door-sized threshold, carving a black vortex as if through thin air.

Teeth gritted, Lanthe said, "Be careful out there, witch."

"I will." She shouldered her pack, readying herself at the portal's edge. "You take good care of my little girl until I get back." *My little girl.* As soon as she said the words, Carrow knew they were true. Ruby was hers. Would always be.

"I will take care of her," Lanthe said, but she glanced away.

The sorceress truly didn't think Carrow was going to make it back?

Before she could question Lanthe, Fegley planted himself in front of Carrow. "You've got six days to get your target back to this portal. Saturday night, witch, no later than midnight, Oblivion Standard Time. Your torque will activate an hour before then. You show without Slaine, and we'll slam the door right in your face. Lastly, don't call him by his name, or he'll know you're a mole. Clear?"

"As clear as you can make it, fuckwit. Anything else?"

Fegley smirked. "Yeah, if the demon finds out what you're planning, he'll cut off your head and mount it on a pike." Carrow was still gaping when the man grabbed her shoulder. "Go to hell, witch. Literally."

Then he shoved her into the abyss.

Wastelands, Oblivion

No sign of Ronath. The afternoon was drawing to a close, and now another interminable night loomed.

Malkom ceased his pacing to gaze out over the desert yet again. He'd had a sense that something momentous was about to occur, a feeling of destiny—which in his case usually meant destruction.

"Face me, armorer!" he roared.

Only the winds answered. With a disheartened exhalation, Malkom turned back toward his lair, eventually snagging a bird for his dinner on his way. Again he recognized that the supply of game was dwindling. Though he possessed unnatural speed, he found it increasingly difficult to sustain himself here.

Snap. The bird's neck cracked in Malkom's fist, and even over the howling winds, he detected the sound. With an easy yank, he severed the head from the body, then lifted the gushing neck over his mouth to sate his vampire need for blood. Back within his home, he'd cook the meat to feed the demon within—

He lowered his arm, his ears twitching. His heightened senses perceived a brief portal opening, a disturbance in the plane below his mountain home. Directly before the forest lay a circle of five boulders, marking a notorious portal's location.

He rose to investigate, tensing to trace to the circle. *Nothing.* Even after all this time, he still forgot that he could no longer teleport. Not since the Scârbă ritual.

No matter. He was fast, could be down in the forest in minutes.

The opening of the portal meant one of two possibilities.

More mortals had been dispatched to the wastelands to capture him. If he'd ever learned how to laugh, he would've now. Whenever they invaded his territory, he'd dismembered every soldier who'd dared set foot on his mountain, piling the mangled body pieces in a gruesome display at the closed threshold.

When the soldiers beseeched him for mercy or screamed their prayers, they always spoke Anglish, the vampires' language, which only sealed their fates.

Though Malkom recognized the tongue, he no longer comprehended it, hadn't spoken it in centuries—but hearing it enraged him.

The other possibility? The portal was being used to dispose of more Lore creatures, exiled criminals.

If so, they'd never know they were about to be judged once more. He sneered, knowing it was an ugly sight. *By me.*

5

Carrow landed so hard atop a pile of old skeletons that her breath was knocked from her lungs and the porous bones were pulverized beneath her.

She lay for precious seconds, enduring that panicky feeling of suffocation. Waiting ...

Once her lungs reset, she sucked in a breath, then immediately began coughing. Though the wind gusted, the air was acrid.

Hauling herself to her feet, she kicked a couple of femurs out of her way and peered around. *So this is hell.*

All around the matching circle of boulders lay a wasteland such as she'd never imagined. Above her spanned a brown sky, swirling with dust and fumes. Behind her, a rocky desert stretched to the horizon. Glowing stones that seemed to have cores of lava dotted the land.

To her right and left, deep chasms crisscrossed the land like scars, wafting plumes of sulfurous smoke. Before her stood what resembled a forest, but the trees were petrified, their color matching that of the scorched bones scattered all over the ground. Nothing green grew here. Everything was just a gradation of brown, dirty white, or ash.

Miles and miles in the distance, far past the forest,

was a single immense mountain with three distinct peaks.

His mountain. Her destination.

Unfortunately, every inch of this place sounded inhabited. In the desert, creatures resembling giant centipedes dipped and tunneled, shifting dunes in a perilous instant.

On either side, the chasms teemed with unseen scrabbling creatures. And even over the wind, she could hear that the forest beyond was crawling with life—not a good thing on a hell plane.

So how was she supposed to get through the creatures to reach the mountain?

Although Fegley's words gave her pause—*he'll cut off your head and mount it on a pike*—she had no choice but to seek out Slaine. Finding him might take her the entire six days.

From those nearby gorges, shadowy figures began to crawl up. Ghouls?

Not them! They were like zombies, mindless walking pathogens bent on increasing their numbers. Contagious through their bites and scratches, the ghouls *needed* to infect others.

Surroundings? Sand centipede monsters behind her; creepy, inhabited woods ahead; ghouls flanking her.

When they began skulking closer, she had no choice but to hasten straight for the murky forest, glancing over her shoulder as she ran.

While the ghouls were resilient, able to lope along after prey for dozens of miles at the same pace, Carrow's own strength and endurance were better than a human's, but not like a Valkyrie's or a Fury's. So how to lose them . . . ?

Just as the thought arose, they began slowing. In fact, once she'd breached the forest, the ghouls halted. Past the line of trees, she turned back. They were prowling at the very edge, wary. Something within had them spooked.

But sooner or later, they'd come for her. Deciding that nothing could be worse than the troop of zombies on her heels, she plunged ahead.

Picking her way over rocks and stone tree trunks, she increased her pace when she could. Her lungs burned, her muscles screaming. . . .

Right when she'd begun to suspect she'd gained a safe distance, she spied more shapes moving amid the trees. A new threat. Numerous eyes glowed back at her from the shadows, beings surrounding her. They were sentient males—she could perceive their emotions.

And the predominant one was lust.

When they closed in, forcing her to stop, she saw there were at least a dozen of them in various shapes and sizes. They were all humanlike, but each had horns and upper and lower sets of fangs. Which meant demons.

She turned in place, drawing a harried breath to speak, wondering if they'd understand English. She knew natives likely wouldn't.

But before she could say a word, the smallest one brandished a spear in her direction. He blinked his eyes so rapidly, Carrow dimly wondered if the world looked like an old-timey film to him. "Is she one of the mortals,

Asmodel?" he asked in English. Non-natives. They were probably exiled criminals.

Like the others, he was dressed in tattered clothes, indicating they'd been here for a while.

The largest one, this Asmodel, said, "Smells like an immortal to me." With the back of his hand, he swiped a line of ropy drool from his mouth. "First female I've seen in the wastelands. Ever."

No females were here? So these were *hard-up* exiled criminals? *Beauty.* Putting on a bold front, she said, "I *am* an immortal, a powerful member of the House of Witches." But she was tottering on her feet, sooty and bedraggled. Scarcely looking like a high-powered witch.

A demon with green skin asked, "Then why have you not smote us?"

Even with her torque deactivated, right now she was a no-powered witch. *Need some happiness here, guys.* "An excellent idea, demon." *Brazen it out, Carrow.* "Though if you allow me to pass, I might consider sparing your lives. Otherwise, I'm debating whether to turn your viscera into nests of vipers or your bones to sand."

Unimpressed, they paid her no heed, arguing among themselves. The gang's intention with her was clear, even before the small one uttered, "I go first."

"The hell you will, Sneethy," Asmodel said.

Carrow shuddered. She had no way to defend herself, and she was surrounded with no place to run. *Brazen!* Raising her palms threateningly, she said, "Then you've left me no choice. Surrender now, or—"

Sneethy called her bluff, merrily yanking free her backpack, scraping her shoulders.

"Hey!" When he dug into it, rifling through her things, she snapped, "Go Yoda someone else's supplies, asshole."

He ignored her, distributing her PowerBars with glee. Those were scarfed down before he'd even held up her canteen with a "whoop!"

But his excitement faded as he sniffed the air. "*It* comes." His low voice conveyed fear—and awe. "Though we haven't crossed into its territory."

So what was *it*?

With darting eyes, the green demon said, "We go now!"

Asmodel stalked closer to Carrow. "I go nowhere without this female." More drool dripped from his lips. "She would be worth her weight in water! Even used."

"You'd risk facing *it*?" Sneethy said.

Apparently so, because Asmodel seized her arm. She kicked down on his instep, but it didn't even faze him. As she fought, he dragged her along deeper into the woods.

"Stop struggling!" he ordered. "You'll be our concubine—or the beast's dinner. And it nears even now."

What in the hell had spooked a gang of demons like this? As they all plunged into a copse of petrified saplings, the fleeter ones darted ahead, the slower ones lagging. The young trees had grown so close, it was like wending through a smoke-laced cornfield. Good cover.

Yet the demons grew more uneasy, drawing their

weapons and crouching low. Asmodel pulled a wooden club from his belt. Sneethy sniffed the air again and whimpered, raising his spear.

The green demon drew a hunting knife and muttered, "It stalks us." A *demon* worried about being stalked?

When she heard a gurgling yell behind them, her eyes went wide. She ceased any resistance, fleeing with them when the gang began running. At intervals, she glanced back, as unnerved as they were.

Then, directly on the path ahead, they came across one of the faster demons—beheaded so recently his body was still kneeling.

As the corpse collapsed, Asmodel sneered, "No, the beast *plays* with us."

Another demon's scream warbled from behind them. They'd barely gone a dozen steps in the other direction when something that sounded like a boomerang sailed through the air overhead. Blood rained down from it.

The *beast* had flung a severed leg like a Frisbee to land in front of them.

Beside the mangled leg lay a pair of demons, one body toppled over the other. And their heads looked to have been severed—not with a sword but with *claws*.

"A single blow took down two." Asmodel swallowed loudly as he jerked her around in a circle, scanning for an escape.

Something had beheaded a pair of immortals with one strike? Then gone to slash off the leg of another? "No, there's got to be more than one," she said. Beings were dying in all directions, screams like a chorus.

"One," Asmodel snapped. *"It!"*

Sounds of carnage echoed through the trees, the cracking of bones and the unmistakable tearing of flesh. She began shaking too hard to run, stumbling twice in rapid succession.

Asmodel promptly abandoned her, taking his chances, sprinting through the saplings.

The few remaining demons followed suit, scattering in different directions. She trailed after Asmodel, the biggest one, while all around her the others screamed.

Then she slowed, squinting in disbelief through the smoke. Ahead, something like a shade seized Asmodel with a staggering speed. Asmodel looked as if he were being lifted by an unseen force. Whatever it was ruptured the demon's body in midair—limbs separated, blood spraying over dust.

He'd never had time to scream.

The shadow vanished. Silence fell. Only the sound of the wind could be heard. Had they all been taken out? Or were they hiding?

What *was* this thing?

She twisted around, her eyes darting. When she reeled back from a nearby sound, she tripped over a legless, beheaded torso, tumbling beside a pool of gore and entrails.

Sneethy. She recognized the spear still clenched in his hands.

Choking back bile, she crawled from the leavings into a patch of petrified brush.

Her first impulse? Ball up there and hide. What use was fleeing? Death awaited in any direction.

Then she grew ashamed. Though young, Carrow was an inducted mercenary of the Wiccae and a leader among their vaunted warrior class. She'd face this beast fearlessly—even to the end.

"Show yourself, coward!" At once, trees began to topple in a line coming straight for her. A monster on its way. Before, it'd been soundless. Now it crashed toward her.

It was playing with her as well.

Carrow would be damned if she was going to sit here, helpless, like some offering to King Kong. For the first time in her life, she had someone depending on her. She would fight.

And if she couldn't match its strength, she'd use other talents. She could be cunning . . . deceptive.

She pried Sneethy's spear from his gnarled fingers. *You're about to see what would happen if Fay Wray were a witch!*

Just as she dragged the weapon into the brush behind her, the attacker plowed into the clearing.

Carrow craned her head up. And up . . . She lost her breath.

The being's body was nearly seven feet tall and splashed with blood. Large horns curved back from above his ears. His lips were parted, exposing upper and lower fangs. Another demon.

And, gods, this one was big. His broad chest and brawny arms were covered in a mesh chainmail shirt, his muscles rippling with strength under the metal. He was clad in leather pants, and they too were spattered in crimson. His long hair was tangled around those horns and hung over his dirty face. A sparse beard covered his cheeks.

Surely, this couldn't be . . . him. Her target. Nothing about his appearance indicated vampirism. *Please don't let it be him.*

When their eyes met, she gasped. His irises were a light blue, as described in the dossier. Severely disturbed? Violently territorial? Affirmative.

The blue flickered, turning blacker by the second, usually a sign of lust or rage in a demon. Neither boded well for her.

Just as she studied his appearance, his gaze raked over her body, over her hiked-up skirt and bared thighs. At once, his horns straightened and flared back, signaling his attraction to her.

When he raised his face, his eyes narrowed, as if with recognition. He clenched his hands into meaty fists, then opened them, splaying his claw-tipped fingers. Again and again he made fists, then released them, like he missed something he'd long held on to.

His shaft was hardening—impossible to miss that. When he sucked in ragged breaths, grasping at his chest, a ridiculous suspicion arose, but she tamped it down.

This demon looked to be on the razor's edge of lust. For all Carrow knew, he'd been out in this wasteland for centuries without a woman, as hard up as Asmodel.

And if she didn't figure out a way around it, this one was about to be on top of her, his hulking body heaving over her.

"I-I'm asking you not to hurt me," she said, studying his expression. His harsh face evinced nothing, no comprehension of her words. So no English. Trothan native? *Check.* His only reaction was an ever-growing erection.

Just as she'd begun to suspect he was beyond any communication, he slammed a fist over his chest, then pointed at her, rasping something that sounded like *"Ara."* His voice was rough, as if it'd been dragged over gravel.

When he stalked closer, she spied a tattoo, a large one that looked like black flames licking up his side— his *right* side.

Hekate help her, this *was* Carrow's target, Malkom Slaine. And the Order had been woefully mistaken. There'd be no coaxing him anywhere.

Change of plans. She wasn't going to *lead* him to the portal. She was going to *lug* his unconscious body there. After repeatedly stabbing him.

But for her plan to work, she needed him to charge her, to fall upon her. Mentally steeling herself, she motioned for him, crooking a finger.

His eyes briefly widened, but he didn't speed up his approach.

Damn it, Slaine! *Charge me!*

6

Malkom had never been so astounded in his ever-lasting life.

On his way down the mountain, he'd caught this female's exquisite scent and had recognized what she was to him—the woman he'd never expected for himself.

With his horns flaring and his loins stirring to mate her, he'd leapt down from on high, then torn through the bone forest. But as he'd closed in on her, he'd also scented the demons surrounding her. While he'd slaughtered them, his heart had begun to beat, his lungs drawing breath, for the first time in centuries.

She was *her*. His. Fate had given him a foreign female with hair like night and emerald-green eyes. Her skin was flawless, as pale as a vampire's, though she had no fangs. She was some kind of immortal, but he didn't know what.

And her *scent*. She smelled as he'd always imagined a woman should. Not like those hardened, hollow-eyed demonesses who'd reeked of the males that'd used them.

Now the reasons Malkom had never had a female no longer affected him. This woman was perfect, her scent was tantalizing to him, and she was *his*.

What use had he for a female? The question no longer mattered. *I claim what's mine.*

She was beckoning him, clearly recognizing him as her male. *She seeks what I have to give her.*

Yet now he was battle-maddened, barely clinging to the last of his control. Demonic thoughts of slaking his lust on this fine creature warred with the vampiric urge to drink her down. He could almost feel his fangs planted into the creamy flesh of her bared thigh.

She moistened her lips and subtly eased her legs open, giving him a glimpse of the dark pink silk betwixt her legs.

Thought fled. He roared and leapt for her.

Just before he was upon her, pain erupted. He gazed down at his side in disbelief. She was jerking a spear up between them, slipped under his chainmail and between his ribs. Her eyes fierce, she buried it deeper.

Tricked. Rage seethed. *Losing control.* She needed to flee from him. *"Cotha,"* he gritted between clenched teeth. *Run.*

This being hadn't even noticed the spear, hadn't registered the pain until she'd shoved it farther into his side.

He'd just continued staring at her with a look of consuming hunger. His desire for her had been so strong it was palpable, making her dizzy.

Now, with his claws digging into his palms until blood streamed from them, he gazed from her face down to the injury, then back up. His eyes boring into hers, he again grated, *"Cotha."*

"I-I don't know Demonish." Ah, gods, only a few phrases! What was he telling her?

He threw back his head and bellowed, *"Cotha!"*

Eyes wide, she dropped the spear and scrambled to her feet. Ducking away, she fled deeper into the forest. She could absolutely believe this male would put her head on a pike.

Within moments, she heard him behind her and tossed a glance over her shoulder, gasping at what she saw. He was *changing.* Through the swirling dust, she spied his upper fangs shooting longer, narrower.

A vampire's fangs. A vampiric demon. And he appeared to be mindless.

She charged up an incline, winding around the lava-filled boulders, fear making her quick. His strength would be unnatural. He'd break her like a matchstick. Sweating, salt stinging her eyes, she shoved her forearm over her face—

Suddenly, he was on the path ahead of her. With a cry, she whirled and dashed for a side trail. After one turn, she realized the path ended in a narrow ledge that tapered out over a fiery ravine.

Dead end.

When he prowled closer, she backed onto the crumbling ledge, chancing a drop that could kill her. *My powers, gods, I need my powers. . . .*

He crouched low and edged toward her, seeming to be in pain, but not from his spear wound. Though injured, he remained hard.

This wasn't how she'd planned her mission! Not

trapped on a finger of rock above a blazing chasm. Not staring into the black eyes of a demonic fiend with razor-sharp fangs. . . .

And the unmistakable need to breed with her.

As he loomed closer, threatening pain with every unconscious flex of his corded muscles, she retreated even farther. Rocks plunged below her. Carrow peered down at the smoke churning from the depths. Would she actually jump to escape him?

No one would ever know where she'd met her end.

When he shoved his hand into his pants to adjust himself, the swollen head of his shaft jutted past the waist. Her lips parted in astonishment.

His erection looked to be visibly throbbing, the tip beading. He absently ran his palm over the uncovered crown, then froze. Slowly, he turned his hand over to see his seed glistening there.

When he dragged his gaze from his palm and faced her again, he looked even more determined to reach her, his onyx-colored eyes burning with intent. And in that second, everything became clear to her.

He *would* be determined. He'd clearly never seen his seed before this night.

Ah, great Hekate, she was his mate.

Though a male demon could experience orgasms, he couldn't produce semen until he'd found his female. He couldn't *release* it until the first time he claimed her. With this first hint of seed, he would believe she was his demon mate.

As well as his vampire Bride. An unmatched vampire male didn't draw breaths and had no heartbeat or sexual ability until he'd encountered his female and become *blooded*.

No wonder he'd appeared bewildered by his breaths. He'd pounded his fist over his chest, over his heart.

Because she'd made it beat.

Had the Order known this would happen? That she'd be his Bride *and* his mate? How could they have? It seemed impossible. So why did she feel double-crossed?

"*Alton, ara,*" he commanded.

Her Demonish was terrible, but she thought he was commanding his female to come—or to *heel*?

"Not until you calm yourself!"

"*Alton!*"

She shook her head, miming that she would jump, hanging a leg over.

With a roar, he lunged to one side to punch a boulder in frustration. It cracked wide like an egg.

His *strength*. He could break her bones with a touch.

She'd heard tales of vampires pursuing their females. They were unstoppable. And she knew that the demon males of some species could be lashed by a breeding drive so strong it made them crazed. Even if they knew they faced certain death following that drive, they couldn't resist it.

He was definitely in the midst of that haze right now.

Would she jump? Rather than have this brute rutting on her? Though his postcoital high might be like happiness, fueling her with enough power to escape him, the demon would tear her with his size. Would she even be conscious to draw the power from him?

Again he eased closer, and again she dangled her leg from the edge—

The outer layer of rock gave way under her foot.

New Orleans, Louisiana
Val Hall, the Valkyrie stronghold

"Nïx, I'm not leaving until I get the info you promised," Mariketa the Awaited told the mad soothsayer dancing around the room. "So let's start at the beginning."

Nïx the Ever-Knowing, better known as Nucking Futs Nïx, cried, "Let's start from the end! It's coming soon, you know." She twirled in circles, her long black braids flying out, resembling copter rotors. She looked like a stoned supermodel, high on runway power, rather than a three-thousand-year-old Valkyrie oracle. Her baby-doll T-shirt said *Carpe Noctem*.

The dozen or so other Valkyrie gathered with them in the great room watched the proceedings intently—they had a stake in Mariketa's quest to find Carrow as well. At least one of their own had been abducted mere miles away from where Carrow had been taken.

So many stolen. Myriad creatures from all corners of the Lore had gone missing, including other witches, one as young as seven. They were rumored to have been captured by the henchmen of an unknown entity, and none of them could be found. The House of Witches, the fey trackers, the powerful Sorceri, none of them could locate their own.

Inhaling for patience, Mari said, "You have to have seen something."

Nïx frowned over her shoulder. "Have to have I?" Spinning, spinning.

"Nïx, stop it!"

The soothsayer slowed to a standstill, casting Mari a hurt look. Then she flounced to an easy chair.

Extracting info from the soothsayer proved difficult at times. At *all* times. And Mari had heard that Nïx hadn't even been lucid for the last two weeks. But Mari had to try—she was beside herself with worry about her best friend.

To search for Carrow, Mari had used all the power she could draw on without risking a mystical backlash. Then she'd called on all thirty-seven covens of the Wiccae to scry. Even with so many talented witches searching, no one could find a trace of Carrow. All they could say was that she was in grave danger.

Thanks for the tip, bitches.

So Mari had gone to the most powerful and famous oracle in the Lore. Her Valkyrie friend. "I got a call that you had information. Nïx? *Valkyrie!*"

"Hmm?" She languidly gazed up. "Then tell me something about Carrow, something that no one else knows."

Tests? Mari felt her heart sinking. Nïx loved to play people. In a small voice, she said, "I thought we were friends."

Nïx's golden eyes flashed playfully. "You are indeed my favorite Wiccan-type person."

"Then why are you making me jump through hoops like everyone else?"

"Not hoops—scent."

"What?"

"Your revealing a secret about Carrow is like giving a scent to a bloodhound. I need something to point me in the right direction."

Things no one knew? Where to start?

Though Carrow was a daughter of Bacchus—not literally—and an impulsive hellion, she was also wicked smart. Folks *never* saw that coming. Also a shocker? There was a method, and a purpose, to her madness. She didn't raise hell for hell's sake.

Carrow's most guarded secret? *It breaks her heart every day that her parents don't return her calls.*

They hadn't called for years. Mari had once walked in on Carrow sobbing over the loss.

Mari gazed around at the Valkyrie, uncomfortable divulging anything private about Carrow. For all these females knew, her best friend had an enviable life— friends, money, parties.

Only Mari and their mentor, Elianna, knew the pain Carrow carried. The party-girl witch who always had a smile on her face was rarely happy. "Very well, Valkyrie. Carrow has an emotion-based power source. She feeds off happiness specifically, but she can't seem to, uh, generate it herself. She's always thinking about how to find more. Like someone on a diet will always think about food."

Nïx squinted at the ceiling. "Carrow is in an environment that she hates worse than anything."

"The woods?" Mari cried. "She can't stand the outdoors!"

"And yet personal preferences rarely figure in my visions, favorite Wiccan-type person."

"Tell me, Nïx, why was she taken there? *Who* took her? Has anything like this happened before?" Nïx had been around for three thousand years. She'd seen a lot. "Have Loreans ever been abducted like this?"

"Yes," the soothsayer answered, adding in a whisper, "by the Order."

"Care to extrapolate?"

"No."

"Tell me who they are!" No answer. "Is it the military?"

Nïx narrowed her eyes at Mari. "Define *military*."

"You know, soldiers, army, et cetera."

Nïx squinted again. "Define *army*."

"At least tell me if they're human!"

"Define—"

"Shut it, Nïx!" She pinched her forehead, then gazed up at the soothsayer. "I can't stand the thought of Carrow out there away from the coven." What if she was somewhere alone and friendless? Because Carrow's childhood had been so seriously screwed up, she didn't handle being alone well.

The soothsayer chuckled. "Ah, Nïxie plays. The Order, also known as the Deceivers, the Summoners, the Collectors, and the Mortals Who Walk on Two Legs, except I made up that last part."

"What do they want?"

"They want all the *freaks* dead. Funny. I don't *feel* like a freak. Unless le freak, c'est chic?" She shrugged. "To be fair, they only rise up whenever immortals do."

"Man, if there's one thing Carrow hates, it's being punished for a crime she didn't commit." Luckily, that didn't happen often, as Carrow perpetrated more than her share of crimes. Her last offense? Stealing a cop's horse to ride into Pat O'Brien's. Carrow's defense? She'd needed an accessory.

Mari had once asked Carrow why she so readily got into trouble with the law—the public indecency and intoxication, the vandalism, and so on. After all, Carrow could harvest power without jail time. "Is it just to get back at your parents?"

Carrow had answered, "At first, yes. Now it's just tradition. . . ."

When Nïx said nothing, Mari grew still. "Immortals *haven't* risen up, right, Valkyrie?"

"Have we not?" She frowned. "I'll have to check my inbox. But I'm fairly certain we were going to, maybe, just a jot. Like against industrial polluters and people who take candy from babies. Those who drive slow in the left-hand lane and men who wear Members Only jackets, naturally."

Mari gaped at the other Valkyrie. Not *all* of them looked surprised. A couple raised their chins. "Have you all gone as crazy as Nïx?"

Though few in the Lore dared to cross her, if anyone would, it'd be her half sisters.

Nïx continued, "Things came to a head with this Order a few years back when they overestimated their firearmy might, and made an incursion against us. Even with their technology, all were massacred. 'Not to be borne!' they said. So now they study us for weaknesses. I can't fault them, really. If humans presented *any* kind of mystery, we'd probably vivisect them as well."

Vivisect? Mari swallowed. Dissecting while the subject was still alive. Her voice broke when she asked, "How do I get to Carrow?" When Nïx merely shrugged, Mari vowed, "I'll go to the mirror, Nïx."

Mari was a captromancer. She could travel through mirrors, could touch them to focus her powers, and could gaze into them to divine secrets. Slight problem with the latter. Though she could commune with a mirror and have Carrow's location in seconds, Mari would likely entrance herself into a mystical coma, possibly forever.

Nïx quirked a brow. "And what would you tell your overprotective Lykae husband? If he found out your intentions, he'd spank you."

Bowen would, in fact, go ballistic if he got a single werewolf whiff of this. He'd never allow it—even though the Lykae had begun to fear that one of their own had been snared by the people who'd taken Carrow.

"Because we are friends, I am offering my services as a surrogate spankee." Nïx said this playfully, but she rubbed her forehead as if it ached.

Mari studied her expression, realizing that Nïx looked *tired*. "I won't go to the mirror *if* you give me something I can use."

Suddenly Nïx tensed. When her amber eyes began to glow, the other Valkyrie eased forward, awaiting whatever foresight—or insight—Nïx was about to divulge.

"They're on an island, undetectable by our kind," she said. "It can't be seen by boat or plane, nor located on any map. To find it, you have to look for something else. To reach it, you have to uncover the key."

Riddles now? "The key? What is it?" Mari demanded.

"Who."

"What?"

"Where? Why? When?"

"Nïx!"

"The key is a *who*. Not a *what*."

"Then who is it?" Mari said. *Oh, gods, please tell me.*

"Don't remember." Over Mari's sputtering, she said, "I recall he's an immortal male. Filled with evil. Obsessed with something as intangible as smoke. Find him, reach the island." She rose. "I have much to do, young Mariketa. And I can't tell you anything more, because I know nothing else." Gazing at the ceiling, she tapped her chin with a claw-tipped finger. "Ooh, oooh, except for the fact that Carrow is soon to die!"

7

Malkom sprang forward, snatching the female's ankle just as she dropped from the ledge. She screamed, was still screaming as he flung her up to safety.

She landed on her belly, clawing at the sand to get away from him, but he clutched her slim leg tight in his fist. Though she thrashed, she gained no ground.

Why was she resisting him? Confusion roiled. *Why can she not recognize me as I have her?*

Her scent was so feminine, so maddening to him. Lust assailed him as he raked his eyes over her back, her narrow waist, her flaring hips. Her body begged to be mated. At the thought of impregnating the female before him, his horns straightened even more, and his shaft pulsed in his trews.

But she surprised him with a mule kick that connected with his mouth, splitting his lip.

No, do not taste the blood. . . .

Against his will, his tongue flicked his lip. One hot drop made him even more crazed. All his vampire instincts rushed to the fore. His newly beating heart thundered, his chest heaving with breaths.

The instinctive drive to plant his seed—the seed she'd brought forth—was overwhelming him. He'd produced it for her, but he couldn't lose it until he was *inside* her. The throbbing pressure turned to pain.

Cannot fight this!

When she kicked out again, he planted himself betwixt her thighs, capturing her wrists behind her back with one of his hands. As she flailed, the remains of her skirt rode up her hips, baring . . . a sight such as he'd never seen before.

Her undergarments were gone. In their place, she had a thin band of shining silk that encircled her hips, then dipped between the curves of her shapely backside.

Astonished, he beheld this vision with his body shuddering and his cock about to explode.

She still resisted beneath him. And some part of him *wanted* to release her, to not do this thing he seemed driven to do.

To *not* use her as he had been used.

But her thrashing goaded the vampire within, made him want to pin her down, made him desperate to drink her. His demonic instinct clamored for him to come inside her body, to mark her neck and claim her as his own.

Both natures commanded him to take her neck.

When she reared back in her struggles, her mane of hair tangled in the brush, baring her neck to him. Beneath the strange collar she wore, the skin was pale and smooth, ready to glove his throbbing fangs.

Never had he bitten another. Reminded of this, rage scorched him inside. A remembered rage. How hard the Viceroy had tried to make him drink.

Now Malkom knew that the long-dead vampire would win. Because there was no way to stop this.

The pain, the frenzy. In Demonish, he rasped, "Forgive me." Then he dropped his body over hers, his head descending to low on her neck. Into her creamy skin, he plunged his fangs.

"*Unh* . . ." He groaned against her as his lids slid closed. Her rich blood streamed into his mouth, even before he sucked her.

Euphoria lit within him with each scorching drop.

Soon the pressure in his cock couldn't be denied. Unable to control himself, he ground it against her backside. The intensity, the mindlessness . . . so much fucking *pleasure*. A single thrust had him coming spontaneously, roaring with his release, snarling yells against her skin. He bucked against her over and over until the pressure receded at last.

Spent, stunned, he collapsed atop her, reluctantly relinquishing his bite. Though he hadn't released his seed, the orgasm had been mind-boggling. And her searing blood continued to dance in his veins. Satisfaction overwhelmed him until he moaned with it.

That had been only the beginning. At last, he'd know a woman. Soon his shaft would be buried in her secret flesh, pumping his seed deep inside her wetness. At the thought, he hardened at once.

Before, he'd been so frenzied that he'd been unable to wait. Now he would claim her slowly.

When he raised up to tell her as much, she struggled beneath him again. He eased his grip so she could twist around to face him. She stared at him with hatred, her vivid green eyes glinting.

Did she still not understand that she was his female?

He captured one of her hands and shoved her palm against his chest, over the heart she alone had brought back to life. *"Minde jart."*

But she cried out in pain. Only then did he realize he'd broken her wrist in the struggle.

He jerked away from her. She was an immortal of some kind—he sensed this. But she was no demoness, and now he'd hurt her with his unnatural strength.

Abomination, his mind whispered.

She rose unsteadily, looking at him as the Trothans had—with revulsion.

When she began backing away, he said, *"Alton, ara."* *Come, female.* But she didn't speak Demonish.

Damn it, 'twas not safe for her out here. In this plane lived a thousand different threats, beasts as well as other demon fugitives. He ran his hand over his face, then tried to communicate in Latin.

In a low voice, she replied in Anglish. He'd heard her talking earlier but hadn't accepted that she spoke that cursed off-plane language. *The one I learned as a boy from my master, his urgent mutterings in my ear. . . .*

The one the Viceroy had tried to force Malkom to speak. Desperate for one less trait to share with the vampires, Malkom had tortured himself to forget that language forever.

How the Viceroy would have relished that Malkom's female spoke it!

"Alton!" Once more, he ordered her to come to him.

Surprisingly, her chin went up, her uninjured hand rising with a lewd gesture.

He comprehended this. Females who were lewd

often came from the lower classes. She could even be
a slave, considering the collar round her neck and her
provocative clothes.

But everything else about her indicated nobility. A
quick cataloging of her unusual dress revealed that her
intricate boots were of the finest leather. She wore a siz-
able jeweled ring, and her ears were pierced for more
adornments. He knew she wore silk, one of the most
valuable commodities in Oblivion.

She spoke again, the sounds clipped. Though he
didn't understand the words, he distinguished the tone.
She'd just given him a command. Definitely not a slave.

Did this highborn think to order him? The demon
urge to master his mate clawed within him.

Dimly he realized she'd begun panting her breaths.
Her green irises soon glimmered with pinpricks of
light, like starbursts. Her visage was marked with aggression, her plump lips curling back from her little
white teeth. But when she spoke, her words were purr-
ing, sounds tugging on his memories.

He recognized the word *vampire* just as he spied
light glowing in her palm.

After the demon-vampire had drunk her and used her
body as his plaything, he'd experienced pure satisfaction for the briefest moment. And she'd seized on it,
fueling her power.

Now she manifested the crackling energy in her
good hand. It hadn't been much to feed on . . . but she'd
make do!

"If you knew what kind of week I've had, you prick!" Carrow bombarded him, laserlike beams exploding from her. They connected with the dazed demon, pitching him into a rock face, the stone crumbling around him. "That's for biting me, Neanderthal."

She'd never been drunk from before. He'd stolen her essence—and possibly so much more. How long would it take before she knew the total damage? "Keep your filthy fangs to yourself!"

She fired another shot and another, until he dropped to his knees, lurching in pain. "That's for breaking my wrist." She wasn't strong enough to kill him, but torturing him was more rewarding than anything she could remember. Yet somehow she forced herself to quit, reserving enough energy for a cloaking spell.

Though Slaine was down, amazingly, he wasn't out. He lay, still conscious, his massive body quaking. He reached for her, so she reared back her leg and punted her pointy-toed boot into his balls.

His strangled bellow was *delicious*.

Then she made herself undetectable. To him, she was as good as vanished. He'd see, scent, and hear nothing. She'd leave behind no trail.

Cloaked like this, she hurried away, cradling her broken wrist, running as fast as she could manage in this strange place. About twenty minutes into her escape, she had to flatten herself against another rock face as he charged past, appearing hell-bent on finding her, his onyx eyes firing with determination.

How had he recovered so quickly? Those beams

should've scrambled his brains. His spear wound still bled, but again, he didn't seem to notice it.

When he thrashed through the woods in one direction, she took off in the other, hoping to gain distance away from his mountain lair.

She forced herself to continue until his roars of frustration grew distant and night began falling. As the brown of the sky darkened to black, the winds increased their howling, the temperature dropping sharply.

Morning on the island must be late afternoon in Oblivion. No wonder they wanted the vemon at the portal at midnight—they hoped to capture him in daylight if possible.

When the dust swirled so hard she could no longer see her way, she found a rock overhang to weather out the now freezing night.

Huddling under the cover, weak from blood loss and thirst, she stared down at her bruised and broken body. She could heal herself with her remaining power, but then the cloaking spell would fade.

Noises surrounded her; the plane was filled with life, even more creatures wailing at night. If her spell wore off, she'd be at their mercy. She raised her fingers to her torn neck. And at his.

No, there'd be no healing, no matter how much pain she was in. Nor would there be any other spells, though she had no water canteen, no food, no blanket.

Now she'd kill for the clothes and gear she'd ridiculed at the facility. When Dixon had outfitted her with an assault pack filled with a Multipurpose Portable Tool Kit, a high-powered flashlight, *twelve* pairs of socks, MREs, and a first aid kit, Carrow had been so smug. "Though I dig the tacticool chic, Dixon, I'm an immortal, remember? Unless that gauze can fix a be-heading. Oh, and twelve pairs of socks? Wool ones for the enchantress? Now you're just being silly, human."

Carrow stared out into the night. Some blister care and wool socks would do her so right just now.

A lone witch torn from her coven. In pain. With no friend to buoy her.

Gritting her teeth, she decided that she'd simply have to buoy herself. She would keep fighting for her life—and for Ruby's.

Yet even as Carrow thought this, a small part of her asked, *But how much more can I take?*

Just before she finally slipped into a fitful sleep, her eyes flashed open. She'd suddenly remembered what the word *cotha* meant.

Earlier, the demon had told her . . . *to run.*

8

For hours, Malkom tore through the brush, relentlessly searching for his female after she'd disappeared right before his eyes.

He couldn't locate her, couldn't scent her, yet he *sensed* she was still on his mountain. Which meant she hadn't returned whence she came—the portal where immortals were disposed of.

Which begged the question: Who in their right mind would *ever* willingly let a woman such as that go?

When he would chase misery and fight an army to possess her?

In the past, he'd had no use for a female, had been pleased not to have one as a liability to protect. But now the knowledge that a creature like her—finer than any he'd ever seen—*belonged* to him burned in his mind, changing everything.

She's mine. So I will keep her. At last, he would be master over another, would guide another's destiny and marry it with his own.

If he had any doubt they would be a match, he quelled it, reminding himself that he was the strongest male in this plane; she was the most beautiful female.

She was his due.

He felt about her as he did about his territory. He'd use his strength to protect both.

But not if he couldn't find her. He spied the tracks of that troop of ghouls as they prowled for her still, as well as the deep prints of a deadly Gotoh. The wastelands swarmed with those vicious creatures, difficult even for Malkom to destroy.

Have to locate her. . . .

In fact, there were countless lethal beasts that were native or had been dispatched here that had bred and populated the plane, making it a death trap, even for an immortal. Even for one with her power, if she wasn't wary.

He rubbed his chest, still astounded by the lightning-like force she'd unleashed. Her kick to his testicles hadn't been mildly delivered either.

What *was* she? Every being he'd ever heard of had been exiled into Oblivion from fabled planes—places of extraordinary rumors that could never be true.

She might be an elemental fey who controlled lightning and utilized cloaking spells. But her ears weren't pointed. She could be a sorceress or a witch. He doubted she was the latter. Malkom had always heard that witches were toothless hags with black hearts, pitiless mercenaries who sold hexes.

Besides, if she could wield those kinds of powers, why hadn't she struck down the demons who'd initially captured her?

He began to suspect she'd had no power then, had leeched it from him, from his release—like a succubus.

With her beauty, she could certainly be one of that

kind. If she was a succubus, she would weaken again, unless another demon inhabitant provided her with "nourishment." There were dozens more of them just beyond his mountain territory, all fugitives like him.

Another male touching what's mine. The idea enraged him, and he ran even faster. Never would another know her perfect body.

And she was perfection. By the gods, she'd been blessed. Flashing green eyes. Buxom curves. Pale skin as soft as the priceless silk she wore. At the memory of her taste, he shuddered with pleasure.

Her blood had been like wine.

His wild search for her had almost taken his mind off his transgression this night. He'd drunk straight from a being. He was a vampire in body and spirit— because he could never go back. Malkom knew he could be satisfied only by drinking from her sweet skin every night.

Part of him blamed her for this fall, for making him lose control. After all, he'd never bitten another before her. Not even when the Viceroy willed it, trying to break him. The years of starvation, the torture.

In the end, Malkom's body had been naught but a husk.

He ruthlessly shoved those memories away, filling his mind with images of her. Yet then came the memory of those green eyes glinting with tears— or narrowed with disgust. Even if the female hadn't understood his words tonight, she'd understood his intent. But his mate had felt no answering frenzy for him.

Perhaps his dual nature had clouded her mind, dulling her inherent need for him. Mayhap she couldn't recognize in him the demon he used to be.

She'd *fought* him. In turn, he'd broken her bones. And now he hazily recalled that he hadn't merely pierced her neck.

Malkom had torn her skin.

He'd harmed the most precious thing he'd ever been given, a woman delivered unto him to safeguard.

Not to ravage.

Never could he have imagined that *both* his demon and vampire natures would rise to the fore. If he hadn't lost control and spent himself against her . . .

He understood why she'd run. Since she didn't recognize him as her mate, she believed him to be no different than the demons he'd saved her from. But Malkom *wasn't* like them.

Somehow he would have to convince her that as his mate, she was his chattel, and by claiming her he would merely be taking what already belonged to him.

But without speaking her language, he could never explain these things. . . .

When the night began to wane, Malkom finally slowed. He gazed round him at the dust-blown wastelands, accepting that he might not find her before dawn.

So he decided he'd do whatever he could to ensure her safety.

To do what he did best.

When he scented the ghouls, he attacked with all the ferocity seething within him.

◆ ◆ ◆

A growling sound woke Carrow the next morning. Her head jerked up—*has the vemon returned?*—but the noise had faded.

Probably her empty stomach.

She rubbed her gritty eyes with the heels of her palms, but she could see little of the area around her. Though the winds had died down, the smoke was still suffocating.

Gods, she was in a bad way, even more exhausted than before. Throughout the night, she'd dozed intermittently in an unsettling slumber, rife with dreams about Ruby and the lives waiting for them back home. She'd been on edge—ghouls had wailed, the sounds chilling her. Then near dawn, they'd abruptly . . . stopped.

Carrow's stomach growled loudly, reminding her that no one was bringing gruel to her cell this morning—and that she hadn't really eaten in over a week. Her thirst was even worse, her mouth as dry as the swirling dust.

She rose with a grimace, her every muscle protesting. With her first step, the blisters riddling her feet threatened to burst. Her healing wrist ached, and smoke burned her eyes and nose.

Ignoring her discomfort, she set out, with no idea of where to go, intent only on sating her thirst and hunger. She figured she was s.o.l. on the former—short of locating the water mines. The ones guarded by Slaine.

But she had to try. Hours had passed since she'd had a drop of water, and last night she'd run for miles in this desert climate. Bad enough for anyone, but especially for Carrow, who hailed from a bayou city known for its moisture.

At every turn there, she was inundated with damp gulf breezes, pounding showers, or sultry humidity.

How Carrow yearned to get herself and Ruby back to the city! To return to their wonderful coven and an existence filled with friends, pranks, and revelry.

For most of her childhood, Carrow had been as good as alone, her neglectful mother and father showing no interest in her. Her toys had echoed in mausoleum-like mansions where "lowly" servants were forbidden to speak to her.

Then her parents had turned her over to the coven at Andoain, the hearth and home where she'd met her beloved mentor Elianna and eventually Mari—a place where Carrow had been enveloped by a sisterhood of witches, cherished and protected.

She desperately missed everyone, but especially Mari.

Though Mari was so full of power—more so than any other Wiccan—she couldn't use the majority of it without gazing into a mirror, her focusing tool. Only problem? Whenever she communed directly with a mirror, she accidentally mesmerized herself, unable to break her gaze.

Carrow had nicknamed her Glitch, short for *glass witch*.

The last time it'd happened, Mari had mesmerized herself so deeply that her Lykae husband had barely broken the enthrallment. Apparently, it'd been a bloody, grueling affair and far too close a call.

If Mari hadn't sent in the cavalry by now, then she wouldn't be able to help without going to the mirror. And if that was the case, then Carrow *hoped* no help was coming.

Don't do anything stupid, Glitch.

Wait . . . had she heard that growling sound again? Not her stomach? The tiny hairs on her nape rose. She scanned around but couldn't see more than a few feet in any direction. *Keep moving.*

Her powers and her cloaking spell were already faltering, which meant that she was no longer invisible. The beasts she continued to hear could find her now. As could those ghouls.

Would that vampire demon search for her during the day, or would the dim sunlight be enough to confine him to the shadows?

She lifted her gaze to the brown, hazy sky and felt no warmth. With the dust buffeted about, he probably could emerge, especially since he was a halfling of sorts.

But here's hoping the vemon holes up.

Just as she was licking her chapped lips, her stomach growled again. Water, food. Gods, she hated the outdoors! She'd always found it hellish—and that was before the outdoors had been situated *in hell*. Bizarre plants sprouted in profusion here, all petrified, of course. Nothing was green in this place.

Keep going, Carrow. One stinging foot in front of the other. She found a rock face and tromped alongside it, figuring she could be ambushed only from three sides.

After an hour of following the rock and "hunting," she concluded that there were no Big Gulps to be self-served or juicy berries to be plucked, no mouth-watering steaks growing on trees or ice cream ripe for harvesting.

Frack.

Half-delirious, she muttered, "I haaaaaate this place."

This was all Slaine's fault. He had to go all batshit crazy on her. Because he'd made her flee, her thirst and every blister on her feet were his fault. Dixon had nailed him dead to rights: brutish, filthy, severely disturbed. *I despise his abominable ass!*

Urban Carrow shouldn't ever be in a place like this, wouldn't be if not for him. She raised her grubby hands to her tangled hair, plucking free *a twig.*

Frack, frack, frack.

She noticed her clunky ring was loose on her finger. The Order's gruel diet had done a number on her previously wood-worthy figure. With a weary sigh, she lowered her hands to stare at her emerald ring.

Carrow's parents had given it to her on her twelfth birthday, directly before they'd abandoned her at Andoain.

Her father had visited there once, years later, to get her into college. Upon leaving, he'd absently patted her on the head, saying, "Send us report cards, and we'll continue sending money."

When she'd dropped out—because there was little happiness to be found on campus during finals—she'd sent a letter to her parents instead of a report card. In it, she'd written: "If you're actually taking the time to read this, then go to hell and shove your money up your asses."

Without fail, the next check had come.

I'd never treat Ruby as they did me. Reminded of why she was here, Carrow tried to reason out a game plan.

Since this demon was violently out of control, she couldn't even approach him, much less communicate with him. The Order's plan—witch lures vemon to portal—was laughable.

She narrowed her eyes. Had those mortals known she was Slaine's mate? How could they have? Unless they had an oracle or some sort of immortal stoolie slipping them intel.

Maybe *that* was why Carrow had been chosen so specifically for capture. It wasn't as if they'd just stumbled across her and decided on a nab. They'd sprung her from County.

If the Order had known, then she surely couldn't trust them.

Yet she had to operate under the assumption that they would let her go. Again she thought, *What are two witches to them?* And Carrow still had no idea where their island was. The Order wouldn't suspect she had the wherewithal to lead anyone back to the facility.

Because she didn't.

Now, Mariketa on the other hand . . .

In any event, this plan of theirs needed tweaking. They were fools if they thought Slaine could be controlled. They wouldn't be able to predict his strength—even an immortal like her had been shocked by it.

Carrow raised her fingers to her neck, to her healing bite mark. It fully sank in then that Malkom Slaine had taken her blood. There were repercussions from that act so risky she couldn't bear to think about them yet.

Which meant the demon was even more dangerous than she could ever have imagined.

Malkom yanked off the last ghoul's head, already scanning for something else to kill.

Seven ghouls he'd destroyed this night. With no sign of her still. The drive to mate with her was there, but something else—some unfamiliar feeling—weighed on him.

He felt as if he were losing his mind, *knowing* she was near, yet finding no tracks, no scent.

Over the course of his search, he'd located only her belongings. Her food, water container, and bag had been scattered in the brush among the demon gang's corpses.

He'd collected all her possessions for her, puzzling over the strange tube of food she'd packed and the peculiar canisters and bottles. But he'd stowed everything near his mine, carrying her full water canteen with him in case he should find her.

Seeing that water container had reminded him that she would already be suffering the dangerous effects of thirst. Dizziness, delirium. Suffering *needlessly.* Malkom was rich in water.

What he wouldn't give to go back to last night. He wouldn't have frightened her, wouldn't have uncontrollably slaughtered those demons.

He tried to tell himself he wouldn't have stolen her blood, but at the memory of that pleasure, he knew he would be lying—

Her scent.

At last! For hours, he'd been unable to detect her, but now he charged headlong in her direction.

As Malkom closed in, he slowed. Better not to make his presence known—she might turn herself invisible again or blast him with her hands.

So he scaled a cliff to follow her from above. At his first sight of her, relief soughed through him. But he kept a vigilant eye on her, ensuring that she didn't come across one of his many traps or some maurading beast. He followed, observing her behavior, puzzling out the foreign little succubus.

Always observing. But this time he enjoyed it. He could watch her for hours, her expressions were so revealing. And though her mutterings were incomprehensible, he recognized the tones. She was no longer afraid—she was *vexed;* kicking rocks, then seeming to curse them.

Even when so visibly exhausted, she was still lovely. Satisfaction swelled his chest as his gaze moved from one exquisite feature to the next. Her lashes were long, her cheekbones high and elegant. Her lips were full.

Before he'd encountered her, he'd never comprehended why males mused on what their mates would look like, what color hair or eyes they might have. As if a male should care more about his female's coloring than he should a fine horse's! Now Malkom experienced an unknown-before pride that his woman was a black-haired beauty.

Though he might have imagined his fated one would be a match for him—a weary and hardened demoness used to deprivation—she was his opposite in so many ways.

She had no fangs or claws, and her skin looked as if it'd never once seen the harsh sun. Whereas he was the son of a whore, he believed she'd been raised as a noble.

Yet she wore a collar, as slaves did. At the thought of owning her that way, his member stiffened. He imagined selecting her, expending as much wealth as necessary to secure her, then taking her back to his lair to enjoy.

In the past, his discipline had kept him from obsessing over intercourse. Now that there was the possibility of claiming her, his eagerness couldn't be stemmed. He wanted the use of her body at his will, wanted to learn her female form.

If he studied her enough, he could figure out how to pleasure a woman. As it was, he didn't even know where he'd begin touching her. He'd never felt a female's body, much less fondled one's sex.

But he had to believe he could find the key to her desires. One of the earliest lessons he'd learned as a youth was that everyone had a key. Were his woman's ears sensitive? Her neck? He imagined piling up that mane of hair and placing his lips on her nape. *Would my hands covering her breasts make her tremble?*

She hissed in a breath, her limping more pronounced. Whether noblewoman or slave, she was clearly not accustomed to a place this harsh. She rubbed the back of her neck, pinching the muscles there. At least her wrist seemed to be healing.

Eventually, she hobbled over to a bone tree stump,

sinking atop it. With a look of dread, she peered at her boots. As she gingerly drew off the first one, she bit her bottom lip to keep from crying out.

The short black hosiery beneath was affixed to her blisters. As she removed the second boot, he winced for her, but she never made a sound. His female was strong in resolve, if not in body.

When she twined the length of her hair into a knot atop her head, he saw the faint outline of his bite. The night before, she'd sneered the word *vampire* just before she'd sent blazing shots to his chest. If that was how she saw him, perhaps she hated them as much as he did.

She'd seemed more furious about his biting her than his shoving against her body for release. He understood her aversion. He'd been drunk thousands of times.

It had never grown any easier to take.

Yet it would be impossible not to enjoy her neck again, now that he'd experienced the bliss of it. He narrowed his eyes. *Give and take.* For years, he'd ceded his blood. *I wear my scars—I am owed!* Her blood would be a small price to pay for his protection.

Malkom didn't know how she'd gotten herself exiled into these infernal wastelands; he *did* know that she was damned lucky to have a strong arm to protect her here, considering her fragile nature and inconsistent power.

Perhaps she needed a token to remind her of how much she needed him.

9

Just after she'd somehow stuffed her swollen, pulpy feet back into her boots, she spied a blur of motion in the smoke beside her, heard a thump. Something had landed a couple of feet away, and it wasn't moving.

What now? Exhaling irritably, she leaned over.

Sightless eyes stared up at her. She scrambled back, tumbling off the stump onto her ass. There lay the head of one of the ghouls from the night before, its throat slashed, slime still oozing from serrated arteries.

She gazed up, squinting through the miasma, detecting a large form on the cliff above her. The demon.

Why would he do this? Was it some sick kind of warning?

Her temper ignited, melting away any fear of him. "What is wrong with you?" She leapt to her feet, ripping open every remaining blister on them. *I am so over this!*

She was exhausted and battered, her temples beginning to pound. Her feet felt like someone had poured acid on them. Her pierced neck was in the itching, reddened stage of healing. "That slime got on my boot! Disgusting demon!"

The last twenty-four hours had been the worst of her

entire life. And he was going to keep at her? "You think a decapitated head will scare me? You think it'll cow me into accepting you? Your 'attentions'?"

She snatched a softball-sized rock from the ground and flung it in his direction, heard a grunt. "I've had stalkers before, you asshole!" Some really demented ones, too. One of them had strangled Mari's cat, leaving it on the front porch at Andoain. Mari had tried to resurrect the poor animal, but the process had devolved into *Pet Sematary* territory, or as Mari had sniffled, "Tigger came back . . . *wrong.*"

To make Mari feel better, Carrow had cursed the stalker to fall in love—with cacti.

When I get my powers back, demon . . .

The thought made her hesitate. Why would she ever expect to get them back here? Everything was just as miserable as she was. Hell, diddling the freaking vemon was her best hope for energy.

No, she wasn't there yet, wasn't ready to accept Slaine's "claim." There had to be another way to save Ruby.

Carrow listened for a response, heard nothing. "Whatever you're going to do, do—it—*now!*"

Again, no reply. As long as she was utterly vulnerable, maybe she shouldn't antagonize the mythical abomination.

She gave a start when he dropped down just before her, crouching beside the head. She braced for another assault, but he merely watched her, calmly appraising.

His eyes were blue, not an enraged black. Instead of the mindlessness of the night before, there was intelligence burning in them, an animal cunning that kept her on edge.

No imminent attack? Could she be so lucky? She let out a shaky breath. Maybe he'd just wigged out because of his vampire blooding?

Able to see him more clearly now, she surveyed his appearance. He'd braided some hanks of his hair as warriors did in olden times, but the rest hung down, covering a good deal of his face. His hair and horns were so sand-coated, she couldn't determine their color. She was going with *darkish* for both.

There were bands of something like greasepaint streaked across his cheeks, reminding her of the camouflage the special-ops boys used on missions. Maybe that was why the vemon had seemed invisible last night?

His jaw and chin carried stubble that couldn't decide if it wanted to be a beard or not. She wished she could see his face clean-shaven—or hey, just *clean*. His nose was crooked, probably from an early break that hadn't healed right. It made him look like a bruiser.

Of its own accord, her gaze dipped to his mouth, a harsh slash with barely noticeable fangs. For some reason those fangs made Carrow think of the women she knew back home who *loved* being bitten. . . .

On the whole, she didn't believe Slaine was hideous, but he wasn't hot by any means. Except in the body department. Again her gaze dipped. She grudgingly admitted his physique was *magnificent*.

While his hips were narrow, his shoulders were broad, real doorway wreckers. His chiseled torso was a masterpiece of flexing ridges, one lean side inked with that flaring black tattoo. The worn leather of his pants encased muscular thighs, and dark leather cuffs circled his brawny forearms and wrists.

She noticed his chainmail and chest had been cut in several new places—and that his left nipple was pierced with a small silver bar. Surprisingly, she found that aspect of the dirty demon . . . sexy. In fact, everything about him from the neck down was.

Her breaths a thread shallower, she met his gaze, then tilted her head. His eyes really were an arresting shade of blue.

Just when she was about to deem one more thing semi-handsome about him, he shoved the head at her and it rolled to her feet.

"Really. *Really?* You crazy—ass—demon . . ." She trailed off, craning her head as he rose to his full, towering height.

He held out his hand, palm up, and grated, *"Minde ara, alton."*

She thought he'd said, *My female, come.* Ah, Hekate, he wanted *his* female, his mate—to claim. She swallowed. He would consider her his property. A warrior like him, in a world like this . . . soon, he'd just dispense with the chitchat and *take* what he wanted. "You jump me again, and I'll tag you in the ballbag just like last night."

His gaze was intent on her face, but not in an admiring way. He looked as if he was anticipating her next move.

Which he could never discern . . . because *she* had no

idea what she would do. Ideas surfaced and resurfaced, decisions and plays analyzed and discarded.

Was the demon her best chance of getting herself and Ruby home?

He was brutal in all ways. He'd thrown a freaking *head* at her. He'd bitten her, *gorging* himself on her blood.

Could Carrow actually surrender herself to him, allowing him to claim her? The night before when he'd been in the throes, he'd broken her wrist in seconds.

The idea of her body naked and defenseless for his use sent chills through her. Chills of *fear*. Only fear.

There *had* to be another way to save Ruby without getting herself mauled by an abomination.

When he began circling her, she pivoted to keep him in sight.

Think, Carrow! There might be another option besides Slaine. She'd quickly encountered other denizens of this plane—perhaps more were nearby? Possibly less hostile than Asmodel's gang? She was on a hell plane with knowledge about a scheduled opening into a relative *heaven*—maybe she could tempt some demons to join her quest.

She could tell them, *Riches and territory can all be yours.* Basically selling them lots in the burbs. *Have you dreamed of a better life with your own backyard?*

The Order wanted her back at the portal with the vemon in tow? Then she could show with an army of plundering demons heaven-bent on a new life in paradise. *We can take over the portal, the entire facility!*

If there was one thing Carrow excelled at, it was creating chaos. She would figure out a way to lose this freak for now, then give herself a day to find other demons.

Growing impatient, he shoved out his hand again. *"Alton, ara!"*

"Come, female?" She crossed her arms over her chest. "You expect me to go with you when you tore my neck with your bite! Should I just forget that you, you *nutted* on me?"

She knew he couldn't understand her words, but it felt good to vent. "Remember that while you were all like"—she imitated his husky groan as he'd had his orgasm—"I was all like"—she whimpered and cradled her hand. "Do you understand me?"

A glimmer in his blue eyes said he might.

"So just stay the hell away from me!" She managed the smallest glow in her palms.

He snarled at them.

"I'm not afraid of you, demon." She straightened her shoulders and raised her chin.

His growl faded and he frowned, taken aback by her reaction.

Standoff. Then he made a play, presenting to her a potential game changer.

Her canteen. He'd had it looped over his back, and now held it out to her with a calculating look in his eyes.

"Give it to me." Instead, he uncapped it and took a swig. She rushed forward. "That's mine, demon." She made a grab for it, but he held it above her head. "Give it back!"

He lowered it enough that she made a futile leap for it. "Oh, fine! What do you want from me?"

Before she could retreat, he cupped the back of her neck, easing the canteen to just before her lips. Apparently, he wanted to hand-feed her the water.

She didn't trust the demon, didn't like him. He was brutish, possibly a hardened murderer. She was tempted to tell him where he could shove that canteen, but she needed the contents too badly.

Humans could die after three days without water— indoors. Carrow had been in hell for more than a day, mostly running, and she was feeling it.

"Very well." She parted her lips, and he pressed the opening against them. Water flowed, hot and metallic. Never had she tasted anything as good.

As she drank, she could feel the liquid already hitting her system, the effects washing over her with the force and speed of a drug rush. Her eyelids slid shut.

Within moments, her headache and twinges ebbed.

He drew the canteen away, but only to let her breathe for a second. "So good," she murmured.

He hastily pressed it back to her lips. She peeked at him, saw how he stared at her, his gaze hooded. He was probably growing aroused by how greedily she hit that canteen.

But she couldn't worry about that. Water ran down her chin and neck, wetting her halter over one of her breasts. *Doesn't matter.*

What was wrong with her? She was being manipulated by a demon, was captive to his whims. He could bite her at any time. *And I can barely keep my eyes open.*

He pulled it away much too soon, his eyes glued to

her sodden top. He got a sinful look in his eyes . . . then he poured water over her other breast. She jerked back, out of his hold, gasping, "Stop that!"

In the middle of a place like this, purposely spilling water seemed extravagant and wicked. She couldn't contain a shiver, and her nipples hardened beneath her halter, right before his transfixed gaze.

He gave a husky growl, emanating a weird sense of happiness. Like awe. Like wonder.

"*Ara, minde jart,*" he finally said, hitting his hand against his chest. His voice had gotten hoarse.

"Female, my . . . heart?" Again, he tried to make her understand that she was his. So he thought that was the only reason she hadn't surrendered to him? "Yes, I know I'm 'yours,' but I'm a witch. And that means that I'm not going to feel about you the same way."

In a patronizing tone, she said, "Fate doesn't force witches to like people who will only hate them. Oh, why am I even bothering trying to explain this to you?" But it occurred to her that if he were as deranged and violent as his folder said, then why was he still attempting to convince her instead of just forcing her? Why not just tie a rope to her collar and lead her away?

If this was truly a pitiless hell plane where one was either owned or a master, then had she just found the sole demon male who would *try* to win her?

Huh. For the first time since she'd arrived in this plane, she didn't feel like death was imminent—

An enormous creature sprang through the air, landing mere feet from them. She peered up in horror.

Spiderlike eyes, pasty gray skin, a yawning, fang-filled mouth. From its carapace, eight thick limbs protruded, stretching twice as long as its body. All over its bumpy skin, parasitic creatures had attached, blood-sucking and bulbous with their harvest.

Its antennae were as long as its limbs, flicking like bullwhips, rippling toward her.

One sliced the air in front of her face. Before she could move, the demon knocked her to the ground with a stiff-armed shove to her chest. She clutched her sternum, hacking for air as he faced off against the thing.

The demon roared at it so loudly that pain spiked her ears. His formidable body tensed to attack, his muscles rigid under his chainmail. He was turning demonic, fangs sharpening and horns straightening.

As she sucked in breaths, he fearlessly launched himself at the gigantic beast, maneuvering the battle away from her. Again she marveled at Slaine's strength and speed. No wonder the Order wanted him. He was by far the most powerful male she'd ever seen.

Wait . . . why was he not tracing? Though many demons and nearly all vampires could teleport, he'd *run* to her rescue and wasn't tracing now.

Just as one slime-filled limb splatted beside her on the ground, the demon glanced over his shoulder at her, his expression wild. His eyes were turning black, the calm blue gone.

Not good for the monster . . . not good for *her*.

The thing went on the offensive with uncanny quickness. She'd never seen, or heard of, anything like this, this *monster* X. The demon had demonstrated his prowess against the gang last night, but could he defeat something so colossal and fast as this?

She wouldn't be sticking around to find out.

Still gasping, she clambered to her feet, then fled headlong—from both of them. Half-blind in the smoke and clumsy with fright, she tried to ignore the pain in her sternum.

Thoughts tangled in her panicked mind. *Run! Has he broken my breastbone? What* was *that creature?* The head had been like a spider's, the body resembling a praying mantis's. Tick-like insects had covered it as they might a mammal.

Are there more of monster X?

The terrain was growing rockier, the brush thinning around larger bone trees. Had she lost them?

Her heart went to her stomach just as her feet left the ground. She screamed until the sudden movements stopped and she could take stock of where she was.

This isn't happening, this isn't . . .

When she felt a hempen rope digging into her right ankle, she accepted that she was indeed caught upside down in a rope snare, swinging from the branch of a tree. Her hair streamed down, and her skirt had hiked to her waist.

The dusty wind kissed the cleft of her ass.

"The last straw!" she screeched as blood rushed to her head. This had to be one of Slaine's infamous traps. "Ugh!" *Hate him.*

All around the edges of this clearing, bones lay scattered. Did the demon just leave his victims here to rot away? When she craned her head up to assess the damage, she felt a chill. The rope around her ankle was stained with old blood.

Need to get free, stat. If she could grab hold of the lead rope above her, she could release the tension on her ankle and get it loose. The rope in her sights, she did a sit-up, stretching . . . "Got it," she said as she wrapped her fists around—

She dropped back down with a *whoosh*. What the hell? The bastard had greased the rope. That demonic, vampiric bastard. If she couldn't get hold of the rope above her, then there was no escape. Which he obviously knew.

She hung limply, swaying from her momentum, cursing Malkom Slaine's very birth, until she felt her ring slipping down her finger. "No!"

But it was gone, helped along by the grease on her hands. "Damn him!" She heard a ping. Following the sound down, she swiped her hair from her eyes with her greasy hands—

Her ring had just beaned a second monster X in the head. Another one of those things was directly below her, gazing up with its mouth wide, its body crouching to spring.

10

Antennae slashed all around Malkom; he dodged them to attack the beast's body.

Now his succubus female could behold his skill. As with the head he'd gifted her, this contest was proof that Malkom could protect his woman and their offspring.

He landed a mighty blow, glancing back. Had she seen it? Was she looking—

She was *gone*? Foolish female! Running from him when the Gotoh hunted in pairs? He had to dispatch this one swiftly.

And then I am going to heat her backside for this!

The beast sprang closer, the tip of an antenna slicing past his face.

"Demon!" she screamed from a distance. A second Gotoh's roar sounded. Which meant it was about to feed on its captured prey.

Though Malkom hadn't killed the first one, he sprinted toward the sound, knowing the beast would follow him, knowing he'd have to fight two.

Gods, to be able to trace. Even with his speed, he might not reach her in time. Pumping his arms . . . faster, faster.

His newly beating heart raced as it hadn't in centuries. Dizziness washed over him, and his vision wavered.

What was this frenzy? The feeling that had weighed on him now escalated. When he recognized it, his eyes narrowed.

This was fear. For her. It'd been so long since he'd felt it that he hadn't comprehended it.

The only people who knew fear were ones who had something to lose.

At last, he *did*. And he'd be damned if anything took her from him.

His fangs sharpened even more, that mindless furor from the night before arising again.

Swinging to avoid the creature's leaps, Carrow repeatedly flung her body upward to try to secure that lead rope. "Demon!" she screamed again. When the thing's claws brushed her hair, she added, "Get your ass over here!"

Slaine burst into the clearing. He scowled, yelling at her in Demonish as he launched himself at the beast.

"Behind you!" she cried when the original one appeared directly after.

He was going to have to defeat both of them—while keeping them away from her.

As he clashed with them below, she hung like a pendulum, helplessly swinging. The second creature kept jumping for her, and the demon kept batting it away while still contending with the first.

With one flick of its antenna, it slit through the demon's chainmail, slashing his chest. He bellowed in fury as blood gushed. But he caught the antenna the next time, using it to force the creature's head down. Hauling it back like a leash, he moved in for the kill, claws bared. A grisly spray of blood erupted. The thing was no more.

One down. But while Slaine had been occupied, the other had begun crawling spiderlike up the tree for her. "Demon! *Eyes up!*"

At once, he leapt for the beast, tackling it away from her. He wrestled it to the ground, evading those sharp antennae as he punched holes in its body. The thing snapped that mouthful of fangs, but the demon was too quick, too powerful. . . .

With a wrenching *crack,* he twisted off the second one's head. Two down. He hauled the twitching bodies away.

Now that the fighting was done, no longer was he roaring or berating her; he'd grown eerily silent as he crossed to the bone tree behind her. She nervously twisted around, pulling her skirt over her ass while keeping him in sight.

He untied the lead rope, feeding out a length to lower her. As he approached her with the line in his fist, she saw he was battle-maddened once more—and getting aroused. The raised outline of his shaft bulged in his pants.

He eased her to a sitting position on the ground, just enough that the pressure was relieved from her ankle. As he stalked closer, she heard his heartbeats *accelerating,* his breaths growing more hectic than they'd been in the fray. His fangs were elongating.

He was about to bite her. Again.

"No, demon!" She scuttled back, but he merely stepped on the rope. "Bastard!" When her palm landed on a stone, she chucked it at him, popping him in the horn. "Snap out of this!"

One's memories could be taken through the blood. The more he drank from her, the more likely he'd be to see hers. He might discover her plan to betray him. *Then he'll behead me, put my head on a pike.* "Don't bite me," she warned.

His eyes now a hungry black and locked on her pulse point, he dropped to his knees before her.

"Don't, vampire!"

He growled at that.

"What? You don't like being called a vampire? Then don't act like one!"

Though she fought him, he looped his arm around her back, pinning her arms to her sides as he covered her body with his own. His erection was like a steel rod as he rocked it against her.

She thrashed as he made her arch up to him, digging her nails into his skin under his chainmail, scarcely breaking the surface. "Damn it, stop this!"

With his free hand, he tugged her hair to the side. When he leaned down to nuzzle her collar higher, she . . . *shivered*?

Before she could analyze her response, he gave a wretched groan and pierced her.

As he snarled in bliss against her skin, she cried out, trembling in confusion.

It doesn't hurt this time.

• • •

Malkom drank deep of her blood, a rich stream of heat sliding down his throat. Shuddering, about to come from her taste, he clutched her closer for more.

Her essence inflamed every inch of his body, stoking his need. *Searing and sweet . . .* His cock swelled, throbbing.

So sweet . . .

He groaned into his bite as he found his release. Over and over, the dry spasms racked him until his eyes rolled back in his head.

The mindless frenzy began to recede, leaving him with that awing sense of closeness, with a satisfaction he'd never known before her.

Once the pressure had finally subsided, he withdrew his fangs. Catching his breath against her neck, he felt her shivering beneath him.

Her head had fallen back, her lips parted. Could she . . . could she have *enjoyed* his bite?

When she angrily shoved at his injured chest, he rose up with an exhalation. *Or not at all.*

Staring straight ahead, she swiped her tangled hair out of her face, streaking her cheek with grease from the rope. Had her bottom lip trembled?

Could any female withstand all that she had without tears? The imprint of his hand on her chest was a glaring bruise. Her fatigue weighed on her so plainly, and his bite had weakened her even more. Now her face had paled.

He'd taken too much. He vowed that he would not suck her so greedily next time, would take but a few sips. *Have to get control of myself.*

Surely she would cry now. Damn it, if she cried, it should *not* be by his doing. Nay, he dreamed of collecting her in his arms and comforting her. He would ask her if she wanted him to take away her troubles, and she would softly nod against his neck.

She could give him purpose.

Yet he didn't have a way of asking her that.

Do I not . . . ? He'd once known her language but had buried it so deeply. He couldn't remember it without recalling his torture—and his childhood. Centuries had passed since he'd spoken it.

With a swallow, he concentrated, staring at her lovely face while struggling to recall words from a language he associated with torment and misery. How to tell her that he didn't wish for her to cry? That he needed to see her safely to his home?

That he would endeavor not to hurt her again?

When she squeezed her eyes shut and clenched her hands, he realized this female wasn't on the verge of tears.

She was on the verge of attack.

And he suspected she'd just become even more powerful than the night before.

Once she opened her eyes again, they were glittering with wrath, brilliant starbursts flashing.

Glorious female. And not a little fearsome.

When she raised her glowing hands, he exhaled, tensing his muscles, bracing for his woman's unholy pique. . . .

11

Slaine's bite hadn't been horrible. And that made Carrow furious.

Luckily, she could now vent her fury because she'd sucked in his happiness as if through a straw. *Power!* A swift, scorching infusion of it. She was even stronger this time.

"You shouldn't have done that again." Was she just like the bite whores in New Orleans who got off on having their blood drunk?

The bite whores Carrow loved to ridicule.

With a wave of one of her glowing hands, the rope around her ankle disintegrated, allowing her to stand. Another wave brought her missing ring flying to her as though magnetized. As she slipped it on, she gave him a cruel smile. "Double, double toil and trouble," she murmured. "Where do you want it this time?"

His tone stern, he said something in Demonish that sounded like an order. Carrow didn't like orders, was accustomed to giving them.

So she fired on him, propelling him across the clearing. He staggered to his feet, looking disappointed with her.

"You think I should respond differently?" She fired

again. "Though I warned you to keep your fangs to yourself?"

When he growled at her, frustration stamping his rough features, she cried, "Then treat me differently, goon! I'm as simple as that."

On her third strike, he tensed his body, bowing up to take the hit directly in the chest, almost proudly. Then he narrowed his gaze on her neck and smirked, as if to say, *It was worth it, honey.*

Her eyes went wide. "Oh, you are so dead," she vowed. "You don't even know how dead you are!" Using the last of her strongest magic, she launched another shot and heard something snap that time. Maybe his ribs? A collarbone?

Yet he was still standing! She'd tapped herself out—no more spells, no more cloaking or firing—and for what?

Gnashing his teeth, he held out his hand to her. As if with great difficulty, he sounded out, *"Home."*

Though shocked that he knew even one word of English, she said, "Go home with you? Not likely." But her curiosity got the better of her. "Oh, so now you know English?"

He frowned.

"Heh. Or not."

Still he tried to communicate with her. He waved a hand at the surrounding area, then ran his finger over his neck.

"You're telling me there's danger around here? *Duh!* How about danger with you? You bit me twice, broke my wrist, and bruised my sternum—all in twenty-four hours!" At the memory of each incident, her temper re-kindled. "Why would I ever voluntarily go anywhere with you?"

With obvious irritation, he made a dampening motion with two flattened hands—to tell her to shut up?

In a tone as dangerous as she was feeling, she bit out, "Did you just shush me?"

He put his finger over his lips, then motioned around them again.

"You *did*! You freaking shushed me? Word to the wise, demon ..." She trailed off when something rustled the brush nearby. Pointing in that direction, she asked, "What the hell is that?"

He glowered at her, as if he'd already explained this.

"Yet another thing that can kill me? Besides *Cloverfield* monsters and demon rapists—present company *not* excluded." Yet as she spoke, she recalled how he'd saved her from the monster Xs and Asmodel's gang.

With difficulty, she acknowledged that she wouldn't have lasted the day without him—and likely wouldn't survive a second night with no magic for a cloaking spell.

She remembered him warning her to run before his first attack. He'd wanted to spare her.

Unless, of course, he merely liked the chase.

Maybe he lost control solely in the heat of battle? Perhaps it wasn't Carrow who'd triggered him last night and today, but the clash with those demons and then the monster X attacks.

More scrabbling sounded, this time accompanied by a new sucking sound—from above. Of all the creatures she'd heard, the calls and cries at night, she'd never heard anything from the sky.

"*Alton, ara.*" He held out his hand for her.

What would Ripley do? She'd face the known rather than the unknown and accept help from unlikely allies. An extra gun was an extra gun, no matter who was pointing it.

Still Carrow was hesitant, absently reaching up to feel the demon's bite. Then she asked herself, *What's more dangerous than Malkom Slaine biting and claiming me?*

Answer: *Everything—else—out—here.*

Case closed.

She had two goals. To stay alive and to free Ruby. Carrow needed him for both. But she knew a male like him would expect sex from the female under his guard.

She would have to manage him, appeasing him short of sex. She ignored what might have been a flutter of excitement at the idea.

"Home," he repeated.

I'll try to establish some ground rules. "No biting." She pointed at her neck, then at his fangs while vigorously shaking her head. "Biting . . . nooo."

He gave her a look of disbelief, clearly taking her meaning—and not liking it. A spate of stern Demonish followed. Was he justifying it? To argue his point? She knew he'd enjoyed drinking her, but was it *this* important for him not to give up?

She made a *peace/viper fangs* hand sign, tapping her neck while shaking her head. "No biting, demon."

He flung his hands out in a *What gives?* gesture.

With her palms on her head, she mimed that the bite had made her woozy and her head hurt.

His lips thinned. Then, with a wary glance upward, he quickly crouched in the dirt, drawing three circles in an arc with lines between them. Once done, he pointed at the indistinct sun.

"Okay. I think I'm with you. Morning, noon, and dusk. This represents a day?"

He held up two fingers.

"Two days? Without biting? No dice, demon." She held up eight fingers.

With a warning growl, he held up five.

Perfect. When she nodded, he held his hand over his chest, his expression pained. He'd just sworn he wouldn't bite her. Though it was obviously a huge concession for him.

Could she trust his vow? In her situation, she *had* to trust this demon to a degree, had to believe he wouldn't bite her.

Her next condition wouldn't be so easy. "No sex."

Not understanding, he shrugged, then motioned for her to hurry.

How to say sex? How to *mime* sex? "Ah, gods, are you really going to make me do this hand gesture?" She made an okay sign with one hand, then threaded the forefinger from her other hand through it.

His eyes widening, he nodded emphatically.

Until she did it again while saying, "Noooo *sex*. NO."

He growled, pounding his fist over his heart again.

"Yes, I know I'm . . . yours. But you're too strong."

She made a muscleman arm, pointing at her bicep, then pointing at him.

"*Fortis?*" he said.

"Latin?" *I suck at Latin.* Carrow just memorized it for spells or used it for fun. More than once, she'd slurred, *Carrowicus much drunkicus* or *Hot-assicus in my greedy handsicus.*

But she thought *fortis* meant *strong.* Maybe. "You"—she pointed at him—"are *fortis . . . maximus?*"

His chin went up, and he nodded arrogantly, as if saying, *Tell me something I don't know.*

She scooped up a twig, pointing to herself, saying, "Me." Then she broke the twig.

He gave another nod of understanding, and again she noted the cunning in his eyes.

"So nooo sex."

Before she could extract that promise, a roar from above sounded. "Oh, shit." With a gulp, she sidled up to him. "And we're off!"

12

*T*his hike is the most enlightening one of my life, Carrow thought as they wended their way up the mountain.

For instance, in the last hour she'd learned how sardonic a lift of a demon's dirty brow could be—when she'd refused to let him carry her as they'd dodged whatever had been approaching. And she'd come to understand how important decapitated heads were.

He'd swiftly collected those monsters' heads, tying them together with a piece of the rope she'd hoped never to see again, then strung them over his shoulder. Periodically, he offered his catch to her.

"No, no, I have a pair just like them at home," she'd said. "I would just regift them." Earlier when he'd thrown that ghoul's head to her, then rolled it to her feet, had it been his idea of a gift? A vemon version of a dozen red roses, meant not to intimidate but to signal his interest and intent?

On the way to his "home," he guided her this way and that, pointing out more of his hidden traps. She used the time to assimilate all that had happened, now that her anger was cooling.

Carrow was one of those people who had bursts of

temper, then later scratched their heads, wondering, *What exactly was I so pissed about?* Yes, he'd bitten her—twice—against her wishes, but she did feel gratitude that he'd saved her life. She didn't know of another male who could've fended off two of those monster X creatures then gotten her away unscathed.

She'd never seen a monster like that before, had never heard of one in all the Lore. When she grappled with the question of what it was, her sharply honed scientifical mind deduced one answer: *manbearpig.* An amalgam, something made by sticking the parts together instead of melding them—just like the vemon.

If a demon and a vampire mated, their offspring would be unique but in harmony, like a Labrador retriever crossed with a poodle. Voilà, labradoodle! But a vemon was a *made* creature, as if one took the front half of the Lab and jammed it onto the back half of the poodle.

In other words, *wrong.*

Maybe that was why Slaine couldn't trace. Though both vampires and demons had that innate ability, vampires could trace easily while demons had to study and train to. Perhaps the two different natures clashed as they tried to do the same thing in totally disparate ways.

She gazed up at him from under a sand-coated curl. "Is that why you can't trace?" she asked him. "The vemon that terrorized New Orleans could teleport. Maybe you just can't puzzle out how?" He frowned at her. "I bet you used to be able to. Must suck not to anymore."

Now that they were seemingly out of danger, for some reason Carrow found herself talking to him. Though she knew he couldn't understand her, she asked him questions, then conjectured answers out loud. She made observations about the terrain, the declining weather.

Occasionally he shrugged without interest.

"I should name you Wilson the Volleyball. You understand as much as Wilson did and respond as infrequently. What's that?" She cupped her ear as if the demon had spoken. "No, no, you're right, Wilson *was* more hygienic."

She didn't know why she found it so pleasing to talk *at* Slaine—her dirty, befanged protector—but there it was. "Once I get back . . ." She trailed off.

When he gave her a questioning glance over his shoulder, she sighed. "Well, things are going to have to change. With me. Right now, if the Andoain coven were *The Love Boat,* I'd be a mix between Julie the recreation chick and bartender Isaac."

Carrow had long been connected in the city, able to uncover all the sins in New Orleans, seeding revelry, then harvesting power from it.

"Now all that's going to be different." She'd have to budget her spells, not use them for frivolous things like better parking places or her fledgling attempts at mind control.

Excitement lacing her tone, she said, "I think I'm going to be ready for a kid after this. If I'd been immersed in my old life when this happened, I probably would've shirked my responsibilities." As her parents had taught her. "But after this adventure, anything will feel easy. Even raising a potentially murderous seven-year-old with control issues."

The demon seemed really keyed up, as if Carrow's chitchat was bothering him. No, that couldn't be right. She wasn't Carrow "Squeaky" Graie. She'd always been told she had a bedroom voice that men found pleasing.

He pointed at her and asked, "Demonish?"

"Do I speak Demonish?"

He nodded.

"Yeah, a little," she answered, then sounded out a few words, asking for some fermented demon brew, their beverage of choice.

In an instant, his body shot through with tension, and he ran a palm over one of his horns. Gaze dipping to her lips, he swallowed.

His reaction was so thunderstruck, she suddenly grasped that her demon drinking buddies had taught her something far more naughty than "Can I have a brew, please?"

In thickly accented Demonish, she'd just asked him, "May I fellate you, if you please?"

Would I please!

Her look of realization, then of irritation, revealed that she hadn't meant to say anything such as this. Someone had taught her the wrong words.

But now Malkom couldn't stop thinking about fitting his shaft betwixt her plump lips. He recalled how greedily she'd drunk from that canteen and nearly groaned imagining her working on his shaft thus. To finally know what that felt like . . .

'Twas almost better when she'd been speaking Anglish!

She crossed her arms and began to do so once more, her tone defensive.

Malkom exhaled, ignoring a twinge in the ribs she'd broken earlier. He hated when she spoke; he loved when she spoke.

The sound of her voice was so damned pleasing to him, especially since he'd been alone for so long. Every word she said was familiar, even with her foreign accent, but after so many years he could associate no meaning with them, only horrific memories of the Viceroy.

Malkom's torture had begun three weeks after the day he'd died. The vampire had released him from that cell after Malkom had killed Kallen, but only to break him.

The Viceroy had been determined to make Malkom more vampire than demon, to make him loyal to the Horde. Only so many Scârbă rituals worked, and Malkom had been a valuable asset, one they wouldn't destroy until there was no hope.

At least, not *fully* destroy.

He'd tried to force Malkom to forget Demonish, to speak only the vampires' language. Each time Malkom refused, he'd had his tongue cut out. When he'd spit blood at them, he'd had his skin flayed to the bone.

Now, to communicate with her, Malkom would have to resurrect his knowledge of that language, braving those memories. He knew he'd pay for it, would be plagued with nightmares.

He gazed over at her, releasing a pent-up breath. Once again, he was struck by her beauty, nigh tripping over his own feet as he stared.

She glanced up at him, pink stealing over her high cheekbones. She tucked her hair behind her ear self-consciously and murmured something with a questioning look in her eyes.

How badly did he want to know what she'd said?

Very badly indeed . . .

She'd just been musing that there were more layers to this demon than she'd initially thought when they reached the opening to a mine shaft.

And here was yet another layer—a barbaric, grisly layer.

In front of the entrance, a dozen pikes rose up like a frontier fort's stockade. Atop the pikes were even more severed heads! Because you can't have too many!

He'd collected them from all manner of creatures—demons, ghouls, and monster Xs. So this was what he did with them. No wonder the other demons feared him.

Fegley hadn't been lying. What a risk Carrow would be taking to march right into this demon's den. If Slaine saw her memories . . .

Pensive, she gazed back down the trap-laden trail, looking out into a black and blustery nightfall. And still Slaine's den was preferable.

When she turned back, he grated, "Home."

He looked proud, pausing to give her time to admire all of his pikes. A large insect crawled from one head's slimy nostril. *Beauty.*

The demon also looked expectant, as if he suspected she would be wowed by his collection.

"Uh, love what you've done. Your curb appeal is unparalleled." She held his gaze. "And I mean that."

He frowned in incomprehension, then ushered her toward the opening. Just before they crossed the threshold, he paused again. With his hand over his chest, he said, "Malkom."

She blinked up at him. Intros? Really? "Okay, then, I'm *Carrow*."

With a nod, he sounded out "Car-row," then led her in.

Had he wanted them introduced before he took her home? Add a layer to the demon's tally.

Inside the mine, out of the wind, the air was as humid as in New Orleans and clean, compared to the dust bowl outside. Those lava-filled stones were dotted throughout, lighting the way—not that he would need help seeing in the dark.

Stone aqueducts lined the walls, with gathering pools at intervals, while broken barrels and ancient-looking carafes littered the sand floor. Where water seeped from the walls and coated those glowing rocks, steam hissed.

So these were the fabled water mines of Oblivion, with water pockets trapped like veins of gold.

As he led her deeper within, the shaft split, and they began following an offshoot from the main tunnel. Soon, she spied an area of even brighter light glowing a welcome up ahead. When they came to the end, she realized this terminus chamber was his lair.

A demon's lair. He truly was a ground-dwelling male. And he wanted to *do* her.

Inside was a collection of those glorious rocks, warming the area like radiators, illuminating it. He had a pallet on the ground, laid out by a fire pit with a spit for cooking. Did he eat meat as well as drink blood?

The pit itself was situated under a crack in the mine ceiling, which must funnel the smoke away. Cluttering the ground were ropes, chains, and blades, likely for those traps he'd pointed out. Large bones were scattered throughout.

Along one wall, cords of firewood were stacked. On another, he'd haphazardly piled up soldiers' assault packs, many of them splattered with crusted blood. There were *dozens*. Were those bones additional souvenirs?

Studying her reaction with that analytical look on his face, he pointed to the packs, opening his mouth as if to say something in explanation. But then he closed it.

When she gave an unconcerned shrug—she couldn't care less that he'd killed those mortals—he ushered her to his pallet, then went to fetch wood for a fire.

The demon had demonstrated courtesy when he'd introduced himself. Now he was displaying hospitality. Yes, he had a tendency to growl at her repeatedly and snap his fangs, but she kept thinking about that head he'd tossed at her.

Since she now knew it'd been a gift of value, she concluded this brutal demon had made an attempt at . . . *courting* her.

If only she could understand him better. The language barrier was a problem. But he knew at least one word of English. Maybe he comprehended more? She needed to find out.

When he returned with the wood and hunched down by the pit, she gazed on, helplessly captivated by his body. The worn leather of his pants lovingly hugged those muscular thighs and narrow hips. His fingers were long and blunt-ended under his black claws.

As he started the fire with practiced movements, the sculpted ridges of his torso flexed under his chainmail, making that winding tattoo shift intriguingly.

That body is too, too much.

But, gods, the rest of him was a disasterpiece of hair and paint. Those braided hanks wouldn't do, hanging over his Valvoline-streaked face like a ratty curtain. And that scraggly stubble on his face? She'd kill to see what lay beneath.

He soon had a blazing fire started, and she leaned forward to luxuriate in the warmth, lids growing heavy. He exhaled, his eyes darkening on her, and a sudden jolt of power hit her like a Mack truck. He was *satisfied* merely having her here.

And just a thread of his happiness had powered her like this?

He was stronger than any other Lore creature, his kind the most vicious. Everything about him was magnified. It figured that he would be able to give her the most power.

She'd bet sex with him would make him *very* satisfied.

The demon was turning out to be an unpredictable, feral, bone-and-head-collecting, sexually ravenous happiness battery.

She swallowed. *All I have to do is plug him in.*

13

My female, in my home. No longer would he pass nights alone down here. He had a mate, a companion.

As she leaned closer to the fire, the light flickered over her raven-black hair, the flames reflecting in her green eyes. She had the sultriest eyes. And he couldn't seem to pull his gaze away.

At last, his woman was with him. Here to be sheltered by him, to be claimed by him.

The idea of protecting her aroused Malkom. As did the idea of providing food for her. He could imagine her expressing her gratitude with her body . . . or her mouth.

Eyes locked on her full lips, he stifled a groan, recalling what she'd said in Demonish. He envisioned her asking once more when she was on her knees, naked before him. In their negotiation earlier, she'd said nothing about his using his mouth on her—or her doing the same.

Malkom had never had his member sucked, had never received that pleasure. *No matter how many times I was forced to wring it from another,* he thought darkly, his muscles knotting with tension before he shook away that age-old resentment.

He'd always wondered how it would feel—wondered

what was so remarkable about the act that it could make a male weak in the knees, could make him crave it again and again.

Could she be coaxed to satisfy his curiosity once and for all?

Maybe she would let him do even more this night? Yes, she'd stipulated no intercourse, but only out of fear that he'd hurt her. Naturally, he'd made no vow about that, because as soon as he'd proved he could touch her without paining her, he intended to take her body.

But he *had* vowed not to drink her, and he would try to honor his oath, at least until he could explain what the act meant to him, and why she could deny him no longer.

On the hike here, he'd realized that with this woman, the Thirst didn't rule him.

The sense of connection did. As he'd taken her neck, he'd never felt more bound to another in his entire existence.

But did I really make her head hurt from drinking her? He thought back to his youth, trying to remember his own reactions. . . .

For now, he'd sate himself on animal blood, would be forced to even this night. Though he'd drunk her blood, he'd lost still more defending her.

Her stomach growled then. Reminded that she must be starving, he shot to his feet, promising to return with a feast of game birds for her to cook.

He held up his forefinger, telling her she should wait there. She would be safe within his den. Beasts avoided this place instinctively. And his foes like Ronath couldn't trace. Even if the armorer had learned that skill in the intervening years, he couldn't teleport directly into the mine shaft, a place he'd surely never been.

When she gave no response, Malkom scowled and held up his finger more insistently.

With a roll of her eyes, she gestured to the fire, plainly saying, *As if I'd leave this.*

Filled with a new purpose, he set out into the night, hunting swiftly, determined to provide for her. A half hour later, on his return, he stopped at a small collection pool to refill the canteen. As usual, he was uneasy beside the water. He began to sweat whenever he neared anything larger than a puddle, had since he was a boy.

For the first time in centuries, he forced himself to kneel so he could look at his reflection. Wondering how she saw him, he peered down.

He had horns and fangs; she did not. While her skin was smooth and clean, his was dirty, his face covered with stubble. His clothes were rough-hewn and tattered.

And those were merely the detractions that could be *seen.*

He could neither read nor cipher numbers, and his birth could not be lowlier. *I was a slave and ill used. . . .*

I killed the only friend I ever had. With a scowl, he hit the water, scattering the reflection.

While he was gone, Carrow peeled off her boots and hose, casting a spell to heal her feet, courtesy of the demon. Once her skin was mended, she wiggled her toes in the fine sand.

And she still had some power left over. If she got enough happiness out of him, she could do some bigger spells, maybe even a three on the Wiccan scale of five. She had a particular one in mind.

Determined to keep some juice on tap, she decided she'd allow herself only one more healing—either the bite on her neck, the bruise on her chest, or her wrist. The wrist was healing on its own, and the bite mark wasn't nearly as bad as the first. This time he'd pierced her skin cleanly, with no tearing.

As if he'd gotten better at it. She shivered again, recalling how it'd felt. A spike of pain, then warm pleasure.

She gazed down at her chest, cringing at the bruised outline of the demon's huge hand. The discoloration stretched nearly from shoulder to shoulder. *Chest it is.*

Another spell, and the bruise disappeared.

Shortly after, Slaine returned with a full canteen and two dead fowl of some sort. They looked like a cross between a pheasant and a chicken.

His eyes briefly widened at her unblemished feet, then he tried to hand the "phickens" *to her.*

"What do you expect me to do with them?" She shrugged with an *I got nothing* expression.

He launched into another spate of low Demonish, this time using her name. She felt like a cartoon dog listening to its owner: "Blah blah blah CARROW blah blah."

"Whatever." She pointed to the canteen.

At length, he handed it to her. As she drank, he ripped off one bird's head as smoothly as pulling a cork out of a wine bottle. When he lifted the body to guzzle the blood, she spit out the water, about to throw up.

With a scowl at her reaction, he took the creatures outside, returning once the cheasants were cleaned, dressed, and doubtless drained.

She turned away as he spitted them over the flames. But once they began roasting, she couldn't take her eyes off them. Though she was starving, and the meat smelled so good, she didn't know if she could eat it.

Carrow wasn't a vegetarian by any means, but if he had handed her those birds before he'd killed them, they would've become pets. Part of her mourned Cluck-Cluck and Chanticleer.

Even so, her mouth watered, her stomach growling loudly, and he smirked, his expression saying, *Bet you're glad you came with me.*

"Lap it up, demon. Any more satisfaction from you, and I'll fry that look right from your dirty face."

As the birds roasted, she padded barefoot over to the pile of soldiers' packs, and began rooting for anything that might make life in hell a shade better.

Every pack had a name tag on it, but instead of Sgt. or PFC, every last tag bore the title Officer, like security guards. Officer Hostoffersson had an all-purpose knife and even a small Dopp kit. *If I bean the demon in the head with that, would he take a hint?*

Officer Lindt had carried no chocolate, but he had a flask. She opened the cap and took a whiff. Had to be Jack Daniel's.

The larger packs contained changes of clothes—black T-shirts, camo pants, socks—and sleeping bags. She'd be trying out one of those tonight. Ah, to sleep under the covers, with food in her belly and warmth all around? Without getting mauled by beasties? *Luxury.*

Surely once she was rested, she could reflect on everything more rationally, could determine the best way to free Ruby and all her friends and allies.

Carrow glanced over at the demon, wondering if he was tired, as well. Did a vampire demon sleep as much as other immortals? She found him staring at her, those blue eyes stark against his streaked face.

"I bet you didn't sleep much last night either, demon. Running around after me. And here I am."

Shrug.

She looked away from him to survey his lair. *So this is where I'll be making time.* The area seemed secure and protected from the elements. As long as the demon was gladdened by her very presence here, she could milk some energy, at least enough to keep him in check.

But it definitely needed a woman's touch. *That's me—so domestic.* With a sigh, she started straightening up. He didn't try to stop her, which was good since Carrow wasn't accustomed to entering into all these negotiations, much less miming them.

Instead he gazed on in fascination as she collected the animal—*fingers crossed!*—bones in her arms, carrying them like firewood to cast out into the main shaft.

Next she coiled the ropes and myriad chains, stowing them and the countless blades in an empty corner. Finished with that, she turned to his pallet. The one he sat on. "Shoo, demon," she said, waving him away. She got the sense that this amused him, but he did move.

She pinched the corner of the worn material, lifting it with disdain, then tossed it out as well.

Once she'd replaced it with a new sleeping bag, she

said, "You can come back now."

But when she selected a second bag to lay on the opposite side of the fire, he finally conveyed an opinion. He smirked, holding up a pair of fingers together, as if saying, *You can set up two pallets if you like, but we'll still be using one.*

Ignoring him, she began unrolling it, but he hastened forward, startling her with his incredible speed. She tripped back, her arms cartwheeling and her ring flying—into the fire. "My ring, my ring!"

He looked from the fire to her with a raised brow.

That ring was the only thing she had of her parents, the only personal gift she'd ever received from them. She clasped her hands to her chest in a pleading gesture.

Sharp nod from the demon. He shoved his hand into the flames, rooting through the embers to retrieve the ring. He held it out to her, then snatched it back at the last minute, blowing on it to cool the band for her.

How could this being—who'd decorated his home with severed heads—also be so . . . thoughtful?

Once he offered the ring again, she breathed a sigh of relief and slipped it back on. But when she noticed the damage to his burned hand, she cried, "You crazy Neanderthal!" Before she thought better of it, she'd knelt beside him and seized his hand in hers.

Malkom's lids went heavy. He felt no pain, only the pleasure of her touch. After being alone so long . . .

Keep your eyes open, Slaine, to enjoy this more.

She spoke, sounding breathless, but he didn't understand her. Still, he suspected this behavior of hers was akin to affection. And he craved *more*. How to get it?

He tried to draw on what he knew of females, to determine how to make this one stay pleased and affectionate.

His knowledge was . . . limited.

He'd barely known his mother. She'd been a whore who'd despised his very existence, selling him into slavery—and eventually attempting much worse. She was no example to him. Then, in the years when he'd been a sequestered slave, he'd rarely even *seen* females, and always from a distance. At fourteen, he'd encountered young highborn demonesses who'd laughed as he'd eaten from their garbage or begged them for a drop of water.

I know naught of females.

As he pondered this, he absently brushed Carrow's hair from her cheek. The touch had been gentle and she looked surprised, maybe even . . . hopeful. Again he marveled at how revealing her expressions were. She was so easy to read; he realized he could learn—from her—how to put her at ease.

I know naught of females. He took her delicately boned hand in his own, pulling her closer. *But this one will teach me.*

What is wrong with me? Carrow didn't know what had possessed her to cross to his side of the fire, much less to touch him. When she tried to extricate her hand from his, he clutched it too hard. "You're going to hurt me again!" She yanked back, freeing herself from his grip.

His eyes darted, his mind working. To her horror, he

shoved his other hand into the fire.

"What are you doing?" she cried, leaping forward, hauling his arm back.

His chin jutting, he presented his latest burned hand to her.

With a defeated exhalation, she took it, skimming her fingers over it. "You'd go through that pain just so I'll touch you?" Sympathy bloomed in her. After centuries alone, he was so starved for attention he'd harm himself, seeking more.

She could relate. . . .

Unbidden, a memory arose of her eighth birthday, which her parents had celebrated with a soiree. The dazzling gathering had been out on their terrace, with lanterns dangling from oak limbs, stretching out over the laughing guests.

Carrow hadn't been invited.

She remembered trembling with desperation, feeling as if she'd die without their attention. She'd ditched her nannies and jumped her pony over the hedge onto the terrace. She hadn't cared if she crashed or made it—either would result in her parents having to acknowledge her existence. *Desperate, shaking, please* look *at me.*

She'd fallen from the saddle, breaking her arm and cracking her skull for her troubles. Once she'd awakened, her parents had already departed for the summer—abandoning her into the care of new, sterner nannies.

When Carrow thought back on her youth, she remembered most that clinging neediness. Sometimes, she still woke with a yawning lack aching in her chest.

And amazingly, anticipating a future with Ruby was the first thing that had ever made that yearning ebb.

"*Ara?*" he rasped.

"What?" He was studying her again. "I'm fine." Even though they didn't speak the same language, when he watched her for every tiny response, she felt like he was "listening" to her better than any man before.

He held up a finger again, then shot to his feet and away from the fire. When he returned, he had her backpack. He must have collected her things last night.

He presented it to her as if he'd known she was sad and wanted to cheer her.

"That was really nice, demon. Thank you." He truly wanted to please her. Which meant he was manageable.

I'm going to get him to that portal, and now I know how.

14

*G*ive and take.

Malkom had given her shelter and a present she'd appreciated, and they'd just finished a bountiful meal he'd provided.

Normally he would've taken the burning spit in his roughened hands and devoured the meat. But for her, he'd cut away a portion, offering it to her on his blade. In time, he'd coaxed her to bite the meat off his knife with her white little teeth. Which had made him stiffen with a swift heat . . .

Give and take. Now Malkom wanted to take something in return.

He was so used to denial, had known a lifetime of it, but no longer could he deny the need to touch her body.

I want to feel a female's breasts for the first time and hear her cries in my ear.

The only time Malkom had ever been in sexual situations, he'd been forced by either hunger, pain, or the threat of both. Never had he voluntarily been with another. Now he wanted to know what it would be like to desire—and then to possess.

Yet earlier, she'd mimed that while he'd known pleasure the night before, she'd received only pain. Twice he'd found release and given her none. He felt his neck heating.

Why *would* she want to receive him?

She yawned, stretching her slender arms over her head, her breasts pressing against her top. Gods, he'd never wanted to see a woman's body so badly. But his curiosity was understandable. He'd never encountered a female like her.

And I will be enjoying her body solely for the rest of my life.

His gaze dipped to the edge of her short skirt, to the shadow beneath it. What would she feel like down there? When he'd been a lad, the idea of rutting atop a female and spending betwixt her legs had aroused him unbearably. He knew females could grow wet inside, but would she be hot? Soft?

He remembered years ago a demon warrior saying, "The only difference between coupling with your fist and coupling with a female is that the fist doesn't follow you around afterward."

Malkom gazed down at his fist, recalling when he'd last brought himself release. Surely she'd be softer than that?

Curiosity. Possibilities. Questions about females he'd forced himself never to consider. If he could convince her that he wouldn't hurt her again, he might at last get the answers.

"Carrow."

"Yep?" She lazily gazed over at the demon, feeling more sated than she had in days. She'd had her fill of fresh water and succulent chickants. Earlier, when he'd handed her meat on a knife, she'd realized he had a thing about hand-feeding her, as if she were a prized pet or something. She'd said, "No plates? No fuss, no muss, huh?" thinking he was kidding.

But eventually she'd eaten every bite he'd offered.

She would be sleepy if it wasn't for the nearly seven-foot-tall demon getting hard right before her eyes.

"Sex," he said. In English.

"Whoa, *what*?" She nearly fell over. She'd thought they'd gone over this. But then, he hadn't promised anything on this score.

"Sex," he repeated. Thumping his chest, he said, *"Nolo fortis."*

She remembered the word *nolo* from all the times she'd pled *nolo contendere*—no wish to contest legal charges. He was trying to tell her that he didn't want to hurt her.

First of all: Yeah, right, she was going to hop back on the trust train with him. And second, even if she believed he wouldn't hurt her, she still couldn't have sex with him. Aside from the fact that she could get pregnant by a vemon, she didn't need to be intimate with him—it would make her mission that much more complicated. She shook her head. "No sex."

He flicked his hands out in that impatient *What gives?* gesture.

Okay, so he wanted to know *why*. Hmm, how to mime *betrayal*? She didn't see that answer forthcoming, so she knelt on the ground, wiping flat an area of sand. With a finger, she drew a profile of the three peaks of his mountain. Beside that she drew a doorway. The last picture was of a house. "*Minde* home," she said.

Curt nod from the demon.

She pointed at him, then herself, then walked her fingers from the mountain, through the door, to the house.

He gave another nod of understanding, but he was quick to point to himself and then her, interlacing his fingers and clasping his hands.

"Together? Yes, we'll go *together*." He would follow her through. There went the first hurdle. Now for the next. "No sex till then."

Scowling demon.

She pointed at the drawing of her house. "*There*. Sex."

She wanted him to leave this plane with her, to go through the portal to her home.

Malkom knew there were other planes, some rumored to be heavenly. When young, he'd heard tales of one with *blue* skies, of all things. Food was said to sprout straight from the ground, there for the taking. No catching or hunting necessary.

Precious water was said to fall from the sky, riches given to all.

But as he'd grown older, he'd realized that all who came through the portal told different tales. Some said the fields were golden, some said green. Some said the "oceans" were blue, some said gray.

Of one thing he was certain. No plane could possibly be worse than this one. Would he go with her? Absolutely. She might have parents, siblings, or friends there. He had no one.

In the sand, she drew the symbols he'd used for a day, then held up five fingers.

She was telling him that he wasn't to claim her until then? The better part of a week? He held up five fingers in blatant disbelief, and her lips curled the smallest bit. "Yes, demon."

He recognized the word and liked it when she called him that. He did *not* like her conditions.

When he asked her in Demonish why he'd only have her there, she merely shrugged, and again he was struck by how little he knew about her. He didn't even know *what* she was, much less what her customs would be.

Perhaps she needed a binding ceremony to make him her husband. Perhaps marrying within her culture wasn't as easy as within his. With a few words spoken . . .

At the end of those five days, would she be as anxious as he? Eagerly leading him by the hand to her home, to her bed?

Would she introduce him to her family? Hardened warriors weren't oft valued in a soft world. Yet maybe her people would appreciate the fact that he'd saved her life.

Dreams of the future, Slaine? He knew better. No longer could he dream without dreading. The two were forever intertwined for him. Every time he'd dared to anticipate a change in his fortunes—even from the earliest age—he'd had his hopes crushed.

When his mother had sold him into slavery, he'd stupidly believed he was going to be *adopted* into a new family. And as much as he'd hated what the master had done to him, Malkom had felt betrayed when that vampire had turned him out in the streets.

But Malkom had made both of them pay, along with the guards who'd delivered him to the Viceroy and eventually the vampire leader himself. All were dead. Except for Ronath.

Reminded of this, Malkom realized he couldn't depart Oblivion when she wanted. Unless Ronath attacked before then, Malkom would be leaving him unscathed, though he'd always meted retribution.

That bastard had cost him his best friend in Kallen. Malkom didn't blame Kallen for what had happened in that cell. Malkom blamed the conniving armorer for the loss.

Nearly as much as I blame myself.

Could he forgo vengeance on Ronath? After awaiting it for so long?

Malkom gazed at Carrow. Hadn't he been awaiting her for just as long, even if he hadn't realized it?

She was no distant dream. She was here, real and tangible, a fantasy made flesh. He feared after one night inside her body, he would surrender his vengeance without a second thought.

One way to find out. . . .

The wheels were turning again. What was the demon deciding?

When Carrow stood, again intending to unroll the second sleeping bag, he scowled.

"No sex," he said in halting English. "No bi-ting." He held up his palm in frustration, so clearly saying, *Then what am I to have?*

Good point, she thought as she knelt on her new bed. The demon had fed her, given her shelter and protection. Though he came from a master/slave culture, he'd actually been negotiating with her, but she knew she was on borrowed time.

Change of plans. "Fine." If she did give him pleasure, he might fuel her with more power. She glanced away and held out her own palm. "Hand shandy, anyone?"

He hadn't moved. *Great.* Was she going to have to mime this one, too? When she faced him, realization lit his expression.

He narrowed his eyes, giving her a look of distaste. As if she'd just cheapened herself.

And Carrow the Incarcerated, party girl without inhibitions, was embarrassed. Then she remembered who she was with. "You're giving me that look when you creamed jeans on me—twice? Maybe *you* should be embarrassed!"

"Carrow," he said warningly.

Yes, he'd injured her and freaked her out, but she no longer believed his behavior was due to malice in his heart—it was because of what he'd become. *He yelled at me to run.*

Which meant that Carrow was the real villain here. She did have malicious intentions toward him. She planned to hurt him worse than he could ever hurt her.

Don't think about that; think of Ruby.

He flicked his fingers at Carrow's shirt, commanding her to remove it. When she merely gaped at him, he hit his fist into his other palm.

The demon wasn't joking around.

Yet the idea of kissing him, or more, when he was so dirty skeeved her. "Look, it's not you. It's *me,* and my inability to dig dirty dudes." Not to mention how filthy she was. Earlier, she'd swiped phicken juice off her chin with the back of her hand.

She had all the materials needed to get them squeaky. She just needed a tub and about fifty gallons of pure, grade A water. "Uh, I don't suppose you have a place to take a *bath*?"

15

She wanted a . . . *bath*. He remembered the word because 'twas so abhorrent to him.

As a boy, he'd been washed by the master's other
slaves, had been wholly dunked in water as he'd
choked and sputtered. He'd screamed with fear over
the bathing, as much as anything else that the master
had done to him.

Malkom would never forget the heavy, alien feel of
liquid over him, or how the lye soap had burned his eyes
like fire.

To this day, he'd never submerged himself.

She mimicked washing her arms. "A bath?"

Yet another habit of hers that was so similar to the
vampires'.

Was this another of her conditions? Then afterward,
she might do more than coldly offer her hand? She'd
wanted to give him that release but to deny him the feel
of her body—and he'd resented it.

Even as his member had swelled for her soft palm . . .

"Water? *To bathe?*" Now she mimicked pouring water over her head.

Oh, yes, wherever she hailed from, she was from a
family of wealth—lots of it. He knew this with all the

conviction of one who'd spent most of his life without *any*. He wouldn't doubt if she were a noble, or even a royal.

Here a carafe of water could buy a slave—and she wanted a barrel's worth of it.

Yet now he was rich in water, could afford her extravagances. When he nodded, motioning for her to follow him, her eyes lit up and she swiftly collected her pack.

Grabbing his pickax, he led her to an area with a bowl depression that had a retaining wall bricked around it. In olden times, the ceiling ten feet above had been pierced at intervals, tapped for the gathering pool beneath.

He stood on the retaining wall and lifted the ax above his head. After a couple of practiced swings at the ceiling, warm water sprang from the rock, trickling into the pool.

She gave a delighted cry as the level began to rise, and he lifted his chin proudly.

"More," she murmured in Anglish. She clasped her hands together in that gesture of pleading.

Though it would eventually fill up the large crater, could he deny her when she asked so sweetly? He was already anxious from his nearness to the water, but when he thought about her disrobing completely—with him watching—he yanked off his chainmail, took up his ax once more, and hacked at the ceiling.

Ah, Hekate, the way his body moves.

His back was bare, the skin damp, and as he swung that ax with such ease, his muscles flexed sensuously.

When a bead of sweat dripped down along his spine, she imagined tracing its path with her finger. The first time she'd ever *desired* to touch him.

Was she actually attracted to a brute like him?

Maybe. But she was just so delighted with him right now. She knew this much water was akin to her bathing in a vat of gold dust at home, and the pool he'd taken her to was perfect, large and oblong, probably waist-deep in the center when filled.

Streams of water rained down from the rock ceiling, spilling from the places he'd pierced, as if from low-pressure showerheads.

When he put down the ax and glanced back, she was biting her bottom lip. From the way he gazed at her eyes, she guessed her irises were sparkling with her interest.

In return, she saw pride in his blue eyes—but she also sensed his underlying disquiet. From the extravagance?

Steam rose from the surface of the pool, reclaiming her attention. She tested it with her fingertips, finding it an ideal bathing temperature. "Thank you, Malkom. But now I need some privacy." She shooed him away again. "You can come back for your turn."

In answer, he crossed his arms and gave a grunt.

"Not going anywhere, huh? Fine." Carrow wasn't shy. A confirmed eighty thousand people had seen her naked. And that YouTube vid was still going strong!

With a shrug, she sat on the rock wall by the water, emptying her toiletries from the PX. As expected, she'd needed them more than a frigging flashlight.

Silly little mortals, step aside, and let the enchantress do like she do.

As the water deepened, she plucked out her toothbrush and toothpaste. Frowning at the tube, she said, "This was full when I left. Demon, did you eat some of my toothpaste?" At his studiously blank look, she sighed. "You *ate* my toothpaste? Well, at least you left half." She loaded the bristles and began brushing while he watched in fascination.

He looked so curious that once she'd finished up, she mimicked brushing *his* teeth. "Brusha, brusha, brusha?" Surprisingly, he seemed . . . interested.

So she signaled for him to sit beside her. When he shook his head, she clasped her hands to her chest. *Please.*

In a grousing tone, he muttered in Demonish, but he did hesitantly sit on the very edge of the pool.

"Here, bare your teeth." To illustrate, she drew her lips back, smiling broadly. "Come on, demon. Baring your fangs? Shouldn't be so strange for you."

Once he did, she carefully ran the brush over his front teeth, letting him get used to the feeling. Since he hadn't bitten anything or growled, she grew more aggressive, going dental hygienist on him.

He had nice even teeth, surprisingly white. In a way, even his fangs were sexy. *Because his second bite aroused you. Shut up, inner Carrow!*

"There, demon. All done—"

Gulp.

"You swallowed it? Gross!" He scowled at her tone. "No more big-kids' Crest for you until you learn to spit." She clucked her tongue. "Well, now your teeth are clean, but the rest of you is caked in dust. Hair hanging all in your face. I wonder if you'd let me cut it? Maybe even shave you? Or would you growl and snap?"

She gingerly lifted a lock of his dirt-coated hair and made a scissors motion. "Can I cut it?" She figured he would put up resistance, thought his kind probably favored having their hair long as per some warrior demon code. But after a hesitation, he gave a nod. So if there was no reason not to cut it, why hadn't he?

Because he's a guy? With no women around, any male she knew would be kicked back in a beer-stained Barcalounger parked in front of a TV, wearing stale track shorts and absently scratching himself.

Now this male was actually going to let her do an extreme makeover, demon edition. Not bothering to hide her excitement, she said, "I'll be right back," then hurried to the soldiers' packs. She grabbed some T-shirts to use as cloths, a comb, a disposable razor, and man soap. She found small shears on the all-purpose knife.

When she returned, he'd already moved off the wall, a wary look in his eyes.

She sat once more, lining up her gear, then patted the stone for him to come sit.

He hesitated before rejoining her.

"Okay, demon. Step one: hair. Commencing." By the time she'd finished unbraiding the ravels, he was nearly quaking. Sensing this was a very delicate time, she moved gingerly. The nervous cast to his eyes made her believe he was allowing her more than he ever had another.

Carrow felt like she was plucking a thorn from a lion's paw.

Though she had to be hurting him as she attempted to work a comb through his gritty tangles, the demon never winced, never made a sound. In fact, he was growing aroused.

His eyes kept returning to her breasts, and he was getting that heavy-lidded look that said he was imagining right then what he'd like to be doing with them. Apparently, the demon was a breast man.

"Eyes forward, demon," she said.

A halfhearted growl in response.

Conceding defeat against the knots, she began to cut some of the worst ones away. Then she shortened his hair in the back to just above where his collar would be—if he wore one.

But when she sheared around his horns, he clenched the rock beneath him. Carrow knew how sensitive a demon's horns were, and this one's were growing, lengthening. His neck went red, and he'd begun to sweat.

When she accidentally brushed one of the hard appendages, the rock beneath his hands crumbled. She glanced at the destruction—and his erection—nervously. "Malkom?"

He gave a nod. *'Sokay*.

She cautiously began again. Once she finished trimming around his face, she drew back for a better look. "*Big* improvement." Yes, his face was still filthy, streaked with camo paint, and covered with stubble, but she could see the basics for attractiveness were there.

Her curiosity was killing her. How far would he let her go? "Now for the rest of you." She ripped one of the T-shirts into four cloths, then lathered soap on one. "This is soap. Your new best friend."

When she ran the sudsy material over his forehead, he closed his eyes, as if savoring even this small contact. She scrubbed the thick layer of dust, revealing tan, smooth skin. Who would've thought it? His brows were light brown with a golden cast.

So help her, if Pig-Pen was a blond . . .

She washed his upper cheeks and his slightly crooked nose, then lathered the rest of his face. She'd never shaved another before—other than for eyebrow pranks—but she figured she couldn't make him look worse than he already did.

So she nervously pulled the razor down his lean cheek. By the fifth drag of the razor, she muttered, "I am a regular 'enry 'iggins." Everything revealed under the disappearing paint and stubble . . . was gorgeous.

Once she'd finished and wiped down his face, her lips parted. *My gods, he's turned up hot.*

The demon had high, broad cheekbones, with shadowed indentations under them. His lips were firm, the bottom one fuller. His jawline was strong, overtly masculine, and his stubborn chin had a cleft in the center. She'd known his bone structure was good, but *damn.* Even his bruiser nose had a rakish cast when taken with his face as a whole.

"Demon?" He wouldn't look at her, and she thought he was holding his breath.

He wanted her to find him attractive, was anxious about it. Which made him seem so normal, vulnerable even, which in turn made her soften toward him.

Before she could think better of it, she cupped his cheek. With undisguised admiration, she murmured, "I don't know what muster is, but you pass it like crazy, big guy."

Now he glanced up. They gazed at each other for long moments. Was she so superficial that his ultimate reveal made him that much more sympathetic to her?

Well, it didn't hurt.

Yet she was also intrigued by his calmness and his cooperation, the steady clarity of his blue eyes. No longer were they black with bloodlust or rage. This demon was trusting her, and she responded to that.

Just then, a trickle of soapy water ran into his eye. His gaze still locked on her face, he didn't even blink.

"Oh, demon! Here." She pressed a dry cloth to it. "Sorry about that."

She almost didn't notice him reaching a shaking hand toward her breasts until too late, but she swiftly backed away. "Ah-ah, we're only halfway done."

Carrow knew she played a dangerous game. Tonight, she intended to release a little of his steam—to show him what he was getting out of their deal. She was ready to pay the piper but had only budgeted so much from her pocketbook. Could he restrain himself?

If not, she believed she had enough power to do a shocker spell on him. She hoped.

In any event, he needed to be clean. Since she'd be rooming with him, she'd tidy him up, just as she had his lair. She was determined to wash every inch of his big body, humming "at the car wash" while soaping him up from tires to grille.

With that plan in mind, she unzipped her skirt, letting it fall to her ankles. Wearing only her halter, bra, and thong, she stepped into the now knee-deep water.

Once she faced him again, he looked dumbstruck, running his hand over his mouth.

When she beckoned to him with a grin, he glanced over both shoulders. Then he hiked a thumb at himself with his cleft chin proudly raised.

And Carrow thought, *I think I just fell into like with him.*

16

M alkom was dazed at the sight of the pert, flawless backside she'd just casually revealed to him.

A reward for his patience? Earlier as she'd unplaited his hair, she'd been in high spirits about the prospect of shaving and shearing him. While he couldn't have been more ill at ease.

After all this time, having *anyone* near him had been strange, much less this female who so effortlessly undermined his control, with her breasts swaying directly before his eyes.

Plus, the water had been mere inches from him.

Yet he'd battled for control of himself, because for some reason, her task had been important to her.

For his troubles, she'd gifted him with that view of her backside.

Now he yearned to touch those pale curves, but she'd removed herself into the water. There, she mimicked that she would wash him, too. He hadn't agreed to this for himself. Yet look how he'd been rewarded for his cooperation so far! With her removing clothing and offering to clean him.

Her hands on him. Water on him.

He would smell like the vampires he'd hated. But *she*

would like him better. To be close to her, could he enter the pool that continued to deepen?

He'd have to undress. When he removed his cuffs, she would see the bite scars, possibly recognizing the marks of a blood slave. The idea filled him with embarrassment.

Let alone stripping completely. 'Twas one thing for other males to see him naked. But a woman? He figured that in all his years a female or two must have—but he'd never known about it, and he surely hadn't volunteered any glimpses of his body.

This one seemed to like the look of his countenance, gazing at him with unhidden approval, which mystified him. Perhaps she could be attracted to his body.

Would *she* undress completely? Show him those breasts he wanted to lick? Remove the silk triangle that covered her sex?

He pointed at her top, then made a couple of quick motions with his fingers.

With a breathless smile, she teased it up so slowly, displaying pink silk, wetted and clinging to her curves. The lace revealed more than it concealed.

His lips parted. The gods amused themselves with Malkom, giving him such a fine female.

Or could she be his justly earned reward . . . ?

For an extraordinary, fleeting moment, he actually felt like the luckiest male alive.

When Carrow drew off her halter, the demon's gaze was searing on her, as palpable as a touch. Brows drawn as if in pain, he gave a low growl and absently palmed the rigid outline of his shaft.

Snagging the shampoo and soap, she beckoned him again with a curled forefinger. But he began pacing back and forth at the edge of the pool. She could see his expressions even more distinctly now, could see sweat beading his upper lip. Realization struck. He was afraid of getting in the water.

His phobia made sense. When would he ever have learned to swim or grow accustomed to large amounts of water?

"Okay, I guess I'll enjoy this all by myself." With just her undergarments on, she waded to the deeper center, dipping below the surface to soak herself completely. She made a big show of lathering her hair, giving a moan here and there as if her military generic shampoo were as orgasmic as a bottle of Herbal Essences.

More prowling.

Once she'd gotten the tangles out of her own hair, she meandered over to one of the still trickling ceiling streams to rinse the shampoo away. When she raised her face to the water and ran her hands over her belly and thighs, she picked up a riot of different emotions from him. One of which was . . . awe.

He gazed at her like he might have looked at his last sunrise.

At last, he trudged to the edge. She eagerly met him there, grasping one of his arms to draw free the laces on his leather cuffs. But that wary cast to his eyes returned. Again she thought, *Thorn from a lion's paw.* "Trust me, demon."

But he couldn't trust her. Ultimately, she was going to betray him. *Don't think about it, just enjoy this time.*

After removing the second cuff, she frowned. The skin on his wrists was marred with bite scars. Vampire bites.

For Loreans, scars only formed before immortality was reached in adulthood. And Carrow knew that sick Horde vampires enjoyed the blood of the young, thought it sweeter.

Had Slaine been a blood slave as a child?

She traced her forefinger over the marks. He wouldn't meet her eyes, and she knew. They'd kept him for blood at some time before he'd fully matured. No wonder he was violent.

Was that why he'd negotiated with her, when probably no other male in this entire realm would have? Because he'd known what it felt like to be powerless?

At that moment, she hated the faceless vampire, or vampires, who'd hurt him, and she felt sympathy for the boy he'd been.

He must have noticed the latter in her expression, because without a word, the proud demon turned to leave.

But she didn't want him to. "Malkom, come back. *Please.*"

He slowed and finally turned. With that calculating look in his eyes, he motioned for her bra.

"You won't return until I take it off? Then I'll give you tit for tat." She raised her brows at his pants.

He reached down to the leather ties hanging low on his waist. With a bob of his Adam's apple, he began unlacing them. *Like he's nervous?* The ruffian, wild-man demon was shy? Finished with the ties, he hesitated.

She recalled the way his hand had shaken as he'd reached for her breasts. Maybe he hadn't been with a lot of women, or it'd been ages since he bedded one. Apparently females were nonexistent in these wastelands—

The demon let his pants drop to the ground. The full length of his erection sprang free, and she gasped. *Oh, my gods.*

Carrow felt the same way she had the first time she'd seen a penis in the flesh. Giddy. And she knew she'd forever be comparing any others to this one.

Demon males were notoriously hung and customarily pierced down south, and this demon was no different. Aside from being almost uncomfortably large, he had four piercings—a sexy foursome of barbells climbing up his thick shaft. The metal gleamed in the low light, making her want to sigh.

But his *size*. Avoiding intercourse with him had been wise. "Am thinking your file is too big for my computer to access, big guy," she absently muttered.

That tattoo on his side snaked down his hip, all the way to his inner thigh, the design and placement intimate. Someone had *lovingly* inked him.

She felt an unexpected flare of jealousy for the women who'd seen his tattoo. Had they traced it with tremulous fingers?

Carrow wanted to follow it with her tongue.

This sinfully gorgeous body and face had been hidden from the world. Malkom Slaine might be a demon non grata, but he was also a diamond in the rough, one that she couldn't wait to feel in her hands. She grew covetous of him, as if she'd just gone speculating in this mine and had hit the mother lode.

When she could tear her gaze upward, she found his eyes were flickering over her face, observing her again, discerning her reaction. He was doing that "listening" thing, likely understanding her better than men who spoke her language.

Once more, he swallowed. How she perceived him was obviously important to Slaine. Was he uncomfortable with his nudity around her? Demon cultures could be such a mix, masters and slaves all driven by sex, yet conservative with it. But she didn't want him uncomfortable.

She cast him an admiring look. "Malkom . . . *fortis,*" she said in a throaty voice. His erection pulsed, and the grim line of his lips eased somewhat.

She played a dangerous game. "No sex?" He'd lose control when they had sex—she knew it. Or rather, *if* they had sex. And the likelihood of him going demonic, vampiric crazy—while brandishing the biggest D she'd ever seen—made her want to cross her legs tight.

He growled, but eventually he nodded.

Deciding to leave her thong on for any additional bargaining power she might need, she unclasped her bra and tossed it on the retaining wall. "Then come—"

He was already on his way.

17

Do not look at the water; keep your eyes on her. Malkom gritted his teeth, refusing to think about the liquid wrapping around his legs, about how unnatural it felt. *No, just look at those beautiful breasts.*

Gods, they were so pale and full, tipped with dusky pink nipples that were stiffening right before his eyes. He clenched and unclenched his fists as he thought about cupping those breasts, squeezing them. . . .

His cock bobbed painfully as he strode toward her. Once he stood before her, he dragged his gaze up to meet hers. Her sultry eyes were heavy-lidded, the irises like starbursts.

She was desirous. Which meant she would have expectations of him that he doubted he could fulfill.

Seduction. *I do not know how to do this.* Would she want to be kissed? 'Twas taboo among the Trothan demons.

She probably thought he'd been with hundreds of females, as most demons his age would have been. She likely believed he was skilled at drawing pleasure from females.

I have no skill and nearly as little knowledge about her body. Yet when a large drop of water coursed from her chest down one of her proud breasts, his apprehensions grew dim. *Have to touch them . . .*

But as he reached for her, she eased away, shaking her head. No, he wanted to touch—

"Malkom, please."

He hesitated. She wanted something of him now. *You have had your turn—now it is hers.* At length, he gave a nod, allowing her to lead him beside a fall of water. He even knelt when she did, though that put the water as high as his navel.

He remained tense when she moved behind him, running the cloth over his back and neck with deliberate strokes. His arms were next as she worked all the way down to his fingers and claws.

When she grazed her fingertips over the scars on his wrists, he recalled her reaction as she'd stripped him of his cuffs. Oh, yes, she'd known what those scars meant. He'd seen the pity in her expressive eyes. Which had shamed him. And those scars marked the *least* demeaning way he'd been used.

How would she react to learning the rest?

As she ran that soapy cloth over any part of him that she could reach, he decided that this bath was markedly different from what he'd remembered. There was no pain or strangling panic. He was still on edge, but his mind was filled with thoughts of her, wondering where she would touch him next, *in what way* she would touch him.

When she looped her arms around him to wash his chest, her bared breasts slipped across his back, rendering him dizzy with pleasure. The feel of those pink tips against him made his cock throb so intensely, he was tempted to begin masturbating under the water to assuage it—

The pad of her forefinger rubbed his pierced nipple. *"Ah, Carrow . . ."* Just when he was about to snatch her into his arms, she stood and began washing his hair, running her nails along his scalp.

For some reason this relaxed him, weakening him until he could barely keep his head lifted. Yet when she all but polished his horns, his shaft pulsed impossibly harder.

How much longer could he endure the building pressure? Had he not come earlier, there'd have been no withstanding this.

But if he touched her, he could hurt her, justifying her fears about his claiming. If he hurt her, then he'd never have *this* again—attention, care, *interest*.

He'd never know what thing she would do next.

With that in mind, he let her guide him to stand, cooperating when she coaxed him to lift his arms, palms against the rock face so water from above would run down over his head.

She knelt behind him, then took the cloth to his feet, working her way up his calves, her destination unmistakable. Would she touch his member? Run her hot, soapy hands over it? When her breast rubbed against his leg, his claws dug deep into the stone beside his head.

This position reminded him of being flogged—or worse. But the torture he'd known before merely had to be endured. Now he had to *deny* what he wanted more than anything he'd ever known.

Each of her touches made his cock strain painfully, every graze as tormenting to him as the bite of a whip.

His seed was rising, feeling like it would erupt against his will. And with it, his demon instinct began burning inside him again. Thoughts of tossing her to the ground ran riot. Of pinning her arms over her head as he plunged his cock betwixt her legs. He imagined tying her wrists behind her back, then laving her sex like an animal at drink. . . .

When her hands reached above his knees, he gnashed his teeth and rammed one of his horns against the rock. Pain tempered his pleasure, buying him precious seconds.

A week ago, if someone had told Carrow that she'd be worshipping a wild-man vemon's naked body, kneeling before it, she'd have laughed.

But worshipping was exactly what she was doing, entranced by every rigid inch of him.

At first, she'd been methodical. Yet then she'd slowed her movements, helpless not to appreciate the masculine perfection of his body—the hollows at the sides of his rock-hard ass, the corded thigh muscles, the sharp rises and falls of his chiseled abs. Those pecs were made for a woman's nails to dig into.

His tan skin was dusted with golden-blond hair on his chest, arms, and legs. A trail of it descended from his navel to the slightly darker hair at his groin.

His shaft protruded from between his lean hips like a rod, his testicles heavy and begging to be fondled.

Carrow couldn't remember ever being this aroused

in her entire life. This demon was raw, uncivilized—and he was making her melt.

By the time she reached his upper thighs, his body was thrumming. She thought he was holding his breath. Instead of touching him higher, she stood and began soaping his lower back and ass, his muscles tensing to her fingertips. He exhaled with disappointment.

Biting her lip, she reached around to work on his lower torso. His stomach dipped and flexed as she ran the cloth down that trail of golden hair. Again, just when she was about to reach his groin, she stopped.

Playing a dangerous game. His low groan grew nearly constant. He glanced over his shoulder down at her. His eyes had turned black once more, gleaming like onyx.

He was about to blow. If he lost control, he might hurt her again, but with a couple of quick strokes, the demon would be done. Time to "wash" between his legs.

With light kisses over his back, she reached down to gently soap his heavy testicles from behind. He jerked, uneasy. Had no woman ever touched him there? Or had it simply been so long ago? She felt sadness to think of him being exiled here by himself for ages.

Tonight she would give him pleasure like he'd never known. *Something to remember you by, Carrow?*

Tamping down the thought, she slipped her hand around his waist, seeking his shaft. She wrapped her fingers around it as best as she could, biting back a moan at the feel of those piercings against her palm.

At her first touch, he jerked again, moving his legs out wider. Then he froze. Tension shot through him, and his erection faltered.

Something was very wrong, his emotions growing *chaotic*. She even detected . . . rage?

Just as she was releasing him to retreat, he swirled around, knocking her hold loose, his clenched hand hitting her bad wrist.

"Demon! You almost rebroke . . ." Words vanished when she glimpsed his face.

His expression was menacing, his fangs sharp. He snarled down at her.

As she backed away, eyes tearing at the pain, he shook his head hard, as if he were coming out of a trance.

Good for you, but I'm still bailing. She turned and hurried toward the side of the pool—

He looped his arm around her waist, dragging her against him. "*Ara* . . . Carrow, *no*," he rasped brokenly. He buried his face in her hair, inhaling her scent. Now his erection came raring back to life, the crown prodding the bottom of her ass.

"Put me down!" The more she struggled, the more she rubbed the tip. "Don't say I didn't warn you." She flooded her body with power, shocking him like an electric fence.

"Carrow!" he bellowed, forced to release her.

Yet she'd barely taken two steps before he swooped her up again.

"You must like pain. However, I—do—not." She shocked him again with even more juice. "Wish I could see the look on your face. . . ." She realized he was simply *taking* it, refusing to release her, so she turned up the volume to high. His forehead fell against her shoulder as he quaked with pain, but he wouldn't let her go.

Soon *she* was defeated, left without power, and still he was standing. *The next time I set out to hurt him, I'm going full guns,* she vowed. She *would* put him down.

He turned her in his arms until they were facing each other, their chests pressed tightly together, his forearm under her ass.

"Let me go *now!*" she all but screamed.

After a hesitation, he let her body slowly slide down his.

The contact of their slippery skin, the gradual descent, the sound of their breaths . . .

Against her will, she felt a spike of desire. And she knew he could tell. He inhaled deeply, his nostrils flaring. Then he hissed out a ragged breath, as if the scent of her were too much to resist. His penis pulsed between them.

When her nipples dragged down his chest, one rubbed directly over his piercing. He shuddered anew. By the time he set her on her feet, he was subtly rocking his hips.

With his jaw clenched until the muscles bulged at the sides, he squeezed his eyes shut—just as hers went wide.

"Oh, my gods! You're about to come?" Earlier, as she'd all but given him a hand job, he hadn't been able to stay erect. Now he was about to blow? "I don't *get* you, demon. Ugh! Just let me go."

His shaking palms covering her shoulders, he set her away. Appearing to gain a modicum of control, he released her and opened his eyes. Whatever he saw in her expression made his gaze dip to her wrist, then to her bite mark.

He parted his lips to speak, then closed them, eyes darting as he so clearly wanted to communicate with her. To explain why he'd hurt her—again?

She was done "listening." Carrow didn't like dirty guys, and she didn't like damaged ones either. She turned and walked away.

With agitated movements, his female donned one of the large shirts from a pack, then stormed away.

Alone. Once more. Malkom punched the wall to keep from yelling with frustration. *Am I destined to be solitary?*

What he wouldn't give to be able to speak to her. He wanted to tell her that he was willing to relearn her language and go without sex or biting for now. He was even considering giving up his revenge.

All this he would do for her, but he needed her to give him new memories to drown out the old. . . .

So many things about this night had reminded Malkom of his past—the water, the scent of the soap, her palm closing over him from behind. Her touch was gentle, completely different from what he'd experienced. Yet even the way she'd steered him had called the master to mind.

Malkom clasped his forehead, grappling to pull his thoughts from the past, realizing that *he* needed to be in control of what happened between him and his female. *He* wanted to guide *her*.

Which was a problem, since he didn't know how.

If only he could have more time with her, a few hours to learn her form, he could get them back to where they'd been just before he'd lost control. And then this night could be what he remembered whenever he thought of sex in the future.

He stalked after her, readying to touch her tender skin.

'Tis not the end.

As she hastened away, she refused to think about that lost look on the demon's face. Refused to think about it—*at all.*

Some inner torment had just been dredged up. Considering that he'd been a slave, she could imagine the *nature* of the torment. Especially when taken with his reaction to her unwitting touches.

Carrow truly felt bad for him, but she had to protect herself. Luckily, she was resolved. *So why am I glancing back?*

She'd only get more of the same if she returned. To be bitten and battered? Just hours ago, her sternum had felt like the landing site of a wrecking ball. And yes, he'd shoved her to protect her, but it was yet another example of how little control he had.

Totally out of control. Like if he were a dog, he'd be the angry-eyed mongrel at the pound, the one that was sure to attack. So why did she have the urge to claim him?

Such a wild, lost male. Another glance back, this time with some lip nibbling. *Eyes forward, slore.*

Damn it, she was still woefully aroused. It'd been weeks since she'd had an orgasm. As she strode down the mine with no bra on, her aching breasts bounced, her nipples hypersensitive. Each step was agony to her still-throbbing sex.

Strangely, her hurting wrist was nearly forgotten—

Without warning, he seized her, tucking her under his arm against his hip, and headed back for the pool.

"Drop me, demon! Now!"

Instead, he carted her right back into the water, setting her on her feet beneath one of the cascades. As she sputtered, he ripped free the T-shirt she wore.

"This is your bright idea?" Surprisingly unafraid of him, she struck his chest with the bottom of one fist. "Way to get back in my good graces, asshole!"

Without even acknowledging her useless hits, he patiently held up his finger. His eyes were flickering back to the steady blue.

"One moment? Forget it, don't wanna stay." At his unbending look, she said, "Listen, I'm sorry for whatever happened to you, because evidently, damage was done. But I'm not your spank moppet or whipping girl, or anything like that—" She squinted at his hand. "Um, where are your claws?" He'd bitten them away. How thoroughly was he planning on touching her?

He bent to drag down her thong.

Carrow's rebellion? Chin raised, she said, "I'm not stepping out of it."

Not a problem for Slaine; he briefly lifted her and removed it, tossing it by her bra.

Then he took one of the cloths, lathering it with the soap, his mien resolute.

"I-I haven't said yes to any—"

He pressed the cloth to her chest, softly rubbing her with easy strokes. Despite herself she was intrigued by this unexpected side of him. Amazingly, she found herself relaxing.

With one hand, he unhurriedly scrubbed. With his other he covered one shoulder, his palm warm over her skin. So lightly, he pressed his thumb against her muscle there, massaging.

When she moaned, he must have taken this as a sign of her surrender, because masculine satisfaction surged through him—fueling her power once more.

The cloth was momentarily forgotten as he used the backs of his fingers to skim her cheek, her jawline, then the length of her neck and lower.

With decisive action, he'd hunted, he'd warred, and he'd protected her. Now he was tentative as he traced the lines of her shoulders, his eyes following his every movement. No man had ever looked at her as he did— like she was the best thing in the world.

He caressed the pads of his fingers over her collarbone so tenderly that she was staggered by his gentleness. Such a killer, such a warrior, yet look at what he was capable of.

He murmured to her in Demonish. She didn't understand the words, but she recognized the tone— wonderment. For the first time in her life, Carrow felt *treasured*. And, gods, that was a heady feeling. *I could get addicted to this.*

From her collarbone, he smoothed his forefinger down . . . down. Just as he was about to reach her nipple, when she was trembling for that contact, he let out a shuddering breath and circled the peak.

She bit her lip. *No, touch me there, demon!*

Instead he returned the cloth to her chest, seeming determined to wash her as she'd done him.

But when she arched her back while whispering, *"Please, demon,"* he groaned, dipping the cloth over her breasts, across her achy nipples.

She gave a cry, earning another lash of satisfaction from him, power pouring from him to her, enabling her magic again.

As her eyes slid shut, she hazily debated: *Heal my wrist, or force the demon to release me?*

Beneath the cloth, his sneaky thumb swept over her nipple. "Oh, Malkom, *yes.*"

Her wrist? Good as new.

18

Determined to wash all of her body, Malkom somehow dragged his hands away from her breasts.

He would minister to her for as long as she had to him. Even if this meant denying his swollen shaft or ignoring the breasts that she offered up.

When she arched her back . . . and they begged for his attention.

So he ran the cloth from her chest to one of her shoulders, rubbing and massaging down to her fingertips. Her other arm received the same attention. He paused at both of her hands, fascinated by how small and fragile they were, comparing their size to his own hands.

Everything about her body was utterly feminine. Her thighs were shapely, her backside generous, her hips flaring out from a tiny waist. He marveled at every sweep of creamy skin, every womanly swell and dip.

He was exploring her—and for some reason, she was allowing him to fully.

Among all his other discoveries, he'd noticed that she had no hair on her legs or under her arms. Aside from her long mane atop her head, and the intriguing patch betwixt her legs, her body was bare.

But he loved how smooth her skin was, how her body was so different from his.

Next came her back. He turned her around, tugging her hair forward over one shoulder. He was tempted to press his mouth against her nape but feared he would alarm her after his earlier bites.

Instead, he worked both the cloth and his bare hand in circular motions from her neck down to the curves of her backside, as if polishing a treasure.

He turned her to face him once more, laying a palm over one of her generous hips to pin her as he ran the cloth upward from her knees. She was shaking under his hand.

"Do not stop me, Carrow," he told her in Demonish, his voice rough. "I will not hurt you again."

The demon certainly had been thorough, washing every inch of her from the navel up—and occasionally lower. He'd even slipped the side of his hand between her cheeks, making her start in alarm, but he'd merely continued his task.

Now he steadily rubbed up her thighs, inch by agonizing inch as he murmured to her in a husky voice. She was shivering, holding her breath, anticipating his "washing" her.

But it wasn't a cloth that touched her there—he'd cupped her in his hot, callused palm.

"Oh!"

Shuddering with pleasure, he rasped, *"Sife ara."* Soft female.

With his other hand clamped over her hip, he held her steady as his forefinger began to investigate her sex, tickling her as it tentatively roved. Between his lean hips, his shaft pulsed with excitement, his piercings glinting across his taut flesh.

Soon, she couldn't comprehend how he'd controlled himself for as long as he had when she'd washed him. Already, she was on the verge, wanting his mouth on hers as she climaxed. "Kiss me."

"Kiiiss?"

Caught up in the moment, she stood on her toes. Holding his face between her hands, she pressed her lips against his.

He froze, clearly not knowing what to do.

"Did I freak you out again?" she asked against his lips, their breaths mingling. His eyes were still open, his expression confounded. Damn it, she'd made a point to let him drive the boat. "Got too excited. Sorry." She began to draw away, afraid he'd start throwing fists. "Won't happen again—"

Like a shot, he wrapped his free palm over her nape, tugging her till their lips met.

Now her eyes widened, but when his lids slid shut, so did hers. She grazed her mouth over his, then again. And all the while he lazily fondled her sex.

Light, fleeting kisses, and flicks of her tongue followed. When she pulled back, his hooded gaze was that of a male who'd just gone to heaven.

She drew in once more, licking the seam of his lips. As they eagerly parted, her tongue darted inside to meet his. He groaned in surprise.

Though hesitant at first, he caught on swiftly. Soon his tongue twined against hers, her moans mixed with his stunned growls as his fingers played.

He cautiously pressed one to her opening. As soon as he'd breached her entrance, she gasped from the delicious fullness inside. But he jerked his hand away, breaking from the kiss.

"What? Why'd you stop?"

He was studying her expression. Fearing he'd hurt her?

"Oh, you didn't hurt me." She took his hand, kissing his palm, then easing it back between her legs. "That's it, Malkom. I should have told you it felt so nice."

When he returned his finger to her core, he slipped it farther within. Her sheath clamped down on it, and his eyes widened with astonishment. She could perceive that feeling of wonder emanating from him.

And she knew. He'd never felt a woman like this. In a hazy part of her brain, she recognized that he was a virgin, at least with women.

"*Ah, Carrow.*" The deeper he pushed in his finger, the more the heel of his palm pressed against her clitoris.

She began to rock against his hand. "Feels so good, demon." Getting closer . . . so close. "Just a few seconds more."

But he withdrew his finger, leaning forward to rasp in her ear, "Sex." His erection pressed high on her belly, insistent. He gripped it in his fist, as if to position it.

"Malkom, no!"

"Yes! *Need.*"

"No!" *Don't ruin this, please, don't ruin it.* "Demon, please."

Just when she was about to retreat, he said, *"Kiss,"* as he cupped her breast.

She exhaled a shaky breath. "Only k-kiss?"

In answer, he rubbed her nipple and licked his lips.

Carrow gazed at his mouth and had to bite back a moan.

Malkom had always thought that females had more control over their bodies, could master their urges. Males were the more animalistic ones.

Gods almighty. My woman is shaking from her need to come.

Of course he'd attempted to claim her!

She was wet, and that meant she needed him inside her. When his member hardened to take her, her sex would grow damp to better receive it.

He and his *ara* were both there.

Yet Malkom had agreed to Carrow's terms, so he would respect her wishes in this. Still, his demon instinct screamed within him to satisfy her. He intended to with his mouth, kissing her body.

He'd start with her soft breasts. On his way down to them, he ran his lips along her neck, nuzzling her collar to kiss the bite mark there. Just as his fangs sharpened, he noticed her sudden tension. *She fears another bite.*

So he hastened down to one of her breasts, his tongue flicking at the moisture still dripping on them from the ceiling above. With a groan, he took one sweet nipple between his lips to suck, eyes sliding shut as it puckered to the tip of his swirling tongue.

When she moaned low and cupped her breast to his mouth, he commanded himself, *Last, Slaine, last! Do not come...*

Oh, yes, his woman loved this as much as he. Malkom would be at her breasts any chance he got. She cupped her other one for him to repeat his attentions.

Yet as he suckled, he scented her arousal deepening. Drawn to that part of her, he kissed lower toward her small patch of silky black curls. Her flat belly dipped as he grazed his lips over it.

Before when he'd felt her inside, she'd been wet like water but slippery like cream. Needing to taste her, he knelt between her legs. She let him hook her knee over his shoulder, unabashed. When he saw her sex, he knew why—she was perfect.

For long moments, he stared, awestruck by her pink flesh, by her glistening folds. He wanted to tell her she was beautiful, again felt frustration that he couldn't.

When he caressed her there, she quivered against his fingers. He gazed up at her. *"Kiss?"*

19

Oh, yes, kiss!

The demon knelt in the water before her, like some wicked god of virility. His horns had straightened and grown duskier as they flared back from his head. His thick hair was drying to a dark blond threaded with golden strands, as if it'd been lightened by the sun. His body seemed to have grown even larger, his muscles bulging everywhere.

Her brawny demon protector was pierced, tattooed, and *sinful*.

And he was gazing between her legs with a transfixed expression, until she was squirming. "Malkom, *kiss*."

He licked his lips in such a feral display of lust, she shivered. Though she was convinced he'd never taken a woman with his mouth, he was heading that way now, leaning in. She felt his breath against her, his firm lips following.

When he gave a testing lick, she held her breath. He'd definitely never done this. Would he like—

"*Carrow!*" he ground out, rocking his hips, thrusting into the water. Then he set upon her, hungrily licking her up and down, groaning against her.

"Yes, Malkom! More . . ." She knew demon males

loved when females guided them by their horns, but when she grasped his, he wrenched his head back with a violent shake, loosing her hands. He cast her a warning look so ominous that she swallowed. "S-sorry, demon."

Still he glowered. Biting her bottom lip, she began petting her breasts for him. Ah, Hekate, she could tell that pleased him.

Mollified, he settled back in. When his tongue snaked over her throbbing clitoris, she cried out and he stilled.

"No, more, *more*. Keep going!"

Her back arched when he made a second foray there. Another firm flick came, then another. "Oh, yes!" she cried, surrendering completely, wantonly rolling her hips up to the demon's mouth.

When he began thrusting his forefinger as he licked, she mindlessly murmured, "You clever demon. It's so good, it's so . . ." Her head fell back. The tension built and built, the coil tightening.

The feel of his thick finger exploring, his wonder, his strong tongue.

"*Alton, ara,*" he grated against her. *Come, female.* But this time the phrase had a completely different meaning. It was a command uttered by a dangerous male who expected her to obey him.

Malkom had planned to feast on her luscious sex until he tasted her coming against his mouth.

She was about to, was undulating to ride his finger and tongue, stealing any control he'd thought he possessed.

Last, Slaine! He feared he'd embarrass himself with her again.

The bud at her apex was sensitive—working his tongue over it made her squeeze her breasts more urgently, made her moans louder. So he circled her there over and over, gazing up at her face.

With glittering eyes, she met his gaze, panting as he plunged his finger inside her channel.

Between licks, he said, "*Alton,* Carrow!"

To see a female coming, my *female . . . to taste it.*

Suddenly, she bucked, her body spasming as she rocked to his tongue. She screamed, "*Malkom!*"

He gave a desperate groan when he felt her little sheath gripping his finger again and again, as if sucking it deeper. Once he tasted her orgasm, he licked in ecstasy, growling with pride and pleasure.

"Ah, demon, yes!"

I wrought this from her. She was so beautiful like this, her body amazing him. *She was made for me alone.*

Eventually she pushed his head away though he still laved. Against his will, he surrendered his prize.

When he stood, trapping her body against the wall, his shaft strained between them. He'd never known it could pain him like this. "Sex, *ara!*" The water running over his heated skin was somehow arousing him even more.

"N-no, Malkom," she said between breaths.

Why can I not mate her? He'd pleasured her hard. He wanted to seize her breasts from behind, holding her steady as he planted his cock into her, deep where he'd licked her softness—

She pressed her mouth to his chest, her tongue darting against his pierced nipple.

His eyes widened. Would she reciprocate? When she brushed her lips lower, his heart thundered so loud he knew she could hear it.

At last! To know what this felt like. . . .

He turned to lean back against the wall. With her collar in his hand, he guided her to kneel between his legs. *"Kiss,"* he commanded in Anglish. She dutifully nuzzled the hair just below his navel, pressing her lips all around.

In Demonish he told her, "Give me this." He fisted his shaft to her mouth. "Take it betwixt your sweet lips."

Peering up at him to gauge his reaction, she daubed her tongue against the crown.

He bucked uncontrollably, nigh coming. Once he'd stilled his hips, inhaling for control, her tongue flicked out again.

His cock pulsed and a bead arose. He bit back a groan when she lapped up that hint of the seed. Voice gone hoarse, he told her, "I will want this from you, Carrow, every day, every night." He stared down into her bewitching green eyes.

Strange beautiful female. She was a gift, a treasure.

"You belong to me." *Never will I be separated from this creature.*

When he threaded his fingers into her hair, she cupped her hand round his shaft, drawing him to her lips. He gave a shout when she suckled the head into her hot little mouth.

Gods, he wanted to savor this, but she'd begun

masturbating him as she circled her tongue around the tip.

With the water running over his body, her tongue swirling and fist pumping, his eyes rolled back in his head.

Cannot withstand this ... for much longer ...

The demon had been so proud at how he'd pleasured her—she could *perceive* his masculine satisfaction. His pride had emanated as strongly as his wonder.

But on the heels of that, she could sense his agony. Her poor demon was about to explode, his engorged penis throbbing against her tongue.

Still, she couldn't deny the urge to tease him to a feverpitch, to make sure he would never forget his first time. His reactions told her this was yet another pleasure he'd never received.

So she eased back to drip water over his length, dotting droplets over each of his smooth piercings. His expression anguished, he rested one hand on her head, the other tightly covering her nape, guiding her head back. He grated in English, "*More.* Be ... good, *ara.*" Telling her not to tease him?

"I'll be good, Malkom," she promised, returning her fist to stroke. But he surged forward, grinding into it. *He's going to come in my hand, he's going to ...*

When she covered the head with her mouth, his legs quaked. His brows drew together as if with pain. Bested by her mouth and hand, the demon warrior gave a helpless groan as he began to come.

The spasms seized him. His massive body jerked.

"Carrow, more!" he bellowed to the ceiling, his muscles contracting in a breathtaking display.

The demon wanted more? She was merciless. Pumping...licking...sucking...

He yelled out until his voice was ragged. Finally, he collapsed back against the wall, tugging her off him. Satisfaction soared through him, and she drank it in.

He was euphoric long after he'd come, possessively cupping her head to his thigh, holding her there as she continued to trace his shaft in fascination.

But then he lowered both of his hands to cradle her face, and she detected another emotion. A pure, raw ferocity.

He gazed down at her not with the expression of a man who was happy with his fate, but with the expression of a man who'd slaughter anyone who tried to change that fate....

20

Late in the night, as he held her sleeping in his arms, Malkom again vowed that he would never, *never* be separated from this creature. *Not while I have a breath left in my body.*

Had he actually wondered what she'd be good for? Only bringing him the most intense pleasure he'd ever imagined! She had wrung so many releases from him, he'd thought he would fall unconscious.

And, in return, he'd made her climax so hard, she'd thrown back her head and screamed.

He had to believe she was as astonished by the pleasure as he was. If she was even half as grateful for it . . .

Though he remained erect for her, she'd pleaded for rest. After going without sleep the night before and his skirmishes during this day, he probably needed to join her.

But Malkom knew he would be plagued with nightmares. And he feared she'd disappear before he woke.

So for now, he relished what had just happened between them—the way she'd trembled against him, her breaths on his damp skin, her bold tongue and plump lips.

He craved kissing her mouth again—and her female

flesh. *Gods, that part of her.* If he'd been fixated on her breasts before, now his obsession was divided. Her channel had hungrily gripped his finger. In five days, it'd squeeze his shaft thus. . . .

At the thought, his enthusiasm waned. *Five days.* Much could happen in a handful of days.

Making plans again, Slaine? He'd foolishly been dreaming of a new future. Would these dreams be destroyed like all the others?

Instead of enjoying his fortune, Malkom was nearly sick, his stomach knotted with apprehension as he gazed down at her face. Her full lips were parted, her lashes a dark sweep above pinkened cheeks. So beautiful it pained him.

'Tis too good with her.

He didn't even know *what* she was, much less why she had come to Oblivion. He'd figured that she was an exile sentenced to this plane. So why was she so certain that she could simply return through the portal?

He was torn. Part of him was suspicious of her arrival. Perhaps she was here by design.

Or perhaps his destined female had been delivered by the hand of fate itself.

Yes, fate. Because another part of him believed she was a reward for all his hardships. *Give and take.*

He was *due* some contentment. And he would work to keep it. Tonight his female had fallen asleep in his arms, *trustingly,* because he'd proven himself.

And more, he'd decided to sacrifice his revenge for her. He'd vowed never to be separated from this woman. Which meant he had to pick one or the other.

Malkom had chosen Carrow, knowing deep in his heart that he would always choose her. . . .

During this night, he'd figured out several things about her. Among them? She was no virgin. She was too confident, too bold. Granted, his experience was limited, but he'd never heard of a virgin who'd guided her would-be lover's finger deep inside her sex.

When she'd come around it . . . He bit back a groan at the memory, wanting to be inside her. Which brought his mind back to her conditions.

He wouldn't judge her because she wasn't a virgin—who was *he* to ever judge another?—but why could he not have her when others had? Why hadn't she done everything in her power to please him, to ensure his protection?

Maybe she sensed how unclean his blood was, or she still feared he'd hurt her. Or was it more? Perhaps she wanted to be wed before he claimed her, or needed permission from an elder or leader to take a male. How else could she have denied them in the water?

Another thing he'd determined? Those rumored heavenly planes—where the air was sweet and the lands gave up food—they had to exist. His soft woman clearly came from a world of plenty.

His thoughts grew dark. What if he followed her to her world, and she forsook him upon hearing about his past? In time, he would remember or relearn Anglish, and then he would have to tell her.

How would he explain what had befallen him? Malkom had been a blood slave, and he'd murdered a royal. He'd been dishonored by his most reviled enemy, outcast by his own people.

Even if she accepted him, her people mightn't give her the approval she awaited, especially since he would be entering her society with no wealth. This mountain was his only territory; if he left it, he would possess no lands to share with her, lands on which to raise their offspring.

Offspring. He'd never had to think about that before. Even if he could have taken a female in the past, he wouldn't have been able to produce seed for her, not until his mate had broken the seal.

Now he might impregnate her. He felt confident that he could protect her and a family far better than his own parents had him.

But what kind of children would I give Carrow? The young of an abomination.

He began to stroke her silken hair, which soothed his thoughts somewhat. Her long mane was cleaned of sand and had dried into glossy waves. He loved the jet-black color, loved seeing those locks spilling over her pale shoulder or streaming through his fingers.

Eventually, his lids grew heavy. But fearing she'd escape him while he slumbered, he reached for her collar. With the band clutched tight in his fist, Malkom finally slipped into a restless sleep.

Dreams of his past surfaced. For so long, Malkom had kept those nightmares at bay. Now they bombarded him.

The memory of the day his mother had sold him to the vampire master arose, as though he were reliving it. He'd been so excited, believing that he was to be adopted into another family. He'd thought he would enjoy endless food, water, and warmth at night.

Malkom would never forget his sinking realization that he hadn't been brought to a new family. The dawning horror as he'd heard screams. He'd seen other boys his age humiliated and abused, his young mind comprehending, *They are going to do that to me.* . . .

On the heels of those scenes came dreams of the Viceroy, who'd tortured Malkom to hold sacred the Thirst. But whenever the vampire had offered demon slaves for him to drink, Malkom had been sickened, fangs gone dull and receding, no matter how badly he'd needed their blood.

I will not feed on my own kind. I am not a vampire!

Each night, Malkom had endured a host of torments. His skin had been flayed from his body with barbed metal whips—or pierced through by his own fractured bones. He'd watched searing pokers slide between his ribs.

His fury over Kallen's death had kept him strong. Never did Malkom let himself forget that he'd been forced to kill his only friend.

And then the time had come when the Viceroy had presented Malkom a slave to drink—one unlike all the others he'd offered, one more valuable than the rest. The vampire had thought Malkom too weak to pose a threat, too numbed to react. He'd been wrong on both counts.

A hazy night of screams, blood splashing the walls . . .

Yet another scene arose. Malkom dreamed of a crying girl combing her black hair in front of a mirror. He saw her reflection as though through her own glinting green eyes.

Carrow? It had to be her as a child. Even amid the reverie, Malkom knew that this scene had taken place, that this was one of her memories, taken from her blood. Some of the vampires had possessed that talent. The Viceroy had. And 'twas his blood that had infected Malkom's own.

I am witnessing her past.

Someone rang a bell, calling for "Lady Carrow." *Lady* meant nobility. He'd suspected she was highborn.

When the bell rang again, this young Carrow dashed the back of her hand against her tears. He could *feel* that she was miserable, heartsick far beyond her years, but he had no idea why.

"All right, all right," she said, drying her eyes, while musing, *I'm actually invited to eat with them?*

Though she spoke and thought in Anglish, he understood the words.

She exited that room into an even larger one, as large as any dwelling in the city of Ash. Her bedroom? Silks draped the windows and her bed, enough fabric to make hundreds of robes. It looked as if all the silk in the world had been contained in that room.

She was rich. So how could she possibly have been unhappy?

From her room, servants escorted her down a hall into a warmly lit banquet room. A table stretched nearly the length of the spacious area, the surface covered with food. Steam wafted from the dishes—what had to be a year's worth of fare—and uniformed servants lined the walls.

At one end of the table, a man and a woman sat

together. As Carrow trudged to the other end, she addressed them in a toneless voice, "Mother. Father."

The woman inclined her head, her many jewels sparkling in the light. "Carrow." But she didn't *look* at her daughter. Malkom wondered if she was blind.

Her father was clean-shaven, his hair short and kempt. Their clothes looked strange to him but were unmistakably well-made.

These are her people, this is her life. Malkom was struck by how clean and plentiful everything was. Silver gleamed, crystal refracting the light from a chandelier above. Clean, shining abundance.

I was clad in tatters, my body filthy, my face unshaven. No wonder she'd bathed him. Even in sleep, he suffered a spike of embarrassment. . . .

Servants rushed to meet their every need, seating and serving Carrow. She didn't eat, merely pushed food around on her plate. Her stomach felt sick, growing worse with each minute her parents spoke to each other in haughty tones, ignoring her.

"Mother, Father," she suddenly said, "I have something I want to talk to you about."

By now Malkom had begun understanding her words from his own previous knowledge of Anglish. With each minute, he remembered more.

"I want to go to Andoain."

Without glancing at Carrow, the father replied, "We're not discussing this with you again. You can't go to spell school because you have no powers yet. Besides, it's for common folk."

Spell school? His mate was a witch, a *channa*. Which

meant that just because fate had marked her as his, she wouldn't necessarily want him back.

"Then I'm going to run away with a pirate," Carrow said. They didn't respond. "I'm going to jump off a bridge and steal your sole heir from you. That's why you had me, isn't it? For an heir? I can't think of another reason—"

Carrow's father snapped his fingers, and two similarly dressed women seized her under her arms.

As she was dragged away, Carrow screamed to her parents, "Look at me, look at me, *look* at me! What is wrong with you?" Her voice breaking on a sob, she said, "Wh-what is wrong with *me*?"

Malkom woke from the dream in a rush, agitated, feeling as if he were behind in some task.

I want to make up for how they treated her. She'd been devastated, truly heartsick. *My mate, ignored, hurt.*

Rolling onto his back, he pressed her sleeping form against his side, and she curled into him with a sigh. He drew her tight against his chest, her body molding so perfectly against his.

He'd had no family. Hers didn't deserve her. *Then we will be family.*

Never will I be separated from her. His voice hoarse, he told her, "Carrow is mine."

He didn't realize until long moments had passed that he'd spoken her tongue.

21

H-o-m-e. With a stick, the demon painstakingly scripted the letters in the sand.

"That's perfect, Malkom." He groused at the praise, but she could tell he liked it.

Three nights ago, he'd taken that stick, twirled it in the sand, and then handed it to her, saying, "Carrow."

And that was how his lessons had begun. In front of the fire, he'd learned to write her name, and she'd taught him how to write his own. This morning, they were working on *home* and *food*.

Carrow had spent these last few days in the mine with him, fed, loved on, protected, and empowered—literally—by his satisfaction.

Though that first morning, she had woken with a heavy sense of guilt. The demon had given her the sexual night of her life—even without actual sex—and had been gazing at her with that same wonder in his eyes.

She'd thought, *Never was he supposed to be like this.* Betraying the crazed vemon who'd attacked her would have been easy. Betraying this tender, proud lover, however . . .

In stilted English, he'd grated, "God morn."

"Good morning?"

He'd given her a patronizing expression as if saying, *That's what I said.*

Carrow had remembered the isolated report of his speaking English. "You know more of my language than you let on, don't you?" What if she could *explain* to him why she was here, even ask for his help? Would she dare risk it?

"Did you once speak English? We've got to talk a lot, then." Like in *Dances with Wolves*, multiple walking-and-talking montages. "Do you like to make the talk?"

He'd understood nothing. So she'd spoken more slowly while assessing his reactions. She'd been able to see recognition with some words, but not enough to truly communicate.

Yet with each hour, he was recalling more. He'd begun speaking haltingly, in that thick Demonish accent.

He knew *please, thank you, are you hungry/tired/ thirsty*? He could understand just about any one or two syllable words. When she'd told him what she was, he'd even understood the word *witch*.

He could also ask her if she was *needing,* as he put it. She refused to teach him the word *horny.* Of course, by now he'd heard her telling him she was about to come so many times that he could inform her of the same in English.

They were rubbing along but not able to talk freely, definitely not enough to test the waters, to see how he'd react to her predicament.

There was a translation spell she could use, but it would take a lot of power and a ton of skill, was consid-

ered a three-out-of-fiver. Even with all the power she'd
been harvesting from him, she wouldn't have enough
juice. Short of a raucous crowd, she'd be a bust.

So she'd been using the power he provided to reinforce her body for his constant—and welcome—
attentions.

Aside from some early stumbling blocks, the demon
loved to touch and be touched. For some reason, this
had made her think of Declan Chase, with his aversion
to contact. Both males had evidently been tormented,
but Malkom still craved physical affection.

Sexually Malkom was a dominant demon to the
core, but he was inexperienced as well. Which made for
more than one tricksy situation.

Still, he'd given her mind-blowing climaxes and a
feast of happiness. The more pleasure she felt, the more
satisfaction he enjoyed, which in turn made her even
stronger.

And *everything* about her seemed to make him
happy.

His reactions to her were so intense, he truly was like
a giant battery for her.

Feeding her from his hand? Made him happy. Waking up next to her? He always looked vaguely surprised
that she was there. Then his face would relax into that
self-satisfied expression, and his happiness would flood
over her like a warm blanket.

Watching her bathe? Made him ecstatic.

He'd joined her every time. Any lingering hesitation
about getting in the water was dwindling. He loved to
bathe her just as she had him, still learning her body as

curiosity lit his eyes. She'd let him examine her freely, glad to give him at least that.

At night, as they lay together on his pallet—no need for a second one after all—he pulled her close, enveloping her in his warm arms, pressing her against his chest. The first two nights he'd slept with her collar clutched in his hand. But now he'd begun to accept that she wasn't going anywhere. *At least not yet,* her mind whispered.

During the days, they ate the phickens and some rock-hard type of tart berry. Just yesterday, she'd gotten him to use a napkin and some plasticware from the packs. *Now we're getting somewhere,* she'd thought. Until that same afternoon when he'd drunk blood from a bird's neck again. She'd sighed. *Rome wasn't built in a day.*

In one of the packs, she'd found clothes for him— black combat boots to fit his big feet, camo pants that actually hit his ankles, and a black T-shirt that could stretch over his brawny chest. Apparently, Hostoffersson had been an immense bastard.

Malkom *rocked* the tacticool. With his golden hair in those warrior plaits, his firm lips and chiseled features, he'd made her heart thump. She'd thought, *I'd have to pry witches off him.*

Now she gazed over at him writing *F-o* . . .

Was she really considering keeping him? As if he'd want her after she betrayed him. In any event, she had no place for him in her world.

He'd be like a bull in a china shop, and her life was already about to change radically because of Ruby.

Hey, from what she'd seen of Oblivion, the Order's facility would be a lateral move for him. Maybe if she told herself that often enough, one day she'd believe it?

He glanced at her then, as though he sensed the serious nature of her thoughts, and she swallowed.

She'd begun to desire *all* of him, fantasizing about making love with him. But two things held her back. He could get her pregnant, and he might hurt her, possibly biting her again.

He'd been working on maintaining his control and was making such strides that she no longer feared when his eyes turned black, now associating the color with his desire. *Steady blue flickering to wicked black.*

But could he maintain control when they had sex?

Merely to cohabit with such a strong being took care on her part, and she'd been using magic just to lessen the risk of an accidental injury. Yet for their "claiming," she would have to surrender herself fully to him, trusting him not to hurt her. She didn't know if she could take that leap of faith.

And of course, there was still the issue of his biting. So far she didn't think he'd dreamed her memories, not that he could have revealed that development with words—or miming—anyway. Yet every time he drank her, it increased the likelihood that he would see them.

For her to explain her predicament to him was one thing. But she feared his seeing bits and pieces out of context. Which again would make him lose control.

She knew he wanted to drink her. She'd caught him gazing at her neck, not necessarily with hunger, but almost with yearning.

One night, she'd awakened to find him pacing, running a hand over his mouth. Keeping her breathing deep and even and her lids barely cracked open, she'd watched as his gaze had darted over her, then up to the ceiling, as if he were seeking guidance. With another look at her, he'd raised his arm to his mouth, sinking his fangs into his own wrist, groaning against his skin. Had he been imagining it was her?

He'd bitten himself to keep from breaking his vow to her.

How much longer could a need like that be contained?

Can I keep my vow another night?

Malkom needed to drink her, not because he thirsted for her blood or wanted to "dine on flesh," but because with each hour, she grew more distant.

She was slipping away from him.

Even as she let him enjoy her body, she often appeared lost in thought, closing off her mind. The more she did this, the more he gazed at her neck, craving that connection that had so amazed him.

Now a disquiet had settled over him, and he couldn't concentrate on the letters anymore. He laid down the stick. She didn't even notice as she stared at the fire.

Malkom was so damned accustomed to loss, yet he knew he would never recover if he lost her. To not have her in his keeping? The mere idea sent his rage climbing.

If only he could communicate with her freely. Yet the more he remembered of her language, the more punishing nightmares of his childhood and torture surfaced.

Still he pushed himself, needing to understand. At

times, just before he brought her pleasure, she'd murmur at his ear. What was she telling him when her voice was almost sad? It made him crazed.

And he wanted to ask her *why* she'd been showing this affection to him. Was it just so he'd protect her? His confidence that she would want the strongest male had now turned to desiring more from her.

Until they could communicate, he'd decided to learn as much as possible about her. Life with the witch was wondrous . . . and odd.

She seemed to have a fixation on cleanliness, scrubbing their eating utensils with her magic and continually washing their clothes.

Each morning and night she'd used the blue stick brush to rub her teeth. She kissed him madly each time he did the same. The scent was sharp but pleasant, and the brushing felt good, as if his mouth were being petted.

He'd stopped swallowing it the second time she'd crinkled her nose and muttered, "Ooh."

And every day, she'd given him writing lessons. He could potentially live for hundreds, if not thousands, of years, and he'd recalled what Kallen had once told him: *"Of course you're intelligent enough to read! Who the devil convinced you otherwise?"*

Malkom might not be learned now, but he *could* be. And whenever Carrow praised his progress or regarded him with undisguised admiration, it brought his mind back to a very brief time, long, long ago, when he'd been proud. He'd commanded armies of demons—and he'd been skilled at it.

I'd almost routed the vampires from this plane with battles I'd won.

In the end, Malkom had done it *by himself,* assassinating the Viceroy so gruesomely that his vampire followers had fled Oblivion in terror.

Despite this, the Trothans had clamored for Malkom's death. At least now he was giving them reason to. . . .

Though his nightmares had returned with a vengeance, these were occasionally quelled by dreams of her memories, always scenes from her childhood. In each one, she'd been indoors, playing by herself in an echoing building. For years, she'd been alone, miserable.

As I was. It seemed fate had paired Malkom with a woman who was perfect for him.

Too perfect?

He ruthlessly tamped down his doubts.

Because he not only wanted her. He needed her.

Whenever they kissed and touched, he was able to shut out thoughts of his past. Everything about his sensual new mate kept him firmly—and feverishly—in the present.

The now familiar scent of her arousal, the look in her glittering eyes when she was needing, the way she nibbled her bottom lip whenever her thoughts grew wicked.

The sound of her abandoned moans as he kneaded her breasts.

She went wild when he licked them, or her sweet sex. He'd wake her from slumber with his tongue delving hungrily.

The witch had brought him more sexual pleasure

in moments than he'd experienced in all his centuries. Her kiss alone . . . it made him feel close to her, almost as much as taking her neck had.

Yet Malkom had stopped pushing to claim her. Now *he* wanted a bond first, because with all the new possibilities between them, one filled him with fear.

Begetting another bastard like himself.

Sometimes he scorned his father more for leaving his son vulnerable than he did his mother for selling hers.

Malkom would never risk the same happening to his own offspring. He intended to wed Carrow at the earliest opportunity—

"Demon," she murmured, finally turning to him. "Portal next night?"

Portal. He knew this word. She used it often enough. "Next night," he agreed. She was keen to get back to her home, had explained that they would leave tomorrow at exactly the middle of the night.

Had he figured out why she was here in Oblivion, or why she believed a portal would open to welcome her back?

No. All he knew was that he was going with her. For now, that was enough.

22

T-minus sixteen hours until they were to leave. And Carrow had feelings for the demon she was planning to betray.

In a moment of desperation yesterday, she'd tried to explain her situation to Malkom, to ask for his help—even though he didn't understand the words *mortals, blackmail, kidnap,* or *daughter.* Eventually she'd drawn a stick-figure Carrow that held hands with a stick-figure little girl, then she'd pressed her hand over her heart.

He'd thought she wanted a baby. When she'd emphatically signaled that wasn't what she wanted, he'd seemed hurt, yanking on his boots and storming off to go hunt.

Now, this morning, she couldn't pay attention to his lesson, was racking her brain for any alternative to deceiving him. Maybe she should have set out on her second day here to find other demons to help her.

But at that time, Malkom had been so brutal, so incomprehensible to her. Betraying him would've been nothing to her. She'd had no idea she could ever come to care for him.

What would Ripley do? She'd definitely rescue the orphaned girl from the island.

Break down the facts, Carrow. Even if she could communicate with Malkom, revealing her plot would have to decrease her chances of getting him to the portal. He might balk. After all, she'd only known him for the better part of a week.

She decided then that revealing everything was an unacceptable risk.

And even if she were certain he'd do it, she'd never be able to convey all the inherent dangers for him. He'd go into that portal either completely unknowing, or partially so.

Carrow pinched her forehead. For a woman not used to feeling guilt over her actions or fear for someone who depended on her, she felt overwhelmed. *Am I doing the right thing?* Most of the time when people were under duress, they could talk to someone, friends or family who could help them make the right choice.

Carrow was flying blind—in uncharted territory.

"Ara?"

She jerked her face up. "Huh? Where were we?"

But his expression had grown serious, the lesson forgotten. He interlaced his fingers and said, "We are bound."

"Bound?"

He collected a piece of rope, knotting it.

"Oh, you mean *bound?*"

He gave a nod, then drew in the sand.

An infinity symbol? "Clever demon, how did you know that . . . ?"

He was gazing at her with a question in his eyes.

"Bound forever?" And somehow she met his gaze and lied, "Yes, demon. Bound forever."

As if to make her feel even guiltier, he gathered her into his arms, cupping her face against his broad chest. His voice a deep rumble, he said, "Carrow is Malkom's."

She wanted to sob.

"Yes?"

"Yes," she answered, wishing that it could be so simple between them. *Demon meets girl. Girl might be falling for demon.*

But then, if not for all the treachery she'd gotten caught up in, she would never have come here to find him, never would have known him.

He rested his chin on her head and placed her hand over his heart. It drummed against her palm.

I made that beat. Maybe fate had been right to match them. Somehow between the two of them, they gentled Malkom's rages. She'd brought him happiness. *At least for a time.*

After midnight, Carrow didn't know if he could ever be gentled again.

She drew back, gazing up at his face. What if it could be simple between them, if just for a few hours? One morning spent enjoying each other—fully—with no thoughts of the future?

He'd been so curious about sex, and so patient with her, that she wanted him to have that experience. But if she offered herself to him, she'd have to trust him not to hurt her.

Do I trust him? Can I? She swallowed. "Malkom, I want you to make love to me."

He shrugged.

"*Sex*, demon."

His body shot through with tension. Sharp nod.

"*Gentle?* Can you not hurt me?" Ah, Hekate, was she actually going to do this?

"Yes." He lifted her into his arms, carrying her to the pallet. "Will not hurt you."

He laid her down, joining her there. Then his brows drew together, as if he'd just recalled something. Was he hesitating?

"You are mine, *ara*. Say this."

At that moment, she was. "I'm yours."

Seeming to make a decision, he removed his shirt, revealing the tan, smooth skin of his chest. Then he eased above her. As she gazed up into the blue of his eyes, any doubts she had faded. *The demon won't hurt me.*

He dipped down to cover her mouth with his own. She loved the way he kissed now. He was aggressive with it, having learned exactly how to drive her wild. Strong flicks, teasing licks that set her body on fire.

As their breaths mingled, she gasped against his lips, "*Yours.*"

She wants me to claim her. Malkom's chest was tight with feeling, his mind filled with thoughts of pleasuring her, so that she'd cleave to him.

"Bound forever," she'd told him. And, gods, he wanted to believe it.

So why did he continue to have the sense that she was slipping away?

As he levered himself above her, the importance of this moment struck him like a hammer blow. But he had no words to express to her what she was about to give him—and how long he'd waited for it.

How long he'd waited for *her*.

He didn't know how to ask her why his heart seemed to stop every time he gazed at her face. No way to tell her what being inside her would mean to him, the trust he would bestow when he gave up his seed. *I could put a babe inside her this night.*

"Witch," he grated. He kissed her palm, then laid it over his heart again, as if she could feel how heavy his chest was. That sense of possessiveness flooded him. With these kinds of feelings and no outlet . . . bewilderment roiled.

She couldn't understand him, and he didn't know what to do.

"Malkom," she breathed, beginning to look uneasy, "y-you have to be gentle."

"Do not . . . want to hurt you."

"The more *needing* I am, the less it will hurt."

Then he wouldn't enter her until he'd made her beg for him to.

Lying in the cradle of her thighs, he removed her top, baring her breasts to him. *Never get enough of these.* He bent down to kiss that tender, giving flesh, knowing how much she desired him to.

Yet once his lips closed around one of her nipples, his fangs sharpened. *Claim her,* his instinct commanded, *in all ways.* As his tongue swirled around the peak, he felt a hot jolt. A drop of blood had hit his tongue.

He rose up, eyes riveted to the line of crimson just above her stiff nipple. Starkness against her creamy breast.

He'd never felt so close to his female as when he'd bitten her. Surely she would feel it too, now that she didn't fear him, now that she wanted his claim upon her.

Must make her mine.

She shook her head, likely to tell him not to bite her, but he cut her off, warning her in Demonish not to deny them this.

Never deny us this.

As he leaned down, she kept shaking her head, shoving against his chest.

"But you are mine!" he told her in Anglish. "*Feel this.*" The connection.

Cleave to me, witch! With a yell, he sank his fangs into one plump breast.

His eyes closed with ecstasy before he'd even drawn from her. When he licked her nipple as he suckled, she tensed beneath him, crying out.

He forced his lids open, alarm flaring. But then he saw her head and arms had fallen back, her lips parted.

When he realized she was coming, he gave a desperate groan, sucking her harder, palm covering her other breast, pinching the tip.

The way her body worked beneath his bite . . . *maddening.* She arched her back and writhed, screaming as she climaxed, whipping forth his own release.

His sac tightened in readiness. *Place your claim.* His cock swelled unbearably. *Plunge it inside her.*

Snarling against her breast, he fumbled for his trews. Too late. Before he could even think of penetrating her, he began coming within them.

He tongued her nipple as pleasure racked him, so strong he jerked from the force of it again and again.

With a final ragged moan, he collapsed over her body, relinquishing his bite with a tender kiss. "Ah, *ara,* you felt it."

23

"You bastard!" Carrow pressed her palm to her breast, flushing from her reaction. "You promised you wouldn't bite me! Does what I want matter *at all* to you?"

The demon stared at her as if dumbfounded, while she was *panicked*. She couldn't catch her breath. There was still time for him to see her memories—out of context—still time for him to balk at the gate and doom Ruby.

"Let me up!" She shoved against him, grappling to get his weight off her. "I trusted you."

"Carrow, I wanted—"

"I *know* what you wanted." She'd offered herself to him, and instead of making love to her, he'd preferred to steal her blood.

That stung so much. At once, she felt both violated and rejected.

"Get off me!" When he wouldn't, fury filled her. She launched him into the wall, feeling stronger than she had in years. And he'd fueled it. Which made her wonder—what in the hell had that bite felt like to him?

Rock dust clouded over him where he'd landed. Had she heard something snap?

As the dust abated, she gasped in horror. She'd launched him *into the blade corner*. His skin was gashed open in a dozen places, blood pouring. On top of that, one of his shoulders had been dislocated, and his right arm appeared to be broken.

Sympathy swept over her, and she rose to see to him. "Malkom, I . . ." She trailed off when blood trickled down her breast and dripped from the peak. Despite his injuries, his gaze was rapt on her nipple, on each droplet of blood.

She dabbed at the puncture wounds, and her regret vanished, resentment and doubt taking its place. *Does he prefer my blood to my body?* "Just . . . just get out!"

He gazed at her with guilt, even yearning in his blue eyes. But above all else, his expression looked disappointed.

Didn't matter how he felt. That bite could spell her doom, Ruby's doom. Ruby, who was sitting inside a cell, motherless, wondering if Carrow would ever return. "Out!"

With a frustrated growl, he left the chamber, *limping* away. How badly had she hurt him?

After he'd gone, she stared at the exit. For as long as she lived, she'd never forget the look on his face. The disappointment in his expression ate at her.

Which confused her. She cleaned up and dressed, then began pacing. He'd just hurt her, so she should want him to hurt in return. Yet he had her so mixed up.

She had the sense that he'd expected something specific from her—she didn't know what. All she knew was that she'd let him down.

Agitated, she crossed to Lindt's backpack for that flask of Jack Daniel's, wondering, *Is it still good?* Of course. Alcohol was preserved in alcohol, after all.

As she stared at the bottle, she wondered how her life had come to this. She had an out-of-control, blood-guzzling demon as a would-be lover, a looming betrayal that she didn't want to deal, and a little girl depending on Carrow to save her life.

She knew without a doubt that Ruby was going to turn her entire existence upside down. And still Carrow missed her like crazy, couldn't wait to get their life together started. . . .

Getting sauced wouldn't help anything. *But it can't really hurt either, can it?* Carrow lifted the flask, knocking back a shot, savoring the burn.

What was she going to do with Malkom? Besides give him over to merciless mortals bent on experimenting on him.

Everything was so difficult between them. Why couldn't Carrow have found a guy like Mariketa's man? Her husband, Bowen MacRieve, adored and spoiled her. He was a gorgeous werewolf who was witty and fun.

Carrow was the mate of a demon who dug blood, possibly more than making love to her. One who couldn't discuss current events or use silverware and had only recently been introduced to hygiene.

Mari had once mentioned that Bowen didn't like to watch the same movies that she did.

Carrow's man? He didn't know what a movie *was*.

She couldn't help but be jealous of Mari. They'd

bonded over the fact that both of their parents had left them behind. It turned out that Mari's had abandoned her to go fight evil and make the world better for their beloved daughter.

Carrow's wanted to play golf on a perpetually balmy paradise plane.

Mari deserved everything fate was giving her. *But I deserve loving parents and a great guy too, damn it!*

Where the hell was Malkom? The clock was ticking, and he was the key to her and Ruby's freedom. *That's the only reason I care where he is.*

Bastard bit her! Again. Chugged her breast like a frat boy on a Natty Lite. *He broke his vow.*

Still, she had a lot of nerve to blame him for that, especially when she was on the verge of *destroying* his ability to trust forever.

Everything was so damned difficult. . . .

At the end of the flask, she concluded that she was now drunk—and that he definitely should've been back by now. Deeming herself powerful enough to fry a monster X if need be, she decided to set out after him. She filched a flashlight, then stumbled down the mine shaft.

Once she reached the exit and the wind hit her face like a slap, she slurred, "Fuggin' *hate* this place!"

She was about to declare her hatred for him as well, but stopped herself. She didn't hate him for what he'd done.

Now that she could see things more drunkenly, she wasn't convinced he'd taken her blood in lieu of making love to her. She suspected his bite might have been a try at closeness, like intimacy for a vemon. *Maybe?*

With a sigh, she unsteadily gestured to herself. "Becauss, less face it, demon hasta be fallin' in love with me by now."

He'd looked so completely staggered by her reaction, clearly expecting her to feel differently about his bite. And she would have if she hadn't been planning to deceive him soon—would've just accepted the pleasure it brought her.

So damned difficult.

"Malkom?" she called, marching out after him. "Where are you?" No response. With his uncanny senses, he should have been able to hear her over the wind. "Demon, come back!"

Finally, she spied his large prints, saw they were accompanied by a blood trail. *Guilty pang.* Down the booby-trapped path she went, trying to remember where he'd pointed out traps.

But it turned out that his contraptions were easy to find. Because they'd all been triggered.

By demons. Now mangled and dead demons. An attack? The dossier had said Malkom guarded the mines. Maybe this was a takeover attempt. Or perhaps the Trothans had come here to capture their fugitive, the one who'd killed their prince?

Farther down the mountain, she could see signs of a struggle. Bone trees had been *felled*. This had to have involved someone as powerful as Malkom.

Had even more demons jumped him? She'd bet they were regretting it now. Malkom was probably out hiding the fresh bodies from her—or cooking them. Who could tell with her man?

She surveyed all the tracks scattered over the clearing. Again, she could make out Malkom's prints, but now she saw lighter boot prints. Even *more* demons?

With ten shots of Jack D in her belly, she was convinced that her scientifical mind could read tracks and deduce a corresponding fight. She was a regular Sacagawea. Even though Carrow had never learned to track.

Deep half prints meant someone lunging, right? There were lots of those. They spun around and around. But she could swear that it looked like in the end, Malkom had just limped away with lighter demons on either side. Then the tracks simply disappeared.

What—the—frack? Had he *allowed* a gang to teleport him away? Even if he was weakened, if he resisted enough, no one would ever be able to trace him against his will.

She had to know what had happened, so she eked out some power to fuel a sobering spell—her least favorite of all spells. On the heels of that, she launched a viewing spell, murmuring, "See here. See Malkom."

A scene began to play out like a show on a TV with fuzzy reception. Malkom was sweating, as if he'd been running up and down his mountain, but he appeared to be returning in the direction of the mine.

Though time had passed since he'd left, he remained thoroughly pissed at himself, ramming his horns into trees. He was still limping, his injured arm hanging awkwardly, and he had dried blood all over him.

Another guilty pang. She'd never meant to hurt him so badly.

Her eyes went wide as the scene continued. More

demons lay in wait for him. Malkom was so injured and distracted that he didn't see them—

Until they'd surrounded him, at least twenty of them. The largest one wore a grand suit of armor and was nearly as large as Malkom. The others called that demon Ronath. From the look on his face, Malkom despised him.

They were here for Malkom, specifically for his capture. If Malkom was a fugitive, had this armored demon come to arrest him?

With hatred seething in his now dark eyes, Malkom said something in a low, brutal tone.

When Ronath responded, sneering some reply, Malkom launched himself at the demon, driving him into a tree.

But Ronath's armor took the brunt of the blow. And unlike Malkom, Ronath and some of his men could trace. Even with Malkom's speed, he couldn't defend against so many as they appeared and disappeared, stabbing him again and again.

Can't watch this . . . can't watch . . .

After several tries, they cast a metal net over him, but they couldn't trace him away when he was resisting so violently.

How much longer could he keep up his struggles? He was weakening—he clearly knew it. Still he clashed with them, and he might have gotten free. But then Malkom froze. His senses were better than the others'. And he'd heard Carrow calling for him, approaching them.

His eyes were calculating, his mind working. Her

lips parted as he stopped fighting them. He'd made the decision to be taken.

Just before they traced him away, he roared twice more to cover her drunken calls. And then they were gone.

Ah, gods, no.

If they'd seized Malkom for that murder, then they'd likely take him back to the nearest city. She hurriedly climbed to a vantage point to gaze out from the mountain.

In the distance, she could barely spy out a collection of buildings rising from the horizon. If the winds had been up much more, she'd never have spotted them.

Surely regicide was punishable by death. She had to go after him. Aside from the fact that she felt guilty as hell for injuring him and then distracting him, she needed Malkom for her and Ruby's freedom.

So she'd go and save him, just so she could betray him?

Are you so cold, Carrow? Not cold, she was *committed* to a little girl who needed her.

A part of her cried, *Malkom needs me, too.* At that moment, she made a promise to herself. If Chase kept his word, then she'd return to the facility for Malkom. "I swear to Hekate that I won't stop until he's freed." Carrow would make everything right. It just might take time. . . .

With that vow made, she focused once more on the problem at hand—some asshole named Ronath.

The sobering spell she'd cast made one sober as

though through the passing of time. Which meant Carrow was now hungover. Which meant . . .

Demons would die today!

How to get to them? Between her and the city was a beastie-filled desert. She'd have to expend beaucoup energy to make herself invincible. Oh, and to float across the sand.

Yes, she'd been using power to reinforce her body with Malkom—and she'd used still more to attack him today. So she wouldn't have enough juice left over from her trek to contend with a town full of demons.

She'd need an infusion. It all would depend on one thing.

Malkom Slaine had better be *happy* to see her.

24

"You've come full circle now, Slaine," Ronath said from outside Malkom's cell, the same one in which he'd been imprisoned with Kallen all those years ago. "And still after all these centuries, you are nothing."

Narrowing his bloodied and swollen eyes, Malkom gripped the cell bars, the wrath inside him burning for release. Earlier, the armorer had ordered his guards to beat him but refused to face Malkom alone—even though Ronath could now trace. "And still you are a coward, one who has always feared me."

When Ronath shrugged, his elaborate armor clanked with the movement. "Your taunts mean nothing to me because we both know that I've won. And you, Scârbă, will always lose. It might take hundreds of years, but you will always fail."

Never had Malkom needed to kill as he did now. Because everything Ronath said was true.

I wanted to live with Carrow. That was all.

Though the idea of being kept from his female made him crazed—he'd sworn he would never be separated from her—he had one consolation. Ronath wouldn't find her. *So I win.* By the time the armorer and his men had finished torturing Malkom and returned to the mountain to begin mining, she would be long gone.

Malkom had made her so furious that there was no chance she'd try to follow him. As if there'd been a chance before the bite. She would make her own way to the portal and leave without him this night. With the power she'd demonstrated this morning, she should be safe.

I would have liked to see her world. To have her show it to me.

Would she wonder what had become of him?

It didn't matter. He would die here, and she would be safe from these demons.

Ronath ran the tip of his bone spear under a claw. "Surely even you can recognize that you were born just to be punished. What I do not understand is why you haven't simply ended yourself. Seems you are more coward than I."

Kallen had once asked him about his will to live, marveling at it, especially in light of Malkom's earlier hardships. This morning, when Malkom had been brought into the city, memories of his imprisonment and his childhood overwhelmed him, until even he had begun to marvel at what he'd survived.

The torture and pain, the unending loneliness.

In this very cell, he'd been trapped with the body of his best friend for days. The brother he'd murdered . . .

Never had he regretted anything so badly. Even before he'd been released, Malkom had realized that Kallen's actions hadn't been the betrayal he thought; the prince had merely decided on a rational course of action.

The better male lives, the lesser sacrifices.

In four hundred years, Malkom had accomplished nothing. Kallen could have achieved so much more.

Yet now Malkom realized that if he hadn't had the will to live that night, he never would have known his witch, wouldn't have been here to save her life.

He pictured Carrow smiling up at him from under a jet-black curl. Malkom had somehow endured long enough to protect the most exquisite woman born, to pleasure her. *I savored her cries in my ear and safeguarded her to the end.*

Gods, how much more easily he would have been able to withstand his past if he'd known she'd be in his future, for even this short a time.

On that night so long ago, Malkom hadn't been willing to die for Kallen, but for the witch . . .

I do it gladly.

Malkom shoved his shoulders back. "You know nothing of my life, Ronath," he said, his tone smug.

"I know it's about to end," Ronath replied, turning to call for the guards. "It's time."

Time to begin the dwellers' grueling ritual. *With me as the sacrifice.* Yet even now, Malkom had only one regret.

He'd broken his vow to Carrow.

She'd been enraged with him. And he hadn't had the words to tell her that he'd bitten her because he was ceding his heart to her. Little by little, 'twas becoming hers to claim.

He'd wanted something of her in return.

Carrow surveyed the demons' city with disgust.

No wind stirred down on this plateau, which should

have been a good thing, but the air smelled rank. And without the billowing dust, the sun beat down. Bleached bones and behorned skulls littered the streets.

Most of the buildings had decayed into ruins, their bricks crumbling and wood splintering.

Even with the full force of Carrow's remaining magic, crossing that hateful desert had taken her agonizing hours. And with each one, she'd become more convinced that the demons had captured Malkom to execute him.

I'll never forgive myself if I'm too late.

Down a main thoroughfare, she saw a crowd gathered in the distance. With the last of her power, she wove a glamour over herself so she'd appear to have a fine cloak covering her body and hair. Beneath it, she would be bedecked in a rich silk gown, gold jewelry, and even a crown.

If she had to interact with demons from a class-stratified society, then she'd look like money and be quick to give orders.

In this master/slave world, perhaps she should even act as if she owned Malkom. Didn't the owner get to mete punishment to her property? She might be able to demand his release under her recognizance.

So says the chick who weekends in Parish Correctional.

Once cloaked, she hastened toward the crowd. The demons were gathered around a bloodstained stage made of stone. In the center of it stood what looked like a pyre platform, except this had *manacles attached.* In the background, colossal statues of horned figures loomed, likely representing the demons' gods.

Piles of blackened bones lay at the foot of the pyre, and charred hands and feet rotted in the manacles. The hands were clenched in fists, the feet curling downward.

The Trothans burned victims alive. Did they plan that fate for Malkom? *Over my dead body.*

The denizens attending this sacrifice had the same shifty eyes as Asmodel, and she perceived in them a sick happiness at the prospect of the upcoming execution.

And these were the demons she'd once hoped to find, to *unite* with? No way could she trust her and Ruby's futures to these dicks.

She felt dirty drawing power from them, from their sadistic *glee.* But she forced herself to, allowing the crowd to begin fueling her.

When she spotted half a dozen swordsmen leading Malkom toward the stage, relief sailed through her to find him still alive.

On the heels of that, her fury at the demons returned tenfold. Malkom had been beaten, and they were hauling him directly out into the sun. The light here still wasn't strong enough to outright kill Malkom, but he was unmistakably exhausted, his skin blistering.

She began pushing through the crowd toward him. But the Trothans were huge, immovable.

The six swordsmen dragged him through a gauntlet of deranged demons who stabbed him with spears fashioned from bones. And at the end of this, they would expect him to be burned alive?

Malkom must have known this was the fate awaiting him, and still he'd surrendered to Ronath.

To protect me.

The swordsmen maneuvered him to the front of the stage, where a chopping block stood. Forcing him to kneel before it, they shackled him to bolts in the stone, securing the ends together with an antique-looking padlock.

She put out a probe. Naturally, Malkom's bonds were mystically enforced. She could open them, but it'd take time.

There was acceptance in Malkom's expression, even when the swordsmen shoved his head to the block and one of them raised an ax.

"What the hell is this?" she demanded of the group of demons closest to her. They scowled down at her, uncomprehending. She needed a new spell, the translation spell, but it required so much power. . . .

The ax came down before she could react. They'd cut off one of his horns.

Though Malkom didn't make a sound, his magnificent body shuddered in the chains, his blue eyes resigned.

The guards swiftly forced his head back to the block. Her stomach churned when they chopped off the second. She knew the horns would grow back, but to lose one—much less two—was supposed to be excruciating.

This torture filled the demons with joy. She gritted her teeth as dirty power coursed through her.

Malkom continued to stare straight ahead, an innate pride lingering in his expression. She perceived no shame from him. Which meant either he'd done nothing wrong—or he was a hardened killer.

Carrow wished she could believe the latter, since it would make her mission easier. But she couldn't. She gazed at him up there, chained, his body covered with gashes.

He was so much better than these people. *Malkom is noble.*

If he'd killed their prince, then the guy'd had it coming.

Malkom must have scented her then, because he stiffened, rattling his chains. Then she got hit with a bolt of something like utter joy.

She swayed and moaned, "Whoaaa." Yet he instantly followed that emotion with a helpless kind of rage.

No takesie-backsies, demon. She'd just scored a spike of uncut, pharmaceutical-grade vemon joy. Delectable power surged inside her. This would be enough for several simultaneous spells, and she'd need them all—protection, language, her continued glamour. As she was hurriedly spellcasting, the demon who'd led Malkom's capture climbed to the stage, dressed in full armor from feet to chin, everything but the helmet.

This Ronath had an air of deviousness mixed with conceit. And she didn't think he could possibly ever have been happier than he was right now. *I'll take a shot of that—and then I'll defeat you with your own delight.*

After quieting the crowd's frenetic cheers, Ronath addressed them: "Blah blah blah MALKOM SLAINE blah blah."

Though she didn't understand Ronath—yet—she knew that whatever he was saying was the *wrong thing*.

She couldn't remember the last time she'd been so infuriated. *Word to the wise, Ronath. Never piss off a hungover witch.*

Or she'll have your head for it.

25

I will heat her backside for this.

How the hell had Carrow made it here across the desert? Malkom had believed he'd separated her from his enemies.

He'd thought he would never lay eyes on her again, had resigned himself. He'd expected her to return to her home, crossing into the portal without a look back.

Then for him to know her scent once more . . .

Foolish female! He quelled the urge to yell for her to run from this place; he must act as if he didn't care about her. Must not to give Ronath this leverage.

Otherwise, they would use her to punish him. Malkom could think of no more effective torment.

At best, they'd enslave her. She would fetch a fortune.

Damn it, why *did she come?* He craned his head to see her better, gashing his neck on the manacle, but he didn't care.

She had concealed herself with a rich cloak over her body and hair, and she seemed to be *floating* through the crowd, which began swiftly parting for her.

Her movements were odd—too smooth yet aggressive at the same time. Malkom swallowed as she neared. Her shining boots . . . weren't touching the ground.

For the first time, he could believe she was one among the eerie witches from olden tales who cooked men's hearts and brewed noxious potions—all for a fee.

When she floated up the steps, he grated, "Carrow, leave . . . this place." But his mouth was almost too dry to speak.

Instead, she stood beside him. When she pulled back her cloak, the crowd grew hushed. He was speechless.

She wore garments fit for an empress, a crown as well. Though his eyes were seared by the sun, he couldn't look away. The light reflected off her gleaming blue-black hair. Her pale skin glowed amidst the filth of this place.

Her green eyes glittered menacingly. She was so beautiful, yet at the same time she looked deadly.

Malkom was awestruck.

"What gives you the right to do this?" Carrow asked Ronath—in *Demonish*.

Now she spoke his tongue? Or was it another spell? Her very voice sounded altered, her words delayed, coming out of her mouth as if filtered.

Ronath snapped his slackened jaw shut, then answered, "What business is it of yours, stranger? This is how we punish criminals in Ash. Especially one like him."

"One like him, Ronath?"

The armorer frowned at the casual use of his name just as Malkom was wondering if she knew the demon somehow.

Ronath recovered, saying, "He owes us his death for a dozen crimes."

He will announce that I was a vampire's whore. Shame scalded Malkom, burning hotter than he'd ever imagined. Carrow would despise him. *Then this will end. I will accept it.*

"There are two murders he must atone for and—"

"*Two* murders?" she said, interrupting him.

Ronath was all too happy to tell her, "He killed our prince. And before that, he murdered his own mother."

Carrow raised her brows at Malkom, but he could deny neither. So long ago, when he'd taken command of Kallen's rebellion, he'd journeyed back to the slums to his mother's hovel. He'd wanted her to see what he'd made of himself. *I wanted her to regret.* Instead, she'd tried to poison him.

How would Carrow react? "*Channa,*" he rasped.

She tilted her head, as if trying to make a decision about him.

Ronath said, "And there are many more crimes."

Just as he took a deep breath to list them all, Carrow raised her gaze—*a decision made?*—and stared Ronath down. "You waste my time. Release him now."

"Release him?" Ronath thought this comical. "Why do you not reveal your name, or join him?"

"I'm Carrow Graie of the Wiccan mercenaries." The crowd grew restless with a witch in their midst. "And I want Malkom Slaine freed. If he killed anyone, I'm sure he had good reason."

Now Malkom's jaw slackened. With her slim shoulders back, she was standing up before all. For him. Aside from Kallen, no one had ever taken his side, ever stood up for him.

"Unchain him. At—once," she ordered imperiously. As Ronath tried to calm the crowd, she turned, catching Malkom's gaze to give him a furtive *wink* of reassurance.

He jolted in the chains, stunned anew. Though his body was a mass of injuries, he began straining against his bonds. Now that she was beside him . . .

'Tis not the end. Not until we say it is.

Ronath demanded, "What business have you with him?"

"He is my male."

Hers? Declared before all! Murmurs sounded in the crowd. They were all shocked that such a female as this had claimed him in public. *I am shocked as well.* If Malkom also claimed her here today . . .

More struggling. The chains began to loosen.

Ronath squinted at Malkom. "Your heart beats." He turned to Carrow. "So you are the whore who brought him back to life?"

With her palms beginning to glow, her expression turned lethal. In a chilling voice, she said, "And you *dare* seek to end it?" A white beam shot from her hand, aimed at his neck.

A hail of blazing light struck Ronath, hurtling his body into the crowd.

Realizing that Ronath would never release him and that she and Malkom wouldn't merely walk away from this place, Carrow let diplomacy fall by the wayside.

And launched a kill shot.

They were running out of time anyway. Malkom was

weakening with every moment in the sun, with each drop of his blood spilled.

The throng began surging up to the stage, yelling for her head and demanding Malkom's sacrifice in the fire.

With one hand, she used magic to propel those demons back; with the other, she directed more energy, beginning to work on Malkom's intricate bonds.

"Carrow, free me," he grated.

"I'm working on it." *Blindly.*

"I will protect you."

"Little busy, love," she muttered as she kept a blood-thirsty demonic crowd at bay while simultaneously picking a mystical lock.

Normally, she would have fallen back to regroup, but she could never leave Malkom without protection from this mob. They looked like they wanted to rip him limb from limb.

"What did you *do* to these people?"

"Kept them without water," Malkom bit out. "They're dying of thirst."

"Ohhh. Good one."

As she was finishing up with the chains, she realized that she couldn't fight off all these raving demons. Neither could Malkom.

Time to freak them out. She began chanting a spell . . . to turn day into night.

Once darkness fell, they stilled. Cries rang out. "Release him!" "We'll all die!" "Let him go!"

Malkom yelled, *"Ara,* behind you!"

Wild-eyed guards stalked her from the back. She blasted them with searing beams of magic, punching holes into their chests, felling them one after the other.

Still she worked to free Malkom. "I've almost got—"

"Carrow, to your left!"

Too late, she pivoted. *Impact.* The air rushed from her lungs and her body slammed back into one of the stone idols. She peered down in disbelief. A spear jutted from her side.

Ronath's spear.

He'd traced to the stage, his armor still smoking from her attack. The metal around his neck had saved him from a kill strike. "You belong with him, witch! Burned in the same fire."

Pain radiated out from her wound. Shock yielded to fury. "You son of a bitch!"

Malkom went ballistic, roaring with rage. His fangs were bared, elongated for a kill. He thrashed with all his strength, nearly getting loose.

"Malkom, I'll be all right."

"Then free me, Carrow! I *need* this."

Only one bolt remained, securing all his chains together. As she tore free the spear, she gritted, "Make him *scream*, love." With a wave of her hand, she removed the final bolt.

Malkom shed his chains, then charged Ronath, claws and fangs bared. *"You will die for harming her!"*

Ronath traced to the side; Malkom anticipated it. When Ronath materialized, he tackled him.

The armorer struggled to defend himself. But even when injured, Malkom was too quick. Too *enraged*. He pinned Ronath, bashing the male's head against the stone. "And for Kallen you will die in agony! He was a brother to me!"

More guards appeared to save their leader. With the last of her strength, Carrow held them back.

When Ronath tried to speak, whispering up to him, Malkom slowed his attack. Yet whatever the armorer said made Malkom roar, "Never!" as he punched his fist through Ronath's chest plate.

The demon screamed in pain; blood spewed upward like a fountain. Malkom twisted his arm and plucked out his still-beating heart—which he displayed to Ronath, squeezing it into a pulp right before his horrified eyes.

Carrow's legs weakened, and she collapsed to her knees. No power left to heal herself. Though she loved to see a good vengeance killing as much as the next witch, they had to hurry. "Malkom, please . . ."

Without another thought, he wrenched Ronath's head from his neck. As Malkom lunged to her, he absently cast it into the dumbfounded crowd. *He cares more about me than even that trophy.*

"Carrow, tell me what to do to help you."

"I'll heal. But we're running out of time." She was losing blood, growing dizzy and cold. Only hours left. On the heels of these trials, could he possibly get them both across that desert? And in time? "The portal . . . we must be there before midnight. Or it will close forever."

With a nod, he lifted her in his arms.

But before they left this place in the dust, Malkom stood before the crowd of freaked-out demons and announced, "She is my female. *Mine*." His voice was surprisingly strong, and the demons quieted. "I claim her before all."

More rumblings and shocked gasps.

Exasperated, Carrow asked, "Was that completely necessary?" Her words sounded weak, reedy.

"Completely." He gazed down at her. "Wife."

She frowned. Had he just called her *wife*? Though dizziness was about to overtake her, she experienced that overwhelming sense of future about him. A shared future. "Malkom, p-please take me home." He drew her tight to his chest. Against his neck, she murmured, "Can you get us there?"

Just as her lids slid shut, he rasped, *"Right now, I can do anything."*

26

His witch had come to Ash to save his life, and she'd believed in him, even in the face of those accusations. Now she was trusting him to get her back across the desert to the portal before it closed.

But how long would her conjured night last? When the sun returned, he could be trapped in the middle of the scorching dunes.

He gazed back at that city, knowing he'd never look upon it again. His female didn't belong in this foul place. And since he belonged with her, then neither did he. He didn't care what he had to do, he'd find a way to get her home.

I will take her troubles away. . . .

With that thought in mind, he braced himself against the pain of his injuries and plowed into the desert.

The sands proved hellish in his condition, and more than once he'd gone to his knees. The creatures inhabiting the dunes had spurred him to his feet. When one attacked, Malkom had secured Carrow over his shoulder then slashed out with his claws, roaring to intimidate the beast. 'Twas enough to keep them at bay.

And by the time Carrow's false night had transformed into true darkness, he had the five stones in sight.

Between breaths, he said, "Carrow, we near. Wake."

She did, gazing around in confusion. She said something, but the words were Anglish. Her spell had worn off, and he didn't quite take her meaning.

He regretted the loss. To hear her voice in his mother tongue . . .

And he'd savored communicating freely with her, even under those circumstances. But her language was coming to him, building faster and faster on itself.

Once he reached the circle, he lifted her bloody shirt to check her side, finding her healing—

The portal began to open, exactly as she'd said.

This time was momentous for him. Ronath was dead, and now a new life with his mate lay within reach. The armorer's last words whispered through his mind: "You will always lose, even if you kill me today. Soon enough, you will lose *her*."

Never. Malkom stifled his doubts. She was taking him to her world. *I do not always lose, Ronath.* Finally, *finally,* Malkom would win.

He was smiling for the first time.

"It opens," Malkom said, his tone excited. "We go together."

Just before them, a threshold was growing, a swirling black vortex.

"Oh, Malkom, you did it." This steadfast demon, who she'd just trusted with her life, had somehow gotten them here on time. Eyes watering, she raised her hand to lay it against his cheek. "And you're smiling."

Though he still sported bruises, he'd never looked more beautiful to her. The winds streamed his golden plaits around his masculine face. His lips curled as his blue eyes flickered over her.

Even as her heart was breaking, she sensed joy filling his. But she could draw no power from him. Already her magic had been doused, her torque reactivated as promised.

If they double-crossed her, Carrow would retaliate with the wrath of a thousand Furies.

She eased from his arms to stand on her own. He didn't seem to want to let her go. *Ah, Hekate, how can I hand him over?* She could imagine an army of soldiers mere feet away, ready to tranquilize him. Though they wouldn't kill Malkom, this betrayal would hurt him so much, maybe irreparably.

No matter if Carrow could find a way to return and free him.

She tried to steel herself, to recall what she was here for. But all she could think about was *his* sacrifice for her. He'd let them take him to that city, even knowing he'd be tortured and burned alive.

Her beautiful, stalwart demon. On impulse, she stood on her toes and pressed her lips to his. When she drew back, his smile had faded and a purely *male* expression surfaced. He looked at her as if she'd hung the moon for him, and he wanted to reward her with hours of hot, abandoned sex.

He believed he would claim her soon. *Because I promised him he could once we returned to my home.* Yet instead of fulfilling the instincts clawing inside him, he'd soon know deception.

With his eyes fixed on her face, he grated, "Bound forever."

Yes, Carrow had long possessed that unique and curious talent—the ability to determine when another had just become a part of her life forever.

From just one meeting, Carrow had known that Elianna would be like a mother to her, and Mari a sister. A week ago, Carrow had looked down at Ruby and seen a daughter.

Earlier, when Malkom had gazed at her, his wife, with such joy, Carrow had recognized in Malkom a partner, a lover.

A husband.

Fighting her tears, she somehow said, "Yes, Malkom." *Think of Ruby, a seven-year-old girl who needs to be free.* "Bound forever."

Malkom had had a long life. *Such as it was,* her mind whispered. She trudged forward and crossed into the brink. Once there, she faced him, meeting his gaze.

I will return for you, Malkom, she inwardly vowed as she beckoned him near. . . .

When Malkom followed the witch, taking her small hand in his, he again thought, *I will win.* This would be a new life for him.

Shuck off the past, the memories, the nightmares.

The portal was churning and black, steeped in power. His heart raced. He'd never crossed one before, but he'd follow his female—his *wife*—wherever she led him.

As he stepped across the threshold, the sun shone brightly, even more strongly than in Ash. Though the light blinded his sensitive eyes and burned his skin, he'd take the pain to be with her.

He blinked at the landscape, seeing a blurring explosion of green all around them, like a wall. *Green?* Scents bombarded him—

The smell of aggression, *enemies.* He jerked his head around, shoving Carrow behind his back. *Can't see . . .*

"Welcome to hell, Slaine," some strange man intoned.

Movement all around them. With his eyes burning, Malkom struggled to analyze the scene. A large, pale-faced man stood at the back. In front of him was a short club-carrying mortal.

More than a dozen mortal soldiers besieged them, weapons at the ready. They were dressed like the ones he'd killed for trespassing on his mountain.

Now they must be bent on revenge.

I've endangered Carrow. Get her away. His gaze darting, he turned back to the portal. Beside the doorway stood a wide-eyed sorceress, but she'd already closed that escape.

The short male calmly ordered, "Seize him."

Malkom drew Carrow closer. "Stay behind me."

But she edged past him to stand next to the sorceress.

"What are you doing, Carrow?"

Her voice a whisper, she said, "Malkom, I'm so sorry." Her eyes brimmed with tears that spilled down her heartbreaking face. Her expression seemed *agonized.*

No. His mind couldn't grasp this, couldn't comprehend . . .

"P-please, just go with them—"

"No, Carrow," he insisted, even as realization took hold, that knot tightening in his gut. She'd lured him into a trap. *"Channa?"*

"I-I didn't have a choice," she said, but he was no longer listening.

"Not you, *not you.*" He gnashed his teeth. *"Not you!"* he roared with fury.

As he lunged for her, he was blasted with some kind of power. Muscles spasming, his legs buckled. And then the pain began.

When the guards surrounded them, Malkom's eyes had been questioning, disbelieving, then anguished. Now they'd shot to black, flashing with an unholy rage.

Carrow screamed as the men opened fire on him with sedation darts, rifles popping. "No, stop this!"

Lanthe held her back. "You can't do anything for him."

But the darts could barely puncture his taut muscles, and he quickly knocked them away. So they opened up with those charge throwers, like flamethrowers with electricity.

He bellowed as they electrocuted him, but he wouldn't surrender. When two soldiers got too close, he leapt forward, claws bared, slashing them nearly in half, slicing through their weapons and their bodies.

Now the riflemen switched to bullets, firing a barrage that nearly put him to his knees.

Tears poured from Carrow's eyes. "No! Please, stop."

She wanted to defend him, to war against these men who dared hurt Malkom. Yet she could do nothing. "Chase, call them off, please!"

The mortal merely gazed on, his wan face impassive.

Lanthe murmured to her, "It's only a matter of time now."

There were too many of them, and Malkom was still weakened from his imprisonment in Ash, from his journey across the desert.

To save me. When she gave a sob, he turned his attention to her. "I will . . . make you pay—"

Another volley of bullets. He convulsed in agony, blood pouring from his wounds and arcing over the ground. Still he fought, futilely striking out until he was so injured he could no longer stand.

They swiftly closed in, securing his wrists in those unbreakable manacles.

With a torque in hand, Fegley sauntered over, placing his boot on Malkom's face, shoving it into the ground. After he'd threaded the collar around the demon's neck, he pressed his thumbprint onto the screen to lock it. "Good job, boys," he said to the guards. "Take him away."

With a smirk, Fegley turned to Chase. "Not as stylish as, say, your black bag over the head, but we do what we can."

The soldiers strapped Malkom to a board, like a gurney with restraints, loading him into one of the trucks. Just before the doors closed, the demon gazed at her with pure hatred, his bloody lips moving as he rasped in Demonish.

"Malkom, I never wanted this. I didn't have a choice!"

The doors slammed. And then he was gone.

Fegley turned to Carrow. "You want your torque off?" He held up his hand, wiggling his right thumb. "Then come to Daddy."

Lanthe nudged her forward. Numb, Carrow crossed to the man who continued to make her life hell.

"Turn around, witch."

After what they'd done to Malkom, she burned to kill Fegley the moment her power returned, but she couldn't until she had Ruby somewhere safe.

When she turned, he snatched her wrists behind her, manacling her. She thrashed from his grip, too late. "What the hell is this, Fegley?" She twisted around to stare down Chase. "Is this just until I get off the island? Or did you never intend to let us go?"

From behind her, Fegley said at her ear, "Bingo."

Lanthe hissed, "You filthy pig," while Carrow rocked on her feet, dazed. All this hurt, and for nothing.

"Chase, don't do this! You gave your word."

Sweat beaded on Chase's upper lip. He sidestepped when a soldier brushed past him, but he said nothing.

Fegley yanked Carrow toward one of the two re- maining Humvees, with a bristling Lanthe following. "Maybe it's out of his hands. Maybe perfect Chase got caught with his hand in the cookie jar."

Carrow gasped as the full realization of what she'd done sank in. *I betrayed Malkom for nothing.* She couldn't return for him and save him from these luna- tics. "What are you going to do to him?" She hadn't al- lowed herself even to speculate about it before.

Fegley was all too happy to tell her, "Cut him wide open, see how he ticks."

Bile rose in her throat, her tears welling again. She was as enraged at them as she was at herself.

Yet then she recognized in an instant of clarity that Fegley wasn't long for this world. A calm washed over her. In a monotone voice, she said to him, "Then I'm going to do the same to you. Cut you open. Slowly."

When he yanked her closer, raising his club, Lanthe muttered, "Leave him be for now, witch. Ruby waits for you to return, asks for you."

And now I can't take her home, can't break Malkom out. "You'll beg me to kill you, will plead for your own death," Carrow continued. "In time, you'll tell me who you love, so I can cut them open, too. It's as good as done. You might as well gut them yourself."

He swung his club at her face; the ground came rushing at her. . . .

27

Consciousness came slowly. After who knew how much time had passed, Carrow woke, cataloging her new injury. Her face was still throbbing from Fegley's hit. *Can't have been out that long.*

She cracked open her eyes to find herself laid out on the bottom bunk in her old cell, with Ruby gazing down at her. "Crow!"

Carrow struggled to wrap her arms around the girl. "Ruby, sweetheart."

"I missed you!"

"I missed you, too."

"What happened to your face, Crow? Why aren't we leaving? Aren't we going home?"

With effort, Carrow rose to a sitting position, wincing in pain. "They lied, Ruby."

"Lied?" The girl's irises shimmered ominously.

"Doesn't mean we'll be here forever. We'll escape, I promise you." Carrow glanced over the girl's head to the bunk across from them, where two new Sorceri females sat. Carrow recognized the pair from the file the House of Witches kept, the file of evil Sorceri to be assassinated at will.

Emberine, the Queen of Flames, and Portia, the

Queen of Stone, partners—and rumored to be lovers—for centuries.

The two were unmistakable. Portia's pale yellow hair was short with black-tipped spikes that defied gravity. Emberine's unruly mane was plaited in the wild Sorceri style, some of the thick braids a brazen titian red, some black. Her metal breastplate was engraved with an image of flames.

Without taking her gaze off them, Carrow asked Lanthe, "What are they doing in here?"

Between the two queens, they could manipulate fire and rock as no others on earth. It was said that Ember had the power of a hundred fire demons, could actually turn herself into a flame. Portia was rumored to be able to move mountains, literally. They used their vast powers mainly for indiscriminate, wholesale carnage.

"They've only been here two days," Lanthe answered, not seeming to like the new additions any more than Carrow did. "We're sort of filling up to capacity around here."

"Yes, we're imprisoned by mortals," Emberine said. "How mortifying." They tittered.

Portia added, "Which has given us plenty of time to bond with little Ruby. What were we talking about just yesterday? Ah, yes, how the House of Bitches can't handle your power."

Ember opened her arms. "Ruby, come sit on Auntie Ember's lap. As you often like to do."

When Carrow's fingers tightened on her shoulder, Ruby frowned up at her.

Portia pointed at Carrow's face. "Nice shiner. It goes with your skirt."

Carrow shot the two killing looks. "I've had a *day*. Do not screw with me." And Fegley's clubbing was merely icing on the cake she'd baked.

She'd betrayed a demon male who hadn't deserved it. *The look in his eyes.* Too late, he'd grasped the power of their weapons. . . .

"Oh, yes, you got double-crossed by the Order," Portia said.

Ember added, "You didn't have to be an oracle to see that one coming."

Once Carrow had finally gotten Ruby to sleep and the Sorceri had turned in, Carrow and Lanthe sat with their backs against the wall—again, *fitting*—watching for any traffic in the ward.

"How was Ruby?" Carrow asked.

"Each night she awakens, still confused about where she is and why her mother isn't here. Each time when she remembers, she cries herself to sleep. She also cried for you."

Carrow exhaled. "I don't know how she won't be messed up after all this."

"I experienced much worse at the same age. I saw my parents' decapitated bodies, saw my sister get her throat slit. And look how wonderfully Sabine and I both turned out."

"*Sabine* and *wonderful*?" Sabine was one of the most feared Sorceri in the Lore. She was the Queen of Illusions, could make her victims see anything she chose, could delve into a person's brain and make their night-mares appear to come to life. Her powers were legion, her vanity nearly as extensive. "Going to need a minute, or a millennium, to try to match those up."

Lanthe eyed her. "So do you want to tell me what went on out there?"

"It started with a ghoul attack," Carrow began, and went on to relate almost everything. Knowing they were being recorded, she left out a few of the intimate details, but she did find herself admitting, "Lanthe, he might have been . . . the one."

"You clearly were for him. I couldn't believe my eyes when I saw the way he looked at you."

"After a few mishaps, he was tender and generous with me. And if anything threatened me, he'd destroy it with a viciousness you'd marvel at."

"Tender to you and vicious to others? He sounds like the perfect male."

"He was." Within that mine, Malkom had been a golden-haired virility god who was both rough and gentle, and determined to pleasure her, to please her in all ways. Outside in Oblivion, he'd been her protector, ready to sacrifice himself for her.

That male was gone, replaced by a seething Scârbă who'd looked like he wanted her heart on a platter.

And who might have murdered his own mother. That tidbit hadn't been in the dossier. And still Carrow thought, *If he did it, then the demoness must've had it coming.*

Lanthe studied her face. "If he was perfect for you before, he no longer is now. You have to get him out of your head, have to move on. You heard him, he wants to kill you. I know this well—there are some things males can't forgive, even of their mates."

"Like Thronos?"

Lanthe shrugged. "Even if you got a chance to tell the demon why you did it, he might just punish Ruby as well, including her in his revenge. He is still a Trothan demon at heart, after all."

"You're right." Carrow hadn't thought about that. "He can't know about her."

"Why did you let yourself come to care for the demon when you knew how this would end?"

"It just happened." She'd already been teetering on the brink when he'd gazed down at her and called her "wife." The pride in his expression had pushed her over the edge. Carrow was a woman not accustomed to being cherished, and he'd made her feel that way, every minute of the day.

"The Order must have known you'd be his," Lanthe said. "I'm becoming more and more convinced they have an immortal informant, a soothsayer able to direct them."

"I'd thought the same."

"There are too many connected Loreans here for it to be coincidence. They use mates and loved ones as leverage to force us to do their bidding. Even to capture our own. That's part of the reason they've been able to fill up so quickly around here."

"What do you think they're doing with Malkom?" Carrow asked.

"They won't kill him. No matter how much Chase will want to."

"What did Fegley mean by Chase and the cookie jar?"

"He tortures Regin repeatedly," Lanthe said. "There's some kind of sick interest going on there. And he's losing favor—inmate whispers say that Chase argues constantly with his superior, some nameless, faceless man who wants to study us. Whereas Chase only wants to exterminate us."

Carrow pinched her forehead, beset with worry for Malkom.

Lanthe patted her shoulder. "Look, what's done is done. You need to focus on keeping Ruby safe and healthy. And, of course, on escaping so you can slay Fegley."

Carrow vowed, "It's going to be bloody—"

Malkom's sudden roar echoed down the ward; she gave a cry. "He's being held here, in this very corridor!"

Malkom had awakened to the thundering of his own heart, finding himself in some bizarre cell, his body riddled with injuries. When he'd comprehended that he was not in his world, not with his woman, a roar of anguish had been wrenched from his chest.

Betrayed yet again. *Not by her, not my female, too.* But now he gazed down and saw that a collar like hers ringed his neck. A slave collar. He gripped it in two fists, yanking with all his strength. Nothing. It budged not one inch.

She'd turned him into a slave once more. . . .

"I will kill you, witch!" he bellowed. Could she hear him? Was she near? He *sensed* that she was, just as he had that first night in Oblivion when she'd concealed herself from him.

It didn't matter where she was; he would pursue her to the ends of this world and any others.

He rose unsteadily on his injured legs, barely able to limp to the wall of glass that kept him jailed. Other creatures from a number of factions were imprisoned behind similar transparent walls, eyeing him warily.

When he pounded the glass with his fists, a male murmured from a distance, "One more hit against that wall, vemon, and you'll be breathing poisoned air." He sounded amused, his accent reminding Malkom of the vampires'. "The mortals diffuse it from the ceiling."

The mortals—the same order of soldiers that had come to his world repeatedly.

What did they want from him? Why had they sent Carrow to Oblivion to lure him out?

Their trap had worked so well. Malkom had wanted what she'd offered so damned badly. Everything between him and the witch over the last week—the best of his life—had been part of yet another betrayal.

At the portal opening, she'd behaved as if she regretted deceiving him, but nothing she said or did could be trusted. She'd also told him they'd be bound forever. And he'd stupidly believed her. When would he learn? *If you believe, then you invite misery.*

Malkom *had* been born just to be punished.

Just not by her. He roared to the ceiling again, his

eyes going wet with loss. *I would relive all those treacheries to take this one back.*

On the heels of that gut-wrenching feeling of loss, fury set in, a wrath demanding to be appeased. He was born to be the punisher as well. Malkom had meted out retribution to anyone who'd betrayed him.

Carrow would fare no differently. He would determine a way to get free, then hunt her down.

Malkom had turned on Kallen, whom he'd loved as a brother. The witch would pay a thousand times over.

Those who betray me do it only once.

28

Screams echoed off the cell walls—captives' shrieks of madness, frustration, and impotent rage.

I'll be joining them soon, Carrow thought darkly. Nearly another week trapped here. How much longer could they continue?

She'd never minded jail before. Because there'd always been an end in sight. Now her guilt over what she'd done to Malkom ate at her. She hadn't heard anything about him, or from him, in days.

And something was coming down the pipeline. Her senses were on red alert. She couldn't rest, couldn't eat the mortals' gruel. The hum from the lights above— so slight for humans—was beginning to sound like a swarm of killer bees to Carrow.

Any plan she devised to escape depended on leaving the cell. Yet not one of them had been allowed outside of it.

Only two things broke up the monotony: finding out gossip from the inmates and watching the traffic in the ward. Again and again, Carrow's friends and allies were led away, only to return *different.*

She and Lanthe tried to shield Ruby from the sight, shoving her behind the metal screen, but the girl refused to mind Carrow, always peering out.

That child was going to need so much therapy.

Now Carrow and Lanthe were sitting in their customary spot against the wall. It was night—they thought—and a storm was building outside, a dull drum on the roof. Ruby sang and played imaginary hopscotch, while the other two Sorceri lay on their bottom bunk, facing each other, whispering and laughing.

Carrow glared over at them together, not buying the whole lovers-for-centuries thing. Being in a relationship that long took a lot of commitment, and she just didn't see either of those Sorceri taking the plunge.

Plus, Carrow would be insanely jealous if it were true. Her eyes watered. *I could've had something like that with Malkom.* Hundreds of years of loving each other . . .

"Carrow?" Lanthe said.

"Huh? Got something in my eye. So what's on the inmate grapevine today?"

Yesterday they'd heard in whispers that Chase and his superior were still butting heads about the overcrowding here. Chase pushed to have all the immortals destroyed, not studied, not weaponized. But so far, he hadn't gotten his way.

And there was talk that the Sorceri species was the next rotation to be examined.

Lanthe answered, "Evidently the Order is now infecting beings to *make* ghouls, hundreds of them. If those creatures escape . . ."

"*If* they escape? Try *when!* Two things that can never be contained? Velociraptors and zombies."

Lanthe tilted her head at her. "It's enough to put one on edge, I suppose."

Carrow knew she was on the verge of losing it, especially since Malkom had gone quiet.

At first, he'd been roaring constantly, even bellowing in English, his vocabulary improving hourly. He'd banged on the walls until the entire building had seemed to shake. He'd been sedated repeatedly, only to wake up more enraged.

Until one morning, he'd grown silent. It'd been even worse for Carrow when his bellows had died down.

Added to this, Ruby was now singing They Might Be Giants' "Particle Man." Over and over. Carrow had taught her to sing it on repeat to annoy *others*—not herself. She muttered to the ceiling, "Amanda, I never knew."

"Particle Man, Particle Man, doing the things a particle can."

Between gritted teeth, she said, "Ruby, stop singing."

She pouted, flouncing to the foot of the Sorceri's bunk. "You said we were going home!" She reminded Carrow of that constantly.

Emberine rose and tsked. "Carrow is mean, isn't she?"

Carrow no longer tried to keep Ruby separated from the Sorceri. Because of their being trapped in a ten-by-ten-foot cell together and all. The two were continually slinking around Ruby, gazing at her with interest, tilting their heads at the girl as if they couldn't quite place something about her.

"You've been sharp with her," Lanthe murmured.

Carrow hissed back, "Don't you feel the tension?"

"From you."

"You're the one who told me to be firmer with her."

"Particle Man, Particle Man—"

Carrow leapt to her feet. "Ruby, damn it! I said *no*."

Lanthe yanked her to the other side of the cell, muttering, "Gods, Carrow, why didn't you just snap, 'Mummy has a headache! Go fetch Mummy's scotch!'?"

Ember cried, "Hide the wire hangers!"

Ruby asked, "Why hide the wire hangers?"

Portia patted her head. "May you never find out."

"I told her not to sing, and she's still doing it"—Carrow leaned around Lanthe to glare at Ruby—"just to annoy me."

"Of course, that's it," Lanthe said. "Not because she's seven, with no toys or anything else to occupy her. Think about it—the high point of our day is when they drag by victims."

Earlier, it'd been Regin again. As the guards had hauled the Valkyrie past Carrow's cell, her normally radiant skin had been ghostly. Blood had streamed from her mouth.

"Carrow . . . is that y-you?" She'd coughed, spattering crimson. "Can't s-see."

Carrow had leapt to the glass, motioning for Lanthe to cover Ruby's eyes. "I'm here!" she'd said, cringing at the V of staples that tracked from Regin's collarbone down toward her stomach. *Vivisection.*

"Kill him, witch!" Regin's voice had sounded crazed, her amber eyes darting blindly and spilling with tears. "Curse Chase. He ordered this." *Never have I seen fearless Regin cry.* "He is Aidan the Fierce. T-tell my sisters."

"Aidan, the berserker?" Carrow had heard Regin speak of him before.

"Aidan the Betrayer," she'd screamed as they dragged her away, "Aidan the Defiler!" To the guards, she'd shrieked, "You fools! You're following one of our kind! You take orders from one of us. . . ."

Centuries ago, Aidan—one of Wóden's berserker warriors—had fallen in love with Regin, one of Wóden's beloved daughters. Aidan had been killed, but he'd continued to reincarnate, seeking Regin in different lifetimes.

Could *Chase* be *Aidan*? And why would Regin believe Carrow could escape before Regin ever could?

Now Carrow exhaled. "You're right, Lanthe. I am freaking out." She pinched the bridge of her nose and lowered her voice. "But I have a male in the same building who wants to gruesomely murder me!"

Lanthe scoffed. "Like I don't?"

"One day you'll have to tell me what went down with you and Thronos."

"What went down? How apropos," she said, her tone cryptic. Before Carrow could question her, Lanthe said, "But that's a story for another time. We're predicting *your* gruesome murder now. And speak of the demon, they intend to bring him out."

"How can you tell?"

"Look, they have twice the number of guards as

usual, and they're heading for the end of the ward. So it's either Slaine or Lothaire."

Let it be Lothaire.

Carrow snapped her fingers at Ruby. "Go behind the screen."

"Crow, I wanna see—"

"Now!"

29

The witch is in a dark building, filled with screeching sounds and intermittent explosions of light. Dressed in skintight leather trews and a skimpy vest, she dances provocatively atop a table with a redheaded friend. Together they tease scores of males.

Drunken from spirits, Carrow leisurely begins unfastening her top. One button, then the next. The crowd cheers wildly, throwing colored necklaces at her, urging her on. She holds the edges of her loosed top together, shimmying forward, working the males into a furor.

When their calls grow deafening, she proudly displays her breasts, shoulders back and chin lifted.

Malkom jerked upright on his cot, waking into a fresh rage. How could she let those men leer at her body like that? Why taunt their desires?

Just as she had with him!

He rose, pacing his cell. Yet another new memory of the witch's. Though they'd begun coming each time he slept, full-blown scenes like this were rare—but always similar. Dimly lit buildings, blaring sounds, her drunken carousing.

Most of the time, there were only impressions, words

whispered in his mind. The witch had oft repeated to herself, *Think of ruby*, while experiencing a keen longing. What did that mean? What was this thing that she yearned for so badly? A ruby? A stone?

He wanted to know so he could deprive her of it, as part of his vengeance.

"Another bad dream, vemon?" the strange male intoned. "It's a hazard of drinking blood."

Days ago, Malkom had matched the voice to a being in the cell diagonal from his—a vampire called Lothaire, one with light red eyes, which meant he was fallen—a crazed Horde vampire.

Like the Viceroy and the master.

Spurred to slaughter that vampire, Malkom had barreled his head against the glass, too late forgetting his horns had been cut. Blood had run from his head. Hadn't mattered. He'd launched himself against the glass over and over until the mortals had knocked him unconscious again.

Upon Malkom's awakening, Lothaire had ridiculed him: "Fool. You sleep excessively for someone who has so much to learn."

Then the cycle had repeated.

Yet soon, Malkom had decided that the vampire was right. He *did* have much to learn. He needed to discover a way to reach the witch and escape with her. And he needed to speak Anglish as well as he understood it, to unlock her language more quickly than he'd ever anticipated.

So he'd stopped fighting and started listening to those around him, observing all he could. At times, he could just make out the witch's voice. She was definitely within this building.

So near . . . She'd given him a taste of her body, he'd taken tastes of her blood, and he needed more—even as he hated her. While he'd been ready to lay down his life for her, had surrendered himself to his worst enemy, she'd coldly plotted his downfall.

Now Lothaire asked, "What did you dream of this time?"

Malkom paced in front of the glass, fully healed now and even more desperate to contend with that vampire, *any* vampire. Desperate for freedom.

Lothaire sighed. "And still you want to kill me? When I know what you are—and where you can find more of your kind?"

More of his kind? Exactly how many were made? "What do you want with me, leech?" Malkom's words came haltingly, but he'd nearly recovered his understanding of this language. As Carrow's memories had begun to accumulate with his own, they'd acted like a puzzle key in his mind.

"You call me *leech*, when you've just woken from a blood-borne dream? You're as much a vampire as I."

"I am no vampire," he grated, even as his mind flashed to that searing image of the witch's breast pierced by his fangs. The crimson drops . . . "I've spent my life ending things like you."

"Your old life, perhaps. But this is a new existence for you. And you need information to survive."

"Information only *you* can give me?" Malkom sneered.

"Precisely. In exchange for your allegiance once we escape."

"Allegiance? The last vampire who sought my loyalty fared ill," Malkom said.

"What did you do to him?"

"He lived to see his blood and most of his flesh painting the walls." The Viceroy had pleaded to die, beseeching Malkom with bloody tears. "Watch that you do not end up like him."

"You're only impressing me. And whetting my appetite."

"I swear allegiance to no one."

"That's your first mistake in our world, *Scârbă*."

Malkom clenched his fists at that word. "You act as if freedom is nigh."

"Perhaps yours. You see, I took something from someone very powerful. Once the waters recede, she's going to come for it. She will unleash hell—since I cannot."

Whatever that meant.

"Now that you're healed, the mortals will begin studying you," Lothaire said. "Whenever you leave your cell, there's a *chance* for escape. Of course, there's a *certainty* of pain."

Malkom worked to block him out, wondering why he'd ever answered the vampire in the first place.

Because he intrigued me with his knowledge of what I am.

"Perhaps if you broke free, you could be reunited with your pretty witch?"

At that, Malkom lunged to the glass. "What do you know of her? Where is she?"

"Carrow Graie is close."

"Where? Damn you, tell me how to get to her!"

"The guards approach. They're going to take either you or me."

If Malkom could leave this cell, would he see her? Since he was able to speak so much more freely, he needed to communicate with her. To tell her that he thought she was more of a whore than his own mother. To inform her that he was going to enslave her, put her in chains, and fuck her tender body raw.

At the thought, he grew hard as stone.

Now he felt relief that he hadn't taken her before. If he'd claimed her that last day, his seed could have been quickening inside her right now. Trapped in this cell, he would have no control over the offspring she carried.

The idea of her growing big with his babe . . .

He slammed his fist into the wall, hating her anew for how badly he still wanted that.

Suddenly he smelled the fog with which they sedated him, spreading through the air.

"Looks like it's to be you, Scârbă."

Finally Malkom might determine why they'd gone to such pains to capture him. And he could begin his search for Carrow.

"Watch out for Chase, the one with the gloves," Lothaire advised. "He is much faster than he appears."

By the time the mortal guards entered to shackle his hands behind his back, Malkom could scarcely lift his head or shuffle his feet. But he wouldn't have fought them anyway. He wanted out of this place.

Down the corridor they led him. He hazily observed more immortals, species after species—

From the corner of his eye, he spied pale skin and jet-black hair.

He swung his head around. The witch. *She is here.* A prisoner like him, standing motionless in the center of a cell.

Though weakened, he thrashed against his bonds. Taking the mortals by surprise, he lurched for the glass that separated her from him.

For a split second, they stared at each other. Even after everything, he desired her, craved her to a blistering degree. "You lied to me! Betrayed me."

Her face lost even more color, and she stepped closer. "Malkom, please—"

"I will come for you!" he bellowed, fighting the mortals. "Make you pay!" He heard a shot and tensed too late. A dart filled him with poison.

He collapsed to his back, keeping her in his sights even as his vision grew dim. . . .

When Malkom awakened, he was strapped to a metal table. The dried blood had been cleaned from his body, and he'd been clad in new clothes, a soldier's trews and shirt like the ones he'd worn before.

Strangers—enemies—had undressed him while he was unconscious. Another indignity the witch would pay for. He strained against his bonds, but they were unbreakable.

A door slid open and the tall man who'd observed Malkom's capture entered the room. Hair hung over his face, seemingly by design. He was dressed all in black—and he wore gloves. *Chase.*

"Why have you taken me?" Malkom demanded, renewing his efforts to get free. He was burning to return and seize the witch. She was here, for some reason imprisoned as he was.

Perhaps she'd failed to bring back the next male her masters had dispatched her to deceive.

"All in good time, Slaine." Sweat beaded Chase's upper lip, and his pupils were dilated. Malkom scented a sickly sweet smell, knew the man was taking some kind of drug.

When a dark-haired woman in a white coat entered, Chase told her, "His blood's been drawn. The second your lab's done, you'll destroy it."

"But his orders—"

"Destroy it!" Chase snapped.

Once the woman collected the glass tubes and left, Malkom said, "What do you want with me?"

"There's much interest in you. In your *genesis*." The man seemed both fascinated and disgusted by Malkom. "Today, you're going to tell me all about it. And tomorrow, my physicians will examine you, to see what makes you faster, stronger."

"So you can make more like me?"

"So we can make sure your kind is never miscreated again. By anyone." Chase had a demented gleam in his bloodshot eyes that even the Viceroy hadn't displayed.

Because the Viceroy had never *despised* the demons he'd tortured. He hadn't cared about them enough to.

"Do you think we're the only ones, mortal or otherwise, who have been seeking you?" Chase asked. "There are only four of your kind known. We have to acquire

all of you, if for no other reason than to prevent someone else from doing it. You have proven the easiest to
catch, since you can't trace."

The others *could*? Was it still possible for him? "Release me. Fight me yourself." Though the mortal appeared unwell, he was tall, his build rangy but strong.

Chase ignored him. "We'll start with the most basic
question. Who made you?"

Malkom gave no answer. Instead he studied the ceiling above him, imagining the expression on the witch's
beautiful face as he tormented her, possessing her body
while stealing her blood.

In a low tone, Chase commanded, *"Answer me."*

"You do not frighten me," Malkom said. "I know
much about torture."

"Then I'm about to teach you more."

30

Carrow was still shaking from her earlier encounter with Malkom when they dragged him by, half-dead, hours later. The whites of his eyes were fully red. Blood streamed from his nose, ears, and mouth.

What had they done to him? Her tears welled once more.

He thrashed to get free, to reach her cell. His voice a weak rasp, he said, "Bound forever, *wife*? Is this what you wanted me for?"

Though he resisted, the guards subdued him more easily, hauling him away, back to his own cell.

As soon as they were out of sight, Ember said, "Wife? The witch is *hitched*!"

Naturally, Ruby had peeked out, witnessing the exchange. "Who was that?"

Ember delighted in answering, "He's your new stepdad. Or rather, your stepdemon."

Portia cried, "Felicitations!"

"Carrow?" Lanthe slanted her an arch look. "Surely you didn't . . ."

Ember laughed. "Yes, do deny it, witch."

"It was one of those demon proclaiming ceremonies," Carrow hedged.

Lanthe relaxed. "So it doesn't count."

Again, Carrow recalled Malkom's expression the first time he'd called her "wife." He'd gazed down at her with such pride, as if he'd carried a treasure. . . . "It counts," she said. "I don't deny it—or him." Even if Malkom was lost to her.

Lanthe gasped.

Ruby frowned with confusion.

Ember snickered, and a haze fell over Carrow's vision.

Malkom's torture, and Regin's as well, these last days of misery, imprisonment with these evil bitches . . . all too much to take. With a strangled yell, Carrow launched herself at Ember, clocking her in the nose.

Blood spurted, but Ember rebounded, screaming thickly as she delivered a blow to the side of Carrow's head. Her ear sang. Damn, that sorceress was fast.

"Stop this, witch!" Lanthe snapped.

Too late. Carrow had already jabbed her fist against Ember's throat; at the same time, the sorceress popped Carrow in the mouth, splitting her lip.

"Portia, do something!" Lanthe said. "They're going to gas us."

"Stop!" Ruby suddenly cried. "Something's coming."

Lanthe grabbed Carrow, yanking her back. As Portia dragged Ember away, her gaze darted all around them, even above them. "The child is right. Evil flies to us on a foul wind."

"Evil flies to us?" Carrow dabbed the back of her hand over her bleeding lip. "Really? And on a foul wind, no less!"

"There's a malevolence nearing us, witch," Portia said. "You can't feel its fury? Your girl did."

Carrow did feel it then. The air around them was thrumming. But from what?

Down the corridor, the ghouls wailed their uneasiness. Gnomes hissed, and a centaur's hoofs clacked against the stone floor.

An outraged bellow sounded. Chase's? He was probably furious that Regin hadn't been destroyed completely.

Outside the storm grew fierce, rain pounding the roof and even the walls.

Ember wiped her nose, muttering, "I *hate* rain." She would.

Lanthe glanced from Carrow to Ruby. "Just in case . . . get ready to *run*."

Carrow helped Ruby put on her boots, then hastily donned her own.

The lights flickered, the feel of power ratcheting up a notch.

"*RIIIIINNNNNNGGGGG!*" some being shrieked.

Icy fear slithered up Carrow's spine. "What the hell is it?"

Lanthe mouthed, "Don't know."

The lights wavered once more, then failed altogether. No backup electricity fired. No emergency lights alleviated the pitch-darkness.

The facility was completely without power. Which meant no gas would disburse to sedate the prisoners?

Carrow jumped when more screams sounded.

"I hear others of our kind," Lanthe said. "Some of them have their sorcery back."

"Then why aren't they escaping?" Carrow asked.

"None would have the ability to break the glass yet, even without a torque," Portia said. "Unlike Ember and me. I've already felt a lovely granite monolith deep in the earth directly beneath us. I'll raise it, rupturing this facility from the inside out. Anything I can't break, Ember will burn."

Lanthe said, "Carrow, hold on to Ruby. Tight."

"Got her." She swooped the girl into her arms.

"*RIIIIINNNNNNGGGGG!*" Whatever it was neared them.

Whispers sounded among the inmates, two words repeated: "*La Dorada.*"

When even the two evil Sorceri looked unsettled, Carrow asked, "Who's La Dorada?"

Lanthe answered, "A sorceress, the Queen of Golds—and of . . . *Evil.*"

Which meant she could manipulate evil better than anyone.

"She walks in apocalypse," Ember said. "I hadn't thought it'd be this soon."

"I have *nothing* to wear," Portia quipped, but Carrow thought it was to cover her anxiety.

Two Sorceri queens with their extraordinary powers feared this La Dorada?

"*RIIIIINNNNNNGGGGG!*"

Whispers sounded once more, another name added now. "*Lothaire . . .*"

Lanthe said, "I think she might be here for the vampire."

For Lothaire, the Enemy of Old?

Portia said, "Before we were captured, we heard he'd stolen her ring, waking her."

"Bet he's regretting it now," Ember said. Then she frowned. "But if he had her ring, then how could he have been taken by the mortals? It's the Ring of—"

Portia slapped her hand over Ember's mouth. "She's coming down the corridor, drawing near."

Moments later, La Dorada limped past their cell. She had a human form, looking like a rotting, mummified corpse brought to life—and soaked in water? Putrid gauze swathed most of her sopping body and trailed behind her. Her face appeared eaten away, and she was missing an eye.

An incongruous gold breastplate covered her chest and a crown sat atop her misshapen head. *The Queen of Golds.*

Wendigos flanked her, their fangs dripping. They seemed to be commanded by her.

Not them. Wendigos were quick, flesh-eating zombies with long, dagger-like claws and emaciated bodies that belied their strength. The only things Carrow feared worse than ghouls were the Wendigos. Both were contagious—a single Wendigo scratch could transform even a Lorean into their kind—but whereas ghouls were nearly mindless, Wendigos were cunning.

With each step, gold flakes and pus seeped from La Dorada's body. The trailing gauze swished from side to side over the stone floor, sounding like a soaked mop.

Carrow didn't know which was more harrowing, La Dorada or the Wendigos who clearly served her.

"*RIIIIINNNNNNGGGGG!*" she shrieked once more.

"You want your ring?" Lothaire's deep voice sounded. *"Then come and get it, you bitch!"*

As La Dorada crept past, Portia's torque dropped from her neck. Ember's as well. Carrow gazed into nearby cells in disbelief. Every being in the Pravus was losing its torque. "What's happening, Lanthe?"

"She empowers evil, manipulates it. And those torques limited the evil immortals could do."

Just like Ruby and Carrow, Lanthe retained her collar.

Portia already had her glowing palms raised, her face sinister as she controlled some unseen mountain of rock.

The floor vibrated beneath them. Just outside their cell, the ground fissured around a burgeoning stone mass.

Ember, too, prepared to unleash her power. Her eyes were alight, her irises swirling, moving like flames. Fire danced above her palms. When she blasted the glass with heat, Carrow dove for the floor, covering Ruby with her body.

The glass exploded, shards raining over them.

"Ember, damn you!"

Under the unimaginable pressure of Portia's rising rock, the steel divider walls began to crumple. The facility's entire structure shifted, more glass shattering as supports buckled.

More immortals freed . . .

"Crow, what's happening?" Ruby whimpered beneath her.

"Here, get to your feet." How much longer until the roof collapsed? "We might have to run for it."

When shouting guards advanced, tossing canisters of gas into their cell, Ember emitted streams of fire, popping the cans back at them.

Portia tilted her head at the men. "These mortals need to get stoned." She waved her hand, and a cement chunk from the floor went hurtling at one of them. Carrow covered Ruby's eyes just as it connected with the force of a rocket. The man's head exploded like a watermelon.

Ember said, "Portia, stop showing off! We have business to attend to." She turned to Carrow. "First off, witch, you're going to pay for striking me."

"If you hurt her," Ruby said with her eyes shimmering, "I'll hurt you worse." Carrow jerked Ruby back behind her.

Why was Ember hesitating? She could burn them all to ashes.

"Leave them," Portia said. "The skirmishes are moving outside, and I'm not attending without my mask and claws. We search for them now."

Ember shot Carrow a look of promised pain, then snapped her fingers at Lanthe. "Come."

When Lanthe remained at Carrow's side, Portia glared over her shoulder. "Melanthe, you traitor. May you rot in heaven." She gazed down the corridor. "With your angel. He'll be coming for you."

Once they'd disappeared, Lanthe said, "There went any power we might have hidden behind. And they're right. Thronos will come after me. As will your, er, spouse, once he recovers enough."

Ruby's eyes darted. "I'm scared, Crow."

Carrow lifted the girl back up in her arms. "I know, but I'm not going to let anything happen to you." When Ruby sniffled, Carrow held her gaze. "Look at me. I will get you out of here—I swear it."

Easier said . . .

Pandemonium reigned in the ward. Ember's flames burned everywhere as she released her trapped Pravus allies. Male immortals carted off flailing females.

Mere feet away, Uilleam the Lykae attacked four of the guards. Though he still wore his torque and couldn't fully turn werewolf, he easily ended the four, biting free one's throat while slashing the others'.

Volós, the leader of the centaurs, trampled anyone in his path, leaving behind pulped corpses. Succubae dragged down mortal guards, raping them in a frenzy. Carrow kept a hand over Ruby's eyes, but their moans rang out as they fed for the first time in weeks.

Lanthe said, "You know, as soon as we step out of this cell, we're in the shit."

"If we can get your torque off, could you do another portal?"

Lanthe had told her she needed to recharge every time she created one. Her expression lit up. "We could walk right out of this place."

"Then we've got to find Fegley." And his thumb. "I think I know where he might be." When the warden had carried Ruby in all those nights ago, he'd entered from a side chamber attached to Chase's office. He could be hidden there now.

"You ready?" Carrow asked.

Lanthe nodded, and they eased out into the maelstrom.

"I told you we'd escape soon," Lothaire grated.

When the building began to shift, Malkom somehow made it to a sitting position, his body in agony. Chase had been right; Malkom had learned much about pain. But he'd endured Chase's tortures, laughing up at him with bloody fangs.

"One way or another, this ends tonight," the vampire said. Whatever being had invaded this place was after the Enemy of Old. In turn, the vampire was pacing, ready for battle—and taunting the being. *"I am ready to have done, Dorada! Face me, crone!"*

Malkom staggered to his feet as the ground quaked beneath him. The metal walls began to warp. The glass of his cell couldn't take much more of this pressure. *Escape is nigh.* He was already envisioning all the ways he'd punish the witch—

His collar abruptly dropped to the ground.

He gazed up. A female of great power was passing his cell. She looked like a walking corpse, surrounded by a pack of Wendigos. *She's rid me of the collar?*

Without warning, another female, a dark-haired sorceress, appeared outside his cell, raising her flaming palms at him. What the hell—

She shot fire at the glass, shattering it to free him. Before she disappeared with a speed approaching his own, she said, "Go find your wife, demon."

"I—*will.*"

Finally, Malkom would have his revenge on Carrow

Graie. One foot in front of the other, half-crazed from his torture, he limped outside.

Chaos. The heat from the fires singed his skin. The groan of twisting metal rang in his ears.

The moaning succubae mating with abandon and the bloody clashes only increased Malkom's madness.

At the sound of a deep bellow, he swung his head back toward the vampire's cell. Directly outside, that dead female stood, commanding her Wendigos to launch themselves at Lothaire. Her grisly face was creased into a smile.

The Enemy of Old was somehow defending himself, tossing the rabid creatures out of his cell again and again. But Lothaire fought a losing battle. "Slaine?" he bit out. "A hand here."

The female swung her head at Malkom, her sole eye riveted to his face. *"RIIIIINNNNNNGGGGG?"*

Malkom shook his head slowly, then turned toward the witch's cell, calling over his shoulder, "Where's your allegiance now, vampire?"

31

"You wanna tell me about Thronos?" Carrow murmured as she carried Ruby and led Lanthe toward Chase's office. "Since we're all on the lam from him?"

"He's broken because of me," Lanthe said quietly. "I 'persuaded' him to dive from a great height. And not to use his wings."

Beauty. "The guys—in fact, everyone here—they do love us, huh?"

Lanthe nodded. "I'm up for Congeniality."

As they approached the end of their corridor, more Wendigos crept through the intersecting hall. Ravenous for blood, bone, and flesh. Their red eyes gleamed in the semi-dark, their wiry bodies hunched, their gaits uneven.

Lanthe and Carrow pressed themselves against the wall, Carrow tucking Ruby's face against her shoulder.

As the creatures scented the air, Carrow's heart raced. *We can't outrun them.* A second passed . . . then another . . . One took a step in their direction—

Screams carried from another corridor, and the Wendigos loped off toward the sound.

Too close. And they wouldn't be so lucky next time.

On that thought, Carrow sped in the opposite direction down the next ward, the one filled with offices and labs. The butchery here was even worse than in their own. Dead humans lay everywhere.

The three stole through a gauntlet of fights, sex, and . . . *feeding*. Rocks still rose, buckling the floor. The entire area was unstable.

At last, they reached the office unscathed. The door had been broken open and now hung askew on its hinges. Ignoring her disquiet, Carrow cautiously eased inside. *Empty.*

Through the window, she saw another turbulent night much like the one Chase had watched there two weeks earlier.

Across the office, the panel door was already halfway open. They slipped inside.

The area looked like a storage room with stacked crates and metal shelving lining the walls. The ceiling had begun caving, with some rafters collapsed, their ends stabbing the floor. Immediately, they heard a man's weeping coming from the back.

They descended a small flight of stairs, then followed the sound to find Fegley trapped, his nearly severed right arm caught beneath one of those colossal rafters. A machine gun lay mere inches beyond his other hand's reach.

"So close, yet so far away." *I couldn't have tortured him better myself.* Well, she *could*. But this would do. She toed the muzzle with her boot. "Aw, it doesn't seem to want *to come to Daddy*," Carrow said, repeating his line. When she kicked the gun away, he cried harder.

From behind them, Lanthe breathed, "Look at this place. These are all our effects."

They were surrounded by the weapons and personal belongings of the prisoners—Invidia whips and antler headdresses, the leather saddlebags of the centaurs, weapons of all kinds.

Though many of the shelves were in disarray, as if someone—or something—had already ransacked the goods, Lanthe was able to find her own things. "My gloves! My beautiful mask." She hastily donned her claw-tipped gloves and cobalt-blue mask.

When smoke began to waft in from gaps in the damaged ceiling, Carrow said, "The fires are getting closer." She could smell the sickening scent of burning flesh. "Let's hurry."

Lanthe hastened over to Fegley. She knelt to yank on his trapped hand, while dodging pitiful slaps from his other. "Even if we bend down, his thumb won't reach our collars, and his left one won't work."

"Heh. That so?" Carrow asked. "If we can't go to the thumb, then the thumb will come to us." She began searching for a blade. "Hell, make it his hand."

Fegley strained his body. "No, don't!"

"Hey, you invited us to the party, mortal," Lanthe said, catching the knife Carrow tossed to her. "Looks like you tussled with the wrong creatures. You had to know you couldn't contain us."

"W-we have for centuries. This is Chase's fault! The ring—he wasn't supposed to t-touch it!"

Carrow frowned. "La Dorada's ring?"

Fegley's eyes looked blank, as if he were confused

about where he was. "If it hadn't been touched . . . He's d-doomed us all."

"You *are* doomed, human," Lanthe said in a contemplative tone. "We're merely going to slice off your hand, but those Wendigos out there will crack open your leg bones and suck out the marrow while you watch." When Lanthe made a Dr. Lecter sucking sound, Fegley whimpered.

Carrow took that as her cue to get Ruby away, saying over her shoulder, "Make it good, Lanthe." *Since I can't.*

Lanthe nodded, knowing what Carrow was giving up.

Ruby said, "We're leaving? I wanna see him get cut up."

Oh, boy. "I do too, honey! But we have to be lookouts." As Carrow wended her way out of the room, she could hear Lanthe saying, "The Libitinae will make you slice open and empty out your own testicles. And if the Invidia find you? You'll live long enough to see one of them wearing your skin. . . ."

Just as Carrow reached the office's outer door, Fegley began screaming.

Carrow peeked out. At the far end of the corridor, she caught a glimpse of *Malkom,* limping through the bloodbath, looking mindless. Though his body had been battered, he was facing off with any beings in his way.

He reminded her of the night she'd first seen him, when he'd attacked all those demons. But now she could witness him dealing that carnage.

That night he'd hurt her unintentionally. Now he *wanted* to.

Wait . . . Malkom's collar was gone? She stumbled back into the room, sinking against the wall. *Ah, gods.* Empowered evil?

No. She refused to believe he was evil. Still, she realized any farfetched hope of communicating with him this night had vanished.

Had she given up on him? Of course not. But for right now, she had to focus on getting Ruby out of a collapsing building and a war zone.

"Witch, I need some help with this zipper," Lanthe called.

Carrow jogged back to her. "We have to hurry."

The sorceress was awkwardly pressing the man's gory hand to the back of her collar. "I can't get his thumb to press flat."

Fegley remained conscious, watching all with a stupefied expression.

Carrow set Ruby down and motioned for the hand.

Lanthe tossed it. A blur of glinting metal appeared between her and Carrow.

"Ah-ah, not so fast!" Ember said triumphantly, holding up the hand she'd just nabbed.

"Where the hell did you come from?" Carrow snapped. The sorceress had been quick *before* her torque had come off. Now her speed was mind-boggling.

"I'm fast as flames, witch. And I'll be keeping this."

Portia traipsed beside her, donning her own mask and gauntlets. "We like the odds, with all of you powerless. Ember, do immolate the warden."

Ember aimed a burning palm at Fegley.

Carrow covered Ruby's eyes just as the man's went

wide. He screamed as the sorceress burned him to cinders.

"Remember what we told you, Ruby." With a last seeking look at the girl, they disappeared.

"What did they tell you?" Carrow demanded, yanking her away from the smoking pile to the other side of the room.

"That I can be like them." She rubbed her eyes against the ash. "I only have to kill a sorceress to become one."

"You're not killing anybody!" Carrow said irritably. "First of all, you're too young. And second, no one's *paid* you to do a hit. We'll talk about this when we get home." She just stopped herself from saying "young lady."

"There goes our thumb plan." Lanthe muttered a curse. "Looks like we're fighting our way out of here." She rooted through a container of weapons, digging out a sword. "Good thing I'm handy with one of these."

"I'm not too shabby myself." Being friends with a legendary swordswoman like Regin had its benefits. Glancing around for a good weapon of her own, Carrow snagged a short sword and sheath, strapping the latter around her waist. Then she stilled. "Wait, Lanthe. Look at the smoke along that back wall. It's getting blown away."

"You think it's another chamber?"

"Could be." They hurried over, shoving away a shelf to reveal another panel. Carrow worked the tip of her sword along its border, levering it open a crack. Lanthe hooked the edge with her metal claws, and together, they heaved it open.

A gust of fresh wet air rushed over their faces, blowing their hair. A tunnel sloped downward before them.

"It's got to be an escape route," Lanthe said. "Probably goes all the way to the shore."

Carrow scanned the area. "But the ground's still quaking. Do we risk the tunnel or the melee outside?" Risk Malkom outside?

"I like our chances in the tunnel," Lanthe said. "And Vrekeners hate anything confined and underground."

Even though Malkom had threatened her, Carrow found it difficult to leave him behind, was gazing over her shoulder. *I'll find him again.* Once she got Ruby to safety. "Then let's do this. Fast." She lifted the girl into her arms. "You ready, kid?" When Ruby worried her lip, Carrow pasted on a smile. "It's a good thing you've got Lanthe and me with you, because your posse is never going to believe the adventure you're having."

Lanthe added, "They'll be eaten up with jealousy, of course."

"So here we go, kiddo." At the entrance, Carrow squeezed Ruby tight, laying a palm protectively over her head. "On the count of three. One, two, *three!*" She took off running, with Lanthe just behind them.

Dust showered them at intervals, but Carrow kept her chin down and her legs moving.

"Air's getting fresher!" she called back. "Almost there!"

Another quake had her stumbling, sidestepping to right herself. "That was a close one—"

Lanthe's scream echoed down the passageway.

Carrow skidded to a stop, speeding back to the

last corner they'd turned. *The Vrekener.* He had his fist gripped around Lanthe's ankle, dragging her bodily back into the smoke. The sorceress was kicking wildly, resisting the limping Thronos, her gloved hands digging into the dirt. Her sword lay just beyond her reach.

"Let her go, Thronos!"

His gnarled wings flared menacingly, spanning the width of the tunnel. He wore no collar.

Carrow set Ruby down, shoving her back under a roof support. "Stay right there!" she ordered over her shoulder as she charged back to help Lanthe.

But before Carrow could reach the sorceress, the Vrekener popped her in the face with one of those claw-tipped wings, knocking her back on her ass. She scrambled up again, drawing her new sword.

When he struck once more, Carrow ducked, sliding under his wing as if stealing home base. She thrust the blade up into his vulnerable skin there.

Blood gushed; he roared in pain, dropping Lanthe's ankle to remove the sword.

Carrow grabbed Lanthe's hand, dragging her up. Yet before Lanthe could get to her feet, Thronos tossed away the sword and clamped his blood-soaked hand over her leg once more.

He wrenched the sorceress back, but Carrow kept a death grip on Lanthe's hand.

When another quake rumbled, Lanthe cried, "Save Ruby!"

"I'll save you both."

In a deafening rush, rocks began to tumble down

from the ceiling, filling the space between Carrow and Ruby.

"Crow!" the girl screamed. "Where are you?"

Carrow jerked her head over her shoulder. She could barely hear Ruby. "I'm coming!"

As she faced forward again, Lanthe yanked her hand away. "Save your girl! I'll be okay!"

Smoke thickened, rubble building around them.

"Crow, hurry!"

"I'm so sorry, Lanthe," she whispered as the Vrekener snatched her friend into the darkness.

Heartsick, Carrow sprinted back to the stones that separated her from Ruby, crouching to dig frantically. "I'm here, baby. Just hold on!"

Though she was able to remove the smaller stones, the boulders wouldn't budge. She clawed at them, gaining no ground. Remembering her short sword, she raced back for it, returning to stab the blade under one of the larger rocks. *Nothing.*

Through a narrow gap in the bottom, Ruby was able to poke out her hand.

Carrow dropped to her knees to take it.

"Don't leave me, Crow!"

"Never! Do you hear me? But I've got to let go so I can find something longer to lever these rocks loose." Like a pipe, or a spear. "I'm going to be right back."

"Nooo!" Ruby shrieked, clutching Carrow's hand, digging her tiny nails in.

Biting back tears, Carrow forced herself to pull free, even as Ruby cried, "No, Crow, no, no, no!" She began hyperventilating again. "Please, please, don't leave me. I'll be good, I w-won't sing anymore...."

"Just breathe, baby. I'm going to be right back!"

"Crow, *p-please*," she begged, sobbing as her little hand blindly grasped.

Forcing herself to her feet, Carrow wiped her eyes. "I'm coming back for you, I swear."

Ruby's hand went limp, and she fell silent.

"Ah, Ruby, no!" Carrow clutched her chest with fear, knowing she could do nothing to help her.

Can't reach her, only one way to help . . . Her mind went blank and somehow she backed away, toward that storage room.

Carrow spun forward, running faster than she ever had, pumping her arms for speed as she maneuvered through the tunnel.

32

Amid the thousands of distracting scents, Malkom finally caught Carrow's, following it down a long corridor into a wood-paneled room. He heard movement in an adjoining chamber and crept inside.

The witch, just there.

She was yanking at the railing of a stairway, gritting her teeth as she used her entire body to pull.

He could have plucked it free with one hand. What did she want with that metal?

Silently, he stalked her. Closer ... His hands shot out, seizing her. "Did you think I would not find you?" His arms trapped her against him.

"No, no!" she screamed, thrashing.

"Shut up!" he roared. *Losing control.* Bloodlust, the battles, the moaning.

The mindless carnage ...

"Malkom, you have to let me g-go!" She was hysterical, yelling at the top of her lungs, flailing until she was hurting her own body.

"You made a vow," he grated between breaths, "that you did not intend to keep." One of her breasts pressed into his palm, her backside rubbing against his cock.

Yank up her skirt and take her against the wall, take what is yours. "You are about to, witch."

"Y-you don't understand, b-back in the tunnel—"

"You are a liar!" He wrapped her hair around his fist. "Say *nothing* to me."

Revenge would be his at last. As he pressed her chest against the wall, he saw her pulse beating in her neck, already scented her blood. How? *Doesn't matter.* He bent her head to the side, shoving her collar up. *The bloodlust . . . cannot fight it.*

With a groan, he sank his fangs into her flesh and drew deep. *Connection. Mine. My woman.* With each drop, power filled him, his injuries mending.

But the mad thumping of her heart made him even more frenzied. He bit her harder, sucking more forcefully.

Until he felt her sob.

He grew still. She was crying—he could feel her beneath his fangs. She'd proved that she didn't cry in the face of fear or even from pain. She'd been *angry* when Ronath had stabbed her with his spear. Yet the witch was weeping now.

Dumbfounded, he slowly released his bite, turning her to face him.

"L-let me go!" She shoved at his face, but her fingertips were ravaged and bleeding. From digging? "Ah, gods, you have to take me b-back to the tunnel!"

What was so important to her? He wouldn't allow her to have *anything* she wanted, would ruthlessly keep her from it. His vengeance was only beginning. He lifted her once more, looping his arm under her legs, clamping her against his chest.

Yet then she whispered, *"P-please, Malkom,"* as she pressed her wet face against his chest. She raised her arms, clasping her hands behind his neck.

And he hated her for that, for seeming to want to be close to him, for reminding him of what he'd lost.

"Take me into that tunnel. Help me. . . ."

He'd go to destroy whatever she wanted so badly. To kill it, as she'd killed everything he'd dreamed of.

When he charged into the blackness, she let out a relieved sob. "Thank you, thank you," she murmured over and over.

You will not thank me for long, witch. He journeyed deep, until he came upon a barrier of rocks. He scented blood covering the outer edges of several. Carrow's blood.

From behind the stones reached a child's tiny hand, one resembling his own female's—soft, pale, clawless. Limp.

Defenseless.

He was so shocked that when Carrow thrashed again, he released her.

She dove for that hand, clutching it in her own, crying over it. "Ruby, hold on, baby!"

Ruby. He remembered the dreams. *Think of Ruby.*

In an instant, he understood. These mortals had held her offspring captive, forcing her to do their bidding. Carrow had tried to explain to him about her baby, had cried as she'd betrayed him.

But she'd had no choice.

The bitter hatred he'd been struggling with began to lift.

'Tis not the end.

She turned to him with tears streaming down her face. "Malkom, please help us."

She will turn to me, and I will take her troubles away. . . .

The demon loomed over her, seething, his muscles standing out with strain. Moments ago, he'd looked on the edge of madness, like a true fallen vampire. Now his brows drew together.

"She's just a little girl, not even eight years old," Carrow whispered. "I can't get her free. I need you to save her."

His onyx eyes flickered.

"Please, Malkom. *Please.*"

At that, he attacked the rocks as though they were an enemy. He dug down, clawing until his fingers bled, too.

Another quake rocked the tunnel. "Hurry, demon!"

Soon he'd busted away a gap in the barrier, large enough for Carrow to ease Ruby through. *Unconscious?* She laid her ear to Ruby's chest, then to her mouth. Her breaths and heartbeat were normal! She checked her head for knots or blood, found neither. "Ah, gods, she's just fainted. She'll be okay."

Carrow gazed up at Malkom like the hero he was, with all the gratitude she felt. "Y-you understand now, don't you?"

He gave a nod.

With her free hand, she cupped the back of his neck,

tugging him down to give him a teary kiss. Against his lips, she said, "I'm so sorry."

When he pulled back, his gaze bored into hers, the message clear.

We'll be finishing what we started.

And she wasn't broken up about that.

Another explosion rocked the facility. He assessed the ceiling. "Not safe in here." Before she could blink, he'd snagged her sword from the ground, stabbing it into the sheath at her waist. "We have to get out."

Clasping Ruby to her chest, she said, "I follow you."

He wrapped his arm around her shoulders, then hurried them out of the tunnel.

Back out in the labyrinthine facility, Carrow searched for Lanthe and Regin everywhere, calling for them, yet hearing no reply. She also kept an eye out for Ember—and Fegley's hand.

But the chaos had gotten worse. Ember's flames soared. Mortal scientists were screaming, creatures feeding on them, ghouls infecting them in large numbers. Soldiers attacked Malkom—a seeming army of them—but he slew them all, protecting Carrow and Ruby.

As they passed the PX, Carrow noticed two fey women she'd seen around New Orleans once or twice. One was tall and lithe, the other shorter and curvy. The pair had just finished stuffing a backpack full of supplies.

Remembering her stint in Oblivion, Carrow paused. She knew how rainy this island was, and she'd sworn that she would never go out into the elements unprepared again. *I didn't even have a child with me then.*

Yet there was no time to pack their own, and the supplies were picked over. When Malkom turned back, she quietly told him, "We need that pack."

He faced the two, saying in thickly accented English, "Your pack. Give it to me."

"No way!" the tall one said. "Go to hell. . . ." She trailed off when Malkom growled and bared his fangs. "Sure thing," she amended, handing it over. "All yours."

Carrow tapped his shoulder. "We need the sweater from one and the rain jacket from the other."

He snapped his fingers.

"This is so uncool, witch," the shorter one said as she shrugged out of her sweater. "We're supposed to be allies."

"Sorry, but I've got a kid to take care of."

Malkom stuffed the clothes into the pack, then strapped it on, leading her away once more.

I could get used to having a demon around.

In the next corridor, Carrow spotted the slimy sidewinder trail of La Dorada heading in one direction, so she pointed Malkom the opposite way.

At last, she spied an exit in the distance, a hole exploded through an exterior wall.

But she hesitated, gazing back for her friends. Carrow worried equally for them—Regin tortured earlier, and Lanthe abducted. "Lanthe?" she cried. "Regin?"

No response. Only the sounds of a battle nearing.

Malkom's voice rumbled from behind her. "We need to get your young away. One hit . . ."

Could kill her.

Carrow turned back. "You're right, let's go."

Outside in the blustery night, a micro Accession raged. And everyone on their side was encumbered by their torques.

Why had Malkom's come off? He was in no way evil.

As soon as they stepped out, the demon froze, astounded.

He's never seen rain before. "Malkom, it's okay." Of course he'd have to experience a gale for his first time. When she laid her hand on his back, he flinched, blinking repeatedly.

"You'll get used to it, demon. But we've got to move now."

The grounds around the facility sloped downward. Hoping to reach the shore, she pointed down. "Go that way."

They followed the descent over treacherous terrain. Amassed fir needles concealed craggy rocks. Downed trees cluttered their way. The scent of decaying matter bloomed with each footstep.

Once they'd gained some distance, the sound of human screams and the baying of ghouls drew her gaze back up toward their former prison.

Cement blocks swirled overhead like a tornado, circling a rising mass of stone. Portia's work. Ember's flames soared, hissing against the rain.

Lightning flashed in the background, punctuating the bizarre scene.

Carrow could hear some female yelling, "Let's do

this! Rock out with your cocks out!" Was that Regin? Or just wishful thinking? "I'm going to grease him right now!" Carrow couldn't be sure.

In any case, gods help Declan Chase if Regin caught up to him.

Carrow squinted, swearing her eyes deceived her when she spied a caped female hastening toward a battle. Surely that hadn't been . . . *Nïx*?

Another section of exterior wall fell. In a wave, creatures escaped: centaurs, kobolds, revenants. Like ants swarming from a mound, *hundreds* of ghouls welled out.

"Ah, Hekate, no," she whispered as she grasped the sheer number. "We've got to put some distance between us and them," she told Malkom. "Let's get mov—"

The earth gave way beneath her feet; within a split second, she tossed Ruby up to him.

He caught the girl's limp form, trying to snag Carrow at the same time, but she'd already slid down into the darkness.

"Keep her safe!" she screamed as she blindly dropped.

He'd just prevented himself from leaping after Carrow. But he held her tiny girl in his arms.

She's trusted me with her young? He had to reach Carrow—without hurting the child.

If he slipped, if he squeezed her too hard for an instant . . . Unlike Carrow, the girl wouldn't regenerate in days if he broke her bones.

Cradling the babe against his chest, Malkom trailed Carrow down, speeding through the forest as fast as he dared, vaulting from rock to rock to be sure of his footing.

He'd never held a child before, and this one was so fragile. *Must keep her safe.* She was the witch's beloved offspring, the reason for her betrayal.

Rain poured, lightning striking. He felt the thunder in the pit of his stomach. The drops unsettled him, his vision blurring from this stray water.

He jerked his head round as he listened for Carrow. He was losing her scent amidst the chaos of smells, the pungent greens of living things. *Everything* here was living. Which meant everything was a potential threat.

As he ran, he spared a glance down at the girl's pale face, recalling how badly the witch had longed for her. *Think of Ruby. . . .* Carrow hadn't wanted to betray him. She'd only wanted her child back.

Now she's trusted me *with such a treasure.*

When he looked up, he halted in his tracks, releasing a shocked breath. Before him was water as far as the eye could see. They were on a cliff that overlooked what had to be an *ocean.*

No time to marvel. *Must get to her.*

At that moment, the child woke and began squirming. Malkom's eyes went wide.

What the hell do I do now?

Carrow jolted to a stop, the momentum flopping her face-first into a puddle of mud. Scooping clumps of it from her face, she hauled herself to her feet, with no idea where to go.

She scanned the area to get her bearings. Trees loomed, dense woods all around her. Over the tempest, she could barely make out the sound of the still-raging battles.

How far had she slid? Should she go uphill since Malkom would be coming down? Calling out to him could be a risk—other creatures might hear her—but she took the chance. *"Malkom?"* The howling winds muffled her voice.

Worry assailed her. Could the demon keep Ruby safe, without accidentally harming her?

"Malkom!" This time she heard movement in the bushes. Towering ferns rustled nearby. "Demon?"

Yellow eyes glowed back. Ghouls. They leapt from their cover, skulking toward her.

"I'm so fucking over this," she muttered as she fled headlong into the forest. The ghouls pursued her, thrashing through the brush.

Soon, it seemed she'd covered miles. How big was this damn island?

She spotted a downed tree that looked familiar. Then a recognizable rock. *Have I been running in a circle?* Son of a bitch! She was right back where she'd started from.

She took off in a different direction. When she heard crashing waves over the storm, she hastened toward the sound.

Just as she caught a whiff of salt air off the sea, a branch walloped her in the face, making her eyes water.

When they cleared, she sucked in a breath and wheeled her arms backward, slowing a skid that was slipping her right to the edge of a cliff.

She stopped herself just in time, dirt clumps tumbling off the ledge. They landed hundreds of feet below in storm-tossed waves.

Cliffs! No gently sloping beach, no pier with a boat. And behind her, the ghouls neared. She gazed back down at the foot of the cliff. Waves crashed over a shelf of rock before the ocean sucked them back.

She was trapped. *A choice.* If she could time a jump perfectly, she might hit one of those oncoming waves. Might not break her legs, her neck . . .

And then she'd be washed out to sea. A jump and possibly death, or a fate even worse. What would Ripley do?

When Carrow spied the ghouls' glowing yellow eyes surrounding her, she whispered a prayer to Hekate, then forced her foot out—over nothing.

33

"I know where they are!" Mariketa bolted upright in bed, waking from a fitful, exhausted sleep.

"*Wha?*" Bowen said groggily beside her. "What's that?"

"There's been an eruption of power! Lore energy." She stumbled from the bed. "I can find Carrow!"

For days, Mari had been racking her brain, desperate to save her friend's life. She'd hounded Nïx for more information, until the soothsayer had simply disappeared.

Now Mari had *felt* where that energy had sprung from. Snagging a pocket mirror from her dresser, she concentrated on the cosmic disturbance she'd felt down deep in her bones. Like an errant thought, the location was flitting away.

Bowen rose, stalking over to her. "Go easy with that, lass," he said warningly. "You will no' look into it."

She shook her head, furiously rubbing the glass with her thumb, downloading the location into the mirror before she lost it forever.

Almost . . . almost . . . got it! She sagged with relief. "Something's happening in the Lore. Something *big*. With that much raw power, it's got to be a concentration of immortals. It must be the Order's island."

"Why do you think that?"

"Nïx said I could locate the island—by looking for *something else*. In other words, tonight I found the *energy*, instead of the *place*." She hugged him. "This is it, Bowen!"

"So what do we do? When do I leave?"

"Well . . ." Mari shuffled her feet. "I don't exactly know how to translate what's in the mirror to a map or coordinates." But with a brief commune with the mirror, she could figure out how to transport them directly there.

Okay, yes, she wasn't supposed to gaze directly at a mirror, given the risk of enchanting herself.

But this would be *such* a quick question, more of a *query* really. Not really even a gaze, but more of a glimpse—

"Doona dare even think about it, Mari." Bowen scowled down at her. "I will no' have you risk yourself."

Though Mari could use mirrors as focusing tools— or, say, to store a cosmic waypoint—she couldn't draw on the monumental power latent in them. It was enough to make her want to tear out her hair.

She gazed up at him, letting him see her frustration. "Carrow's my best friend, a sister to me. And she's not the only witch missing." Amanda and Ruby, Carrow's cousins, couldn't be found either. "Bowen, I can't just sit here and do nothing. Nïx predicted Carrow's death!"

"And she might as well have predicted that Bowen's curvy redhead would get enchanted forthwith. No' a chance of this, witchling. I'll smash every bluidy mirror in this place and tie you to the bed."

He was clearly still miffed about the last time she'd gotten enchanted. Bowen had stepped between her and the mirror, rescuing her, but now he threw a mantrum whenever she even hinted that she might commune with one.

Just because she'd accidentally bored holes into his body—with her eyes.

"If I can't transport us there, then who will?" Mari demanded. "We'd have to find someone who can trace or open a portal not to a place, but to *energy*, based on nothing more than what I sensed in a dream, even though he or she could be captured by sadistic mortals bent on vivisection."

"Lass, we'll find a way. There's got to be somebody in the Lore who's crazy enough for even that. We will no' rest until we've run them down."

Mari frowned. Crazy? She couldn't quite get enough air as the answer hit her. She knew someone who was *certifiable*. He was also an immortal male, filled with evil, and obsessed with something as intangible as smoke.

The *craziest*. "Ah, Hekate, I know who the key is!"

Malkom didn't have time—or the words—to calm the girl.

"Put me down!" she shrieked.

He set her on her feet, keeping a grip on her shoulder as he straightened.

She gaped, no doubt uneasy with his size—

With a scream, she booted his shin. *Or not.*

He growled, crouching before her. "Stop, girl!"

She kicked again, screaming words he didn't understand. But he could make out *Crow* again and again. "Carrow?"

She paused her assault on his leg. "Crow. Carrow." She had a fierce look in her eyes. Green eyes like the witch's. "What have you done with her? Have you hurt her?" Another kick to the shin.

"Did not hurt her," he said in measured English. "But she is—"

"You're Malkom! The demon she captured."

He scowled. "Carrow is mine." He hit his chest over his heart. "She's . . . my wife."

"You don't have to talk so slow. I'm not a baby, you know." At his bemused look, she said, "Where's Lanthe, then?"

"Do not know her. I must find Carrow. We have to go *now*."

She crossed her arms over her chest. "I'm not going with you. You yelled at her earlier. You said you were going to make her pay."

He couldn't deny that. "'Twas true. Until *you*."

"I don't know why she misses you."

Misses me? "She fell, Ruby. She could be hurt."

The girl's eyes went wide. Then she turned on her heel and *set off*.

With a growl, he snagged the back of her shirt. "You have to stay with me."

"Goin' to save her."

He swiftly caught her up, seating her above his hip. "As—am—I," he bit out.

"Okay, I'll go with you. But if you try to hurt her, I'll kill you."

"Understood, child."

Amidst all the other scent threads, he again caught a teasing hint of Carrow's. Then he scented ghouls. *Below* them? He gazed down over the ledge.

And lost his breath.

The first step was terrifying, the plummet even worse. *Falling . . . falling . . .*

When Carrow plunged into the water, the freezing temperature ripped the breath from her lungs. Desperately swimming from the depths, she burst up to the surface, sucking in air, exhaling with a scream.

The wave that had cushioned her fall now seized her, hurling her away from land.

Had she heard Malkom's bellow?

Live, Carrow! The words replayed in her mind. *Ruby needs you.* She began weakly paddling, doing no more than keeping herself afloat. Salt water stung her ragged fingertips before her skin grew numb with cold. Her teeth chattered, her muscles becoming sluggish. The force of the current couldn't be fought.

Would she be cast out to sea? If the island compound was truly a thousand miles away from land, would she drift for days before someone found her? Months?

As an immortal, she wouldn't die from exposure. Sharks were another matter. *Don't let those rumors be true.*

She heard movement from just behind her. Ah, gods, no! The ghouls had jumped as well and now were caught in the same current.

As they were all swept along parallel to the shore, those fiends clumsily paddled and thrashed about, wailing.

Then they caught sight of her again. They were so stupid, so aggressive, without even the sense to get to safety before attacking her.

As the rain and waves boiled all around her, the ghouls somehow neared. The largest slashed its claws out at her.

She kicked back just in time. *Live, Carrow!* Another swipe, another near miss—

A fin glided past her. A second joined it. The rumors were . . . true?

Soon sharks swarmed them. The largest ghoul disappeared before her eyes, yanked down into the depths. Was a shark beneath Carrow even now, eyeing her legs?

Floating with her face barely above the surface, she forced herself to remain motionless. When a shark bumped her, Carrow stifled a scream, somehow holding herself still.

Her strategy worked; she bobbed quietly, while behind her, one frenetic ghoul after another was snatched down. Though the shore was still in sight, she couldn't risk swimming to it.

Even as rain pelted her upraised face and danger surrounded her, the bitter chill made her eyelids feel so heavy. Floating . . . numb.

In time, she was no longer cold, just so sleepy. *Hypothermia.* She lost the battle to keep her eyes open.

Close them just for a moment.

♦ ♦ ♦

Malkom had watched her jump from the cliff, had seen the water flinging her body like a giant fist. His heart had dropped when the ghouls followed.

And Malkom *couldn't* follow, not with her child.

Holding the girl tight to his side, he sprinted along a more solid-looking trail that wound down to the water.

Running, praying . . .

"Hurry, demon!"

Reaching the sloping ground beside the waves, he set the child down and ran along the edge, peering out.

The great water crashed against the edge of land in deafening bursts, swirling and swelling like angry wraiths. He couldn't see her.

"She's there! Just past the waves." The girl pointed. "Swim for her, Malkom!"

Can't swim. But when he caught sight of Carrow, motionless in the water, he charged into the freezing depths—

The bottom disappeared. Heart racing, he kicked to stay above the surface, gulping breaths, swallowing stinging water. *Can't breathe . . .*

Dizziness washed over him, and his vision wavered. He shook his head hard. Then it happened again. Yet somehow he'd maneuvered closer to Carrow.

He felt the ends of her hair just as he saw a ghostly fin break the surface. He snagged the witch, trying to hold her while flailing his free arm and kicking frantically to keep them above the water. *How to return to the land?*

Another fin rose and dipped. Creatures were circling

them, which meant predators. Which meant fangs or claws, or both.

He shook her. "Carrow, wake!" She wasn't breathing? "Witch?"

One of those things came from beneath them, knocking into him with the force of a Gotoh. Another driving hit nearly pried Carrow loose from Malkom's arms before he gripped her against his body.

The next strike shoved them below the surface. Malkom's feet briefly scraped the bottom. Going against all his instincts, he let himself sink among the creatures. Once his feet connected to the bottom again, he kicked with all his strength, surging out of the depths into shallower waters. Through the frothing waves he hauled her away from those things.

Back on land, he dropped to his knees with her, lowering his head to her chest. "Carrow!" She still wasn't breathing. No heartbeat. "No, *no!*" She couldn't die like this.

She is already dead. He knew this, could see—could *sense* she was gone.

But Carrow was an immortal, so she would revive. Right? *And what do I know of witches?* He couldn't say that her kind could come back.

"Carrow, wake up!" Her parted lips were blue, her face ashen. His bite mark was stark against her neck. "Wake now, witch!" *I cannot lose her again.*

Grabbing her by the shoulders, he shook her until her head lolled. "Breathe!" he roared. Water trickled from her mouth. "Come back, *ara!*" Collecting her into his arms, he cupped her head to his chest, smoothing her hair from her face. *"Carrow, I plead to you . . ."*

The girl was hitting his arm, screaming at him. "Blow air in her mouth, Malkom!"

Had he heard her right? Desperate, he put his lips to her cold ones, exhaling.

34

Blackness receded in a rush as air filled her lungs, pushing the heavy water up. *Lungs too full, strangling—*

She opened her eyes. Malkom's mouth was pressed to hers? She knocked him out of the way, hunching over to hack up the seawater.

As he rubbed her back with his big hand, she wheezed on the stone-laden beach. Sand gritted in her eyes, her teeth chattered around rattling breaths, but she was alive. "R-ruby? Wh-where is she?"

Ruby rushed into Carrow's arms. The girl was conscious, safe.

"Are you okay, Crow?"

Carrow held her tight, shuddering with relief. Over the girl's shoulder, Carrow met Malkom's gaze. "Malkom, you kept her s-safe." She mouthed, "Thank you."

He gazed away, looking uncomfortable with her gratitude. Then he tensed, his eyes going black and fangs lengthening.

The surviving ghouls had begun loping ashore.

Malkom rose to his full height, roaring at them until her ears hurt.

Amazingly, they cowered, scuttling back into the

waves. She remembered that the ghouls in Oblivion had been afraid of him, too. Never in her life had she met an immortal who could frighten them.

The monster that monsters feared.

She and Ruby both gaped up at him. Ruby whispered loudly, "He scared 'em away, Crow."

"I-I saw that, honey."

Ruby was shaking, soaked through. Though Carrow could scarcely imagine getting to her feet, she knew she had to. They had to keep moving. *I've got a little girl to protect.*

But where to take her? Carrow swiped her forearm over her face, squinting through the persistent rain at their surroundings. The rocky beach was part of a small cove. The forest bordered it. Mountain peaks soared in the background.

"She n-needs shelter and a fire," Carrow told Malkom. "She'll grow too cold. Will you help us again?"

A sharp nod.

As ever with things concerning the witch, Malkom's thoughts were in turmoil.

She'd asked him to get them somewhere safe, but he knew nothing about these lands. Falling back on habit, he'd begun heading for higher ground, had led them for more than an hour.

He glanced over at her now. She was petting the girl's damp hair as she murmured reassuringly to her. The child looked like a tiny Carrow, a doll in her image, a *deela*.

Though he'd offered to carry both her and the girl,

Carrow insisted on holding her, saying that she would be shaken.

Shaken? *He* was still shaken from seeing Carrow lying lifeless, with her face so pale. Her heart had been still in her chest. She hadn't been breathing, until he'd given her breath.

The least he could do, since she'd first given it to him. Earlier, when he'd realized that Carrow hadn't wanted to betray him, he'd been so damned relieved. His rage had been like a noose around his neck, easing its bite.

But now that he'd had time to come to grips with everything, he wondered how he could ever trust her again. Although he understood why she'd done what she did, the fact remained that she'd led him to what could have been his death. And his rancor over that had begun to grow.

A drop of water splatted him in the face. This place she'd taken him to was an alien world of green and water. The stories had been true. Yet even faced with all these new wonders, Malkom's gaze wouldn't stray long from the witch.

She looked exhausted, but she was putting on a smiling face, chattering to the girl. "Do you think your posse will believe that there were sharks?"

Sharks. Those powerful beasts in the water. He'd asked Carrow if there were creatures that strong on land, and she'd told him that there should be only Lore creatures from the cages. When she'd added that he would be more powerful than any of them, he'd nodded in easy agreement.

He could protect the two witches from any of those beings—unless those creatures joined forces.

The girl whispered at Carrow's ear, "Why can't he swim? Everybody can swim."

Carrow stumbled a step, knowing he could hear a whisper from a mile away, much less from three feet. "Um, he comes from a place where there's very little water. So no need to learn."

The girl yawned, the subject forgotten. "Are we going to go home now?"

"We're going to do everything we can to get back. I promise you."

Home. Back to the child's father? It struck him then that Carrow had a man, a sire for her offspring.

'Twas one thing to know that she'd been with another male, but this reminder that one had planted his seed within her was too much.

Jealousy scalded Malkom, and his claws drew blood from his palms. He wanted to hate this other man's get.

But couldn't. The child reminded him too much of Carrow when she'd been young.

Have I rescued them only to turn them over to some other man? One who hadn't protected them from this Order in the first place? One who'd given Carrow the baby she obviously adored?

The male would want them back.

Malkom's fangs sharpened. The male would die.

Once the numbing cold of the water had worn off, Carrow's battered body and injured fingertips had grown agonizing. Her waterlogged boots were weights on her feet and her legs were like jelly. Still, Carrow carried Ruby while trying to keep up with Malkom.

The girl had started drowsing against her shoulder, waking up in a rush, then falling back asleep.

In the distance, the war continued with explosions of light and sound, the ground still vibrating beneath their feet. Bands of creatures passed too close for comfort, running or galloping, probably bent on marauding.

They'd passed none of the witches' allies.

The air around them was crisp and laden with fog. The air between Carrow and Malkom remained brittle and tense. *What is he thinking about all this?*

His shoulder muscles bulged with tension beneath his black T-shirt. Earlier, she'd noticed that he was dressed in new clothes, and his horns had almost grown back. Now his injuries had faded.

Beautiful, heroic male.

He'd mentioned her promise of sex. Would he expect it later tonight?

Carrow knew that she and the demon wouldn't just automatically go back to the way they'd been. But she'd hoped that once he understood *why* she'd had to betray him, his resentment would ease.

It seemed to have been buried deep, simmering beneath the surface.

Ruby finally fell asleep and remained that way. Her arms went limp, her face slack as it pressed against Carrow's shoulder.

Carrow waited a few minutes, then murmured, "Thank you again, Malkom."

At length, he grated in rough English, "You should have told me."

"How? Besides, I had no idea how you'd react. If you'd refused . . ."

"You knew how I felt. About you. Likely, I would have done anything at that time."

Felt. At that time. Past tense. "I never wanted to hurt you, but Ruby's life was on the line. Some things you just can't risk. If it makes any difference, they'd promised to release us." She met his eyes. "And I'd vowed to come back for you."

"Should I believe that?" He looked like he wanted to.

"Believe it or not, I wouldn't have stopped until I'd gotten you free."

He gazed away. "Why did those mortals want me?"

"I guess because you're unique in the Lore."

"And their aim?"

"They want to war with our kind, to stamp out immortals. We know very little about them. I was captured only three weeks ago."

"You told the child you would try to take her home. Where is it?"

"A place called New Orleans. Which must be *very* far from this island."

"Island," he repeated thoughtfully. "Water all round. How big is the water to cross?"

"Thousands of times bigger than your mountain."

He slanted her a disbelieving look.

"It's true . . ." Hearing what sounded like a small plane taking off, she gazed up, holding her hand over her forehead to shield her eyes from the rain. She caught sight of a prop plane, and her heart fell. *There goes a way home—*

Winged demons attacked it in the air. Dozens of them, all members of the Pravus, tore at its fuselage. The craft nosedived, crashing in the distance into a ball of flames.

"Well, scratch that escape route." She worried her lip. And they absolutely *had* to escape.

Although she felt safer with Malkom, there were still threats out here. He could defeat several opponents at a time, but maybe not a dozen demons, especially if they could trace. In other words, they were as much in danger now as when they'd been locked up.

And the Order would doubtless send in reinforcements. From what Fegley had said, this organization of mortals was more far-reaching than she'd ever suspected. They weren't going to merely hand over their island.

Worse than all this? La Dorada could still be here. Carrow absently muttered, "We've got to get out of here."

"Will your *people* not come for you?"

"Maybe. If they can find us here. I think the facility, maybe even the entire island, has been cloaked," she said. "But with this much power flowing and this many immortals active in one place, maybe the coven can pinpoint the location."

"Why do you and the girl still wear your collars?"

"Ours didn't come off. Only those of our enemies did. Anyone evil. And then yours, for some reason. Maybe because you're a vemon. I don't know."

"So certain I am not evil?"

"Yes. I am."

He narrowed his eyes. "You had your collar in Oblivion. Why were you able to do magic?"

"They turned it off while I was there."

"Of course they did," he said, his tone seething.

"Malkom, again, I want you to know—"

He raised his hand to quiet her, saying under his breath, "I smell food cooking."

Suddenly Carrow was ravenous.

"Come." He followed the scent, leading them downhill closer to the water than they'd been before.

Soon they saw light in the distance. An old-fashioned cabin stood on a wooded cape, nestled among the trees. Smoke curled from a crooked stone chimney.

Did the property belong to the Order? Some kind of auxiliary structure?

Through a dirt-caked window she could see shapes moving within. There appeared to be three beings who had taken up residence.

"Await me here." Malkom stalked inside. As Carrow watched in amazement, he simply evicted the occupants—what looked like two shapeshifters and a nymph. He tossed the shifters bodily from the cabin, and the nymph tore outside after them, fleeing.

All three were naked, likely going at it before they'd been interrupted. Though Malkom had probably gotten an eyeful of naked nymph, he looked unaffected as he stood on the covered front porch, motioning for Carrow to join him.

As she hurried toward the inviting shelter, she again thought, *I could get used to having a demon around.*

The aged exterior was cedar shake, with rusted metal tools and tongs dangling from the ceiling of the covered porch. A harpoon hung above the low doorway. A whaling cottage?

The interior was cobwebbed and rustic, seeming from a bygone era. In front of the stone fireplace lay a moth-eaten rug. The earlier three squatters had left their clothes strewn over it. What looked like a roasting hare sizzled over the flames on a spit. She guessed they'd gotten bored waiting for dinner to cook.

"Malkom?" *Where'd he go?*

She found him in a compact back room adjoining the main area. Inside the chamber were a dusty rocking chair and two spartan beds, positioned against opposite walls, with their mattresses removed. Instead of wooden slats, rope nets stretched across the bed frames.

Malkom had already spread a blanket over one net, motioning for her to lay Ruby down. He'd set the feys' opened pack against the wall.

She turned to thank him, but he'd already left. "Okay," she said with a sigh, laying Ruby down. The girl was still shivering. *Gotta get her out of these clothes.*

Carrow had just finished changing her into the short fey's baggy sweater when Ruby woke.

"Where are we?" She glanced around with a groggy frown.

Lacing her voice with enthusiasm, Carrow said, "Our own cabin in the woods. Right on the beach." She dusted off the back of the rocking chair, hanging Ruby's clothes to dry. "We're safe as kittens here."

"Where's the demon?"

"He's just outside."

That seemed to reassure her.

"Are you hungry, honey?"

"Just really tired. Will you stay here while I go to sleep?"

Carrow wanted only to curl up next to her and get unconscious for two days. But she forced herself to plaster on a smile. "I will," she said, removing her own soaked boots and hose. "And I won't leave this little cabin until you wake up."

"I'm glad you came back to get me in the tunnel." Ruby offered her hand.

Carrow took it in her own. "Ruby. *Of course.*" The fear Carrow had experienced this night had been worse than any she'd known before. To leave Ruby behind amidst all that danger?

The hardest decision she'd ever made.

As Carrow had run, she'd thought, *This is what parents do.* Sometimes they were forced to make potentially life-or-death decisions for the children they cherished most in the world. Even though it might be horrifying to do so. "But don't forget, the demon helped us."

"I don't like him," Ruby whispered loudly. "He can't swim, and he talks really slow and weird."

Yes, he did speak slowly, but Carrow thought his Demonish accent was sexy. "I didn't like him at first either. Give him a chance. Remember, he saved both of our lives."

"Did he really marry you?"

"Did he mention that?" At Ruby's nod, she said,

"It's complicated, honey. Besides, even if we were, he wouldn't want to be any longer."

"But if you're married, then Ember's right. He's my stepdemon, and I'm going to have to live with him, too." She pouted, which was totally understandable, all things considered.

Of course Ruby would be nervous about her future. *With so many questions that I don't have the answers to.* "How about this—you know that house on the corner just down from Andoain, the one that can't be sold because of all the noise and fumes coming from the coven?"

"Uh-huh. It's got the big trees."

Carrow had been scoping it out because it had a pool and she was tired of sneaking dozens of witches into King Rydstrom's New Orleans pool house and residence. Plus, he'd busted them that last time. "I'll buy it, and it'll be our own clubhouse-slash-pad." It was conveniently located only a few houses down from Mariketa and Bowen's place. "You can decorate your room any way you like."

"What about the demon?" Ruby asked suspiciously.

"We could invite him over." Would he accept Carrow's invitation? Just now, he'd looked like he couldn't stand the sight of her. "We could teach him what movies are."

Her lips parted. "He doesn't know?"

Shaking her head, Carrow slowly said, "He's probably never tasted ice cream."

Ruby seemed to be giving this possibility serious consideration—until her eyelids slid shut.

As Carrow watched her drift off, her own lids grew heavy. Again, she thought about how much she wanted to join Ruby in sleep. Or to lie on Malkom's solid chest, with the steady drum of his heart beneath her ear. Carrow nearly moaned at the prospect of being close to him again.

But she had to get something settled with him tonight. They needed a plan. *And I need to explain to him that I never wanted to hurt him—*

"She sleeps?" he said from behind her.

Carrow jumped. "How did you get in so quietly? Never mind. Yes. She's got to be exhausted."

"I will get more wood for the fire."

"You're going back out there? Malkom, can't it wait?" She gently extricated her hand from Ruby's, rising to stand before him. "We need to talk."

He shrugged, turning toward the other room, and she followed.

"Sit." He motioned to the stone hearth. When she sank down in front of the fire, he used a purloined knife to cut a hunk of meat from the hare. "Eat."

For some reason, like Ruby, she was no longer hungry. "I'm fine. You take it."

He gazed at the bite mark on her neck. "You need it more."

So she leaned forward to nibble off his knife, but he simply handed it to her. *The hand-feeding days are so over.*

He stood once more, pacing the length of the room and back. Looking just to the right of her, he grated, "Where is her father, Carrow?"

35

"Her father?" The witch rubbed her forehead. "He's dead. I believe he died before Ruby was born."

"You *believe*?" She didn't even know where the sire was?

Her eyes widened. "Oh, wait. Malkom, there's something I need to tell you. Though Ruby is related to me, I'm not her mother."

He tensed. "Another lie?"

"I never said she was. But it doesn't matter, she's mine now. I'm adopting her. And what's more, I love that little girl like she was my own."

"Where's her mother?"

"She died three weeks ago, killed by the Order."

"You have no other children?"

Her brows drew together. "No."

"Is there a male? That you are bound to?"

She stood, meeting his eyes, so direct. "That depends."

"On what?"

"On how angry you are with me." She sidled closer to him, her movements graceful.

He hated how she still affected him so effortlessly. He crossed the rest of the distance to her. Cupping her nape, he gazed down at the face that had bewitched him, the eyes that haunted him. His voice hoarse, he said, "What do you want of me?"

"I want to earn your forgiveness." Her breaths had shallowed, pink tingeing her high cheekbones.

"You have it. I understand why you behaved as you did."

"Then I want a chance to earn back your trust."

Not so easily done. He released her, turning to peer out the window. With his finger against the glass, he followed a stream of water outside. *Amazing.* Water everywhere, and glass even in this modest structure. "I thought things were a certain way. With us. They were not. Now I do not know."

"I care for you. That hasn't changed," she said. "If anything, my feelings have grown stronger."

"How much was . . . real?"

He knew she'd understood what he was really asking when she answered, "Malkom, I've never known more pleasure with another man."

How badly he wanted to believe her. But he was inexperienced, and she could have feigned that pleasure, with him none the wiser. She could be lying right now.

"What do *you* want of *me*?" she asked.

"You are my female. Fate has bound you to me. So I need to protect you."

"And claim me?"

Lust shot through him, and he hardened with a swift heat.

"Or drink me?"

He hissed in a breath, his mind fixed on that last day they'd spent in the mine. Seared into his memory was that vision of her—fresh from her orgasm with beads of crimson slowly slipping past her nipple. His bite mark had been like a brand on her flesh. "And you would let me take your blood? When you would not before?" He tried to recall his taste of her tonight, but only saw a haze.

"Now I understand why you do it." She was just behind him. "It's to feel close to me, isn't it? I will never deny you that again."

Never deny them. . . .

"Malkom, I would give anything to feel that close to you. I've needed you." When she laid her palm on his back, then her cheek, he stiffened. "Haven't you needed me?"

She wanted him, wanted him to possess her at last. So why did he feel such foreboding? Such fury?

Ignore it. Take her, bury yourself in her body. But she could deceive him again, as easily as before. Only this time, if he claimed her, she could be carrying his babe.

He'd rather not have a child than have one out in the world, vulnerable, without him there to guard it, providing for it. He wouldn't be like his own father, who'd left Malkom to the whims of a whore, to be bought and sold.

Though he might understand why Carrow had done as she had, he couldn't merely forget the pain of the last week, the mistrust of the last four centuries. "I spent these days hating you. I imagined doing things to you . . ."

"That would make my skin crawl?" she finished.

He turned to face her. "Yes." He'd been anticipating them right when his collar had fallen off.

"What would you have done in my situation?"

"The same. But I also would not expect to be forgiven. I would not expect to be trusted," he said, thinking of another question he wanted her to answer. "Why did you come to Ash? Did you intend to rescue me from the Trothans only to hand me over to the mortals?"

"No. I would have come for you no matter what. I felt awful about hurting you—"

"Yet you decided to do worse to me?" He ran his hand through his hair, still unused to his regenerating horns. *Another pain that I endured for her.* "Do you know what the armorer said just before I killed him? He told me that I would lose you."

"I'm not lost, Malkom. I'm right here."

He exhaled. "And I am weary, witch. Go tend to your young and leave me be."

She drew back her head as though slapped. "Very well. But I will win back your trust. If it's the last thing I do." She returned to the back room. He heard the ropes tighten as she joined the girl in the bed.

He stared at the rain on the window for long moments, waiting for her to fall asleep. As usual, his eyes were greedy for the sight of her.

Once he heard her breathing was deep and even, he returned to watch them in slumber. Carrow had her arms wrapped tight around the little one.

The witch would do—*had done*—anything to protect that child.

When he'd been Ruby's age, he would've killed for someone to take an interest in his well-being, much less vow to protect him—no matter what the consequences.

I would have thought her an angel.

If Carrow had been the heartless female he'd supposed her to be, then she would never have taken that mission to lure Malkom here.

Maybe 'twas not over yet.

The knot in his gut remained. *And maybe you are a fool.*

In what looks like an abandoned city, the witch and her army face off against a horde of centaurs, fire demons, and Invidia.

She is confident of her abilities, knows that they'll have a victory—or go down in history.

"Wait for my signal!" she orders over her shoulder as she advances. Though flames light the night and explode all around her, she marches forward. She knows fear, yet she continues in the face of it.

Foolhardy witch. Even in sleep, Malkom began to sweat, heart racing for her.

In her hand, she pulls up concentrated magic. It sparks, but is cool to her, a welcome pressure above her palm.

"Now!" she screams, hurling the magic. An arc flares from her hand toward a distant structure. In a heartbeat's time, the blast renders the building to rubble.

But her enemies have focused on her. Fire demons trace around her, a dozen of them with flames ready. Before she can retreat, they strike, fire streaming toward her—

Malkom woke, shooting upright from his spot against the cabin's outer door.

He ran his hand over his face, gazing out into the stormy night. 'Twas only a dream. And obviously she'd recovered. So why was he filled with apprehension for her?

He had no one but himself to blame for witnessing that battle, had welcomed her memories. Though dreading the nightmares from his past, he'd sought dreams, needing to know more about her.

With his latest taste of her blood, he'd been rewarded with new memories, dozens of scenes. That battle in particular.

He leaned back against the door, piecing together what he'd learned. Carrow was a commander of the Wiccae, heading an entire contingent of witches. She was both reckless and victorious in war.

When fully powered, she was able to pitch building-crushing bombs from her hands.

And that is the life she wants to return to?

A life he wasn't a part of.

He glanced back in Carrow's direction. So close. Yet loneliness weighed on him, worse than any of his nights in that infernal mine.

Because now I know what I am missing. . . .

36

"Crow, are you awake?"

"Why do kids ask that when they know you're not?" She cracked open her bleary eyes. "No. Really."

"I'm hungry. And that demon's gone, so I can't get him to fetch me something."

"Ruby, he's not a dog." She rose from the net, wincing at her body's chorus of twinges. The floor was going to be freezing on her bare feet, and there was no enticing aroma of coffee to coax her out of bed. Still she rose. *Have more than myself to look out for now.*

Carrow had always been fiercely defensive of her coven, raring on the front line in any conflict. But looking out for Ruby was different, the need to do right by her even stronger. *Because she's depending completely on me.* "Was Malkom here when you woke up?"

"Nope."

"Oh. Well, let's see what we can find." She rooted through the feys' pack, finding only two energy bars and a few packs of energy gel.

Again, there were no multipurpose tools or weapons of any kind. But there was shampoo and soap aplenty. The feys were just as silly as she'd been when packing.

Carrow held up her find. "You wanna chocolate-chip

energy bar or some energy gel?" She might have been worried that they'd run out of food, but she knew Malkom could catch more.

"The bar."

As Ruby ate the chocolate chips off the bar, Carrow peered out the window, hoping to catch a glimpse of him. Surprise—it was still raining!

Fern fronds climbed upward like trees, stretching as tall as she was. Lichen seemed bent on covering every inch of rock, battling with fungi for dominance.

At the shore in the distance, all appeared harsh, scoured by wind. Here within the trees, fog subdued the scenery, muting it.

She realized Malkom wouldn't have to fear the sun here today, could travel comfortably under the cover. And in the interior, the forest was just as dense as here. *So how far would he go?* she mused as she began exploring the cabin.

First thing she noticed? Nonpoisonous spiders and centipedes filled the place to the rafters. *Good thing witches like insects.*

The sole closet contained a coil of rope, some life jackets, and a pile of decomposing blankets. At the bottom was a bucket and an old-timey wooden tub.

In the cooking area, she found a rickety stove, a couple of rusting food tins, and an assortment of mismatched pots and pans. Twine, clothespins, a whalebone comb, and a moldy deck of cards were in one drawer.

Another stroll to the window, another eager scan. No Malkom.

Carrow needed to talk with the demon so she could

run her new plan by him. She thought they should get this place fortified, and then he could venture out to search for a way off this island, looking for allies, a boat, a severed hand, anything.

She suspected that Lanthe was still here. Though Thronos could fly, there was no way he could go a thousand miles over an ocean with a passenger, especially not when he was so broken, his wings twisted. If Malkom could rescue Lanthe, then they might be able to track down Fegley's hand.

Long shot? Absolutely. But Carrow didn't exactly have any short shots to choose from. . . .

Still he hasn't returned. She needed something to take her mind off him, something to keep her occupied.

So she strung up a line of twine in front of the fire, using the clothespins to hang up Ruby's damp clothes.

Which took ten minutes. *What to do now . . . ?* Her gaze fell on Ruby, hopping after a centipede on the floor.

"You need a bath, kiddo."

By dint of Herculean effort, muffled curses, and trial and error, Carrow procured water from a trough outside, warmed it on the stove, and filled the wooden tub.

"I'm kind of getting handy," Carrow said as she began washing Ruby's hair with the feys' shampoo. "*Little House on the Prairie*-esque, even. We're just like pioneers, except we don't have to wear bonnets, right?" Ruby gave a half smile.

I'll take it. The first smile she'd seen from her since their ordeal began. "Look at that. I almost forgot you had dimples." Carrow ran her forearm over her brow. "Come on, let's get you rinsed off."

After the bath, once Ruby had been fed, washed, and dressed, with her hair combed out, Carrow gave a mental hat tip to moms everywhere. She also felt a flare of alarm that Malkom still hadn't returned.

"What're we going to do now?" Ruby asked.

"Maybe check out the beach?"

"It's raining outside."

"No prob." Carrow helped her don the tall fey's rain jacket, but it swallowed her, looking more like a poncho. After rolling up the sleeves, Carrow said, "Let me see you rock the poncho. Who rocks the poncho?"

"I do!" Ruby put her hand on her hip and flipped her hair. *Adorable.*

"Come on, you," she said, grabbing Ruby's hand as they tromped outside into the fog. One side of the cape was wave-tossed, the other smooth. They headed for the windward shore.

The beach there was eerie to Carrow, forlorn even. Giant whalebones arced up from the rocky ground, while ragged seaweed lined the edge.

Carrow was used to Gulf Coast beaches, full of fun, sun, and sometimes drunken nudity. *This is not my scene.* She recognized this like a malamute plopped in a desert.

As if reading her mind, Ruby said, "I wanna go home."

"Me too. I'm going to talk to the demon about it when he gets back." She gazed around. Hours had passed, and still no sign of him. Maybe he'd just left them behind? Said to hell with her and her kid? No matter that she and Ruby were defenseless without him?

"*Now* what do we do?"

"I don't know, honey." Or maybe he'd been way-laid by a covey of nymphs? *Fornicating with them in the rain. His magnificent body damp and flexing with strength.* "I'm coming up with an idea as we speak," she lied.

"What if he doesn't come back?" Ruby asked.

Then they'd be totally and unequivocally hosed. Carrow could try to find Regin or Lanthe, but she would have to bring Ruby with her into the mountainous interior. Worse would be to leave Ruby here. *What if I never made it back to her?*

"I don't know. We'd probably be in a pickle." Last night Carrow had thought that she could get used to having a demon around to do things for them. Now she chafed at how dependent on him they'd become. For the thousandth time, she yanked at her torque. She needed her powers back *now*!

"Should I be nicer to him?"

"You should be nicer to him because he's a good guy." Carrow sighed. He *was* good, a bighearted, proud demon. She knew better than to believe he would abandon them or leave them unprotected while he bedded nymphs. Which meant . . . he could be hurt. "Maybe he's at the cabin, waiting on us."

The demon wasn't at the cabin. Now her worry went into overdrive.

She'd just slipped Ruby the last energy bar to de-chip and anxiously dealt a hand of go fish when the door swung open. He was safe! She leapt to her feet, rushing toward him.

He glanced over his shoulder, then faced her with a frown. "What?"

You're safe. "I was worried. Where'd you go?" She blinked up at him, trying to listen to his reply. *Safe. With us.*

"Searching for a better place to stay." He was soaking wet, but the grim set to his lips had eased.

Carrow tilted her head. *I think he likes it here. Thank goddess for that.*

He edged away from her, putting down some supplies he'd collected—ropes and a shovel. Then he shook his hair out, like an animal, making Ruby giggle around a mouthful of chocolate chips.

Had he just given a half smile before his face grew stern again? "You will remain here," he said. "This is safest."

"Okay, whatever you think."

"But others might come. I'll set up traps, block off this branch of land."

"A peninsula," Carrow absently corrected, then wished she hadn't. "Um, it's a peninsula of land."

"You're gonna make traps?" Ruby asked with wide eyes. "Can I see?"

"Honey, I'm sure he'll be busy."

"The child can come with me."

"She doesn't have to go, Malkom. It could be dangerous."

He glowered. "I would never let her get hurt."

"I know that." She trusted him implicitly, especially after he'd gotten her safely back to Carrow last night, a miracle in itself. "I just—"

"We will be back in an hour or so." He motioned for Ruby, who ran to him so fast she almost forgot her rain jacket.

Carrow wasn't invited? Leaving the little lady back at the homestead? *Bite your tongue.* She forced a smile that made him frown again.

At the doorway, he paused and asked over his shoulder, "Do you need anything?"

You. Being loving again. "I'm good for now." When they left, she glanced around the cabin.

I wonder if I can fit in that tub.

37

Information. He wanted it and thought the girl could give it to him—though he hadn't encountered a child in centuries and had no idea how to deal with one.

But how difficult could it be?

As he strode down a natural trail, she jogged to keep up, out of breath, yet still chattering. She reminded him of the witch in Oblivion, talking to herself as they'd hiked to his mine.

What doesn't remind me of the witch? He'd spent the morning fruitlessly searching for a more defensible position, all the while thinking about Carrow until he'd wondered if he could go mad from it.

In his dank mine, Malkom had stared at her for hours, trying to determine what she reflected on when her eyes had grown soft. He'd found it so damned exciting to be with her. Rewarding.

Now what he felt for her was so raw it frightened him.

"Find a place to sit," he told the girl. "I'm digging here." A pit trap would do nicely on this path.

If not for the concentrated number of immortal enemies, he'd have considered this island a good place to live. Mist cloaked the sun, and even if it emerged as it had the day of his capture, Malkom could keep beneath the cover of trees. The vast forest surrounding them teemed with animals, sluggish creatures that seemed to go out of their way to be seized. Even more jumped in the water, taunting him to catch them.

Already, he'd drunk more blood than he would have over several days in Oblivion. . . .

The child sat on a root that grew above the ground. "Why're you digging there?"

"Good place for a trap. So others cannot get to the . . . *peninsula*."

"Why?"

"Anyone who wants to come to the house will have to walk on either this path or one other."

"Why?"

Ignoring her questions, he began shoveling. "So tell me about Carrow—"

"You really can't swim? What's your job? You look like a fireman." Her eyes lit up. "Firemen have deaf dogs." She sighed. "I want a dog."

She must have caught her breath. Malkom tried to keep up with her words, growing more alarmed by her each second. "Ruby," he said, injecting a note of sternness into his tone. "I want you to answer some questions about Carrow. Does she have a man?"

"Like a boyfriend? Crow's got tons of boyfriends. They're always coming around the coven."

He clenched the shovel handle, just preventing himself from rendering it to dust. *I will put their heads on pikes.*

"Crow's one of the most beautiful witches we've got in our coven." Getting a sly look about her, Ruby said, "You think she's pretty, too."

"She is"—*beyond compare*—"appealing enough," he said. "Do others think well of her?" Or was she as hated as he'd been?

"Everybody loves her because she's fun. Everybody wants to be friends with her."

Malkom knew how much *fun* she was. He'd seen her disrobing for hundreds of males, was certain any one of them would want to *befriend* her.

He stabbed the shovel down. "How long have you known her?"

"I've known Crow forever. She's always bringing me things," she said. "But she's rutterless."

"What does that mean?" he asked, astonished when water began to trickle up from the bottom of his hole. 'Twas everywhere here. Malkom was beginning to love this place of plenty.

When he was young he'd wanted three things. A home that no one could ever force him to leave. As much food and water as he could ever enjoy. To be noble and respected like Kallen.

Here he could satisfy at least two of those desires.

"It means she didn't have anything," the girl said, then added proudly, "Not until me."

Malkom began to put it together. Carrow's own parents had treated her so callously that the idea of mothering a child in need called to her. Could he hate her for this?

For that matter, could Malkom turn his back on this girl? She was seven years old. *Roughly my age when I no longer had a mother, my age when fate began punishing me.*

"What happens when you return home?" he asked her. "Who will provide for you?" When her brows drew together at the question, he said, "How will you buy things?"

"Carrow makes a fortune off her spells."

A fortune. He'd known she'd come from money, but he hadn't wanted to acknowledge that she had wealth in her world—whereas he would not.

"We're going to get a pad."

"A pad?"

In a singsong tone, she answered, "A house. Like a lily pad. We're going to have parties. It has a pool. She said we can invite you over."

Invite him over. The witch didn't plan to *reside* with him? On this island, she would be forced to. Here, *he* could provide for her. He had no guarantee of it in her world.

The girl had collected some insect on her hand, letting it roam as she tilted her hand this way and that. Weren't little females supposed to be scared of such creatures? He thought back, searching his memory, but he could recall only the young demonesses who'd laughed as he'd eaten from their garbage. He remembered being stung with humiliation.

He shoveled harder, wanting to lose himself in his task.

"You really come from a world with no water?" she asked. "Do you miss it?"

Without looking up, he said, "There was little water. And no, I do not miss it."

"I bet you miss your friends. I miss mine."

Digging faster. "I had no friends."

"What? You *have* to have friends. You don't have a gang? I have a gang of witches. We meet in the attic. Elianna—she's my nanny—she says we're going to take over the world." Ruby took a breath, then said, "Did you have a family?"

"None. I left no one behind." His pit was as deep as his chest, water now past his ankles.

"No parents?"

Exasperated, he ceased digging. "No, Ruby, my mother was killed, and—"

"So was *mine*," the girl interrupted in a shocked tone. "The humans did it." She gazed away, her bottom lip trembling.

Malkom's eyes went wide; he dreaded her tears more than he would a kick to the teeth.

When Ruby stemmed her tears, wiping her nose on her sleeve, he felt abject relief—and a grudging respect for the girl.

"Did the humans kill your mom, too?"

He exhaled. "No, child, it happened long ago."

His respect for Ruby grew when she murmured, "I'm going to hurt the people who did it."

"I believe you will one day," he said honestly. And who would make sure she was prepared to exact her revenge, skilled and strong enough to punish without being harmed herself? "But you cannot go after them, unless you're ready and know you will win."

She canted her head. "How will I know?"

I could make sure. I could help you get vengeance. "I am sure your coven will teach you. Or Carrow will."

"You know, you're just like me. We both lost our moms and now we both have Crow."

Wanting to change this subject, he asked, "What are your powers?"

"I'm like Crow, in the same three castes as her." When he motioned for her to go on, she said, "Warrior, enchantress, and conjurer. But I can't do anything with this collar on." She glared down at it.

He'd already known Carrow was an enchantress, just hadn't known that was a literal power. He wished he could believe that she'd enthralled him to desire her, but what he felt for her was too consuming to be a mere spell. "Carrow's magic seems to come and go." Last night, she'd told him that her collar had been turned off in Oblivion. So why had her magic been so unpredictable?

"I guess." Ruby shrugged. "If she doesn't have a source."

"A source? Of power?"

"I'm not supposed to tell anyone."

Eking out an awkward smile, he faced her. "But 'tis only me, child."

With a suspicious expression, she said, "Why'd you tell me you were married to Crow?"

His shoulders stiffened, feigned smile gone. "I *am*."

"I asked her if you were."

In as unconcerned a tone as he could manage, he asked, "And what did she say?"

"She said that even if you were, you wouldn't want to be with her."

So Carrow hadn't denied it. And last night, she'd acted as if she'd wanted him to claim her. When he'd told her to leave him alone, he'd seen her disappointment.

It would be easy to believe she wanted to start a life with him. Easier still to believe that she'd been ready to feign affection for his protection.

Sounds familiar.

"But I think you do want to be with her," Ruby said. "You were sad on the beach last night when she was hurt."

Sad? He was nigh out of his mind with worry, anguished.

Yet there were two issues with the witch. Malkom couldn't bear to lose her; he was *definitely* going to lose her. Once she found out about his past or returned to her home ...

And he didn't know if he could ever believe in another again. It only brought misery.

I will get through this hour by hour, denying myself what I want most.

"We talked about you last night."

"Did you?"

"Yeah, if you're married to Crow and she's adopting me, then you do, too. You're my stepdemon."

"Stepdemon?"

"Yeah, like a stepdad who's a demon."

Stepdad was some kind of father? Why had Carrow told the child these things? To put pressure on him? She had a lot of nerve, assuming he'd provide for her *and* her adopted one. Without even asking him.

Malkom ran his hand over his face. Why would Carrow want *him* for this role?

Why do you think, fool? She and the child were both defenseless here.

When Ruby's stomach growled, he immediately looked up. "You are hungry."

She grinned sheepishly. "Uh-huh."

He gazed from his half-finished pit back to the child, then exhaled. "What do you usually eat, then?" He would return and complete this later.

"I like dinosaur chicken nuggets, pizza sticks, tangelos, and organic juice boxes."

Puzzled, he asked, "Are those things *here*?" She shook her head. "We could catch something to eat."

She shot to her feet, eyes wide. "I love catching things! I catch frogs and spiders and green snakes!"

"Very well." He took his shovel, climbing from the pit. As he passed her, she stuck her hand up to him.

He frowned at it. "What? Did you hurt yourself?" Carrow would have his head—

Ruby slipped her tiny hand into his.

He gazed down in consternation, about to draw away. Why would the child do such a thing? *I do not understand this.*

She peered up at him. "Aren't we going?"

Though he felt a hint of that uncomfortable tightness in his chest, he said, "We are going, *deela*." And he kept her hand in his grasp.

Carrow was pensive in the wooden tub, and not just because she was afraid of getting splinters in all the wrong places.

Earlier she'd tried yet again to get her torque off, this

time using rope and a tourniquet system. She'd almost asphyxiated, yet the collar hadn't budged. With a bitter curse, she'd accepted that she would be magicless until she returned home.

Now she sat with her knees to her chest, lathering her hair, contemplating how she might get back in the demon's good graces. She was used to being well liked. She didn't go around putting mittens on destitute kittens or saving nuns from a nuclear winter, but she tried to do right. Surely the demon would thaw to her, would recognize that she'd acted out of necessity.

Though he was angry with her, she knew he still cared. She recalled his reaction on the beach, faintly hearing him pleading for her to wake up. Just thinking about that made her toes curl.

But she didn't have time to let things sort themselves out naturally. She'd realized two things today. First, this being powerless and dependent on a male sucked worse than being in the "great outdoors." And second, she needed the demon to be firmly on their side—now—so they could escape this place as soon as possible.

Among all the other threats, La Dorada could still be out there, with her trained Wendigos.

When Carrow was little, she used to have nightmares about those creatures. They were ravenous, eating any living thing they came across, mortal or immortal, falling upon it in a frenzy. And worse than being eaten alive was joining their number. Sustain a single bite or scratch, and within days . . .

Carrow trusted Malkom to keep her and Ruby safe in the short term, but how long would it be until the contagious members of the Lore overran the entire island?

She scooped water up over her head, beginning to rinse her hair, imagining what would happen once the three of them returned to New Orleans. What would Malkom's life be like? She knew he'd have a job at least. With his strength, speed, and healing ability, he'd be so in demand as a mercenary it wouldn't even be funny.

Would the other demons who lived there accept him as one of their own? The witches would, eventually. Mari and Elianna would adore him once they heard he'd saved Carrow's and Ruby's lives repeatedly—

Ruby's shriek rang out.

Carrow bolted out of the tub, suds dripping down her face as she blindly sprinted out of the cabin and down the stairs. Outside in the sprinkling rain, she heard another shriek.

"Ruby!" She followed the sound through the woods to the calm side of the cape, screaming, "Where are you?" Brush scraped her bare legs. "Ruby! Answer me. . . ." Carrow trailed off when she spotted them, her tension fading as she took in the scene.

On the beach, Ruby squealed and laughed as she dodged fish flapping all around her feet.

Malkom was shirtless, knee-deep in the water, easily hand-catching them to toss up on the shore. And Carrow could have sworn he'd been sporting a grin until she ran out.

Carrow ran her forearm over her eyes, stepping back behind a waist-high bush. She wrapped her other arm over her chest. "You scared me."

"We're fishing, Crow!"

And I nearly had a heart attack, Ruby. "That's good, honey." Her irritation vanished when she realized this had to be Ruby's first real laugh since her mother had died.

Carrow gazed at Malkom, wanting to thank him again, but his heated look robbed her of breath. Ruby hadn't seemed to notice—or care—that Carrow was naked.

But Malkom...

As he hastily backed into deeper water, his eyes flickered black, his lips parting. And gods, she responded. His tanned skin was damp, the sculpted muscles in his torso flexing with his movements, that tattoo twining up his body. *I used to follow it with my mouth.*

Once she could pry her eyes upward, even his face made her want to sigh. His blond stubble, those chiseled features, that wicked mouth. But when she bit her bottom lip, he jerked his gaze away, scowling.

Oh, well, Rome wasn't built in a day, she thought breezily, delighted to see his interest was as marked as ever. He definitely still wanted her. "Fish on," she called. As she sauntered back to the cabin, she felt his eyes return to her, burning like a brand.

38

The witch, naked to all the world. Her face pinkened from her bath. Tendrils of black hair clinging to supple skin. And the brush she'd hidden behind had revealed as much as it'd covered. . . .

If Malkom could get that image out of his head, he thought he might find this night enjoyable, relaxing even.

After he and the witches had eaten *fish,* he'd sat in front of the fire, watching Carrow and Ruby playing cards on the rug, a game called blackjack. They were wagering seashells. Either Carrow was letting the child win or she was a poor player indeed.

They'd asked him to join them, but even if he'd been inclined, he couldn't read the symbols.

So he'd reflected on his day, realizing it hadn't been miserable. The girl was bright and had proved to be agreeable company. This island was a paradise, filled with all the things they needed to survive and even to thrive. The air was clean, the water from the cloudy sky sweet.

Which meant he couldn't hate the witch for where he'd ended up. However, for her deceit . . . that was another matter.

And still he wanted her just as much as before. Hell, more so.

Now he regarded her expressions, watched the firelight on her shining hair. He missed touching her, missed taking her neck. Or breast. He missed merely sleeping with her against him—

"So, you two were busy today," she said.

Ruby answered, "We put traps out, and now nobody can get here. And tomorrow, we're going to string pots that will make a lot of noise if anybody gets too close to our *ter'tory*."

At that, Carrow grinned in his direction, as if she wanted to share her amusement with him.

"The *peninsula* is closed off," he said stonily. Preparing for an attack was normal for him. Relaxing with others like this, hearing their laughter, was foreign. "You should be safe." And if anything approached by air, he would hear its wings from a mile away.

"Then, Malkom, I have a favor to ask you," Carrow said, taking another card. "I need you to search for a way to get us off this island."

To get them to the home she spoke of. Malkom knew it surely couldn't trump this place of plenty, with food all around. He'd scooped the night's meal straight from the water! "What do I know of that, witch? 'Tis not my world."

"You could venture out and try to find any of our allies, or maybe a boat. Perhaps there's another island nearby—this could be one of a chain. And as you said, we should be secure here until you return."

"I will consider it." He would *never* consider it.

The child asked, "Why can't you just trace us away? Demons can trace, can't they?"

"I could, long ago. But I no longer have that talent."

"Why?"

"Because I am not truly a demon anymore."

"Then what are you?"

"Ruby, I'm sure he doesn't want to talk about this," Carrow said, clearly growing nervous.

The witch had all but signed Malkom up to be a protector for the child but hadn't revealed what he was? Out of shame?

The old anger simmered up, that rage he'd felt at being turned into an abomination against his will. Made into something hated.

Carrow acted as if she could accept it, but she didn't want others to know.

"I became a Scârbă," he said.

"What does that mean?"

Something that must not be. Neither a true vampire nor a demon. "A vampire demon."

"V-vampire?" Ruby's eyes went round. "You drink blood?"

"I do," he said. "I have drunk Carrow before."

Ruby swung her gaze to Carrow, who looked like she wanted to throttle him.

"Did it hurt, Crow?"

"Yes, witch, did it hurt?"

She faced him with a determined glint in her eyes, then turned to the girl. "No, honey. It's like a hug. It's what Malkom and I do when we want to feel close to each other." She turned to him once more. "Isn't that right, demon?"

His lips parted.

"In fact, I could use a bite right about now."

Woman, I would kill for another taste of you!

Their gazes held.

"Why didn't you tell me?" Ruby demanded. "I'm not supposed to talk to vampires. Unless they're married to Valkyrie."

After a laden moment, Carrow dragged her gaze away to answer Ruby. "Because I wasn't sure that Malkom wanted you to know. Besides, he's not a vampire."

"He's not?"

I'm not?

"Nope. You remember how Peter Parker got bitten by a spider and had superpowers?" The girl nodded. "But he's not a spider, is he?"

"Of course not!"

Who is Peter Parker?

"Malkom got some superpowers from a vampire, but he's still a demon," Carrow said decidedly.

"Ohhh, so he's like a superdemon."

Carrow's lips curled at him. "The stuff of legend, honey."

Malkom sat there, wound up with tension, grappling with what Carrow had said. Was that truly how she saw him? Not as something *less* but somehow as something *more*?

In that cell with Kallen ages ago, Malkom had vowed

to find a way to become fully demon again. In Oblivion, he'd even briefly considered asking the witch to help him. *Now I do not know. . . .*

"So, are you going to let me win back my shells?" she asked the girl.

"But I want Malkom to play," Ruby said with a pout.

He and Carrow shared a look. Would she tell the child he couldn't read the symbols?

"They might not have cards where he comes from. Maybe he could team up—"

"With me!" Ruby bounded over to him, dropping her cards all over to grab his arm. "You can be on my team." She pulled him until he relented and joined them on the floor.

Carrow looked surprised. "Okay, then. The object of the game is to get to twenty-one points without going over."

"The cards with people on them are worth ten." Ruby displayed a card that depicted a crowned man.

Carrow said, "And aces can be one or eleven."

Ruby showed him a card that looked like all the rest. "This is an ace. It's got an A on it."

Reading *and* ciphering. Any remnants of his relaxation disappeared.

"Ruby, since you're on vacation from school, why don't you do all the adding? Ask Malkom if you can."

"Can I, Malkom?"

He gruffly replied, "As you will . . ."

The next hour flew by in a haze of numbers and even some amusement. Additional rules to the game were revealed, which made it even more interesting. Soon he could recognize aces, and he'd even learned some of the number symbols—easy enough to deduce when Ruby counted on her fingers with many of the cards.

At one point, the girl had cried, "Double down!"

He'd frowned at their *hand*. "What does that mean?"

Between peals of laughter, she'd said, "I don't know!"

But in the end, he and Ruby had won more than they lost, and Carrow had finally run out of shells.

"You guys were merciless. But I want a rematch soon." She turned to him, caught him staring at her before he gazed away. More softly, she said, "That was fun."

Surprisingly, it had been.

Though the child's energy had begun to wane, Ruby said, "We can give you more shells." She scooped up a handful, solemnly offering them to Carrow.

"Nope. Time for bed."

The girl grumbled but did rise. "Good night, Malkom." She leaned in and kissed his cheek, then trudged toward Carrow.

"And to you, *deela*," he muttered brusquely, not liking Carrow's delighted smile.

"Come on, kiddo." As she squired Ruby to bed, she glanced over her shoulder. "I'll be back in a minute." She bit her bottom lip in that way that drove him crazy.

Gods, he desired her, still craved her, but taking her would be reckless. *Cannot do what my father did.*

Then stay away from her.

◆ ◆ ◆

As per Ruby's request, Carrow had promised to hold her hand until she'd fallen asleep, assuring her that she and Malkom would be close by if she woke up.

Naturally, when Carrow was dying to get back to Malkom, the girl had been chatty, talking about her day with him. Already, Ruby nursed a serious case of hero worship for the demon.

Makes two of us. When he'd freed Ruby from those rocks . . . no one else could have done it.

Once Ruby had drifted off at last, Carrow crept out of the room, her heart racing.

He was gone.

Earlier, by the fire, he'd been looking at her with that dark, hungry expression. She hadn't known if it was an invitation or not.

Assuming it was, she set out to find him, wearing only a sweater, her leather skirt, and a blanket wrapped around her. She found him on the calm side of the cape, deep in the water he'd earlier fished.

"What are you doing?"

His breaths fogged over the freezing water. "Learning to swim."

"I could have taught you." She laid out the blanket, sitting down to wait for him.

"I figured it out." He seemed to have gotten the hang of it, swimming with fairly sure strokes. Eventually, he made for the shore.

She was just about to ask him if he was cold when he rose up, naked and magnificent. Her lips parted. Not cold at all.

As he stalked toward her with his long-legged

strides, she nearly whimpered with need. Water lovingly sluiced down his torso, drops clinging to chiseled abs before reaching his muscled thighs, his narrow hips . . . and between. He stiffened under her gaze, his length distending.

He'd gotten her used to enjoying him almost hourly. Now she'd gone a week without him. She needed release—but she also merely wanted to be close to him again.

"What do you want, witch?"

"To talk to you. Have you thought about my plan?"

He reached for his clothes. "I told you I will consider it."

"Just look at me." A shake of his head. "No? You couldn't keep your eyes off me tonight."

Finally he faced her. "You are the one who put us in this situation. I am just trying to get us through it."

"By not talking to me? By not touching me?"

He stabbed his legs into his pants, hissing in a breath as he fastened them over his erection.

She rose, sidling closer to him. "I know you still care about me. When I'd drowned, you were a mess. You were relieved to see I was going to be all right."

"I did not want my fated female to die, no."

And he's learned snarkiness!

She touched his arm, but he flinched. "What can I do to earn back your trust?"

"Leave me be, so I can think on my own."

"Okay. If that's what you want. I just thought you needed more, from the way you looked at me."

"And what if I did need more? What would you offer me, *wife*?"

"Sex. I'm offering to have sex with you."

He gave a bitter laugh. "All you would be doing is keeping a vow you already made."

"That's true."

"If you are so eager for it now, why did you not let me claim you in Oblivion?"

"I don't have sex with just anyone, Malkom. You were out of control at first, frightening me at times. And then when I did offer, y-you bit my breast!"

"Which I paid for dearly."

"Yes, you did. But the fact remains that I offered myself to you because I had feelings for you. Undeniable ones."

In a scoffing tone, he said, "You were that sure of me in Oblivion? When you had no fated tie to me?"

"I was well on my way to being sure. I trust my instincts. And they were screaming that you were the one for me."

"A pretty story from a deceptive witch."

"Malkom, I know it'll take time for you to trust me again. But I also know it *will* happen. Maybe we can enjoy each other until it does? I'm asking you to make love to me."

"So I will continue protecting you? You are offering yourself up to a demon you seek to use. Just as before, witch. Nothing has changed."

"I'm offering because I desire you so much." She took his hand, kissing his callused palm before trailing it down her chest, her belly. . . . "Touch me. See how much."

Seemingly of its own will, his hand continued down. At the leather hem of her skirt, he hesitated.

Carrow didn't think she breathed until his hand disappeared beneath her skirt. She trembled as his palm grazed up her thigh.

When his fingers met the wet folds of her bare sex, his brows drew together, and he cast her a look so fierce, part scathing, part adoring.

A wild, lost male.

"I miss the way you touched me, Malkom. The way you *kissed*," she breathed. She was wetter than he'd ever felt her, quivering with need.

His nostrils flared at the tantalizing scent of her arousal. "Damn you, witch," he bit out, unable to stop his fingers from stroking her slick flesh. His cock shot even harder for that damp heat.

She leaned into him, laying her palms flat on his chest. Against his skin, she murmured, "Will you kiss me?" Then she licked his pierced nipple.

He shuddered, cupping her head tight to his chest with the crook of his arm. "Again," he rasped brokenly as his fingers continued rubbing betwixt her thighs.

Her tongue darted out, flicking till his knees went weak.

"You want my kiss?" He released her. "Come to me."

She stood on her toes, leaning up to him, but when she licked her plump lips, he was helpless not to meet her, slanting his mouth over hers. He groaned against her, having missed her lips over the long days and nights in that cell.

He could fool himself, letting himself believe that they were truly close, that they had no history. Yes, he could pretend that there was nothing between them—nothing but need. He kissed her harder, his tongue thrusting against hers.

She'd begun moaning, soaking his fingers. When he realized she was about to come, he drew his head and his hand away.

In truth, there *was* nothing between them but their need. No bond, no trust, no future.

She sagged against him, brushing her kiss-swollen lips again his chest. "I want you," she whispered. "Please make love to me."

He stared at the trees above as a soft rain began falling, misting his face. Lust clawed at him—but if he didn't trust her, then how could he do this with her?

I have to know my offspring will be wanted and taken care of.

Earlier, he'd remembered there was a way he could take her and still prevent a child. But it might take more control than he had. *Mustn't bite her, then.* Else he'd definitely spill inside her.

So 'tis done? He would have her this night?

Before when he'd thought he would claim her, his chest had been full of emotion, unbearably so. Now it felt hollow inside.

Just enjoy this, as any other male would do.

Finally, he would know what it was like to desire and to possess.

He gazed down when she began caressing his chest. His stomach dipped as she lightly dragged one fingernail above the top of his trews, back and forth through the trail of hair just below his navel. His cock strained to her touch, the crown jutting past the material.

"Oh, Malkom." She sucked in a breath. "Stop me if you don't want me to touch you, love. Otherwise . . ."

Stop her? He wanted to shove her cool hand into his trews, make her fondle his heated shaft and soothe his aching testicles.

When the pad of her finger met the sensitive tip, he groaned, knowing he was nigh defeated. She began rubbing the head, up and down the slit, coaxing until it gave up drops of seed for her.

Defeated.

Grabbing her wrist, he pulled her hand away, then lifted her into his arms. He carried her to the blanket, laying her down to yank and tear her clothes from her.

Once she was stripped before him, he sat back on his haunches, releasing a pent-up breath. He stared, staggered by her beauty, feeling almost drunk on it.

The mist dampened her flawless skin. Her creamy breasts rose and fell with her panting breaths, her nipples stiffening as if to beg for a lash of his tongue.

Her heavy-lidded eyes seemed to glow with her desire. "Malkom, please don't stop now." She was squeezing her thighs together, her body subtly rocking with need.

"*Ara,* I have never . . . I do not know . . ."

"You can tell me anything."

"I have never done this and . . ." He wanted to get it right. To not hurt her, only to pleasure her—

She wordlessly drew up a knee, parting her legs to reveal her glistening curls.

A growl was ripped from his chest. As he yanked off his pants, he told her in Demonish, *"I am defeated, female."* Naked, he dropped to his knees beside her. *"Tonight I must have you, else die from the wanting."*

39

Malkom rasped words to her that she didn't understand. But no matter the meaning, she knew they were words of feeling, convincing her that she hadn't lost him forever.

As he knelt before her, he again reminded her of a virility god. His towering body flexed with cords of muscle. His horns had nearly regrown and now flared back, darkening.

His damp blond hair whipped across his cheek, his blue eyes flickering to that intense black.

Yet as her gaze followed the golden trail of hair leading down to his shaft, his size gave her a moment of hesitation. If he wasn't gentle, he would definitely hurt her.

Trust him, you've wanted this.

When he lay beside her, she leaned over to stroke him.

But he cast her that stern look, slowly shaking his head. In English, he grated, "No more of your touches, witch, lest I finish in your hand." Then he gathered her wrists to pin them over her head. With his free hand, he readied two fingers to enter her, biting free his claws.

She shivered in anticipation, her sex clenching for

those fingers inside her. "Then touch me, demon," she whispered, letting both of her knees fall wide.

With a groan, he cupped her with his rough palm, covering her possessively as he slid his forefinger inside her.

"Yes!" She welcomed the insistent stroke, even as she'd begun panting for more.

He dipped his head to nuzzle her breasts, his hot tongue flicking one of her nipples. With his brows drawn tight, he closed his lips around the swollen peak, muttering mindlessly to himself about how sweet she tasted . . . how he'd dreamed of her scent.

By the time he returned with a second finger, she was nearly on the verge.

"Tell me you are ready." Before he took her other nipple, he rasped, "I want to be . . . claiming you." He gave a decisive thrust with those two fingers. "Ah, *fucking you like this*." Another unyielding thrust. At his words, she grew even more aroused, and he could feel it. "My female is slick, needing her release."

"Yes, I'm ready." She sounded as desperate as she was. "Please, demon . . ."

He moved between her legs, his tanned skin sheening in the rain, his shaft jutting eagerly. His eyes were now black as onyx and burning with intent.

So gorgeous. *And about to be mine.*

He gripped himself in his fist, positioning the broad crown against her entrance. "Tell me you want me, witch."

"I want you, Malkom." She moaned when the head nudged inside her. "I've never wanted like I do now."

♦ ♦ ♦

As Malkom gazed down at where their bodies were about to join, he swallowed, nervousness and excitement warring within him. "At last to have this."

At last to have my wife.

"Yes, yes," she murmured, her hips rolling wantonly.

With each undulation, her sex moistened the head of his cock, giving him a taste of what he might yet feel, spurring him to thrust. He wanted deep within her, wanted his shaft to be covered in that wetness.

"Just please go a little easy at first."

As water drops collected over her pale skin, he began to press forward, groaning from the heat that greeted him. When her sheath enveloped the head, he watched, unable to catch his breath as he inched through her tightness. *After so long wondering . . .*

"Slow, demon." She grasped his shoulders as she maneuvered beneath him, wriggling her hips as if to receive him better. "Please."

Slow. Somehow. He clamped the backs of her thighs with shaking hands. Spreading her legs even wider, he painstakingly squeezed in deeper. His cock had already begun throbbing, bordering on pain. He wasn't even halfway in.

And still he watched their joining. A feeling like grief seized him when he realized that he'd never fit her. That her tender body had not been made for one like him.

"Witch, I cannot . . ." Yet her eyes were still desirous, heavy-lidded. "Do you not . . ." What to ask her? He could barely formulate thoughts, much less words. "I do not hurt you?"

"No, Malkom." She shook her head, and the exquisite scent of her hair nearly felled him.

Truly? If she had no worry, then his was relieved. Carrow would know about these things better than he.

"You feel wonderful," she added, biting her bottom lip.

My gods, so do you, woman.

His resolve renewed, he pressed forward. Sweating as he mounted her, he sank his aching shaft deeper.

"Demon, you're almost . . ." She gasped when he'd gone as far as her body would allow, gloved within her heat. "Ah, *there!*" She arched her back, and her sex slipped along his cock.

His eyes nearly rolled back in his head.

"Carrow!" Dizzy with pleasure, he rasped, "There is nothing better." He wanted to savor this, to revel in the connection. But instinct drove him, commanding him to thrust. He withdrew his hips and bucked for the first time. The bliss of it wrenched a roar from his chest. His back bowed.

Another thrust.

Gods almighty. He'd never *lived* before this moment.

With a ragged groan, he gazed down at her, telling her in Demonish that she was soft, perfect.

That this was heaven.

He stretched his body over hers, heaving forward, needing to do this *hard.*

Okay, now he was hurting her.

"Easy, demon." He didn't seem to hear her. At first

it'd been so good, but he was growing even thicker. She was pinned on his length, could feel him throbbing inside. "Please, c-can you just give me a second?"

Seeming to wake, he rose above her with an incredulous look. But he did go still.

Denying his instinct was obviously agonizing. His jaw bulged at the sides. The muscles in his torso, arms, and neck were tensed, the ridges sharp. "You are hurting," he grated, his accent more marked than she'd ever heard it.

"Yes, a little. I need to get used to you."

Sweat beaded his chest and forehead. "What . . . what do I do?"

"Would you kiss me here again?" She cupped her breasts in offer.

His brows furrowed as if she'd just struck him out of the blue.

With a desperate groan, he gripped her breasts with his big palms, kneading them as he took one peak between his lips. His greedy mouth sucked until it was almost agony.

She arched her back again. "More, demon!"

He moved to her other breast, still kneading the first, pinching the nipple he'd left aching and damp.

Soon, she was panting, now craving the thickness wedged within her. "Malkom, now," she pleaded, rocking her hips to urge his own. "I'm ready."

In answer, the demon gave a measured thrust.

Pleasure radiated throughout her body. "Ah, yes!" No pain. Only rapture. *"More . . ."*

Another forceful stroke.

With nothing to distract her, Carrow noticed how perfectly he ground against her clitoris with each thrust. How his sweat-slicked hips rubbed between her sensitive thighs.

How he filled her so deeply, she felt as if he were a part of her. One being, unending.

"Cannot stop again, witch," he growled against her nipple.

When he drew his hips back, she cried, "Whatever you do, don't stop!"

Now his female wanted him to continue. Grappling for control, determined to feel her come, Malkom did.

He bucked against her, once and again, until he found a driving rhythm.

"Drink me," she moaned as their skin slapped.

He rose up on straightened arms. "What did you say?" Another plunge of his cock made her plump breasts quiver. The tips were puckered, still moist from his tongue. Had he heard her right?

"Take my neck . . ."

"Cannot." Already, he doubted he could deny the tugging grip of her sex in the final moments.

Much less while her blood coursed through his veins.

Her head thrashed. "Suckle blood from my breast, like you did before."

"Carrow! Be *silent*," he hissed, even as his gaze was riveted to that soft, giving flesh. So easy to pierce her pale skin. To drink from her, pleasuring her.

What would it feel like to have his fangs and his shaft within her body, both gloved by her sweet skin?

He shook his head hard, struggling to outlast her, to keep from tasting her. Her throaty moans had grown constant, her nails digging into his back, clutching him close. She was on the edge, and he was determined to take her over. *Cleave to me, witch. . . .*

Pounding betwixt her legs, driven by her lush heat, he gripped her nape, yanking her up. "I cannot give you up. *Never* will I release you."

Cleave to me!

"Demon . . ." Her anguished expression transformed to one of ecstasy, her eyes glimmering like stars. "Oh, you're making me—" She threw back her head and screamed, "Malkom! Yes, *yes!*"

He felt her squeezing as she began to come, clenching round his shaft as he'd imagined so many times.

But 'twas all so much better than his fantasies. Her scent, her cries, the way her body writhed wildly beneath his. Plunging into the wetness of her orgasm . . .

"Gods, *Carrow!*" he bellowed. He was about to explode, the seal soon to be broken, his semen climbing. For four hundred years he'd waited to ejaculate, to offer his seed to another.

When he'd grown so large he could barely thrust inside her, when he was about to come harder than he ever had in his life, his mind whispered, *Nothing but need.*

40

"Wh-what?" Carrow didn't understand. "What did you do?"

Malkom had *pulled out*?

He'd finished on her belly, heaving over her as he'd yelled her name. And it felt like a slap in the face. He hadn't even broken his demon seal, hadn't ejaculated with his release.

Now he collapsed atop her, his heart like a drum, his hips still languidly rocking.

Be glad, Carrow. You don't need a baby. So why did she feel like crying? "Okay, you can get up now."

He raised his head as if with difficulty, the corners of his lips curling. "I do not know if I can move, *ara*."

That half grin was almost her undoing. He looked so boyish, his face relaxed, his eyes now that steadfast blue.

"At least not until I take you next." He began hardening atop her.

"Get off me."

He frowned at her tone, levering himself up on his elbows. "I have hurt you?"

He had, just not in the way he thought. She scrambled back, out from under him.

"*Channa*, what? Did I do . . . wrong?"

"Just give me a second, Malkom." She couldn't even process this. The best sex in her entire life, the strongest emotional connection she'd ever felt, and he'd gypped her. Why would he do that? *How* could he do that?

He'd seemed utterly lost right before he'd come.

But then, he didn't trust her. And deep down he could even hate her. Probably both.

All she knew was that he'd defied his demon instinct, denied himself that kind of pleasure, to make sure she didn't get pregnant with his baby.

Though he'd vowed never to release her, never to give her up, he might hate every minute of having her.

"Why will you not look at me?" he asked when she began dressing. "Are you angry about how I ended? Is that wrong to your kind?"

"I just didn't expect you to do that."

"I know. 'Twas nigh too good to pull away."

She muttered, "Second slap of the night," then added, "Yet somehow you found a way to."

"You are upset about this? I did not know you wanted a child."

Once dressed, she faced him. "I didn't. I don't!" She brushed her damp hair from her forehead. "I don't necessarily want a kid, but I thought you needed to break the seal and obey your instincts and all that. Since I'm your mate."

"Those drives were . . . pressing," he said, sounding as if he'd just uttered the understatement of the century. "I am very stunned I could deny them."

"If those drives were *pressing,* then your motives for

pulling out must be as well. Look, I understand why you did it. If you got me pregnant, then I could blaze and you'd never know where your all-important heir went to."

He frowned at some of her words, then seemed to take in her meaning. "An heir to what, Carrow?" he snapped. "I left any wealth I had behind, for you!" Clearly reining in his temper, he said, "I am speaking of how my child would be treated."

"What?" Third slap of the night. "You think I would mistreat my own baby?"

"Just as you said, some things you cannot risk. I must be there to protect my offspring."

"From whom?"

"From anyone or anything," he said. "Ruby has no parents and is dependent on fate—dependent now on my goodwill."

"Your *goodwill*?" She wanted away from him. Unfortunately, in this case at least, she wasn't stupid. There'd be no flouncing away, not when she had Ruby with her. Malkom was right—they'd have to stay with the big gun for as long as he'd let them.

No matter that he'd just made her feel dirty and lacking. *I want my powers back!*

"You know 'tis true. And I would not have my own so vulnerable."

"You forget—Ruby has me."

"Do you think I could *ever* forget that, witch?"

Carrow had heard of loves that could trump all obstacles. But then she'd also heard that there were things couples couldn't come back from.

She was beginning to fear that she and Malkom might not get past this.

He stabbed his legs into his pants once again. "You are angry with me and have no right to be."

"And you're treating me like some evil bitch who'll abscond with your kid. I'm not like that. I'm actually not that bad a person." She knew he'd had a tormented life, knew he'd experienced hardships she couldn't even imagine. Carrow could understand his mistrust. *But I don't know what to do about it.* "Will you ever see past what I was forced to do? Or will you always think I'm a liar?"

"What would you do then, if my seed took?"

"I wouldn't keep your child from you." As if she even could. It struck her that Malkom was in their lives now. For better or worse, he was on this plane and would never willingly be parted from her.

Maybe he was right to keep an emotional distance. Their relationship was likely doomed.

So why had she felt that unwavering certainty about him? *Husband,* her heart seemed to cry even now.

"You said you'd wanted me to claim you in Oblivion," he grated. "You could have gotten pregnant then. Did you give no thought to that?"

"I did."

"And?"

"And I thought that my life was already changing radically because of Ruby. And that little girl fills me with contentment like I've never known. So why wouldn't another child do the same?"

"So 'tis all about *your* happiness. You would have

raised *my* child while I was imprisoned in that place?"

"I know you don't believe me, but I vowed to my goddess Hekate that I would come back for you. I swore that I wouldn't stop until you were freed. I don't know what to do to convince you of that."

He looked like he wanted to believe her so badly. Then his expression grew closed-off once more.

"I asked you a question before, and I want the answer," she said. "Yes or no. Will you ever see past what I was forced to do? Because I'm beginning to suspect you will always hate me, will always think I'm deceiving you."

"And what would you do if that were the case? Nothing will change by my answering either way."

Still he'd evaded the question. She pinched her forehead. "Then what do we do now?"

"We did things your way; now we will do them mine," he said, his tone as cold as frost. "I am going to protect you. I will even protect your adopted one. Expect nothing more."

Her lips parted. When he was done with her, Carrow's heart would be as broken as his was. Maybe worse. She asked softly, "Will that be enough for you?"

"It must be for me, as well as for you. I usually kill those who betray me. Count yourself lucky."

41

I've been taking my knocks, Carrow mused, staring at the peeling ceiling above her bed. While Ruby snored from the other bed, she thought back over the last three days on the island.

Malkom had been so kind to the girl, but he'd been icy to Carrow, barely speaking to her, barely looking at her. He refused to sleep inside, preferring to camp out between the neck of the sandy peninsula and the cabin. She liked to think he did this solely to protect them, instead of to distance himself from Carrow.

With Ruby, he was all patience and kindness. And the girl was fascinated with her "stepdemon." Apparently, she'd explained the term to him—and he hadn't denied the title.

Ruby had fun with him, following him everywhere, and he didn't seem to mind. Several times a day, Carrow saw the big demon on his way to some task with a tiny witch huffing after his long-legged strides. He'd taught the girl how to tie special knots, and together they brought back fish and berries.

Carrow could tell he even enjoyed it when Ruby sang "Particle Man." But it made sense. He'd been alone so long, the sound of a child singing must be pleasing, no matter the tune.

Last night, Ruby had asked for *Malkom* to hold her hand at bedtime. Carrow had stood at the doorway, watching as he'd patiently waited for Ruby to fall asleep. He'd gruffly told her, "Dream well, *deela*." Demonish for *doll*.

With each second he'd remained at that bedside, Carrow had become even more convinced that Malkom was the one. . . .

Sometimes Ruby would report in on things they'd done.

"I'm teaching him to read," she'd said yesterday, her tone filled with importance. "Because I read waaaaay better than him."

"You didn't tell him that, did you?"

"Only twice."

Ruby continually pressured Carrow to leave, reminding her several times a day, "You promised me you'd take me home."

"I know, baby, but it's complicated."

"I miss my friends. I miss Elianna."

Elianna, Carrow's mentor and substitute mother, was a half immortal who aged but never died. The old witch always wore an apron with pockets full of mysterious spellcasting powders, and every time Carrow hugged her, those scents wafted up. To this day, Carrow associated the smells with warm hugs and unconditional love. "I miss Elianna, too. And Mariketa. But we'll see them soon."

In turn, Carrow was pressuring Malkom to help

them escape this place, but he kept blowing her off. She thought he feared that she'd leave him once they'd returned home. When in truth, if he treated her half as well as he had in the mine, then she'd be stuck to him like epoxy.

She didn't see that forthcoming. After they'd made love the first time, Carrow had awakened with her body well pleasured, even as her heart had still hurt. She'd been so stung that she hadn't sought him out for any more of his attentions.

But last night as she'd lain awake during a storm, he'd appeared in the doorway, limned by the flashing lightning. *"Come."*

She'd missed him like an ache, finding it impossible to deny him. Filled with excitement, she'd followed him out. As the rain fell, he'd taken her against a tree, then from behind, then with her writhing in his lap. She'd lost count after that, but each time he'd taken pains never to come inside her—or to bite her.

This morning, Carrow had been cross-eyed with exhaustion and pleasantly surprised when he'd come to the cabin early, getting Ruby fed and taking her out—as if he'd wanted to let Carrow sleep late.

Such a thoughtful gesture, a *husbandly* gesture. But later, when she'd thanked him, he'd coldly denied that he'd done it for her.

Yes, she'd been taking her knocks, singing "Tub—thumping" to herself as she'd held her tongue and plastered on smiles. *I get knocked down, but I get up again. . . .*

She'd first started falling for him because she'd felt

cherished. Now this disdain was killing her. It constantly reminded her of her childhood.

When she was young, she'd thought if she was good and made her parents proud, they would thaw toward her and give her love. Now she'd begun to accept that they *never* would.

Would Malkom?

Yet his behavior had made her realize something. She'd done wrong by him, and if his treating her like this for a time would help them get past her betrayal, then she could endure it.

However, there was no reason for her to endure it from her parents. She'd gazed at her emerald ring, the one tie she had with them. What if she just admitted defeat? Relinquished all hope?

Then she'd wondered, *What if Malkom* never *gets past my betrayal?*

That would be a problem, she thought as she rose to go find him.

Since Carrow had already fallen in love with Malkom Slaine.

Two witches were making Malkom rethink everything he'd known. For a demon of his age, this was an uncomfortable process.

They'd settled into a routine of sorts. During the day he fished and checked the perimeter traps with Ruby tagging along. Once done, the girl would teach him to write a few words in the sand. At night, he dreamed.

Memories from Carrow had begun suppressing his

own nightmares from his past. And not all of her memories were filled with loneliness, carousing, or wars.

He'd witnessed much more from her life—visions of *cars,* great *bridges,* and *boats* as big as mountains. He'd seen her home, a manor called Andoain, the place she'd spoken to her parents about. It was filled with other witches and surrounded by unusual creatures.

But Malkom had also begun to suffer a recurring nightmare about journeying with her to her lands. As soon as he got there, she whispered, *"I'm so sorry, Malkom."* Or, in another version, she didn't apologize; she laughed at him just as those demonesses had when he'd been starving as a boy.

Carrow had admitted that she'd been well on her way to wanting a future with him, even before they'd journeyed through that portal. *You were well on your way, witch, but I was there.* He'd cared about her when he'd blindly followed her. And he hurt all the worse for it—

He heard Carrow approaching.

"Why don't you ever stay inside with us?" she asked from behind him.

He shrugged.

"Do you mind if I sit?"

Sit. Talk to me. Say the one thing that will ease my mistrust. Malkom didn't *want* to feel like this, but four hundred years of misery couldn't be cured by a few days with her. Old fears died hard.

Sensing she was about to leave, he grated, "Sit."

She settled next to him on the sand. "I need to know when you're going into the interior to search."

He wouldn't be. Because Malkom would *not* be returning her to her old home. If he did go off to "search," he'd just return with word that there was no way to escape.

This place was paradise. For the first time ever, he was utterly satisfied with all that belonged to him.

Though he'd had no choice about coming to this island, he would choose to stay, seizing another territory to guard, one with ample room to run, water, and food.

Food from the *sea*. Fishing for his mate and their young one was satisfying.

More importantly, 'twas a place without the screeching sounds and blinding lights of her home. Without the *wars*.

"Why are you so eager to return?" he asked her. "Is it so bad here?"

"I have to get home. That's where my life is."

"You are my female. Your life is with me."

"Then let's spend our lives together. In New Orleans," she said brightly. "Malkom, you would be happy there with us. But you'll have to trust me."

Just accept what she offers, a part of him commanded. If she betrayed him again, he would survive. Yet then he pictured how she'd looked today, smiling down at Ruby as they'd collected shells.

No. No, I would not.

If he let himself love Carrow and she forsook him again, he would *not* go on. So to trust her in this would be to trust her with his very life.

Now the situation was even more complicated. He

was growing to care for the witch's adopted one, too. If Carrow forsook him, she'd take the child with her.

Which was unacceptable. He'd already decided that if Carrow could adopt Ruby, then he could as well. If the girl needed a mother to love her, then she also needed a father to protect her.

Father. A new purpose for him, a new name. Something to take the place of bastard, slave, murderer. A whore's get . . .

When he didn't respond, she asked, "And what about Ruby? Her friends and school are back home."

"The girl will adjust. Just as I've had to do again and again."

"I want more for her. I thought you would, too."

"Tell me how I can trust this next world you want me to go to. The last time I trusted you to take me to a new place, I did not fare well."

"But you're better off now, aren't you?"

"If I am, I've certainly earned my good fortune," he said, recalling his capture and Chase's torture. Reminded of that man's disgust, Malkom said, "In your world, would your people accept what I am?"

She gazed away. "Your kind isn't . . . well, there are those who'll want to make you an enemy just because of what you are. But we won't know if they can be made to see differently, not until we try it."

"Your home cannot possibly be better than this." The blinding lights, the sounds, her *behavior* . . .

"Maybe not better, but different. We belong to a coven there, and Ruby needs to learn from them. Malkom, she could grow up to be dangerous. The Sorceri showed a disturbing interest in her," she said. "And I have a bad feeling about this place. A sense of something coming. More mortals will return here. And the dangers on this island are greater than there could ever be at home."

"Ah, you have a sense, then?"

"So you're not going to believe that either?" Her cheeks flushed with anger. "If you think I'd lie about a potential danger, then I'm beginning to wonder if we truly can come back from this."

"'Tis convenient. Your *sense*."

"La Dorada could still be out here. Remember her? That ghastly woman who crept through the ward, wreaking havoc?"

"She did not bother me. Aided me, in fact. She is not a concern."

Carrow narrowed her eyes. "You seem utterly convinced that this island is better than my home. Have you dreamed my memories?"

"Yes," he answered shamelessly.

Her lips parted, but she quickly collected herself. "What have you seen?"

You, dancing upon tables. "Glimpses of your world. Cars and gadgets. Enough to know I'd prefer it here."

"What have you seen of my *life*?"

Why not tell her? "I saw your wars. Saw you fighting recklessly."

"There aren't *that* many wars, Malkom."

"I saw you disrobing for strangers."

She didn't even have the grace to flush. "Have you seen me with another man?"

Malkom dreaded that possibility. "No, I have not.

But what I have seen is damning enough. Why would you behave like that?"

She shrugged casually. "A lot of reasons. I was single—unbound—and it was exciting. I'm not shy, and our culture is fun-loving and free. Plus, I get power from it."

Now it was his turn to be shocked. "That is your *source*?"

She nodded. "Happiness. Revelry. They give me power." She tilted her head at him, her green eyes appraising. "Malkom, I'm not going to apologize for that, or for anything I've done."

When his scowl deepened, she said, "You're four hundred years old. I'm not yet fifty. So don't judge me for having fun when I was young and single. And don't judge me for securing power that's there for the taking."

Don't judge her? Who the hell was *he* to ever judge another? "Would you intend to continue doing that?"

"Only the week directly before Ash Wednesday." At his frown, she explained, "It's a citywide celebration. Wild revelry. And I'd hope you'd be right there with me." She eased in closer to him. "If you've seen my memories, then it's only fair that you tell me about yours." She traced her fingers over the scars on his wrists.

When he recoiled, she drew her hand away. "You will never learn to trust me, will you?" Her expression grew saddened. "So it's not that you assume this island is a better place to live—it's because you're afraid I'll betray you once we get back? You had no intention of ever going to search, did you? No intention of ever helping us off this island?"

"No. I did not."

She gasped. "Do you expect me to keep this torque on forever? To live helpless and vulnerable without any magic? I am a *witch*, Malkom!"

"Vulnerable? You have my protection—I pledged it. And no matter what, you would be in less danger here than in your world, amidst *your wars*."

"Will you ever move past this anger?"

He shrugged.

"Damn it, demon, tell me. Will you ever trust me again?"

"I do not know."

"Just answer me!" she cried. "Yes or no?"

Old fears died hard. "No."

Her hand flitted to her forehead. "Then you're going to continue to freeze me out? Distance yourself? You're treating me like my parents did." She gave a bitter laugh. "At least I've given you reason to."

So that's how she viewed his behavior? Likening it to her cold and haughty parents? His first impulse was to deny being anything like them. But hadn't he been cold?

At least I've given you reason to. . . . He *was* treating her as they had. How could he, when he knew firsthand how heartsick their neglect had made her?

What was his neglect doing to her now?

She'd done nothing wrong with them, nor was she truly culpable for what she'd done to Malkom. She'd sought only to save an innocent child, the little girl he too wanted to call his own.

"We can't be trapped here because you fear I'll leave

you once we return home," she said. "Did you never think I could leave you here?"

His body tensed, and he bared his fangs. "Try it, witch. Always I will come for you. For you both. Nothing will stop me!"

She dropped her face into her hands. "What is *wrong* with me?" He barely heard her mutter, "Falling for someone who can't love me back."

"Love?" he spat. "You want that from *me*?" His heart seemed to stop.

Maybe he should tell her everything. If he dreaded her reaction, then he should just get this out of the way. She was going to forsake him eventually. *And I will not care because she has already betrayed my trust.*

She raised her head. In a deadened tone, she said, "Yes, Malkom, I want you to love me."

"You know nothing about me! But you will." He would reveal his sordid past, sparing no detail, so she could understand the male she'd wed. "After tonight, you will know everything."

42

You will know everything. . . . His expression was cruel, as if he planned to hurt her with whatever he was about to reveal.

But he was already hurting her. He believed their relationship hinged on his past and how it affected him. Instead, it should be about *their* pasts, shaping their future together. And just as he had difficulty trusting her, she had difficulty being driven away, ignored, rejected. . . .

"Then tell me, Malkom. I want to know."

Though his demeanor was aloof, his irises flickered black, belying his calm. She knew in an instant that he'd never told another what he was about to confide in her.

"My mother was a whore," he began. "I have no idea who my father was."

Carrow had already known that. She debated telling him, but decided to hear it from him. "Go on, please."

"When I was a boy, she sold me to a vampire master who used me for blood." He looked to the right of her as he added, "And for . . . sex."

Ah, Hekate, was that why he'd killed his mother?

"She knew what that vampire would do to me. And still she made me his slave." Lips drawing back from his fangs, Malkom said, "And the master raped his slaves repeatedly."

"Malkom, I—"

"Let me finish," he snapped.

"I'm sorry, go on."

"But that was not enough for the vampire. He shared me with his sick friends. He liked to shame me, to make me shame myself in front of them. In time, I hated myself even more than I hated him."

Carrow's heart was breaking for this demon. She'd suspected he'd been abused like that, but hadn't imagined to what degree.

"I did whatever that vampire wanted of me," he told her. "I was his whore, and in time, he believed I was an eager one. If I felt pain, I ignored it. If I knew disgust, I learned to hide it."

His expression grew even more haunted, his eyes now fully black, as if he were reliving that misery. Carrow wanted to hold him, but she knew he wouldn't accept comfort from her now.

"Never did the master see how much I despised him. And still he eventually kicked me out to starve in the streets. I was stunned, could not comprehend what I had done wrong. 'Twas years before I realized I'd grown too tall and big to please him."

"Wh-what happened then?"

"I healed, I survived. Somehow my body even thrived. But my mind was never right. I knew I had to kill him." He'd begun speaking in a monotone voice, as if reciting a logbook of events. But she could *feel* the pain he'd buried so deeply. "The last thing the master saw in his life was my face. After that, I killed a lot of vampires. I loved to do nothing more. Soon Prince Kallen heard of me. We became friends." Malkom added in a mutter, "I could not believe he wanted to be my friend. I'd never had one before. Or since."

Don't cry for him—he'll hate you for it.

Wait, they'd been friends? Carrow dreaded hearing more, knew the ending to this story from the dossier: Malkom had assassinated Kallen the Just.

"Kallen was aware of my lowly birth and that I'd been a slave. But it mattered naught to him. He was the first person who ever gave a damn whether I lived or died. For years, we fought the vampires, side by side as brothers, until we were captured because of a traitor— Ronath the Armorer."

Ronath? Then he'd died too quickly.

"The vampires' leader, the Viceroy, made Kallen and me into abominations. Scârbă. Then he imprisoned us together with no food—or blood. He told us that only one of us would ever leave that cell. The one who drank, or the one who killed."

Hatred for those long-dead vampires seethed inside Carrow. How much Malkom had suffered at their hands.

"Kallen was not as strong as I was, not as used to hunger. He needed blood more than I did. I should have realized that then, should have given him what he needed. I have never regretted anything more than what I did in the cell that night."

"He tried to drink from you?" So the prince had succumbed to bloodlust and turned on the man who'd looked up to him, who'd *loved* him. And Malkom thought he was in the wrong.

"Of course he tried to drink from me! We were maddened with thirst. Kallen was my best friend, and I destroyed him—"

"Malkom, he didn't leave you a choice."

"There is always a choice!"

"You just said you were maddened by thirst."

"I did not *drink* him, witch—I killed him, because I thought he had betrayed our friendship. I've never drunk anyone before you."

Never before me? He'd resisted that long? "How did you escape the Viceroy?"

"He wanted me to become loyal to the Horde, to become more vampire than demon. He tried to force me to drink from demons. I resisted for years, withstood his torments. But one night, he presented me with the neck of a demon boy, one who was my age when I'd first ceded blood. I could sense the child's fear, could scent it, and it felt so *familiar.* A rage such as I've never known rose up in me, and I gave myself over to it. I broke free, slaughtering that vampire."

Torments? For years? And then she'd turned Malkom over to Chase for more. . . .

"Last came Carrow Graie," he said softly, his voice full of menace, "a witch as beautiful as she was deceitful. She made me care for her, then tricked me, luring me into a trap to be enslaved yet again."

Ah, gods, he considered her no better than the others.

"Anyone who has ever betrayed me has paid with his

life. With my bare hands, I killed the master, the Viceroy, Kallen, and Ronath."

"And your mother?"

"When I was grown, I visited her hovel to show her what I'd made of myself, to make her regret. When she served me poisoned drink, I forced her to finish the cup."

Carrow's heart fell when she recognized why Malkom had returned to see that demoness. He'd still been seeking a mother's love, even if he hadn't realized it then—or now. And his mother had answered his longing with a deadly poison.

Malkom mistook her silence. "'Twas no less than she deserved! Now all of them are dead but you."

"D-did you want to kill me?"

His gaze held hers. "I thought about it. Had you not been my fated one, I would have."

She understood so much more about him now. His reaction during their bath in Oblivion. Why he didn't want to impregnate her.

How could he trust Carrow with a child of his when he'd been left by his parents to be brutalized again and again? His own mother had sold him as a slave and tried to murder him. Why should he expect different from Carrow?

Malkom had the deepest, most far-reaching trust issues of any person she'd ever known. And Carrow had betrayed him, a male who'd been shaped by betrayal.

She glanced at his wrists. He had far worse scars on the inside. *And I've ripped them wide open.*

"Now what does the witch think of her *husband*?"

43

Malkom braced himself for her disgust, even as he knew he shouldn't give a damn what she thought. *She* had wronged *him*.

Still, as he watched her seeming to formulate a response, he regretted telling her. He could not take her disgust, could not bear it from her—

"I appreciate your confiding in me about your past," she finally said. "It explains a lot. But it doesn't affect my feelings at all."

He exhaled a breath he hadn't realized he was holding. Then his anger fired. "How can you say that?" he snapped. "Your words are false, meant to deceive me again. How could you not be disgusted?"

"I'm not. I feel pain for what you've suffered and want to comfort you, but my feelings for you haven't changed in the least."

Maybe she didn't understand how bad it'd been. *How dishonorably I behaved.* "I scavenged refuse, eating from filth. I murdered my best friend, the only one who was ever good to me in my entire life." He grated, "I behaved as if I loved every second the master violated me, acted as if I were eager, craving whatever he and his friends did to me."

Though she didn't gaze away, her eyes watered. "I wish I could have saved you from that. Could have rescued you from him."

He shot to his feet. "What is *wrong* with you, woman?" He ran his hand over his face. "No, I know. You treat me just as I treated my master, feigning love to gain protection, acting as if I do not disgust you."

"I'm not feigning anything, demon! You were a child! You did what it took to survive. And thank the gods you did. You grew into the noblest, bravest man I've ever known. Because of your strength and will to live, you were here to save me and an innocent little girl from dying."

Noblest? Malkom shook his head hard. "You said the mortals wanted me, a Scârbǎ, because I am unique. You and the girl might not even have been taken but for me."

"I may have been a pawn, but I believe they wanted Ruby anyway. She was going to be captured regardless. And if not for you, she would have died that night. Why don't you remember events like that?" She gazed at the sky, then turned to him once more, her eyes stark. "I regret hurting you, but I do *not* regret being sent after you. The very thought of never knowing you makes me feel sick inside."

He clenched his fists. *It does me, too.* What would it take for him to lose this knot in his gut, this bitter doubt?

I do not want to feel this way anymore. . . .

When he didn't reply, she rose. "Malkom, I'll go. But there's something you should know." She waited until he'd met her gaze to say, "If you told me these things to drive a wedge between us, then you've failed. All you've done is make me care for you more."

Which makes no sense to me! After dredging up all these memories, he ached inside. He wanted to hurt her, to shake away that mask of concern and empathy. *I will never believe again.*

As she turned back for the cabin, his hand shot forward, snagging her ankle to pull her to the sand. "I'm not done with you, wife."

She twisted around to face him. Instead of being outraged or wary, her expression was fierce. "Good, because I will *never* be done with you, Malkom." She eased her hand to his face, resting her palm against his cheek. Her eyes began to soften as she gazed up at him.

Every time she looked at him like that, his rancor grew. "The only reason you accept one like me into your bed"—he forced her hands over her head, pinning them with one of his—"is that you know you will be vulnerable without my protection." He recognized this as well as he would his own harsh reflection in a pool. "And when you are safe in your home, you will have no need of me."

"That's simply not true."

"Prove it," he said, his voice cruel. "Prove to me why a highborn woman so fine as you"—he clawed her shirt open to expose her breasts, giving each a brusque squeeze—"would want to lie with a male like me."

"Malkom, I want to lie with you because I desire you so much."

At her ear, he rasped, "You truly crave the bastard son of a whore rutting betwixt your pale thighs?" After tearing off his own shirt, he shoved her skirt up to her waist, baring her sex. "Wouldn't you be suspicious, if you were me?" He yanked his pants down to his knees, then maneuvered his body over hers.

"I crave *you*. I always will."

When he positioned his cock at her entrance, she began panting, growing wet for him, which only infuriated him more.

"You like being *fucked by a Scârbă*?" He wrapped her hair around his fist. "Look at me! Truly look. Tell me what you see that others cannot!"

"I see my husband."

With a yell of frustration, he entered her with one unrelenting stroke. Though his thoughts were in turmoil, pleasure rocked him. He threw back his head, biting back a groan.

She gasped at the intrusion, sucking in a breath. Then she whispered, "I love you."

He stilled, gazing down at her. "What did you say?"

The demon's body was a mass of tension, like a bomb about to explode, but she still repeated, "I love you, Malkom."

"Shut up!" He shoved inside her so hard, her teeth nearly clattered.

"But I do."

"Stop saying that," he commanded, bucking his hips, driving his shaft deep within her. He looked down at her as if he hated her, as if he wanted to punish her for loving him—even as she could sense his emotions, could sense how much he yearned for her too.

"Are you trying to hurt me?"

He quaked above her. "It'd be nothing more than you deserve." His flickering eyes were filled with more pain than she'd ever seen in another. Then his gaze fell to her neck. "If I bit you, would you still tell me you love me?"

Yes, always. "Try it and see."

"You'd probably come for me again. Isn't that right, witch?"

But instead of taking her neck, he went to his knees, releasing her hands. Gripping her ass with splayed, clutching fingers, he positioned her so he could sink even farther inside.

Seated deep, he pumped inside her like a piston, his rigid muscles flexing under sweat-slicked skin. She tried to raise her hips up to meet him, seeking his next determined thrust, but he was too strong.

The friction . . . his growls of pleasure . . . the thick heat swelling within her.

Just watching his body move like this was about to send her over the edge. Her hands were drawn to him, palms caressing his sheening chest, then dipping down his torso.

With each of her strokes, with each of his relentless plunges, tension built inside her, spiraling, until she throbbed. "Demon!" she cried, desperate for release. Her head thrashed as the pressure within her gathered, readying to explode.

At last, the pleasure seized her. Scorching. Boundless. "Ah, gods! *Malkom, yes!*" Her back arched, her nails digging into his hips, wanting more, wanting him even deeper.

"I feel you," he bit out between clenched teeth. "Feel you coming round me." At the last minute, when she was certain he'd remain within, he jerked his hips back.

With an agonized yell, he shoved his shaft over her belly, mindlessly grinding atop her for his final shuddering throes.

When he collapsed over her, she gazed above him at the misty sky, tears welling as she hurt for him—hurt *with* him.

At her ear, he grated, *"I'm still not done with you, wife."*

When Carrow woke just before dawn, a cocoon of fog had wrapped around her and Malkom. The last time she'd checked on Ruby, it'd been raining. Now all was still and soft.

Malkom remained asleep, which wasn't surprising. He had to have exhausted himself in the previous hours of sweating, frenzied—and, she hoped, cathartic—sex.

Yet never once had he hurt her.

And at the end of the night, he'd turned on his side so he could enfold her in his arms, clasping her tightly to him. His body still shuddering, his voice raw, he'd said, *"A witch holds my life in her palm. Ara, I live or die for you."*

Now she gazed down at him. His brows were drawn, his eyes moving behind his lids. His lean cheeks were covered in blond stubble.

So beautiful. Her wild, lost male. How could this demon who'd known so much hurt and shame be so proud and good?

She grazed the backs of her fingers over his face, repeating his words, "Carrow is Malkom's."

Wanting to get back to her own bed before Ruby woke, she reluctantly extricated herself from his arms, earning a soft growl, though he slept on.

She dressed in tattered clothes, then made her way to the cabin, reflecting on the secrets he'd confided, the revelations of all that had been done to him.

In the past, she'd wondered if hatred and abuse might be preferable to neglect and abandonment. At least then she might have found out why her parents hadn't loved her.

After hearing Malkom's tale, she knew how fortunate she'd been. She'd been able to find a new family—a mother, sister, daughter.

And now a husband.

Carrow was lost for him. She admired him, respected him, loved him.

She felt as if they'd turned a corner. He'd let out all his frustrations, told her his secrets. It had to have bonded them. She'd become certain that he could get over her betrayal.

But could he get over the rest—the four centuries of expecting and receiving duplicity—without breaking her heart first?

When he woke, she would tell him that things were going to be different. She wouldn't tolerate him saying cruel things to her—or about himself. He was her husband, and she'd be damned if she let anyone call him those things, not even Malkom himself.

Going forward, she would show him that he was

more than his past. Did Carrow believe that the love of a good woman would heal all his wounds? Counteract years of abuse?

No. But the love of a good woman and a new daughter, the respect and gratitude of a witch coven, the eventual welcome into a community of immortals—well, these things couldn't hurt.

She intended to fight his doubt, calling on all her available resources to kick its ass to the curb. If he thought his past was stronger than their future, then he'd never seen a witch hell-bent on saving her demonically proclaimed marriage.

Heartened by her decision, she rubbed her thumb over her ring.

Am I not more than my past as well? She was ready to fight his doubt, but not her own?

Though the ring wasn't as loose as it'd been, she realized it no longer fit her. She removed it, clasping it in her palm as she detoured to the beach.

Standing before the roaring surf, she peered down at it.

Carrow was done.

She'd made this resolution before, but invariably, as time went by, she would try to contact her parents. Always she'd held on to this damned ring, held on to unfounded hope.

Done. She threw the ring into the waves.

At once, she gasped, tempted to dash into the water and find it. But she stopped herself. Tears welling, she raised her face to the mist. *Good-bye.*

Turning on her heel, she headed back to the cabin.

With every step she took away from her past, she felt lighter, as if a crushing weight on her chest were dissolving. The longing, the bafflement, the *desperation*—all . . . ebbing.

She sighed, feeling as if she could finally breathe after so long.

In the bedroom, she tugged Ruby's blanket higher, leaning down to brush a kiss over her forehead. *I'm going to take care of you, Ruby. I always will.*

Satisfaction coursed through Carrow, a flare of power surging within her. Though doused by her torque, it had arisen . . .

From within me?

With a bewildered laugh, she climbed into the other bed. All her life, she'd been waiting for this answer. Carrow had always known she could feed her powers from *anyone's* happiness. She'd just never figured it could be her own—because she'd never been truly happy.

Not until she'd let go of her past and welcomed a new future.

She stared at the peeling ceiling, which looked so different from when she'd left it. *Because I'm different now.*

Then she *smiled*, was still smiling when she gradually drifted to sleep.

But not long after, she bolted upright in bed, just as Ruby did.

"Did you feel that, Crow?" the girl murmured. "Something bad's coming."

44

"What do you want with me, Mariketa?" Conrad Wroth said as he traced with his wife into Andoain's great hall.

As soon as Mari had been able to locate them—a feat in itself—she'd asked them here to meet with her and Bowen. "I need a favor," she said, beholding the towering, red-eyed vampire. *The key.*

Conrad was an immortal male, filled with evil—in the form of a vampire's blood-borne memories—and he was obsessed with Néomi, his phantom Bride. Who was as intangible as smoke.

Fortunately, Conrad owed Mari big-time. The ballerina Néomi, now one of Mari's friends, was alive only because of her.

"Name it, then," Conrad said, his Estonian accent pronounced.

"Well, it's like this," Mari began, "you know how Loreans have been abducted by this weird order of mortals? My best friend Carrow was among them. But I've located where they're all being kept."

Though Mari had been able to sense a cataclysmic Lore disturbance, she could get no second opinion or reading from other witches. She couldn't find Nïx anywhere, so no backup from her.

In the eyes of the Lore, Mari's mystical waypoint was only a baseless hunch.

She felt like the plucky seismologist who'd seen a blip of untold strength but couldn't get anyone to believe the *big one* was coming.

"What does this have to do with me?" Conrad asked.

Bowen said, "We need someone to teleport me to Carrow."

"Us," Mari corrected. "Teleport *us* to Carrow."

Clasping her upper arm, Bowen said, "Damn it, lass! We have talked about this."

They'd been going round and round. Her wolf was nothing if not overprotective.

"And I will no' allow—"

"How did you find them?" Néomi interrupted, softly but sternly, her French accent coloring her words.

Mari said, "I detected the immortal energy within the place and was able to download the location into a mirror. Full disclosure: it felt like a freaking Lore world war was going on."

Conrad and Néomi both remained quiet. At length, Néomi said, "You know how deeply we are in your debt."

Not even a year ago, Conrad had brought a dying Néomi to Mari. She'd risked everything to save Néomi, using more power than she'd had to give to transform her into a phantom, an immortal who could become corporeal or intangible at will.

"But this sounds like a suicide mission," Néomi continued. "If he can somehow trace to this energy you speak of, what if it's in the middle of the ocean, or in a sunny desert?"

"I firmly believe that it's on an island."

Conrad asked, "Can't someone fly over the coordinates first?"

"Nïx told us it couldn't be seen from a plane," Mari hedged, since, of course, there were no coordinates. Which had hardly helped her prove her case to her immortal allies.

"Vampire, we need someone to get us *on the ground*," Bowen smoothly said, "so we can search the island on foot."

Mari added, "Conrad, it has to be you."

"How would he know where to go?" Néomi asked.

Mari carefully gazed away as she held up a small pocket mirror. Before this week, she'd never achieved so much magic with so little mirror. "I created a trail to the energy, like a portal, and stored the directions to it in this mirror. I believe if you gaze into the glass, it will act like a mystical GPS system to guide your teleportation." *Patent pending if this badboy works!* "It's possible you could trace directly there."

Conrad gripped Néomi's small hand. "If something happens to me, who will take care of my Bride?"

Mari hated to pressure him, but this was for Carrow. "Conrad, you wouldn't have a Bride right now if not for me."

The vampire gazed down at Néomi with such a consuming look that even Mari sighed. "I'll do as you ask, witch." Just when Mari felt a welling of relief, he said,

"But I go alone. I can trace across the area much faster. Can cover more ground."

Bowen shook his head. "We doona know exactly what you'd be tracing into. Did you no' hear the *Lore world war* bit earlier? At the very least, you can expect those mortals to be there in full force."

"*Alone,*" the vampire repeated.

"But how will Carrow know you are a friend?" Néomi asked him. "Your eyes are red."

Conrad was a true fallen vampire, his eyes bloodred from drinking victims to death. But he'd been brought back from the brink by Néomi and three stubborn Wroth brothers.

Mari said, "I could tell him something only Carrow would know. And show him pics so he'd recognize her."

"Are you certain, *mon grand*?" Néomi asked.

He nodded, saying simply, "Mariketa bids this."

"Very well." The dancer stood on her toes, reaching up her free hand to thread her fingers through his black hair. "Then bring Carrow back. And come home safely to me."

"I will return with her," he told Néomi. Then he faced Mariketa. "To pay on a debt so dear that it can never be settled."

Malkom woke late, blinking against a heavy bank of morning fog. He'd just dreamed a memory of Carrow's, one that he hadn't experienced before.

When he'd been in chains, humiliated in front of all the citizens of Ash, Carrow had looked up at him with realization. *Malkom is noble,* she'd thought.

He sat up, staring out into the gray mist, staggered

yet again by her. In the past, he'd longed to be noble. He might not actually be, but for his lady to deem him so?

'Tis well enough for me.

Then his heart sank. She had thought that *before* last night, when he'd proved he was anything but.

Why could he not stop punishing her? Did he mean to take out *all* his pain on her, centuries of it?

He sank back, throwing his arm over his face. The things he'd said to her, the things he'd *done*. He'd revealed secrets he'd never told anyone—not even Kallen. And then he'd taken her in the dirt like a common whore.

He suffered from remorse so acute it physically pained him. *Get to Carrow. Apologize. Make her understand.* With those thoughts in mind, he rose and dressed, hastening to her.

As he came upon the cabin, the fog burned off, the sun appearing for the first time since their escape. Already it'd begun burning his exposed skin.

Shading his sensitive eyes, he saw that the door was open. Inside, the two witches were darting about. *Packing?*

His heart dropped to his stomach. Carrow was leaving him? He'd told her too much. *I bared my soul, and of course, she found it lacking.*

He grew panicked at the thought of losing the family he'd only just found, wanting to take back his careless words and actions. *You've finally pushed her away, Slaine.*

He strode up the stairs. *Do not look at me as the others did, channa.* He couldn't handle that from her, couldn't live with the fact that he'd spurned her and brought this upon himself.

She'd donned her sword and boots. It sounded as if Ruby was scurrying about in the back room. They truly were leaving him.

He swiped his forearm over his eyes and swallowed, wanting to say something, but he couldn't trust his voice. Then Carrow saw him standing in the doorway.

He didn't take a breath, dreading . . .

"There you are." She crossed to him, rising up on her toes to kiss him.

Once her lips brushed his, he groaned in relief, yanking her into him. He tightened his arms around her as he took her mouth.

She sighed, responding so sweetly.

Until they heard straining noises coming from the back.

Carrow pulled away with a sheepish smile. Then she called out, "Do you need some help, Ruby?"

In an exasperated tone, she replied, "I told you I could do this."

Hunched over and huffing with exertion, the girl dragged out the pack. She hauled it to his feet, then stood fully, placing her hand on her lower back. Her face was bright red from the effort. "I packed it for you!"

"Am I . . ." He cleared his throat. "Am I to come, then?"

Ruby frowned, glancing from Carrow back to him. "Duh."

"What a great job, baby. Now, go grab a couple of lucky shells for our trip."

As soon as the girl had left, Carrow wryly said, "There might be a dead fish in there 'in case you get hungry.'"

Now that his panic had eased, his ire grew. "Where do you think you are going? The plan you laid out was for me to search."

"I had a premonition that something bad is coming here. I don't know when or how, and it could be hours or days. But we've got to leave. We'll keep to the trees to avoid the sun, and we can travel through the night, but we're running out of time." When he said nothing, she added, "Look, if you don't believe me, you can ask Ruby—"

"I will go with you."

"You *will*?"

He could see now that he had no choice but to go. Just as she'd said last night, the witch didn't have to wait to get home to leave him. She could do it just as easily here.

And he couldn't keep her and the little one prisoners forever.

Carrow's eyes lit up. "Y-you trust me?"

Malkom . . . didn't. He'd finally realized he was incapable of trust—short of some kind of irrefutable proof that he was never going to obtain. But the alternative to leaving with her was losing her, so he would choose the lesser of two evils. He would make this leap. "I want to return to your home with you and Ruby."

"You're going to be so happy with us! I promise you."

While she was delighted, he was filled with misgivings. He'd been given too fine and good a female. One he could never believe would truly love someone like him. Fate's cruelest jest so far—

A clanging sound rang out. *The pots hitting each other.* Carrow's eyes went wide. His fangs sharpened.

"Ruby!" she screamed, sprinting outside.

45

As Carrow ran for Ruby, Malkom faced off against the intruders at the neck of the peninsula, waiting for them to reveal themselves.

She'd just reached Ruby at the beach, snatching the girl into her arms, when the creatures swarmed into their sanctuary, a ravening tide of fangs and insatiable hunger.

Wendigos. With their dagger-like claws and emaciated bodies, their clothes ripped to shreds. Already their rancid stench pervaded the area.

There were scores of them. More than La Dorada had with her. Their sheer numbers overwhelmed Malkom's traps. How could there be so many of them?

The answer came to her as Malkom roared, charging them with a breathtaking ferocity.

They'd infected others, increasing their number.

To keep the beasts away from Carrow and Ruby, Malkom met them in the sun. Would he know they were contagious? "Don't let them touch you, Malkom!"

One scratch or bite . . .

"Help him, Crow!" Ruby's eyes were gleaming as she frantically tore at her collar. "We have to help him!"

Though he battled the Wendigos savagely—snapping their necks while dodging their claws—the sun was taking its toll on him. Soon he was surrounded.

I can't draw them over here, can't risk Ruby. "Stay here!" Carrow ordered her as she unsheathed her sword.

One of the beasts twisted its head toward them. It loped forward, fangs dripping. Twenty feet away, ten . . .

When it launched itself at Carrow, she ducked and sidestepped, swinging for the back of its neck. She beheaded it, but more turned toward them.

"No!" Malkom yelled. *"No, here!"* He provoked them to attack only him, yet still half the tide veered in Carrow's direction.

"You stay behind me, Ruby! If I get into trouble, run for the calm beach and get into the water. Do you hear me?" Carrow glanced back when the girl didn't answer. Ruby was slack-jawed.

A vampire had appeared behind Carrow—one with red eyes. Reeling in shock, she raised her sword. Just as she was about to swing, she realized he looked familiar. But she couldn't tell when he was shading his face, recoiling from the intense sunlight.

"Mariketa sent me to retrieve you. I am Conrad Wroth," he grated as his skin began to blister. "For hours, I've searched this island." He looked it, was sweating and dirty as though he'd traveled for miles. "I'm to tell you about the Mardi Gras float you hijacked?"

"Ah, Hekate, you're legit."

"Who is he, Crow?"

"He's been sent by Mari!"

The vampire's fangs had lengthened, his eyes darting. He hissed in pain as more blistering appeared. "I can't . . . stay much longer, witch. And the beasts near."

"We can't leave without that demon over there!" Carrow pointed, but Malkom was so overrun they could barely see him. "Just bring him to us, vampire! Please." When he shook his head in a twisting, deranged kind of way, Carrow screamed, "*Malkom!*"

"Demon, over here!" Ruby cried.

As more Wendigos neared, Carrow raised her bloodied sword again, glancing over her shoulder. "Vampire, take the girl back to Mari! Send help to us if you can."

Another twist of his head. "I'm to return with *you.*" Conrad snagged Carrow around the waist, picking up Ruby with his other arm.

At that moment, Malkom turned, caught sight of them. His eyes went wide, and he bellowed, "*No, no!*" He plowed toward them, but he was besieged. . . .

"*Malkom!*" both she and Ruby cried.

Carrow reached for him, yet Conrad held her tight. When he tried to trace, she resisted him. "Malkom, hurry!"

The vampire's skin smoked, then caught fire completely.

Mariketa glanced around at the crowd that had gathered in the meeting hall at Andoain—a collection of factions from the fey to the Valkyrie, from the Lykae to the nymphs and more. Just about every species from the Vertas side was represented.

In the three hours since Mari had dispatched Conrad to retrieve Carrow, all these beings had heard about it. *News traveling at a supernatural speed.* Now anyone with friends or family thought to have been abducted had teleported, portaled, or driven here.

The gathering reminded her of a Super Friends meeting, except instead of the Hall of Justice, they'd descended on Andoain, with its ornate old couches, altars for tables, giant hearth, and even bigger karaoke stage. Nothing matched except for the coven's four professional-grade poker tables—and the spoof cauldrons.

This was the first time in ages they'd used the hall for anything but girls' night out.

Dozens of beings lined the walls or sat stiffly on the antiquated settees. One couple sat atop a woofer.

With so many different creatures here rubbing together—some allied only through ties with another common faction—Mari was pleasantly surprised at how well everyone was behaving. So far only a few *nut up or shut up*–type ultimatums had been issued.

Of course, she'd taken precautions in case things got ugly.

"How much longer until the vampire is expected to return, witch?" Sabine, the Queen of Illusions, demanded imperiously, every inch the sorceress, from her crimson mask and elaborate crown to her claw-tipped gauntlets. Her husband, Rydstrom—another of Mari's good friends—had his big hand splayed possessively over her hip.

People quieted to hear Mari's answer, gazing at her. Among them were Bowen's cousin Garreth and his Valkyrie wife, Lucia the Huntress, both looking exhausted. Mari knew they'd been searching nonstop for Regin all over the world. Garreth was also here because his cousin Uilleam was missing.

Myst the Coveted and several other Valkyrie sat on

the settees, awaiting news of Regin the Radiant as well.

The demons, the Lykae, the Valkyrie . . . all of them were expecting Mari's magic to, like, *work*. After all the years when it *hadn't*, she was having stage fright. There was a reason she'd been called *Awaited*.

"Uh, soonish," Mari answered, though she had no idea how long. She'd thought he would be back by now. *Have I sent Conrad on a suicide mission?*

She glanced over at Néomi anxiously pacing, shifting from her pretty and vivacious corporeal form to her pale, ethereal phantom state.

Had Mari just widowed her?

Bowen sensed her nervousness and looped his arm protectively around her shoulders. "Doona worry, witchling. This will work out."

More minutes passed. More rumblings sounded. *"How much longer will it take?" "How do we know the witch's magic will work? The captromancer can't even face a mirror." "Where is Nïx? She should be here. . . ."*

Bowen turned to the crowd. "Any more lip, and I'll toss you out on your arses. You're here now only because Mariketa wills it."

Mari gazed up at him. *Gods, I adore this wolf.* He was the Keymaster to her Zuul. She couldn't think of a better guy to have in her corner—

"Wait!" Mari straightened. "I feel a disturbance." The air began to diffuse. "Something's coming."

"I smell smoke," Bowen muttered. "Whatever it is, it's comin' in hot."

46

A red-eyed vampire has Carrow and Ruby.

Carrow struggled to get free, her fingers outstretched as she reached for Malkom.

Ruby flailed, screaming for him.

Though the vampire's skin had caught fire, still he would not release them.

Malkom slashed through the Wendigos, evading their attacks. As the creatures began to feed on their own fallen, slowing their advance, Malkom jerked his head around, searching for a way out of the circling horde.

"Malkom, hurry!" Carrow screamed.

Frustration strangled him, his fists clenching. *Can't get to her.* Gods, to be able to trace.

Then remember how! Never more desperate, never more frenzied, he struggled to recall—as he hadn't been able to in centuries.

Remember, Slaine . . .

He tensed every muscle in his body. *Reach her.* Dizziness assailed him; confusion followed. *I've felt this.* In an instant, he realized he'd experienced the same sensation when he'd run for Carrow during the Gotoh attack. And when he'd somehow reached her in the water amidst the sharks.

Both times he'd been panicked to get to her. *Remember now—or lose her.* With a yell, he strained again.

The Wendigos began tightening their circle once more.

Must . . . reach her.

Then came that unforgettable feeling of floating. He'd begun to disappear! No, only a waver. Leveling his gaze on Carrow's beautiful face, he attempted once more.

Disbelief.

He'd vanished. No time to thank the gods before he'd reappeared, claws bared, ready to slay—

They were gone. The vampire had traced them away, could have taken them anywhere. Malkom's legs threatened to buckle.

A vampire has my family. The thought repeated in his disordered mind. He should have found a way to take them from here! Carrow had warned him again and again.

Now his selfishness had cost him everything.

Madness threatened, nigh overwhelming him. *Keep your wits about you, Slaine.* The vampire wouldn't kill Carrow and Ruby; he could've done that at once. So he'd abducted them for some purpose.

Which meant Malkom would have time to find them.

But how? Have to get off this fucking island!

I can trace now. Yet a vampire or demon could only teleport to places he could see or remember.

Do I not remember her life? He could go to the land of her memories, find her coven, launch a search. *When I find that vampire . . . he'll beg to die.*

Malkom spied a mountaintop in the distance, tracing there out of the oncoming rush of Wendigos.

He needed to buy himself time—to remember a place he'd never been.

By the time the vampire transported Carrow and Ruby to Andoain and dropped them unceremoniously, his skin was fully aflame.

While she and Ruby coughed from the smoke, he merely took the pain as his red eyes scanned a crowd of immortals.

"Néomi!" he bellowed. The phantom gave a cry and ran for him, batting at the flames, extinguishing them.

Clearly uncaring of the damage he'd sustained, he rasped, "*Koeri*, I *need* you."

Néomi swallowed, looking part apprehensive, part excited. "Of course, *mon coeur*." He yanked her into his arms, planting his fangs into her neck. Then they *disappeared*.

"Wait, *no*," Carrow cried. "Where'd he go? I need him to get back!"

"Get back?" Mari said. "What are you talking about? I barely got you out."

"Crow, he's in trouble!" Tears streamed down Ruby's face. "We need to help Malkom!"

"Who's Malkom, Ruby?" Mari asked. "And what's on your necks? Carrow, what's on your sword?"

Brown Wendigo blood covered it. "There's no time to explain! Where will the vampire go? We have to find him."

Mari shook her head. "Conrad's a special kind of loopy. He won't be right from that for days." To Ruby, she said, "Hey, kiddo, why don't you go with Elianna and get washed up?"

Elianna hurried over, but Ruby flung herself away. "I want to g-go after Malkom!" Her breaths were shallowing.

The girl was hysterical; Carrow was nearly there. She dropped her sword, crouching to grab Ruby's shoulders. "You know how I came back for you twice? I will find Malkom. I swear to you, I'll bring him home."

"Come, sweet," Elianna said, reaching for her.

Ruby's face had gone red, her chest heaving, eyes shimmering. She was about to pass out again. *"I want him back NOW!"* Her shriek was earsplitting. *"Now, now, now!"*

"There, child," Elianna murmured, laying her hand on Ruby's forehead. At once, the girl fell unconscious, and the old witch swooped her up into her arms. "A little mystical Benadryl never hurt anyone," she said, heading upstairs. Over her shoulder, she added, "Ruby will wake in a couple of hours. I suggest you retrieve whoever it is that she wants by then."

Carrow surveyed the faces in the room, seeing more witches, nymphs, some of the noble fey, Valkyrie, Lykae, and more. Then she spotted King Rydstrom and his fellow demons. He could trace! "Rydstrom, I need you to trace me back to the island. Right back to where I was!"

Mari said, "Carrow, I can only direct Rydstrom to the island—and that's if he can follow some *really* vague directions. I can't get him exactly back to your location. Apparently, it took Conrad more than three hours to reach you from where I'd sent him."

Even with Carrow's limited knowledge of the island, she couldn't outpace a tracing vampire. More than three hours to get to Malkom . . .

Have to get started now! "Mari, pull up the directions—Rydstrom is tracing me. And get this thing off my neck!"

Rydstrom's sorceress queen, Sabine, demanded, "Is Lanthe there?"

"Yes!" Carrow answered. "Somewhere." At Rydstrom's quizzical look, she hastily explained, "We got separated. I'm sure we can find her within a day or so. If we leave right now!" Turning to Mariketa, she snapped, "Mari, my collar—I need it *gone*. It's binding my powers."

"I'm on it!" Mari said, rubbing her thumb over a pocket mirror while studiously gazing away. "Damn, Carrow, that is some serious mojo."

Rydstrom crossed his brawny arms over his chest. "So if you weren't just with Lanthe, then you can't say for certain that she's even still on this island."

No time to convince him, to explain Thronos . . . Carrow couldn't catch her breath, feeling as if she were about to hyperventilate like Ruby.

"We'll go in when Mariketa scries for her specifically," Rydstrom decided. "It will ultimately save us time."

Typical logical Rydstrom. "No, damn you! Now!" If anything happened to Malkom . . . She clutched at her chest, thinking about Malkom in the midst of all those creatures. "We're leaving this fucking minute!"

Sabine shot to her feet, her anger making the room appear to rock. "You didn't just talk to my husband like that."

"I did. And you'll get him to cooperate if you ever want to see your sister again!"

"Now you're threatening me?" Sabine narrowed her eyes behind her mask. "I'll turn your mind inside out." She held up her glowing palms, poised to strike.

"You think Mari didn't bind any mystical offensives within our coven?" A quick glance at Mari. "You did, right, Glitch?"

Wide-eyed, Mari nodded. "Between that and your new collar, the best you two can do is catfight."

In his arrogance, Malkom had thought he could protect them from anything.

Now a *vampire,* one of Malkom's most reviled enemies, had stolen his family right in front of his eyes.

You will always lose.

No, he *couldn't.* Not this time.

Concentrate. He closed his eyes, dragging up memories from his dreams. He didn't want to go to the pulsing, screeching tavern. He needed to reach Andoain to alert her coven, to get their help in locating the vampire he'd soon rip limb from limb.

Focus, Slaine. . . . Malkom felt himself tracing once more. Having no idea where he would end up, he let himself go.

He appeared in a new land—at *night.* 'Twas warm here, even though the moon was high.

Before him stood a sprawling home with a shimmering blue pool and a grove of trees. He shook his head hard, astonished his tracing had worked. Could this be Andoain?

His brows drew together. This home was unoccupied. No lights burned. No food scents or movements came from within. It didn't look like the Andoain of Carrow's memories.

How to find her?

Emptiness. Wind blew through those trees, bringing a hint of rain. Lightning struck in the distance, nearing swiftly—

A woman's yell sounded. *Carrow's!*

He traced through the grove in that direction, disappearing and reappearing. Each time, he materialized ever closer to her. Soon he'd located the house she was in.

Every time the lightning blazed, he saw a different facet of the home. In the dark lulls, he perceived an imposing building surrounded by a black fence. During the strikes, he saw a timeworn structure with animals teeming around it. Snakes slithered in the yard. Insects and other reptiles abounded.

Malkom stalked closer. Small black animals—*cats*—swarmed outside, wrapping around his legs.

He could scent Carrow and the little one inside, among dozens of other beings. He didn't smell that vampire from before, but other immortals were within.

Carrow's voice was distinct now. She didn't sound afraid; the witch sounded *furious,* railing at others. Was there no threat?

He traced inside, about to take her and Ruby from this place when he heard, ". . . *you want your wife unharmed, then get me back to the island!*"

47

When silence fell over the crowd, Carrow glanced up from her grappling—powers bound—catfight with Sabine. Immortals were backing away from her in a wave.

That's right, I'm bringing the rain! "Rydstrom, damn you, just trace me to the island!"

"Rydstrom, stay out of this," Sabine snapped, taking a cheap shot to Carrow's kidney. Even with her exceptional powers bound, Sabine was still a fierce scrapper. But Carrow was fighting for the man she loved.

Another tag to Carrow's kidney. "Bitch," she hissed, driving her elbow into Sabine's torso. Lucky break—Carrow had nailed her solar plexus!

Sabine gasped, robbed of breath. Carrow took the opportunity to dive for her sword and spring up behind her, placing it at her neck. "The blood of a Wendigo coats this sword."

Rydstrom's lips parted, his eyes sharply turning black. "Just . . . just calm yourself, witch." He held up his hands as he eased closer. "Think about what you're doing. You'd sacrifice our alliance?"

"Don't you people get it? I'll sacrifice *anything*!" Carrow cried. "Rydstrom, what wouldn't you do for this woman right now?"

"There is nothing," he rasped, "nothing I wouldn't do to get her back. I will trace you."

In a weird tone, Mari said, "So this Malkom guy—is he really big?"

"He's Malkom Slaine, my *husband*. And it won't matter how big he is if I don't get to that goddamned island in time to save him from a horde of Wendigos!"

Without warning, Carrow felt a jolt of unfettered joy, just as she heard a male say, " '*Husband*'?"

Over her shoulder, Carrow glared. "Yeah, that's what I—" It was Malkom, directly behind her, emerging from the shadows. As he stepped into the light, her heart went to her throat. "How did you . . . who brought you?"

"I brought myself, witch," he said, his voice hoarse.

Carrow was about to run to him, then she remembered the bristling sorceress she had at sword point. "I'm sorry for this, Sabine. But he's my male, and you'd do the same for Rydstrom." Carrow released her, tossing the sword away. "Truce. Or I won't help you find your sister."

Sabine whirled around, her lips thinned. "I demand a rematch with our powers."

"Are you kidding?" Carrow scoffed. "You'd annihilate me."

The only thing greater than Sabine's powers was her vanity. She smoothed her red hair, clearly mollified. At length, she said, "Truce."

With that, Carrow ran for Malkom, and he met her, opening his arms to her, clutching her tightly.

Holding his face, she rained kisses on his forehead, his cheeks, his lips. "Did you get scratched or bitten? Because I'll keep you locked up until I can find a cure—"

"I am unscathed. I traced away from them."

"How? How did you find me here?"

"I figured out how to trace and followed your memories. I told you I'd come for you. And for Ruby." He surveyed the room. "Where is the little one?"

"She's right upstairs, waiting for me to bring you back," Carrow said dryly. "You have just arrived at a meeting with my allies. Wherein I was politely asking them to return me to the island."

"You . . . you called me husband. In front of all." His blue eyes darkened.

Oh, how badly this demon wanted to believe in her. "Because you *are*. And you always will be." She stood on her toes, cupping his face. "I was out of my mind, Malkom. Out of my ever-living mind to get back to you."

Another wave of that joy hit her. "I will not doubt you again, *ara*."

"I won't give you reason to. But I warn you—I'm not letting you out of my sight from now on." When the corners of his lips curled at that, she said, "I love you." Then she showed him how much, pressing her mouth to his for a desperate, breathless kiss.

Yet then he tensed, drawing her away. Like a shot, he tossed her behind him.

A vampire had appeared. Nikolai Wroth—one of Conrad Wroth's brothers and husband to Myst the Coveted.

Without warning, Malkom attacked, gunning for Nikolai.

"Malkom, wait!" But he'd already lunged for the unsuspecting vamp, tackling him to the ground with a force and speed few had *ever* witnessed.

Garreth MacRieve said, "Bluidy hell, what *is* he?"

Rydstrom said one word: "Vemon."

"Here?" Garreth bellowed. "And near my woman!" He charged for Malkom. Rydstrom was right behind him.

"No, he's with me!" Carrow cried. "Stop!"

With his fangs and claws bared menacingly, Malkom fought them all, holding them off.

But Nikolai had only just gotten his bearings to begin whaling on Malkom. Rydstrom, a rage demon, hadn't gone fully enraged yet. When Malkom clocked Garreth in the face, the Lykae muttered a stunned *"Goddamn?"* then sprang back into the fray, morphing to his werewolf state.

Three different species, ganging up on her man. "Let—him—go!" No response. "He won't hurt any of you."

Malkom chose that moment to raise his brows in disbelief. *Won't I?* Then he slashed out with his claws. Gods, he was strong. Murmurs sounded, incredulous whispers.

Lucia the Huntress said, "Witch, do you not understand what he is?" The Valkyrie drew her bow on him. "I've faced his kind before. And barely escaped with my life."

Sabine said, "Even if I wanted to break this up, my powers are bound. Do let boys be boys."

Myst had drawn a sword, striding forward to end this.

Carrow turned to a wide-eyed Mariketa. "He's my husband, Glitch. Please help me."

"You're sure about a . . . a *vemon*?"

"Never been more sure."

Mari nodded. "But we have *got* to catch up tonight, 'kay?" With a wave of her hand, she flung the four males in opposite directions, pitching them into the walls.

Mouthing "thank you" over her shoulder, Carrow hurried to where Malkom was already on his feet for more. "Malkom, wait! I told you these are my allies."

"You ally with *vampires*."

"The red-eyed one from earlier was sent to save me," she said. "You just ambushed his brother, Nikolai."

"A leech risked his life to save yours?"

"Yes. He's a staunch ally."

"And the rest?"

Carrow surveyed the other immortals, as though seeing them through his eyes. Mari and Bowen, both staring at Carrow and the vemon. Lucia and her winded husband Garreth. The bleeding Wroth brother, spoiling for another round, held back by Myst. Rydstrom, Sabine, and so many more.

Carrow shrugged. "I'd fight alongside all of them."

He exhaled. "Very well." Standing stiffly, he faced his opponents. "Then I . . . apologize. I do not seek to war with my wife's allies."

Carrow knew how hard that had been for him to apologize, especially to a vampire. Luckily, the three appeared to . . . not want to murder him in that instant.

Making light of his attack, she said, "Everybody here brawls all the time. You'll fit right in."

"If we're not to kill the vemon," Rydstrom said, "then you should alert us in advance."

Carrow gazed up at Malkom, grinning like a fool. "I had no idea he'd show."

"Okay, so everybody's cool?" Mari asked around. "Then can we please find out what happened on the island—while I work on your *really*-hard-to-get-off collar?"

"Are you okay?" Carrow asked Malkom. "Do you need to rest?"

He gave a sharp shake of his head, pulling his shoulders back.

So Carrow related everything that had occurred within the facility, from their capture and imprisonment to their escape via La Dorada.

Had Lucia and Garreth shared a worried glance at the mention of the Queen of Evil?

Once Carrow had finished, Lucia asked, "Did you see Regin?"

"She's there, and I believe she's gotten free."

Lucia sagged against Garreth. Then she said, "What do you mean, *you believe*? Why weren't you two together?"

"I didn't have a lot of say about, oh, anything. My power was nil." She flicked her collar, saying, "I'm not wearing this for flair. Look, Lucia, I know you're worried. But Regin was alive." Carrow thought back. "She did want you to know that *Aidan* was there. She said that I was to curse him. He hurt her. Repeatedly."

"Aidan? Dear gods."

Sabine said, "And what about my sister?"

Carrow said, "A Vrekener named Thronos took her."

"*What?*" The house appeared to rock again. "Thronos? Then Lanthe's definitely still on that cursed island. I will turn the Vrekener's mind inside out, show him nightmares he can never recover from." She added in an absent mutter, "Just as I did his father."

Rydstrom told Sabine, "*Cwena*, the witch will scry for Lanthe—"

"And what about Uilleam?" Garreth demanded. Turning to Bowen, he said, "He's your cousin, too. Get your wife to scry for him first."

Lucia said, "I've been around the world looking for Regin for weeks. Mariketa should locate her first."

A chorus of other voices rang out, immortals who wanted their loved ones found.

When Mari put her hands over her ears, Carrow cab-whistled for silence. "She can't scry for everyone's exact locations. It'd take her weeks. And even you guys can't afford that kind of overtime." She turned to Mari. "But you could get a ballpark for dozens, right?"

"I could tell you who is on that island. But not precisely where."

Carrow continued, "And even if she could locate one or two, anybody who goes to retrieve them will be in danger from the moment they set foot there. The Pravus immortals all have their powers. *None* of the Vertas do. La Dorada might still be skulking around for all we know. Plus, the humans will surely return to take back their facility."

"So you're calling for a war," Garreth said, looking like he was hot on the idea.

"And where is Nïx?" Lucia asked. "Shouldn't we get her foresight before planning anything?"

Carrow shook her head. "There's a chance that I saw her on the island. I can't be sure, but I think it was her."

Garreth demanded of the crowd, "Then who will storm this place with the Lykae?"

Carrow smiled, setting them up for the kill. "And how are you going to get there, wolf? The island has some kind of mystical cloak over it."

"Nïx told me no one can see it by boat or plane," Mari said.

Sabine flicked her claw-tipped hand at Malkom. "This . . . *being* can return us. I'll pay him his weight in gold."

Malkom stepped forward. "I will go, relaying people there. And I do not want your gold."

Under her breath, Carrow said, "Um, demon, we're mercenaries here." She squired him to the side of the room. "If you want to join the family business, you gotta make them pay, okay?"

In a low tone, he said, "'Tis the only way to get them to accept me."

And Carrow knew how he longed to be accepted. "I think you'll be surprised, big guy. But for now, let's concentrate on feathering our nest, then work on the acceptance, all right?"

When he grudgingly agreed, Carrow turned to the others and raised her voice. "Mari will scry tonight, Malkom will prepare for mass teleporting, and I'll draw up schematics of the island. We'll try to contact Conrad and see if he has any intel we can use. Then we'll come up with a battle plan and leave at dawn."

Mari added, "Anybody who wants on that island, I have some paperwork and payment options."

Carrow nodded. "Tomorrow morning, we go to war."

Malkom tensed beside her. "We?" he growled, tracing her outside.

She blinked up at him. She'd thought he was going to be unstoppable *before* he could trace. "Malkom, if you go, then I do, too. Remember the *I'm never letting you out of my sight* part from earlier?" He opened his mouth to argue, but she said, "If you're happy, then I'll be strong enough to watch over you as well as you do me." As soon as things calmed down, she'd explain that she'd learned to empower herself, that between his happiness and her own, she'd be one formidable Wicca. "So I'll just have to make you ecstatic."

"Witch, you already have." He drew her close, resting his chin on her head. "When I heard what you said in there, in front of everyone?"

"I would die for you, Malkom. Can you trust that? Can you believe in me again?"

Against her hair, he murmured, "Right now, I can do anything."

48

Though Malkom and Carrow still had much to discuss with the immortals downstairs, he couldn't be easy until he saw Ruby with his own eyes. Carrow had told him, "She freaked out, shrieking for you. I mean, I knew you'd made an impression, but Elianna had to mick her, knock her out."

So they started for Carrow's room to check on the girl. On the way, he gazed around at all the new and peculiar things he saw. Carrow's memories had prepared him for much, but still, this proved bewildering. He itched to investigate everything unfamiliar.

They'd just passed through the doorway leading to a spacious suite when Carrow's torque dropped to the ground.

"Ah, Mari, thank you," she murmured, kicking the band away.

He could sense magics flowing through Carrow, now uninterrupted—just as he sensed them steeped in every inch of this coven.

Magics surrounding him. 'Twas not so disturbing as he might have imagined.

She rolled her head, massaging her nape. "Gods, that's nice to get rid of."

Eyes fixed on her bared neck, Malkom skimmed the backs of his fingers down that pale length. Their gazes met.

"Crow, is that you?" Ruby sleepily asked from the bed.

Carrow bit her bottom lip. With a sigh, she crossed to her. "It's me, honey." She sat beside the girl.

"Did you get Malkom back?"

He drew closer, easing down beside Carrow. "I am here, *deela*."

Instantly, Ruby's face lit up into a smile. "Crow, you swore you'd bring him home!" She launched herself at Malkom, hugging him with all her might.

Over the girl's shoulder, Malkom met eyes with Carrow. She'd promised her new daughter to bring him back, had been ready to fight her own allies to reach him.

Earlier, with her every word, his jaw had slackened. He'd wanted to have proof of her affection, to be certain of it. Now her feelings—and his place in her world—were abundantly clear.

His chest had grown tight, even as the knot in his gut had disappeared.

"Actually, he brought himself home," Carrow said. "He can trace now."

Ruby pulled back with narrowed eyes. "But is he staying?"

Carrow gazed at him as well.

He answered, "From now on, I stay with you two, my wife and our young one. 'Twill always be so."

Ruby laughed, bestowing another hug, while Carrow's eyes flickered amidst tears. "We wouldn't have it any other way, demon."

He'd just committed his life to theirs, had told his wife and adopted daughter in so many words that he would be with them, protecting them till the day he died.

Still he felt no apprehension about their futures, only anticipation. *To dream without dreading . . .*

Carrow slipped her hand in his, then said to Ruby, "Hey, your gang is downstairs. They've missed you. I was thinking a slumber party and pizza, if you aren't too tired—"

"They're here?" Ruby scrambled to the floor. "I have to show them Malkom!"

Show me to them? She is . . . proud.

"Well, we can't keep them waiting," Carrow said. "Go get Mari to pop off your torque. Unless you want to keep it on until you're eighteen, 'cause I'm okay with that."

"Crow!"

"All right, all right. Hey, before I forget to tell you, while you're in spell school tomorrow, Malkom and I are going on a mercenary gig. But we'll be back by dinner."

"Okay. Can we have chicken dinosaurs?"

"I'm sure Malkom would love to try them." She grinned up at him. "He does so enjoy his phicken."

"I like this bed," Malkom told Carrow, his voice rumbling with contentment.

Carrow glanced over at him from one of her closets. While she'd been readying her clothing and supplies for their new job, he'd lain back in her bed with his arms crossed under his head and a light sheet covering his body. His feet stretched out over the end of her California king.

How could he look so absolutely right among all her things? Especially when males didn't usually go tromping around inside Andoain, much less a giant demon at home in a witch's bed.

In the hours since the other immortals had left, he'd examined most of her belongings, the plumbing, the air-conditioning, the TV, myriad appliances.

And he'd been "shown" to Ruby's friends. Carrow would never forget his reaction when Ruby had proudly introduced him as her stepdemon. He'd been briefly surprised, then moved. The same as when she'd declared him her husband.

He'd later admitted, "I have rarely been introduced as 'my' anything. 'Tis welcome now."

Ruby's friends had gazed up at him with owl eyes, but eventually they'd gotten used to him. When they'd learned he'd never had pizza before, they'd all waited with bated breath to see if he'd like it. Carrow thought he'd exaggerated his reaction just a jot for their enjoyment and loved him all the more for it.

Now the slumber party in the attic was in full swing, music blaring from the karaoke machine, kids laughing.

Malkom grinned, seeming to love the noise. *So long was he alone . . .*

"What else do you like?" she asked, determined to make him happy in her world.

"Showers."

She quirked a brow. "You liked what we did to each other in the shower." That had only been the appetizer to the main course she planned. Beneath her unassuming robe, she wore her raciest lingerie.

"'Tis true," he said with a shameless grin. She loved it when he smiled. Tonight, he had often, awkwardly at first, but he was getting the hang of it.

"Is this where you want to live?" he asked.

"Actually, I've got my eye on a house right down the street." She hurriedly piled up her folded clothes for tomorrow. She was gearing up tonight because once she got into that bed with him, she didn't intend to leave it until they departed bright and early. "It's got a pool."

"I think I traced there earlier. I must have seen it in your memories." Then his demeanor grew stern. "I will want to purchase it for my family."

"Baby, if you get Lanthe back for Sabine"—she slapped her hands, rubbing them together—"then it's ours, all ours."

He relaxed again. "The rage demons seemed decent enough."

As Carrow had caught up with Mari and Elianna, Malkom had been waylaid by the demons.

"And what were you talking to them about for so long?"

"King Rydstrom wishes me to war with them in the coming Accession."

"Did you tell him it'll cost him?"

Malkom nodded. "The king told me I had a clever—and violently devoted—wife. I was prideful."

She patted her hair. "I *try*. You're going to make a fortune as a mercenary, you know. Guarding people, fighting battles."

"And what were you talking to your friends about?"

"About how you and I are going to be Ruby's parents." Elianna and Mari had been completely supportive, pledging to help Carrow as much as she needed.

Then the three of them had teared up as they'd raised a glass to Amanda, a small tribute until a proper service could be held. Carrow had added a silent thanks to her cousin for having such a remarkable kid.

"I also told my friends how much I adore you," Carrow said.

"This is mutual."

"Oh, and how I think you're utterly fantastic in bed."

He scowled at that until he saw she was dead serious. Then he gave a modest shrug. "Also mutual."

"We've already gotten two wedding gifts. Elianna put a mystical noise dampener on our room, so no one can hear me having my wicked way with you."

He raised a brow, his erection already tenting the sheet in readiness.

"She also conjured you a new wardrobe." Carrow opened her second closet to display all his new clothes. At his amazed expression, she said, "They'll all fit. Eli's a genius at stuff like that." Absently adjusting the silky black ribbon tied around her wrist, Carrow said, "And Mariketa gave us a present, too. Something *very* valuable. But it's a surprise."

She wondered how he'd react to that gift. *I'll know soon enough.* "By the way, we're going to have a wedding celebration here at the coven when everything settles down." She might have felt a pang that her birth parents wouldn't be there for the festivities, but luckily Carrow's entire *family* would be. Mari, Elianna, Ruby, and Malkom.

"I liked the witches."

"Because they were all whispering about how gorgeous you are, and you could hear every word," she said as she finished prepping. Carrow had noticed his neck had gotten red, and he'd looked flummoxed a couple of times.

"I am only interested in one witch. Come to me, *ara*."

She sauntered over to the bed. "You like my bed, showers, and my coven. But how do you like this?" She let her robe pool at her feet, revealing tight black garters, fishnet thigh-highs, a black silk bustier, and a matching thong. *Hey, it's his welcoming party after all.*

He swallowed, brows drawn. "Gods almighty, woman." With that incredible speed, he swung his legs over the side of the bed, snagging her around the waist.

She gave a delighted cry as he pulled her onto his lap.

With clear fascination, he fingered the lace edge of her bodice. "I like very much."

"So do you want to know what Mari gave us?" She held up a wrist, displaying the ribbon. "It's enchanted with a contraception spell. A *very* coveted gift."

When he frowned, she leaned forward, murmuring, "You can come inside me, and I still won't get pregnant."

"But I want to—"

She interrupted him with a brief kiss. "Let's get settled into the new house with Ruby first. So she can get used to life with us." Carrow knew that there would be adjustments and rough patches ahead. She didn't think the little girl had fully comprehended her mom was gone.

When Malkom was still hesitant, she said, "Ruby's going to need all the attention we can give her. And we've got plenty of time. Since we're going to live forever and all."

He exhaled. "Very well. We are agreed. For *now*."

"Then let's see if this ribbon works," she purred at his ear, making his erection pulse beneath her. "You don't have to hold back tonight, Malkom. I'm stronger, and I want everything you have."

"I want to give it to you, wife." He curled his fingers under her chin, drawing her in for a kiss. He grazed his lips against hers so tenderly, with teasing flicks of his tongue. Then he grew more aggressive, deepening the kiss while pinching her nipples through the silk, until she was squirming over his shaft.

"Spread your legs," he said against her lips.

When she did, he lazily petted her panties. "These are damp."

"Then you should take them off me—"

Rip. She trembled when he tore them free.

His fingers returned to stroke, and his lids went heavy when he found her so aroused. Satisfaction soared through him, and she felt it. "Oh, demon! I want that, too. All of you. *Now*."

"Must make sure you're ready," he said, his voice husky. After biting off a claw, he delved his forefinger between her folds. He slipped it deep as his thumb began circling her swollen clitoris.

With a sigh of pleasure, she gripped his shoulders to lean back, letting her knees fall open in surrender.

Slowly thrusting and softly circling. Over and over. He watched as his fingers played, spreading her, rubbing. And beneath her ass, his shaft stirred against her sensitive skin.

"Demon," she whispered, already nearing her peak. "I'm close. . . ."

He stopped at once, withdrawing his fingers, making her whimper.

"Straddle me," he commanded as he sucked his glistening finger, shuddering with pleasure at her taste. "My female is delicious."

Shivering, she maneuvered herself over his lap.

Once she was poised above his shaft, he fisted it with his free hand. "Come to me. Take me into that sweet sex."

"Malkom," she gasped, lowering herself. When the crown breached her entrance, he growled, ripping the cups from her bodice so he could suckle her, licking one nipple while rolling the other between his wet fingers.

She couldn't hold on. "Ah, gods!" With only the tip inside her, she began to come, her slick orgasm sending her slipping down his length. She wanted to throw back her head to scream with pleasure, but he rose up from her breast to meet her gaze, his hands capturing her face.

With his teeth clenched and sweat beading his brow, he forced her to stare into his flickering eyes as she slid along his beautiful cock, crying out with every inch.

Pulsing thickness within . . . waves of gripping heat.

Gazing at him as she came made her feel bare to him. The act was searingly intimate—and even more arousing.

By the time the spasms had finally ended, when he throbbed deep inside her, she was already on the verge again.

Laying his palms over her hips, he rasped, "I'm not done with you." Then he wrenched her down while surging his hips up, sending her spiraling into another climax. . . .

This time Malkom let her throw back her head as she came, savoring her abandon, her body's eager surrender. Her long hair brushed his thighs as she screamed his name, her pale throat working.

Her neck was fully bared to him—no collar. His aching fangs went sharp for that flesh, craving relief as much as his shaft did. But he would never again take her blood without asking.

When she faced him once more, she panted between red lips, her eyes like stars, glittering from her pleasure.

He grasped her finger, pulling it to his mouth to nick it on one fang. Then he held her bleeding finger between them. "'Tis to be your choice, *ara.*"

They both stared at the bead welling, the stream gliding down.

"But I want *all* of you, demon," she said breathlessly. "Every part of you." Before his riveted eyes, she painted the crimson along her neck, beckoning him. "I *need* your bite as much as you need to give it to me."

"*Witch!*" he growled as he swung her around to the bed. Still wedged deep inside her, he laid her down beneath him, then raised himself on straightened arms.

As his hips rolled between her thighs, he stared down at her. Three weeks ago, he would have thought this a fevered fantasy—the most exquisite female he'd ever seen, offering her neck while he drove in and out of her luscious sex. "You are too beautiful to be real, channa."

"Drink from me, Malkom. Taste me. It's yours, whenever you need."

Gods, could she truly be his? A woman to accept everything about him? He caught her neck in the crook of his arm, using his forearm to press her head to the side. Leaning down, he licked the blood from her neck, fangs sharper than they'd ever been. With a snarl, he plunged them into the tender spot between her neck and her shoulder.

Her body shot tense when he sucked her. "Malkom! It's . . . ah, gods, demon . . ." She cupped his head to her neck, pressing his mouth closer.

She feels it, too.

That closeness, a bond he'd never imagined, was even stronger when he was inside her. With her essence coursing through his veins, and his hips pounding against her, he had to fight not to come.

As he surged over her, riding her tight sheath, pleasure rocked him down to his bones. To finally know this, to share it with her.

Last, Slaine, last! This is actually happening. . . .

"Malkom, I'm close!" He felt her words as much as heard them. "Demon!" she screamed as she began to orgasm.

The clenching of her sex robbed him of his will-power. Now that he was to give her his seed, he noticed the way her sex milked his cock, demanding its due.

Too much pressure . . . about to explode. He released her neck, his back bowing from the intensity as his semen rose within him.

"Come inside me," she said, panting. "I need to feel it. *Give me all of you.*"

Her words sent him over the edge. "Can't keep it in . . . ah, no longer!" Helpless to stop it, he slammed his body between her thighs, taking her harder than he ever had, until . . . in a blinding rush . . .

He was released.

"*Carrow!*" he bellowed as he began to ejaculate. Again and again, his shaft shot deep into her heat. *Pumping . . . ecstasy . . .*

As he mindlessly thrust, filling her womb, she cried out, "I feel it inside me. Malkom, you're so hot . . . like a brand." Her knees fell wide as she fisted the sheets, coming once more.

Just as the tension left her body, he groaned, emptying the last of his seed. They lay for long moments, catching their breath. He could scarcely formulate thought—the connection had been too complete, the pleasure too consuming. *I feel nigh dumbstruck.*

"Demon," she gasped, sounding dazed.

"I couldn't have imagined that," he murmured. "'Twas pleasure with no equal."

He'd fully claimed what he wanted most in this world. His woman. And he felt . . . *whole*.

Again, those once-confusing emotions hammered inside his chest, clamoring for release. Before, he hadn't understood what he'd felt, hadn't had the words to tell her.

Now he did. He raised himself up on his elbows to gaze down at her. "I am in love with you, Carrow." He tucked a lock of her black hair behind her ear.

"Malkom, I love you so much." Her eyes glinted. "I always will."

As he beheld the face of his wife, he saw that love in her expression, love there for the taking. He'd wanted proof, and there was no denying what he saw so clearly.

In what felt like a far distant life, Malkom had once been told he'd never win.

Now his heart was full as the truth struck him. *But somehow I have won* her.

A future with her spread out before him. Dreams to come, dreams to come true.

POCKET
BOOKS

Kresley Cole

PLEASURE OF A DARK PRINCE

Never far from her bow, Lucia the Huntress is as mysterious
as she is beautiful. But the secrets she harbours could destroy
her – and those she loves – and every day brings more danger.

It isn't safe for her to be with Garreth MacRieve, yet
whenever she sees the fierce werewolf with his smouldering
eyes, she finds herself surrendering to his kiss.

From the shadows, Garreth, prince of the Lykae, has long
watched over Lucia, the lovely little Valkyrie who alternately
maddens him and inflames his lust. He aches to claim her as
his own and keep her safe from harm, but first he must
convince her to accept him as her guardian. To do that he'll
exploit Lucia's greatest weakness – her desire for him –
whatever the cost.

ISBN: 978-1-84983-036-2
PRICE £6.99

POCKET
BOOKS

Kresley Cole
NO REST FOR THE WICKED

A vampire warrior who yearns for death . . . Three hundred
years ago, Sebastian Wroth's brothers forced him to become
a vampire – a nightmare in his mind. Shamed and alone, he
longs to die. Until an exquisite creature comes to kill him,
inadvertently saving him instead. A beautiful assassin
dispatched to destroy him . . .

When Kaderin the Cold Hearted lost her two beloved
sisters long ago, a benevolent force deadened her sorrow,
accidentally extinguishing all of her emotions. Yet whenever
she encounters the vampire with his grave eyes, her feelings –
particularly lust – emerge multiplied. For the first time,
she's unable to complete a kill.

The prize is a key powerful enough to resurrect her sisters.
Not understanding the key's import, Sebastian hinders
her against other opponents by using her new feelings to
seduce her and earn her love. But when Kaderin is forced
to choose between finally killing Sebastian and reuniting
her family, how can she live without either?

ISBN: 978-1-41650-988-2
PRICE £5.99

POCKET
BOOKS

Kresley Cole

A HUNGER LIKE NO OTHER

A mythic warrior who'll stop at nothing to possess her . . .
After enduring years of torture from the vampire horde,
Lachlain MacRieve, leader of the Lykae Clan, is enraged
to find the predestined mate he's waited millennia for is a
vampire. Or partly one. This Emmaline is a small, ethereal
half Valkyrie/half vampire, who somehow begins
to soothe the fury burning within him.

A vampire captured by her wildest fantasy . . .
Sheltered Emmaline Troy finally sets out to uncover the truth
about her deceased parents – until a powerful Lykae claims
her as his mate and forces her back to his ancestral Scottish
castle. There, her fear of the Lykae – and their notorious dark
desires – ebbs as he begins a slow, wicked seduction
to sate her own dark cravings.

An all-consuming desire . . .
Yet when an ancient evil from her past resurfaces,
will their desire deepen into a love that can bring a proud
warrior to his knees and turn a gentle beauty into
the fighter she was born to be?

ISBN: 978-1-41650-987-5
PRICE £5.99